Kind of Cruel

SOPHIE HANNAH

Kind of Cruel

HODDER &
STOUGHTON

First published in Great Britain in 2012 by Hodder & Stoughton
An Hachette UK company

1

Copyright © Sophie Hannah 2012

The right of Sophie Hannah to be identified as the Author of the Work has been
asserted by her in accordance with the Copyright, Designs and Patents Act 1988.

A CIP catalogue record for this title is available from the British Library

Hardback ISBN 978 0 340 98069 9
Trade paperback ISBN 978 0 340 98070 5

Typeset in Sabon by Hewer Text UK Ltd, Edinburgh

Printed in Great Britain by Clays Ltd, St Ives plc

Hodder & Stoughton policy is to use papers that are natural, renewable
and recyclable products and made from wood grown in sustainable forests.
The logging and manufacturing processes are expected to conform to the
environmental regulations of the country of origin.

Hodder & Stoughton Ltd
338 Euston Road
London NW1 3BH

www.hodder.co.uk

For Juliet Emerson, who helped me to solve many
mysteries, both autobiographical and fictional

If you ask someone for a memory and they tell you a story, they're lying.

Me aged five, curled in a ball behind the doll's house, hiding; scared the teacher will find me, knowing it's going to happen, trying to prepare myself – that's a memory.

Here's the story I turned it into: on my first day at primary school, I was furious with my mother for leaving me in a place I didn't know, with strangers. Running away wasn't an option, because I was a good girl – my parents were always telling me that – but on this occasion I objected so strongly to what had been inflicted on me that I decided to protest by absenting myself from Mrs Hill's classroom as thoroughly as I dared. There was a large doll's house in one corner of the room, and, when no one was looking, I tucked myself into the space between it and the wall. I don't know how long I stayed there, hidden, listening to the unappealing noises my classmates were making and Mrs Hill's attempts to impose order, but it was long enough for my deception to start to feel uncomfortable. I regretted hiding, but to show myself suddenly would be tantamount to confessing, and I had no desire to do anything so rash. I knew I'd be found eventually, and that my punishment would be severe, and I became increasingly scared and agitated, crying quietly so that no one would hear. At the same time, part of me was thinking, 'Say nothing, don't move – there's still a chance you'll get away with it.'

When I heard Mrs Hill tell all the children to sit cross-legged on the carpet so that she could take the register, I panicked. Somehow, although I'd never been to school or even nursery before, I knew what that meant: she was going to call our names, one by one. When I heard mine, I would have to say, 'Yes, Mrs Hill'. Wherever I was, I would have to say it. The possibility of remaining silent didn't occur to me; that would have involved a level of deceit and rebellion I wouldn't have been prepared to contemplate, let alone attempt. Still, I didn't move from my hiding place. I have always been an optimist, and wasn't willing to give up until I absolutely had to. Something might happen to prevent Mrs Hill from taking the register, I thought: a bird might fly in through the classroom window, or one of my classmates could suddenly fall ill and have to be rushed to hospital. Or I might come up with a brilliant idea in the next three seconds – some amazing exit route out of this mess I'd got myself into.

None of those things happened, of course, and when Mrs Hill called my name, I decided the best course of action was a compromise. I said nothing, but raised my hand from behind the doll's house so that it was clearly visible. I was doing my bit, I thought – admitting to being present, raising my hand responsibly – yet there still remained the miraculous possibility that no one would notice, that as a reward for declaring myself, I would get to miss the entire school day. And then I could turn up the following day and do exactly the same again. That was my fantasy; the reality was that Mrs Hill spotted my protruding arm at once and demanded that I come out from behind the doll's house. Later, she told my mother what I'd done and I was punished both at school and at home. I don't remember the punishments.

How much of that story is true? At a guess, I'd say most of it. Ninety per cent, maybe. How much of it do I remember? Hardly any. Two emotional states, that's all: the mixture of fear and defiance I felt while I was behind the doll's house, and the terrible humiliating defeat of having to come out and face the class. Everyone knew I'd taken a risk, then lost my nerve and given myself up. I remember feeling shamed by the memory – seconds after the event; a memory within a memory – of my stupid bet-hedging gesture of staying hidden while silently raising my hand. I was pathetic: too good to be naughty and too naughty to be good. I remember wishing I was any other child in the class, anyone but me. I'm pretty sure I had all those feelings, though at five I didn't yet have the vocabulary to describe them.

The problem – what prevents me from being certain – is that for forty years, my story about what happened that day has been trampling all over my memories, so that by now it has effectively replaced them. True memories are frail, fragmentary apparitions, easily bulldozed into submission by a robust narrative that has been carefully engineered to stick in the mind. Almost as soon as we've had an experience, we decide what we would like it to mean, and we construct a story around it that is going to make that possible. The story incorporates whichever relevant memories suit its purpose – positioning them strategically, like colourful brooches on the lapel of a black jacket – and discards the ones that are of no use.

For years, I told a different version of my first-day-at-school story, a version in which I emerged from my hiding place with a cocky smile on my face and said with absolute confidence, 'What? I wasn't pretending not to be here. I put my hand up, didn't I? You never said I couldn't sit behind the doll's house.' Then one day I caught myself mid-anecdote and thought, 'Can that really be what happened?' Sometimes we need to demolish our endlessly told tales in order to get to the real memories. It's a bit like stripping layer after layer of paint off a brick wall. Underneath, we find the original bricks – stained and discoloured, in poor condition after years of not being able to breathe.

The funny thing is that, now, both versions of the story – the one in which I brazen it out and the one in which I'm humiliated – feel like memories to me, because I have told both so many times, to myself and to other people. Each time we tell a story, we deepen the groove it occupies in our mind, allowing it to burrow further in and seem more real with each telling.

A true memory might be a fleeting image of a red coat, a lemon tree (you don't know where), a strong feeling, the name of someone you used to know – just the name, nothing more. Genuine memories do not have beginnings, middles and ends. There's no suspense, no obvious point to them, certainly no moral lesson learned – nothing to satisfy an audience, and by 'audience' I mean the teller, who is always the first audience for his or her own story.

All this can be applied to Christmas 2003 and what happened at Little Orchard, which – as you've probably guessed by now – is not a memory but a story. Hopefully, it's a story that can be used to retrieve a few memories embedded within it, and maybe some rejected ones too, ones that didn't fit with the overall flow and were ditched accordingly. As an experiment,

I'm going to assume, for the time being at least, that the Little Orchard story is one in which every detail is false.

None of it really happened. Nobody woke up on Christmas morning to find that four members of their family had disappeared.

I

Tuesday 30 November 2010

Look: there is nothing special about this place. Look at the gaps between the bricks in the gateposts, where the pointing has fallen out. Look at the ugly UPVC window frames. This is not a place where miracles happen.

And – because I'm more than willing to shoulder my share of the blame in advance – there is nothing special about me. I am not a place where miracles happen.

This isn't going to work. So I mustn't be disappointed when it doesn't.

I'm not here because I think it's going to help. I'm here because I'm sick of having to plaster a receptive smile on my face and make pleased and surprised noises when yet another person tells me how brilliantly it worked for them. 'You should try hypnosis,' says everybody I meet, from my colleagues to my dentist to parents and teachers at the girls' school. 'I was really sceptical, and only went as an absolute last resort, but it was like magic – I never touched cigarettes/vodka/cream cakes/betting slips again.'

I've noticed that anyone who advocates a wildly implausible solution to a problem always stresses how cynically unconvinced they were at first, before they tried it. No one ever says, 'I was and am exactly the kind of desperate idiot who's ready to believe in anything. Weirdly, hypnotherapy really worked for me.'

I'm sitting in my car on Great Holling Road, outside the home of Ginny Saxon, the hypnotherapist I chose quite randomly. Well, perhaps not entirely. Great Holling is the nicest village in the Culver Valley; might as well go somewhere picturesque to waste my money, I thought. Very few places are so idyllic that one notices a backlash against them – people describing them as being 'not the real world' or 'up their own arse' – but it's almost a cliché around these parts to thumb your nose at the beautiful seclusion of Great Holling by opting, instead, to live in a noisier, dirtier place that, coincidentally, contains cheaper houses. 'But even if I could afford to live in Great Holling, I wouldn't. It's just too perfect.' Yeah, right.

Still, maybe I should be more trusting. Plenty of people have money and choose not to use it to improve their situations. Some fools I know hand over their hard-earned cash to quacks and ask to be mesmerised, hoping they'll come round to find that all their problems have disappeared.

Ginny Saxon's address, like her brand of therapy, is a con. She doesn't live in Great Holling. I have driven all the way out here on false pretences – even more false pretences than a silly placebo treatment, I mean. I should have looked more carefully at the address and realised that the double helping of the village's name within it – 77 Great Holling Road, Great Holling, Silsford – was protesting too much. I am not in Great Holling, but on an A-road on the way to it. There are houses on one side, including Ginny Saxon's, and brown and grey sludgy-looking fields on the other. This is agricultural land masquerading as countryside. In one of the fields there's a building with a corrugated metal roof. It's the sort of landscape that makes me think of sewage, even if I'm being unfair and can't actually smell any.

You are being unfair. What's the harm in having an open mind? It might work.

Inwardly, I groan. The disappointment, when this charade I'm about to participate in leaves me exactly as it found me, is going to hurt – probably worse than after all the other stuff I've tried that hasn't worked. Hypnotherapy is the thing everybody does as a last resort. After it, there's nothing left to try.

I look at the time on my car clock. 3 p.m. on the dot; I am supposed to be arriving now. But it's warm in my Renault Clio, with the heater on, and freezing outside. No snow here, not even the kind that doesn't settle, but every night snow is forecast with a little more glee on the part of the local news weather lady. The whole of the Culver Valley is in the grip of that peculiarly English weather condition – inspired as much by schadenfreude as by sub-zero temperatures – known as 'Don't think the snow won't come just because it hasn't yet'.

'On the count of three,' I imagine saying to myself in my best deep hypnotic voice, 'you will get out of your car, go into that house across the road and pretend to be in a trance for an hour. You will then write a cheque for seventy quid to a charlatan. It'll be ace.' I pull my written instructions out of my coat pocket: Ginny's address. I check it, put it back – a delaying tactic that establishes nothing I didn't already know. I'm in the right place.

Or the wrong one.

Here goes.

As I walk towards the house, I see that the car parked in the driveway is not empty. There's a woman in it, wearing a black coat with a furry collar, a red scarf and bright red lipstick. There's a notebook open on her lap and a pen in her hand. She's smoking a cigarette and has opened her window, despite the temperature. Her ungloved hands are mottled from the cold. Smoking and writing are obviously more important to her than comfort, I think, seeing a pair of woolly gloves lying next to the Marlboro Lights packet on the passenger seat. She looks up and smiles at me, says hi.

I decide she can't be Ginny Saxon, whose website lists giving up smoking as one of the things she can help with. Sitting in her car outside her house with a fag in her gob would be an odd form for that help to take, unless it's a carefully thought-out double bluff. Then I notice something I couldn't see from the road: a small free-standing wooden building in the back garden with a sign on it saying 'Great Holling Hypnotherapy Clinic – Ginny Saxon MA PGCE Dip Couns Adv Dip Hyp'.

'That's where it all happens,' says the smoker, with more than a trace of bitterness in her voice. 'In her garden shed. Inspires confidence, doesn't it?'

'It's more attractive than the house,' I say, slipping easily into nasty-girl-at-the-back-of-the-school-bus mode, praying that Ginny Saxon won't pop up behind me and catch me slagging off her home. Why do I care about ingratiating myself with this chippy stranger? 'At least it hasn't got UPVC windows,' I add, aware of the absurdity of my behaviour but powerless to do anything about it.

The woman grins, then turns away as if she's had second thoughts about talking to me. She looks down at her notebook. I know how she feels; it would have been better if we'd pretended not to notice one another. We can be as sarcastic as we like, but we're both here because we've got problems we can't sort out on our own, and we know it – about ourselves and about each other.

'She's running an hour late. My appointment was for two o'clock.'

I try to look as if this doesn't bother me; I'm not sure I succeed. That'll mean . . . Ginny Saxon won't be able to see me until four, and at ten past I'll have to leave if I'm going to be home in time to meet Dinah and Nonie off the school bus.

'Don't worry, you can have my slot,' says my new friend, tossing her cigarette end out of the window. If Dinah were here, she would say, 'Go and pick up your litter, right now, and put it in a bin.' It wouldn't occur to her that she's only eight, and not in a position to give orders to a stranger more than five times her age. I make a mental note to retrieve the cigarette stub and put it in the nearest wheelie bin if I get the chance, if I can do it without the woman seeing me and taking it as a criticism.

'Don't you mind?' I ask.

'I wouldn't have offered if I minded,' she says, sounding notice-ably jollier. Because she's off the hook? 'Either I'll come back at four, or . . .' – she shrugs – '. . . or I won't.'

She closes her car window and starts to reverse out of the drive-way, waving at me in a way that makes me feel I've been conned – a mixture of flippant and superior, a wave that seems to say, 'You're on your own, sucker'.

'Do come in out of the cold,' says a voice behind me. I turn and see a plump woman with a round pretty face and blonde hair in a ponytail so limp and casual that most of the hair has fallen out of it. She's wearing an olive green corduroy skirt, black ankle boots with black tights and a cream polo-neck top that clings around her waist, drawing attention to the extra weight she's carrying. I guess that she's between forty and fifty, closer to forty.

I follow her into the wooden building, which is not and has clearly never been a shed. The wood, both inside and out, looks too new – there are no marks to suggest that a muddy trowel or an oily lawnmower has ever lived here. One wall is covered from top to bottom with framed botanical prints, and there are curvaceous sky-blue vases filled with flowers in three of the room's four corners. A white rug with a thick blue border takes up most of the wooden floor. On one side of it, there's a maroon leather swivel recliner chair and matching footstool, and on the other, a brown distressed leather sofa next to a small table piled high with books and magazines about hypnotherapy.

This last detail irks me, just as it annoys me when I go to the hairdresser and find piles of magazines about hair and nothing else. The symbolism is too crass; it smacks of a desperation to ram home one's professional message, and always makes me think, 'Yes, I know what you do for a living. That's why I'm here.' Do I really need to immerse myself in exclusively hairy thoughts while I wait for a suet-faced teenager to ram my head into a basin and pour boiling water over it? What if I'd like to read about the stock market, or modern ballet? I wouldn't, as it happens, but the point is still valid.

Hypnotherapy is, admittedly, marginally more interesting than split ends (though, in fairness, at least my quarterly visits to Salon 32 leave me in no doubt that an actual service has been performed).

'You're welcome to have a look at the books and magazines,' Ginny Saxon says, more enthusiastically than is warranted. Her accent is what I think of as 'media' – it doesn't belong to anywhere, and tells me nothing about where she's from. Not the Culver Valley would be my guess. 'Borrow as many as you like, as long as you bring them back.' Either she's putting a lot of effort into her act or she's a nice person. I hope she's nice – nice enough that she'll still want to help me even when she realises I'm not.

Pretending to be a better person than I am is exhausting; having to make a constant effort to produce behaviour that doesn't match my mental state.

Ginny holds out a magazine called *Hypnotherapy Monthly*. I can't not take it. It falls open at the centrefold, home to an article called 'Hypnotherapeutic Olfactory Conditioning Examined'. What was I expecting: a full frontal shot of a swinging stopwatch?

'Have a seat,' says Ginny, indicating the swivel recliner and foot-stool. 'Sorry to keep you waiting an hour.'

'You haven't,' I tell her. 'I'm Amber Hewerdine. My appointment's for now. The other woman said I could have her slot, and she'll come back later.'

Ginny smiles. 'And then she said?'

Oh, God, please don't let her have heard our entire conversation. How thick are these wooden walls? How loud were we?

'I didn't hear anything, don't worry. But from what little I know of her, I'm guessing she said more than what you've told me.'

Don't worry? What the hell is that supposed to mean? Last night I asked Luke if he thought a person would only train to be a hypno-therapist if they enjoyed messing with people's minds, and he laughed at me. 'God help anyone who tries to tangle with yours,' he said. He didn't know how right he was.

'She said, "Either I'll come back at four, or I won't",' I tell Ginny.

'Made you feel like an idiot for sticking around, did she? Relax. She's the idiot. I don't think she'll come back. She chickened out last week as well – booked an initial consultation, didn't turn up for it. She hadn't given me any notice of cancellation, so I billed her for the full amount.'

Should she be saying these things to me? Isn't it unprofessional? Will she bitch about me to her next client?

'Why don't you tell me why you're here?' Ginny unzips her ankle boots, kicks them off, curls herself into a ball on the leather sofa. Is that supposed to make me feel less inhibited? It doesn't; it irritates me. I've only just met her. She's supposed to be a professional. How does she dress for a second appointment – camisole and knickers?

It doesn't matter; there isn't going to be a second appointment.

'I'm an insomniac,' I tell her. 'A proper one.'

'Which forces me to ask: what's an improper insomniac?'

'Someone who has difficulty falling asleep, but when they do, they sleep for eight hours solid. Or someone who falls asleep straight away, but wakes up too early – four a.m. instead of seven. All the people who say, "Oh, I never sleep properly" and it turns out they mean they wake up twice or three times a night to go to the loo – that's not a sleep problem, that's a bladder problem.'

'People who use "insomniac" to mean "light sleeper"?' Ginny suggests. 'Any little noise wakes them? Or who can only fall asleep if they've got earphones piping music into their ears, or with the radio on?'

I nod, trying not to be impressed that she appears to know all the people I hate. 'They're the most infuriating of pretend insomniacs. Anyone who says, "I can only get to sleep *if*" and then names a requirement – that's not insomnia. They satisfy the "if" and they get to sleep.'

'Do you resent people who sleep well?' Ginny asks.

'Not if they admit it.' I might be too exhausted to be nice, but I like to think I'm still reasonable. 'What I object to is people who don't have a problem pretending that they do.'

'So people who say, "I sleep like a log, me – nothing wakes me" – they're okay?'

Is she trying to catch me out? I'm tempted to lie, but what would be the point of that? This woman doesn't have to like me. She's obliged to try to help me whether she likes me or not. That's what I'm paying for. 'No, they're smug beyond belief,' I say.

'And yet if it's true – if they *do* sleep like logs – what should they say?'

If she mentions logs again, I'm leaving. 'There are ways and ways of telling people you're a good sleeper,' I say, perilously close to tears. 'They could say, "No, I don't have a problem sleeping", and then quickly point out that they have plenty of other problems. Everyone has problems, right?'

'Absolutely,' says Ginny, looking as if she has never worried about a single thing in her entire life. I stare past her, out of the two large windows behind the leather sofa. Her back garden is a long, skinny strip of green. At the far end, I can see a small brown patch of wooden fence, and fields beyond it that look greener and more promising than the ones I saw on the other side of the road. If I lived here, I would worry about a developer buying up the land and cramming it full of as many houses as he could squash in.

'Tell me about your sleeping problem,' Ginny says. 'After that build-up, I'm expecting a horror story. There's a wooden lever under the arm of your chair, if you want to lie back.'

I don't want to, but I do it anyway, putting my feet up on the footstool so that I'm almost horizontal. It's easier if I can't see her face; I can pretend I'm talking to a recorded voice.

'So. Are you the world's worst-afflicted insomniac?'

Is she mocking me? I can't help noticing I'm not in any kind of trance yet. When's she going to get started? We've got less than an hour.

'No,' I say stiffly. 'I'm better off than people who never sleep. I sleep for stretches of fifteen, twenty minutes at a time, on and off throughout the night. And always in front of the TV in the evening. That's the best chunk of sleep I get, usually, between eight thirty and nine thirty – a whole hour, if I'm lucky.'

'Anyone who never slept would die,' says Ginny. This throws me, until I realise she must be talking about the insomniacs I mentioned in passing, those less fortunate than me.

'People do die,' I tell her. 'People with FFI.'

I sense she's waiting for me to continue.

'Fatal Familial Insomnia. It's a hereditary condition. As diseases go, it's not much fun. Total sleeplessness, panic attacks, phobias, hallucinations, dementia, death.'

'Go on.'

Is this woman a moron? 'That's it,' I say. 'Death's the last item on the agenda. Not much tends to happen to them after that. Which would be a relief, if only they weren't too dead to appreciate it.'

When she doesn't laugh, I decide to take it darker. 'Course, for some people, FFI would have the added bonus that all their family die too.' I listen for her reaction. One small chuckle would make me feel so much more confident about her. Is she secure enough in herself and her abilities to let that one pass, to let my joke be a joke? Only a desperate therapist would pounce on such an obviously frivolous comment at this early stage.

'Do you want your family to die?'

Predictably disappointing. Disappointingly predictable.

'No. That's not what I said.'

'Have you always had trouble sleeping?'

I'm not comfortable with how quickly and smoothly she's changed the subject. 'No.'

'When did it start?'

'A year and a half ago.' I could give her an exact date.

'Do you know *why* it started? Why you can't sleep?'

'Stress. At work and at home.' I put it in the broadest possible terms, hoping she won't ask for more detail.

'And if a fairy godmother were to wave her wand and remove the sources of that stress – what do you think would happen then, sleep-wise?'

Is it a trick question? 'I'd sleep fine,' I say. 'I always used to sleep well.'

'That's good. The causes of your insomnia are external rather than internal. It isn't that *you*, Amber Hewerdine, can't sleep because of something *in you*. You can't sleep because your current life situation is putting you under unbearable pressure. Anyone in your predicament would be finding it difficult, right?'

'I think so.'

'That's better. That's the kind of insomnia you want.' I can hear her beaming at me. How is that possible? 'There's nothing wrong with *you*. Your responses are absolutely normal and understandable. Can you change your life situation to eliminate the sources of stress?'

'No. Look, I'm not being funny but . . . don't you think that might have occurred to me? All those nights I've lain awake, dwelling on everything that's wrong . . .' *Don't get emotional. Think of this as a business meeting – you're a dissatisfied customer.* 'I can't eliminate the causes of stress from my life. They *are* my life. I was hoping that hypnotherapy might be able to . . .' I can't say what I was going to say. It would sound too ridiculous if I put it into words.

'You're hoping I can deceive your brain,' Ginny summarises. 'You know, and it knows, that it has reason to be anxious, but you're hoping hypnosis might hoodwink it into believing everything's fine.' Now she's mocking me for sure.

'If you think that's such a ridiculous proposition, why did you choose this line of work?' I say curtly.

She says something that sounds like, 'Let's try the Tree Shaker.'

'What?'

I must have sounded alarmed. 'Trust me,' Ginny says. 'It's just an exercise.'

She'll have to settle for my acquiescing without further argument. Trust is too precious a commodity to demand from a stranger.

'You'll probably want to close your eyes – it might make it easier.'

I wouldn't bet on it.

'You might be relieved to hear that you won't have to speak hardly at all. For most of the time, you'll just be listening and letting memories come to mind.'

That sounds easy enough. Though 'hardly at all' suggests that I'm going to have to say something at some point. What? I'd like to be able to prepare for it.

When Ginny next speaks, I nearly burst out laughing. Her voice is slower, deeper, more trance-like, similar to the joke-hypnotist voice I had in my head: *You are falling into a deep, deep sleep.* That's not quite what Ginny's saying but it's not too far off. 'And so I'd like you to focus on your breathing,' she intones, 'and the very top of your head. And just . . . let it . . . relax.'

Why is she doing this? She must know that she sounds like a cliché. Wouldn't she be better off talking normally?

'And then your forehead . . . let it relax. And moving down to your nose . . . breathing slowly and deeply, calmly and quietly, just let your nose relax. And then your mouth, your lips . . . let them relax.'

What about the bit between my nose and my lips, whatever its name is? What if that part's rigid with tension? She missed it out.

This is hopeless. I'm rubbish at being hypnotised. I knew I would be.

Ginny has reached my shoulders. 'Feel them drop and relax, all the pressure melting away. Breathing slowly and deeply, calmly and quietly, letting go of all stress and tension. And then moving down to your chest, your lungs – let *them* relax. There's no such thing as a hypnotised feeling, only a feeling of total calm and total relaxation.'

Really? Then why am I paying seventy quid? If all I have to do is relax, I could do that at home on my own.

No, I correct myself. I couldn't. Can't.

'Total calm . . . and total relaxation. And moving down to your stomach . . . let it relax.'

Septum. No, that's the bit between your nostrils. I used to know the name of that indentation between the nose and top lip. What do people mean when they talk about someone's elevens being up? No, that's the groove at the back of the neck. It looks more like the number 11 the closer a person is to death. I'm almost certain the same isn't true of the . . . philtrum, that's what it's called. Now that the name's come back to me, I have a clear picture of Luke announcing it triumphantly. *A pub quiz. The kind of question he always gets right, the kind I'm useless at.*

I force myself to pay attention to Ginny's droning voice. Has she got to my toes yet? I haven't been listening. She could save time by grouping all the parts together and instructing the whole body to relax. I try to breathe evenly and keep my impatience at bay.

'Some people feel incredibly light, as if they might float away,' she's saying. 'And some people feel a heaviness in their limbs, like they couldn't move even if they wanted to.'

She sounds like a children's TV presenter, doing 'light' and 'heavy' voices to match her words. Has she ever experimented with a more deadpan delivery? It's something I've often wondered about actors on Radio 4: why doesn't anyone tell them the phony voices really don't help?

'And some people feel a tingling in their fingers. But everybody feels lovely and calm, nice and relaxed.'

My fingers are tingling quite a lot. They were even before she said it. Does that mean I'm hypnotised? I don't feel relaxed, though I suppose I'm more aware of the buzzing neuroses in my mind than I was before, more intently focused on them. It's as if they and I are trapped together in a dark box, one that's drifted away from the rest of the world. Is that a good thing? Hard to see how it can be.

'And now, breathing slowly and deeply, calmly and quietly, I'd like you to imagine the most beautiful staircase in the world.'

What? She's springing this on me with no warning? A dozen desirable staircase images crowd into my mind and start scrapping with each other. Spiral, with wrought-iron fretwork? Or those open, slatty steps that look as if they're floating on air, with a glass or stainless steel balustrade – nice and modern, clean lines. On the other hand, a bit soulless, too much like an office building.

'Your perfect staircase has ten steps,' Ginny goes on. 'I'm now going to take you down those steps, one by one . . .'

Hang on a second. I'm not ready to move anywhere yet. I still haven't got my staircase sorted out. Traditional's the safest bet: dark wood, with a runner. I'm seeing something stripy . . .

'As you descend, I want you to see yourself drifting down into calm, and into relaxation. So, moving down one step – calm and relaxed. And moving down another step, taking another step towards peace and towards relaxation . . .'

How can she be going too fast while speaking soporifically slowly?

What about stone? That's also traditional, and grander than wood, but possibly a bit cold. Though with a runner . . .

Ginny's ahead of me but I don't care. My plan is to take all the time I need to get my staircase designed – if I cut corners at this crucial stage, I'm bound to regret it later – and then leap down to the bottom all in one go. As long as I get there when she does, what difference does it make?

'And now you're taking the last step, and you've arrived at a place of total calm, total peace. You are completely relaxed. And so I'd like you to think back to when you were a very small child, and the world was new. I'd like you to remember a moment when you felt joy, such intense joy that you thought you might explode.'

This throws me. What's happened to the staircase? Was it just a device, to get me to the calm, relaxed place? I have already missed my chance to produce a joyful memory; Ginny has moved on, and is now ordering me – if a demand made so drowsily can be considered an order – to remember feeling desperately sad, as if my heart was breaking. Sad, sad, I think, worried about having dropped behind. She moves on again, to angry – incandescent, burning with rage – and I can't think of a single thing. I'm about to miss my third deadline. *Might as well give up.*

As she progresses from fear ('your heart pounding as the ground seems to fall away beneath your feet') to loneliness ('like a cold vacuum all around you and inside you, separating you from every single other human being'), I wonder how many times Ginny has recited this spiel. Her descriptions are pretty powerful – perhaps a little too powerful. My childhood wasn't especially dramatic; there's nothing in it, or in my memory of it, to match the kind of extreme states she's describing. I was a happy child: loved, secure. I was heartbroken when my parents died within two years of one another, but I was in my early twenties by then. Should I ask Ginny if a memory from adulthood will do as a substitute? She specified early childhood, but surely a more recent memory would be better than nothing.

'And now I'd like you to imagine that you're drowning. Everywhere you turn, there's water, touching every part of you, flooding into your nose and mouth. You can't breathe. What memory springs to mind in connection with that? Anything?'

My philtrum would be getting soaked. Sorry, that's all I've got.

What's Ginny aiming to uncover here? I'm not thinking about feelings any more, I'm thinking about submarine disaster movies.

When she tells me to imagine myself in a burning house, trapped by flames, I feel sick in the pit of my stomach. This is so seriously lacking in feelgood factor that I'm praying I'll be handed an evaluation form at the end of all this so that I can make my objection official.

I don't want to do this any more.

'Okay, that's great,' Ginny says. 'You're doing great.' I hear a slight sharpening in her tone, and I know the moment has come: audience participation time. 'Now I'd like you to let a memory come into your mind, and tell me about it. Any memory, from any time in your life. Don't analyse it. It doesn't have to be significant. What are you remembering, right now?'

Sharon. I can't say that. Unless I've misunderstood, Ginny wants something new from me now, not leftovers from the last exercise.

'Don't try to select something good,' she says in her regular voice. 'Anything will do.'

Right. Nice to know how little all this matters.

Not Sharon and her burning house. Not unless you want to leave here in pieces.

Little Orchard, then. The story of my disappearing relatives. No death, no tragedy, only a never-to-be-solved mystery. I open my mouth, then remember that Ginny told me not to pick something good. Little Orchard is too showy and attention-seeking. She won't believe it genuinely 'came up', and she'll be right. It's permanently 'up' in my mind; I wonder about it constantly, even now, after so many years. It gives me something to do, when I'm lying awake at night and I've already worried about every aspect of my life that can be worried about.

'What are you remembering?' Ginny asks. 'Right now.'

Oh, God, this is a nightmare. What should I say? Anything, anything.

'Kind. Cruel. Kind of Cruel.'

What does that mean?

'Can you repeat that?' says Ginny.

This is really strange. What just happened? Ginny said something odd, but why would she ask me to repeat it? I wasn't paying attention; my mind must have drifted off for a second, back to Little Orchard, or to Sharon . . .

'Can you repeat those words?'

'Kind. Cruel. Kind of Cruel,' I say, not sure I've got it right. 'What does it mean?' Is it a magic spell, designed to drag recalcitrant memories to the surface?

'You tell me,' says Ginny.

'How can I? You were the one who said it.'

'No, I didn't. You said it.'

There's a long pause. Why am I still horizontal, with my eyes closed? I ought to sit up and insist that this stranger stops lying about me.

'You said it,' I snap, annoyed that I should have to convince her when she must know the truth as well as I do. 'And then you asked me to repeat it.'

'All right, Amber, I'm going to count to five to bring you out of hypnosis. When I reach five, I want you to open your eyes. One. Two. Three. Four. Five.'

It's strange to see the room again. I pull the lever under the arm of my chair and it tilts me upright. Ginny is staring at me, not smiling. She looks worried.

'I didn't say anything,' I tell her. 'You said it.'

~

In my haste to escape, I nearly run into the woman with the red lipstick. 'All better?' she says. The sight of her shocks me; at first I can't work out why. How could I have erased her from my mind so completely? I ought to have known I might open the door and find her here, waiting. My brain is not operating at its usual speed; I'm not sure if it's tiredness or the after-effects of hypnosis.

Her notebook. You forgot that you saw her writing in her notebook. What was she writing?

I struggle to pretend nothing has changed: my customary reaction when I'm ambushed by the unexpected.

It doesn't work.

Why would Ginny Saxon pretend I'd said something I hadn't? Before today she didn't know me; she has nothing to gain from lying about me. Why is this only occurring to me now?

I should say something. Red Lipstick Woman asked me a question. *All better?* In the hour since I last saw her, her bitterness has transmuted into good-humoured resignation: she doesn't believe that Ginny is capable of curing either of us, but we must participate in the charade all the same. I stare at the clouds of breath in the air between us and imagine they are a barrier through which words and understanding cannot pass. I can't speak. Day is already turning into night; the fields look like flat dark cloths spread out beside the empty road. They make me think of the magician we hired for Nonie's seventh birthday party, the black satin throw he draped over his small table.

What's wrong with me? How long have I let this silence last? My thoughts are either moving too fast or unbearably slowly; I can't tell the difference.

Her hands mottled from the cold, black woolly gloves on the passenger seat beside her, a notebook open on her lap, words on the page . . .

I resist the urge to run back to the warmth of Ginny's wooden den and beg for her mercy. I went to her for help – help I still need. How did I end up calling her a liar, refusing to pay and storming out in a rage?

Kind, Cruel, Kind of Cruel.

'An hour ago you could talk and now you can't,' says Red Lipstick Woman. 'What did she do to you in there? Blink your answers – two for yes, one for no. Did she programme you to assassinate her political enemies?'

I can't ask. I have to. I might only have a few seconds before Ginny summons her inside. 'Your notebook,' I say. 'The one you had in the car. This is going to sound strange, but . . . were you writing some kind of poem?'

She laughs. 'No. Nothing so ambitious. Why?'

If it wasn't a poem, why the short lines?

Kind

Cruel

Kind of Cruel

'What was the name of that guy who dictated a whole book by blinking his left eyelid?' she asks, looking over her shoulder towards the road as if there's someone there who might know the answer. She doesn't want to talk about what I want to talk about. Her private notebook; why would she?

'"Kind, Cruel, Kind of Cruel" – is that what you were writing? I'm not asking you to tell me what it means . . .'

'I don't know what it means,' she says. Reaching into her hand-bag, she pulls out a packet of Marlboro Lights and a silver lighter. 'Apart from the obvious: kind means kind, cruel means cruel, etc.'

'Could I have seen those words in your notebook?' *And you have the right to ask this because?*

I wait while she lights a cigarette. She takes two deep drags, savouring each one: an advertisement for the bad habit of which she hopes to be cured. Though I suppose I shouldn't assume that's why she's here.

Assume nothing. Especially not that you must be right, and the person trying to help you must be a liar.

Why do I have the sense that she's stalling? 'No, you couldn't have seen those words,' she says when she's ready. 'Maybe you saw them somewhere else. Since we're asking intrusive questions, what's your name?'

'Amber. Amber Hewerdine.'

'Bauby,' she announces, startling me. 'That was his name – the blink-writer.'

I'm going to have to press the point; I can't help myself. 'Are you sure? Maybe you wrote it a while ago, or . . .' I stop short of suggest-ing that the words might be there without her knowing, that someone else might have written them. That's crazy – crazier than the idea of Ginny brainwashing would-be assassins in her back-garden treatment room in the Culver Valley. I don't trust my judgement at the moment; everything that comes into my mind must be forced through the filter of normality and plausibility. *Don't ask her if she shares the notebook with anyone; no one shares their notebooks.*

I decide my best bet is to be as straightforward as I can. 'I remember seeing it.' *Like you remember Ginny saying it and asking you to repeat it?* 'Like a list: "Kind" on one line, then a couple of line spaces, then "Cruel" underneath, and "Kind of Cruel" a few lines beneath that.'

She shakes her head, and I want to scream. Can I call two people liars in one day, or is that excessive? It occurs to me, way too late, that I ought to tell her why I'm asking. Maybe that would make a difference to her willingness to talk. 'I'm not prying,' I start to say.

'Yes, you are.'

'I've never been hypnotised before.' I didn't realise how pathetic that would sound until I said it. She flinches. *Great.* Now I've embarrassed us both. 'I'm trying to check my memory's working properly, that's all.'

'And we've established that it isn't,' she says. Why isn't she more freaked out by this, by me? I know how oddly I'm behaving, or at least I think I know; her matter-of-fact responses are making me doubt it.

Kind, Cruel, Kind of Cruel. I can see the words on the page, and more than that: an equally strong image of myself looking, seeing. I'm part of the same memory as the words; I'm in the scene. So is she, so is her notebook, her cigarette . . .

'You're describing lined paper,' she says.

I nod. *Pale blue horizontal lines, with a pink vertical line running down the left hand side to denote the margin.*

'The pages in my notebook aren't lined.'

Which ought to be the end of the matter. She's looking at me as if she knows it isn't.

If Ginny didn't say those words and ask me to repeat them, if I didn't see them written down in this woman's notebook . . .

But I *did*. I know I did. Just because I was wrong about Ginny doesn't mean I must be wrong about this.

'Could I have a look?' I ask. 'Please? I won't read anything. I'm just . . .' *Just what? Too stupid and stubborn to take her word for it without checking?* Why don't I care that I'm behaving outrageously? I can't take this any further; I have no right to. 'Show me any page, and if it hasn't got lines on it—'

'It hasn't.' She glances at her watch, nods towards the garden. 'I'd better go in. I'm more than two hours late for my appointment, and sixty-five minutes late for yours. And even if most of that lateness isn't my fault . . .' She shrugs. 'Believe it or not, I'd rather carry on talking to you. And I might show you my notebook one day, maybe even one day soon – but not now.' She gives me a loaded look as she delivers this peculiar speech. Is she coming on to me? There must be a reason why she isn't as angry with me as she would have every right to be.

Maybe even one day soon. Why does she think she's going to see me again? It makes no sense.

Before I can ask, she's walking past me and into Ginny's back garden. Watching her move convinces me that I couldn't do anything so ambitious; I stay rooted to the spot. Maybe I'll wait for her to come out in an hour. Except I can't. I have to get back for the girls. I need to leave now, or I'll be late. Still, I don't move – not until the sound of knocking galvanises me and I realise that in a matter of seconds, Ginny will open the door of her wooden office. I can't let her see me here, not after the way I yelled at her. If there's one thing I am absolutely sure of, it's that Ginny Saxon must never see me again, and vice versa. I'll post her an apologetic note with a cheque for seventy quid pinned to it, and then find a different hypnotherapist – one closer to home, in Rawndesley, who has never seen me behave like an obnoxious brat. Luke will laugh and call me a coward and he'll be right. In my defence, I could point out that, as cowards go, surely the paying, apologising kind are the best.

Who am I kidding? I'm not going to tell Luke how badly I behaved.

You never do. I push the thought away.

Inside my now freezing car, I rest my head on the steering wheel and groan. Ginny could have argued with me, but she didn't. She agreed to waive her fee for the session, since I clearly felt badly let down by her. Maybe I'll send her a cheque for double the amount I owe. No, that looks desperate; might as well change my will, leave her everything on one condition – that she promises not to spend the rest of her life thinking I'm the biggest arsehole she's ever met.

It's nine minutes past four. If I set off now, I'll make it. If I stay here another ten minutes, then drive dangerously fast all the way back to Rawndesley, I'll make it. I won't even need ten minutes, because Red Lipstick Woman will have locked her car, and I'll be back in mine and heading home thirty seconds from now.

I don't know what it means. She said it as if she was more frustrated than I was by her inability to understand the words in her notebook; she didn't seem to care if I knew it. Then why deny having written them?

Without allowing myself to think about what I'm doing, I get out of my car, cross the road and walk up Ginny's drive, exactly as I did an hour ago. I'm glad it's dark, glad Culver Valley County Council is more scared of the anti-light-pollution lobby than of their opponents, who petition endlessly for a solid flank of lamp-posts along every rural A-road, so that pensioners and teenage girls can see the muggers and rapists lying in wait for them.

There are no criminals anywhere in sight, I'm happy to report. Only a crazy woman in search of a notebook.

Everything will be fine as long as Red Lipstick Woman has remembered to lock her car; I will be prevented from doing something insane and illegal. What law would I be breaking, I wonder. Something to do with trespass, probably. It can't be breaking and entering if I don't break anything. Unlawful entry?

I try the driver door. It opens. Immediately, I feel more unlawful than I have ever felt. My gasps of breath hang like foggy graffiti on the air: visible evidence that I am here, where I shouldn't be.

All I've done is open a car door. Is that so bad? I could still close it and walk away.

And never find out if you saw the words you think you saw.

What if they're not there? Will I go back to believing they must have come from Ginny – that she asked me to repeat them and then, for some impossible-to-imagine reason, denied it?

The notebook lies open on the passenger seat, next to the black gloves. My hands shake as I reach over and pick it up. I start to flick through the pages. There's lots of writing in here, but I can only make out the odd word; the sky is too dark, nearly as black as the surrounding fields. There's a light on in the car – it came on when I opened the door – but in order to benefit from it I'd have to . . .

Don't think about it. Just do it.

My heart pounding, I sit in the driver's seat, leaving the door open and my legs outside in the cold, so that only part of my body is doing something wrong. I open the notebook again. At first I can't concentrate; my focus is on my out-of-control heartbeat, which feels as if it's about to spring out of my mouth. Will I be found at five o'clock, dead from a heart attack in a stranger's car? At least I've shaken off my post-hypnosis stupor, finally – nothing like a bit of law-breaking to detrancify the mind.

There's no such thing as a hypnotised feeling. That's what Ginny said. I'm no expert, but I think she might be wrong.

When I'm calm enough to concentrate, I see that the notebook is full of letters, if you can call something that isn't addressed to anyone or signed from anyone a letter. Which you can't, I don't think. My guess is that these diatribes were not written for sending but to make the writer feel better. Each one is several pages long, angry, full of accusations. I start to read the first one, then stop after a couple of lines as a tremor of panic rolls through me.

What the hell am I doing? I'm not here to immerse myself in a stranger's bitterness – I need to find what I'm looking for and get out of here. Now that I've glimpsed the verbal wrath Red Lipstick woman unleashes on anyone who crosses her, I'm even less keen than I was to be caught rifling through her possessions.

I flick through the pages quickly: diatribe, diatribe, diatribe, shopping list, diatribe ... After a while I stop looking at the content. There is too much writing on these pages for any of them to be the page I'm looking for: one with only five words on it, surrounded by lots of space; a mostly blank page.

I'm an idiot. These pages aren't lined. Why wasn't that the first thing I spotted when I opened the notebook? Why am I still sitting here? Can hypnotherapy cause permanent brain damage?

I carry on flicking through, although I'm guessing the notebook is unlikely to develop lines at its halfway point.

Give up.

Just one more.

I turn the page, barely see the words before I hear the click of a door opening. *Oh, no, oh, God, this is not happening.* Harbouring an overpowering desire for something not to happen feels the same as forbidding it to happen. The drawback is that it doesn't work.

I'm trapped in an elongated rectangle of light. The woman whose car I have invaded is marching towards me. Trying to work out if I'd have time to get out and run away before she reaches me, I end up staying where I am. Why did I take such an insane risk? How could I be so stupid? Dinah and Nonie will be getting off the school bus at half past four, and I won't be there to collect them. Where will I be? In a police cell? My stomach churns in sudden, urgent pain; adrenaline forces beads of sweat through my skin. Is this a panic attack?

'Put down my notebook and get out of my car.' Her efficient calm chills me. There's something wrong about this situation, wronger than me being here without permission. She ought to be angrier. *She ought to be inside.* Why did she come out? Was it a trap? Maybe she knew what I was likely to do – knew it before I did, even – and deliberately left her car unlocked, giving me the opportunity to incriminate myself, and her the chance to catch me.

Ginny Saxon stands in the doorway of her wooden room, watching us. 'Everything okay?' she calls out. I can't look at her. I stare at the open notebook in my hands.

Then I close it, pass it to its owner.

'Go home, Amber,' she says wearily, as if I'm a naughty child whose detention has come to an end. 'Stay at home. We'll do the explanations part later, shall we?'

I've no idea what she means, but I'm more than happy to make both our lives easier by getting the hell away from her, away from Ginny, away from 77 Great Holling Road, the scene of too many catastrophically humiliating events for me ever to be willing to come back here.

~

Back in my car, I force my mind to go blank. If I'm thinking anything, it's 'Drive, drive, drive'. I can just make it in time for the girls, if I'm ruthless. As I approach the Crozier Bridge roundabout, I get into the lane on the far left, the only one that isn't clogged with queueing cars. Once I'm on the roundabout, I swerve over, attracting irate beeps from other drivers, and get into the lane I need to be in. I perform the same stunt at three more roundabouts and save nearly ten minutes of queueing time.

You are ruthless, and not only today. Don't try to pretend this behaviour is new.

Hypnotherapy seems to have amplified the voice in my head that's always trying to make me feel guilty. Or maybe it hasn't. It's certainly magnified my paranoia.

Drive, drive, drive. Drive, drive, drive.

My heart rate finally slows to a manageable level when I realise that I will, after all, be there in time to meet the bus. I've never missed it yet, not once, and I'm determined that I never will. The downside of seeing off my bus-related worries is that there is now space in my mind for other thoughts.

She lied to me.

The words were there in her notebook, exactly as I said: 'Kind,

Cruel, Kind of Cruel'. Written as a list on an otherwise blank page. No printed lines, true, but apart from that detail my description was spot on. So why did she tell me I couldn't have seen it?

I need another perspective on this to orientate my own – not that I know what mine is yet, other than confusion. If I tell Luke what happened, he'll tell me it's obvious why Red Lipstick Woman lied. Since Little Orchard, his default mode has been to listen to whatever's puzzling me, then deny the existence of the puzzling element in case I become obsessed. 'You're looking at it from the wrong angle,' he'll say. 'It would have been odd if she *hadn't* lied. She doesn't care if your memory's misfiring – why should she? All she's going to care about is preserving what's left of her privacy. She's written something weird in her notebook, you've seen it, and she doesn't want to explain what it is. No mystery there.'

Song lyrics? A poem? A description of her emotional state, or her personality? It was kind of her to let me have her appointment, cruel of her to sneer at Ginny for basing her hypnotherapy practice in a shed in her back garden.

Kind of cruel to lie to me about what she'd written in her notebook?

I shake my head, disgusted by the absurdity of my line of reasoning. How many people write lists of their own character traits in notebooks that they carry around with them?

Jo's the person I'm itching to discuss it with, but I'm not going to allow myself to ring her as soon as I get in, however much I'd like to. On a day when I've already done too many bad things, I'm going to exercise some self-restraint for once in my life and stop myself from adding another to the list. Since Little Orchard, I have often drawn other people's inexplicable behaviour to Jo's attention and asked her if she can think of any reason why someone might behave so bizarrely. I do it to make her feel awkward; I am trying to tell her without actually telling her that I have not forgotten her and Neil's mystifying disappearing act that Christmas – never referred to by any of us and never accounted for.

If Jo is conscious of my hidden agenda, she's expert at conceal-ing it; my frequent observations about the irrationality of this person or that person never seem to throw her off track. I'd like to think she's as aware as I am of all the important things we don't say to one another when we get the chance – aware, crucially, that these gaps between us are her fault – but I'm starting to wonder if she has deleted Little Orchard from her mind, and is genuinely oblivious to its continued occupation of mine. From the way she says, 'That *is* odd' and 'What a weirdo!' when I describe the strange behaviour of my various colleagues, it's pretty clear she's offering that response as someone who wouldn't dream of behaving so oddly herself.

I arrive at the corner of Spilling Road and Clavering Road at my usual time of twenty-eight minutes past four. Dinah and Nonie's school bus has two drop-off points in the centre of Rawndesley – here and the station car park. The station is the more popular one, but for me this one has two advantages: hardly anybody uses it, and it's no more than five or six strides from my front door. Luke and I bought number 9 Clavering Road just over a year ago in order to have somewhere big enough for the girls to move into. I was determined to buy the biggest house I could afford; nothing else mattered. It still doesn't. I don't care that the carpeting throughout is hideous, synthetic and bright red, or that all the curtains are faded floral and so heavily swagged that you can barely see any window between the loops and folds of fabric; I don't care that we can't afford to replace any of it. What I love about my house is that even though it's on a main road, even though I live with three other people, two of whom are children, I can always find a silent, empty room when I need one. Luke's and my old house had a ground floor that was entirely open plan apart from a downstairs loo; this one has floor after floor of square rooms with closable doors. When I mentioned this to Jo as a major attraction, it was obvious she disap-proved. 'Who do you want to shut out?' she asked. She didn't say so, but I knew she doubted my ability to look after Dinah and Nonie properly – Saint Jo, who believes no one can nurture quite as well

29

as she can, who loves nothing more than to surround herself with as many dependent relatives as possible.

I told her the truth: that the only person I want to shut out – need to, sometimes – is myself. I remember what I said. I chose my words carefully to tempt her interest: 'My mind can be a harsh environment. Sometimes I need to take it far away from the people I care about, to make sure I don't contaminate anybody.' Jo's reply shocked me. 'Ignore me,' she said. 'I'm just jealous. Dinah and Nonie are amazing kids. You're so lucky.' At the time, I laughed and said, 'As if you haven't got enough people on your plate.' It was only later, lying awake that night in bed, that I replayed the scene and decided I was angry with her – or rather, I decided I ought to be, I would have every right to be. I spend a lot of time wondering how I ought to feel about Jo, while having no idea how I actually feel.

She called me lucky, knowing my best friend was dead, knowing that Luke and I probably wouldn't now have children of our own. She avoided responding to what I'd said about feeling the need to shut myself out because she didn't want our conversation to go beyond the superficial. She never does any more; I'm convinced that her apparent determination to spend every waking hour catering for at least ten people is an escape strategy – how can anyone expect you to engage in meaningful conversation with them when you're dashing around your too-small kitchen putting together a cream tea that would make the Ritz Hotel's equivalent look paltry?

I look at my watch. The bus is late. It always is. We've been told in an official letter from the school that while we must be prompt and prepared to wait for up to twenty minutes, the bus will never wait for us. If we are not there to pick up on the dot of half past four, the children will be returned to school and put in something called 'Fun Club'. I was instantly suspicious when I read this: if things are fun, one doesn't generally need to be 'put in' them. I wanted to write to the school and point out that its bus needs a lesson in give-and-take, but Dinah forbade me. 'You're going to need to fight the school over more important things,' she told me, as if toppling the board of governors was something she'd been

mulling over recently, even if she hadn't yet wholeheartedly committed to the plan. 'Save your energy for a fight that matters.' This made
me smile; it's something Luke and I are always telling her. 'Just make
sure you're on time for the bus. It's easier for us to be on time than
it is for any other family at the school,' she added, sounding like a
headmistress. I submitted because I was so relieved to hear her
describe us as a family.

Luke and I didn't know when we bought our house that the girls'
school bus dropped off and picked up right outside; when we found
out, Luke said, 'It's a sign. It's got to be. Someone's on our side.' On
yours, maybe, I thought. The kind of Someone he had in mind would
have had access to information about me that I was fairly sure
would result in an instant withdrawal of all supernatural support.
Knowing I couldn't say that to Luke, angry to be trapped with a
secret I hated and wished would go away, I snapped at him unfairly.
'Would that be the same Someone who let Sharon die?' He apolo-
gised. I didn't and still haven't.

Another cheery memory. Ginny Saxon would be proud.

I can say sorry to strangers, and even send them cheques for
seventy pounds that I've told them they don't deserve, but I can't
apologise to my own husband, not any more; I would feel like a
hypocrite. Any 'sorry' I might say would be nothing more than a
shield for the 'sorry' I'm not saying, the one I can never say.

Hypnotherapy and me are a bad match, I decide. I need something
that's going to pull me out of my endlessly churning interior world,
not plunge me deeper into it.

I've never been less in the mood to make polite conversation than
I am now, so Sod's Law dictates that, on the exterior world front,
today there are three mothers waiting on the corner for the bus.
Usually there's only one, who cuts me dead because I once said the
wrong thing. I've forgotten her name and the name of her shaggy-
headed child, but I think of her as OCB, which stands for organic
cereal bar. She brings one every afternoon for her son, whose hair,
she once told me, has never been cut because she can't bear the
thought of vandalising any precious part of him, and certainly not

when he's perfectly happy as he is, and why should she, purely for the sake of convention and to please the bigot contingent? She detained me for nearly fifteen minutes with a full explanation that veered into gender-role-redefining manifesto towards the end, even though I'd been polite enough not to ask her why her son resembled a sheepskin rug.

Before she decided I was beyond the pale and not worth talking to, I learned a lot about what it means to be a parent from listening to OCB. It seems fairly straightforward: if you have a child that behaves like a savage, deflect attention from his shortcomings by accusing the teachers of 'pathologising' him and failing to meet his individual needs, especially if these include the need to poke other children in the eye with a fork. If your son fails a test, accuse the school of being too outcome-focused; if he is lazy and says everything is boring, blame the teacher for not stretching or stimulating him in the right way; if your child is not particularly bright, couch the problem in terms of the school failing to identify and plug a 'skills gap'; crucially, ostracise anyone who dares to suggest that some gaps – those belonging to clever children, specifically – are easier to fill with skills than others, and that, hypothetically, a teacher might try endlessly to lob into the chasm some fairly basic proficiencies and fail to lodge them there, owing to an inherently unsympathetic micro-climate of massive stupidity.

I probably shouldn't have said that, but it had been a long day, and my freedom went to my head – the freedom of being a guardian and not a parent. I can see exactly how Dinah and Nonie make life harder for themselves, their classmates and their teachers, just as I can see their talents and their strong points, the personal and intellectual qualities that are going to make life easier for them. I feel no urge to feign modesty about the good or pretend the bad doesn't exist, not having made the girls myself, and so I don't need to enter into any reciprocal delusion-bolstering deals of the sort that many of the parents rely on: 'It doesn't surprise me *at all* that Mr Maskell hasn't spotted that Jerome's gifted, Susan – he hasn't noticed that Rhiannon is either.'

Dinah and Nonie are first off the bus when it arrives, as they usually are. I hang back behind the mothers, as per Dinah's instructions. In the very early days, she told me that I wasn't allowed to run forward and give her a hug or a kiss, that Sharon hadn't been allowed to either – any display of affection in a public place is embarrassing and therefore forbidden. I am, however, allowed to smile enthusiastically, and this I do as the girls walk towards me with quick neat steps, like purposeful businesswomen on their way to an important meeting. I can see from Dinah's face that she has something significant to say to me. She always does, every day. Nonie is worried about how I will react to whatever it is, and how Dinah will react to my reaction, as she always is. I can feel myself mentally limbering up as they approach, knowing that whatever's about to pass between us will seem to fly by at a million miles an hour, and I'm going to need to be on my toes, mentally. Luke has the knack of relaxing with the girls; he can coax them into winding down in a way that I've never been able to. My conversations with them often feel like super-fast games of verbal ping-pong, in which I'm desperate to let them win, but never quite sure how to.

'Are you and Luke ever going to have a baby?' Dinah asks, handing me her and Nonie's book bags; it is my job to carry them to the house.

'No. Why, what makes you ask that?'

'Someone on the bus asked us, because you're not our mum and dad. This girl, Venetia, said that if you had a baby of your own, you'd love it more than you love us, and Nonie got upset.'

'If we did have a baby, we wouldn't love it any more than we love you,' I say to Nonie, making sure to look only at her, knowing Dinah's pride would rebel at the slightest suggestion that she too might need reassurance. 'Not one single bit more. But we're not going to have a baby. We talked about it, and we decided. We're going to stay as we are: a family of four.'

'Good, because there'd be no point,' says Dinah.

'In our having a baby?'

'No. It'd only grow up and work in an office. Has anyone from school phoned you today?'

'No,' I say. 'Should they have?'

'Dinah's in trouble, and it's not her fault,' says Nonie, picking at the skin on her lip.

'I told you.' Her sister turns on her. 'Mrs Truscott didn't ring because she knew Amber'd stick up for me.'

'Stick up for you over what?'

'Is Luke home yet?' Dinah ignores my question, unwinds her school scarf from round her neck and hands it to me along with her gloves.

'I don't know. I've not been into the house, I've only just—'

'I'll tell him first and then I'll tell you.'

'That's stupid,' says Nonie. 'He'll tell her.'

'*I*'ll tell her. But she won't worry as much once she sees Luke thinks it's funny, which he will.'

All this before we get to the front door. 'What's wrong with working in an office?' I ask as I fumble in my handbag for my house keys. 'I work in an office.'

'It's boring,' says Dinah. 'Not for you, if you like it – that's fine. I just mean, when you think how many people work in offices – almost everybody – *then* it's boring. It'd be silly to have a baby just so that it could grow up and do a boring thing that too many people do already.'

I drop my keys on the doorstep, bend to pick them up, say, 'People do different things in their offices – interesting things, sometimes.' I notice I'm not demanding to know what Dinah is putting off telling me; I also like the idea of waiting until Luke's here to soften the blow by finding it hilarious.

'I'm going to be a stonemason, like Luke,' says Dinah. 'I could take over running his business when he gets too old. He's quite old already.'

Can girls be stonemasons? Luke is forever lugging around huge chunks of York and Bath stone that I'm sure no female could lift. 'Last week you wanted to be a baroness,' I remind Dinah as I unlock the door. 'I think that's a better fit, I have to say.'

Nonie hangs back. 'How much money have we got?' she asks. OCB, who is conducting an inventory of Sheepskin Rug's possessions on the pavement nearby, adjusts her stance in the hope of hearing my reply.

'That's a funny question, Nones. Why?'

'Enver in my class – his mum and dad have got so much money that he won't ever have to get a job. We haven't got that much, have we?'

I try to usher her inside, but she sticks determinedly to the doorstep. 'You don't need to worry about money, or about getting a job,' I tell her. 'You're a child. Let the grown-ups do the worrying.' Her frown lines deepen, and I realise I've said the wrong thing. 'Not that Luke and I have anything to worry about. We're fine, Nones, financially and in every other way. Everything's fine.'

'I'd like to get a job when I'm older, but I don't know how to,' she says. 'Or how to buy a house, or a car, or find a husband.'

'You're not supposed to know about any of that stuff yet. You're only seven,' I say.

She shakes her head sorrowfully. 'Everyone in my class already knows who they're marrying, apart from me.'

'Dinah – airlock!' I call out, seeing that the inner door is wide open, the one that's supposed to stay shut until the outer door's closed. 'Come on, Nones, can we go in? It's freezing.' She sighs, but does as she's told. Disappointment rises from her small body like steam. She hoped to be able to solve her matrimonial problem before crossing the threshold, and it didn't happen; now she's having to go inside with it still unresolved.

I give her a hug and promise that as soon as she's old enough, I will find the most amazing, handsome, clever, kind, rich, wonderful man for her to marry. She looks delighted for a second, then worried. 'Dinah'll need one too,' she says. Nonie's obsessed with fairness. I restrain myself from voicing my sudden strong hunch that Dinah will need at least three, as I hang up coats, arrange discarded shoes in pairs and pick up the envelopes that are scattered on the floor. One is from Social Services. I wish I could tear it up and not have to read what's inside.

I'm about to close and lock the outer door when I hear a voice say, 'Amber Hewerdine?' I look outside and see a short, wiry man with black hair, dark brown bloodshot eyes and sallow skin. He looks as if he's been doing too much or too little of something. Automatically, I wonder if he sleeps well. 'DC Gibbs,' he says, producing a card from his pocket that he holds in front of my face.

That was quick. Aren't mistakes meant to take a while to catch up with you? Obviously the in-denial period of imagining I might get away with it has given its appointment to the horrible retribution that was booked in for a later slot.

'Put that thing away,' I tell him, looking over my shoulder into the house. Thankfully, we seem to be alone; he missed Nonie by a few seconds. 'Listen, because this is important – more important than me looking at that woman's stupid notebook,' I hiss at him. 'I've got two girls inside who *cannot* find out that you're a cop. Okay? If they see you, you're selling something: double-glazing, feather dusters, take your pick.'

'Kind, Cruel, Kind of Cruel,' he says, and I have that unnerving feeling again, the same one I had outside Ginny's house, when I was caught in the act: *this is wrong*. His reaction is off by a few degrees. Why isn't he telling me that helping oneself to the contents of someone else's car is a serious offence? Why is he quoting those strange words at me? Then it hits me, what the problem is: this is like something that would only happen in a dream – a stranger accosts you outside your house and says the very words that have been going round and round in your mind.

'What does it mean?' he asks. *In a dream, neither of you would know what the words meant.*

'You're asking the wrong person,' I say.

'Amber?' I look over the DC's shoulder and see Luke walking towards us fast. He must sense that something's wrong. I feel irrationally encouraged by the idea that there are three of us now, and two of us are on my side. Luke smells of sweat, and of the dust that's coating his skin and clothes; he's been at the quarry all day.

'This guy's police,' I tell him, mouthing the last word. 'Go in and keep an eye on the girls, tell them I'm talking to someone from work.'

'What's going on?' he asks us both, as if we're conspiring to exclude him.

'I need to talk to your wife,' DC Gibbs tells him. To me, he says, 'You can agree to come in or I can arrest you – your choice.'

'Arrest me?' I laugh. 'So that you can ask me why I looked at some woman's notebook?'

'So that I can ask you what you know about the murder of Katharine Allen,' he says.

What is the difference between a story and a legend? In which category does Little Orchard belong? I'd say it falls squarely into the 'legend' category. It has a name, for one thing: Little Orchard. Those two words suggest more than a house in Surrey. They're enough to call to mind a complex sequence of events and an even more multi-layered collection of opinions and emotions. Wherever we have a mental shortcut phrase for a story from our past, that provides a clue that the story has become a legend.

Does it matter that, apart from one Italian nanny, the only people who know it are all members of the same extended family? I don't think so. For all those people, it stands out. It will always stand out. It's unique: a banned story, one they have tacitly agreed never to mention to one another and one that, as a result, they probably dwell on far more than they would if they were allowed to discuss it freely. It is certainly the most intriguing story the family owns – a mystery that seems unlikely ever to be solved. No progress has been made towards solving it in seven years, and the reasons why this is the case are almost as interesting as the mystery itself.

What sort of mind would invent something so bizarre, and why? If I'm pretending, for now, that the story – the legend – is a lie from start to finish, then that's a question that has to be asked of every event, every utterance and every emotion within the overall sequence – asked, and if possible, answered.

First, though, we must look at the sequence. Which is a practice we've grown unused to, ever since Little Orchard acquired legend status. When a story becomes a legend, our mental shortcut phrase tends to evoke not what actually happened, stage by stage – that would be far too labour-intensive – but a convenient wrapping that covers the whole. For Little Orchard, several obvious wrapping concepts spring to mind: 'We'll probably never know', 'It only goes to show that you can never truly know a person, however close to them you think you are', perhaps even the treacherous 'We're better off not knowing', since many people collude with whoever is attempting to pull the wool over their eyes.

Do you see what I'm saying? How a memory loses itself within the hard shell of a story, and how a story is then further twisted out of shape and consolidated in its most easily consumable form when it becomes a legend?

I want to take the Little Orchard legend back to the level of story. Treating it exactly as I would a work of fiction, I'm going to tell it as if I don't know any of the characters in it – I haven't met any of them yet, and so I trust no one character more than the others. I'm also going to bring to the story the same expectation I would bring to a work of fiction: that I can and will find out exactly what it all means, that any other outcome would be an outrageous betrayal on the part of the storyteller. Like all mystery stories, this one must have a solution. Not knowing, never finding out, is unacceptable. I am stressing this before I start to describe what happened; in doing so, I am signalling to the solution that I know it's there and I expect it to reveal itself when the time is right.

December 2003: Johannah and Neil Utting, a married couple in their mid-thirties, splash out on hiring a big house over Christmas, one that can accommodate all their relatives. It will be their Christmas present to everybody. Their own house is too small, with only three bedrooms.

After searching on the internet, Johannah, known as Jo, chooses a house called Little Orchard in Cobham, Surrey. It has five double bedrooms and four twins, which is perfect. The whole extended family is invited, and everybody accepts: Neil's brother and sister-in-law, Luke and Amber; Jo's mother Hilary, Jo's sister Kirsty and her brother Ritchie; Neil's parents, Pam and Quentin; Jo and Neil's nanny Sabina, their five-year-old son William and their newborn baby, Barney.

On Christmas Eve, Sabina stays in with William and Barney while everyone else walks to the nearest pub, the Plough, to have dinner. Everybody seems to have a good time. Nothing out of the ordinary happens. At about ten thirty, the party returns to Little Orchard. William and Barney are fast asleep. Pam and Quentin, Neil's parents, are the first adults to go to bed, shortly followed by Sabina, the nanny. Neil, Luke and Amber decide to call it a night half an hour later. Amber and Luke hear Neil say to Jo,

'Are you coming to bed?' and see him look puzzled when she says, 'No, not yet.' Amber and Luke are surprised too. Neil and Jo always go to bed at the same time – they are 'one of those couples', as Amber comments to Luke later. Neil seems put out by Jo's negative response. He shrugs and stomps off upstairs. Everyone listens to his footsteps, which echo through the house for a long time. He and Jo are in the master suite, on the top floor.

Amber and Luke say goodnight and head upstairs to their bedroom on the first floor, leaving Jo, Hilary, Kirsty and Ritchie downstairs in the lounge.

The next morning, Christmas morning, four people who should be there are not. Jo, Neil, William and Barney have disappeared. So has their car. Sabina, the children's nanny, is mystified. Jo would never go anywhere without her, she says, not if the children were going. 'Even if William or Barney were ill, and needed to be taken quickly to hospital?' Hilary asks. 'Especially then,' says Sabina. No note has been left anywhere in the house. All mobile phones are checked, but no explanatory messages have been left. Jo's handbag and Neil's wallet have gone, but all the Christmas presents are still there, wrapped and waiting beneath the tree. Most of them are for William and Barney. Sabina bursts into tears. 'Jo would never take her boys away on Christmas morning before they'd opened their presents,' she says. 'Something has happened to them.' She tries to ring first Jo's mobile phone and then Neil's, but both are switched off.

Sabina and Hilary want to contact the police, but the others persuade them that it's too soon, and would be, at this stage, an overreaction. By two o'clock, everybody has come round to their worst-case-scenario way of thinking, and Sabina makes the call.

A detective turns up, asks a lot of questions, says he thinks it unlikely that Jo, Neil and the boys have been removed from Little Orchard against their will. Sabina accuses him of not having listened properly. She tells him to go back to the police station and recharge his solitary brain cell. He nods and stands up to leave, as if he thinks this is a sensible suggestion, and says he will call round again the following day to see if Jo and Neil have been in touch. At the front door, he pauses to announce that Christmas – especially Christmas spent with one's entire family – can be a very stressful time of year; he tells everybody to bear that in mind.

The rest of the day passes in a blur of tension and misery, punctuated by occasional hysterical outbursts from Pam and Hilary, William and Barney's two grandmothers, and from Sabina, who keeps saying that she will throw herself off a tall building or swallow a bottle of pills if anything has happened to Jo, Neil and the boys – that's how much she loves them. Luke gets angry and snaps at her to 'give it a rest with the suicide talk'. Pam remarks, at one point, that Kirsty is lucky. 'Ignorance is bliss,' she says. 'She doesn't even know they're missing.' Does Amber wonder about what Kirsty does or doesn't know? She doesn't even know if there's a name for what's wrong with Kirsty; Jo has never volunteered the information.

No presents are opened and no turkey is eaten. That night, nobody sleeps well. Pam and Hilary don't sleep at all.

The following morning, Amber comes downstairs at quarter past seven and finds Jo in the kitchen with William and Barney. The tips of the boys' noses are red, the lenses of Jo's glasses misted over. They look as if they have just walked in. Neil's jacket and mobile phone are on the counter. 'Wake everyone up,' Jo orders, before Amber has a chance to ask her anything. 'Get everyone together in the lounge.' She doesn't look at Amber as she says this.

Amber does as she's told, and soon the whole family plus Sabina is assembled in the lounge, not daring to move, waiting for the announcement that will explain everything. Jo and Neil are heard whispering in the hall, but no one can make out what they're saying. Luke and Amber exchange a look that says, 'This had bloody well better be good'. Only Sabina is irrepressibly relieved and happy, clapping her hands together and saying, 'Thank God they are back safe and sound.' Pam and Hilary have bypassed the relief stage altogether, and are waiting in petrified silence for some piece of catastrophic news to be delivered; both are certain it's on its way.

After keeping everybody waiting for nearly fifteen minutes, Jo finally appears. 'Neil's taken the boys upstairs for a bath,' she says. 'They were filthy.' She sighs and stares out of the window at the split-level garden that looks like an enormous grass staircase, with a perfectly square lawn on each step. 'Look, I know you've all been waiting and wondering, but if it's all right with you, I'm going to keep this brief.' Jo sounds like a politician at a press conference. Almost as if she has listened to herself and not liked the way she sounded, she changes her tone – makes it warmer, more personal. Now there is plenty of eye contact. 'I'm really sorry about yesterday. Neil's sorry too. We're . . . sorrier than we can say. Truly. We know how worried you must have been . . .' She pauses. Her eyes fill with tears. Then she sniffs, pulls herself together. 'Anyway, the important thing is that there's nothing wrong and nothing for any of you to worry about. Everything's fine – and that's the truth. And I promise we will never mysteriously vanish again. Now, please tell me we can forget all about yesterday and have our Christmas Day today instead.'

'Of course, Jo,' says Sabina. 'We are just happy you are all okay.'

'We're more than okay.' Jo looks at each of us in turn, trying to drive the point home. 'We're fine. There's no problem, there's nothing we're not telling you. Honestly.' Her voice is full of warmth, confidence and authority – the sort of voice you want to trust.

'Fair enough,' says Ritchie. Hasn't he noticed that Jo has told a very obvious untruth, in her bid to be believed? *There's nothing we're not telling you.* Of course there is; everyone listening knows there is. No one points this out, however. Everyone assumes Jo meant to say that there was nothing *significant* she and Neil were withholding.

'Well . . . thank goodness,' says Pam. Quentin nods. Hilary is busy wiping Kirsty's mouth and doesn't say anything.

Amber and Luke exchange another look. Luke opens his mouth to speak – to demand a proper explanation, he tells Amber later – but Jo cuts him off, saying, 'Please, Luke, don't make this worse for me than it already is. Can't we put it behind us? I've been so looking forward to being here with everyone. I can't bear to think that I've ruined Christmas.' She attempts a joke: 'If you knew how much Neil and I paid for this place, I promise you you'd understand.'

Luke wouldn't have let Neil get away with it, but this is Jo – a woman trying not to cry, trying very obviously to put a brave face on something. Luke doesn't want to make her break down in front of everyone by pushing her to reveal details she doesn't want to share. He also gets the impression that most people in the room would rather not know; if they are not party to the problem, they can't be expected to contribute to its resolution, and doing nothing is always easier than doing something. And, given Jo's reluctance to talk about it, it could well be deeply private – even more reason to steer clear. Luke can feel everyone around him deciding to take Jo at her word and believe that everything is 'more than okay' and 'fine'.

Amber is thinking along the same lines: if it were not something private, Jo would tell them. She's not generally a secretive person. If it hadn't been an unavoidable emergency, Jo wouldn't have taken her branch of the family and disappeared without a word of explanation to anybody. Jo is neither thoughtless nor unreliable. It is inconceivable that she would do such a thing.

Officially, the incident is never mentioned again. In fact, it gets several more mentions over the years, most of which Jo and Neil know nothing about. Amber keeps track of the references, like a sort of unofficial verbal cuttings agency, which is both appropriate and easy because Amber is often the person who brings it up. Two years after the event, she finds herself alone with Sabina and dares to ask her if she knows any more than the rest of them do. 'No,' says Sabina. 'In Italy, I would know. English families don't talk about anything.' Amber believes her.

About a year later, Amber confides in Pam, her mother-in-law, that she still often wonders what really happened, still wants to know. 'Well,' says Pam, wrinkling her nose as if Amber has raised a distasteful subject. 'You do and you don't, really.' Amber thinks this is a ridiculous thing to say. What on earth is it supposed to mean?

Luke is the only person with whom Amber can talk freely about Little Orchard, though it annoys her that he often appears to be humouring her. He is no longer interested. As he puts it, 'The moment's passed. It was a blip, that's all. Neil and Jo have been fine ever since. What does it matter any more?'

It matters to Amber. So much that she has even considered asking William, now twelve, if he can remember anything of that night. Why?

Amber is reluctant to claim sole ownership of her curiosity. She suspects everyone is secretly desperate to know; certainly all the women who were there. Hilary and Sabina have both wondered ever since that night – they must have; how could they not? – whether the happy-seeming surface of Neil and Jo's relationship is nothing more than an optical illusion. Pam, before she died in January from liver cancer, must have wondered too.

And is Amber really the only member of the Little Orchard party who still listens carefully whenever William and Barney open their mouths, in case they let a clue slip out? If something strange is going on between their parents, or in their home, there's no way that, bright as they are, they're unaware of it.

Why doesn't Amber simply ask Jo straight out, if she's so curious? Maybe, after all these years, Jo would simply laugh and tell her. And even if not, surely the worst that would happen is that Jo would say, 'I'm sorry, that's private.'

When Amber thinks about it, she realises that she knows the answer to this question, and, as answers go, it's a baffling one. It isn't that she is worried Jo won't want to tell her. On the contrary, and odd though it sounds, *it is Amber who doesn't want to tell Jo*. She feels as if that would be a terribly impolite, almost a violent thing to do. Jo appears to have erased the incident from her memory entirely. She walked out of the lounge at Little Orchard on Boxing Day 2003, having made her announcement, and immediately – instantaneously – created an alternative version of the universe, one in which *it did not happen*. That is the world in which she now lives happily, and for Amber to ask her about Little Orchard would be to drag her out of it. 'Like going up to someone you see having fun at a party and telling them that you happen to know they were a victim of genocide in a previous life,' says Amber to Luke, who thinks she is being melodramatic. His take on it is different: 'I still don't see why they didn't just make up a plausible lie, if they didn't want to tell us the truth,' he says. 'That's what I'd have done.'

Which rather goes to prove my point: that there's nothing most of us love more than a plausible lie. A good story, in other words.

2

30/11/2010

It was nearly over. Detective Constable Simon Waterhouse grinned to himself. It hadn't started yet – the emergency meeting he'd called, with no authority to do so, was still waiting for him to arrive – but Simon could taste the finish. He was going to find out who had murdered Katharine Allen and why, within a few hours if he was lucky. It felt good to be speeding towards that knowledge – towards anything, if he was honest. He hadn't realised until today how much his own slowness had depressed him. He'd spent most of his life hesitating, imagining that he needed to win some kind of theoretical argument before acting. It seemed obvious to him now that a wiser strategy was to do almost anything, quickly. The wrong action leading to the wrong result was a swifter route to where you wanted to end up than no action and no result. Fast-forward motion was all that mattered.

There had been none in the Katharine Allen investigation for nearly a month. Now, thanks to Simon, there would be. Impatience hummed in his veins, a force field of restlessness that wasn't too far removed from extreme boredom, the kind that starts to fizz and explode around the edges, that would do anything rather than remain within its confines. Simon had no idea if his transformation into somebody more reckless than himself was permanent; Charlie had called it insanity, trying to talk him out of it. Running along the corridor to the CID room, Simon pictured himself strolling back in the opposite direction with a satisfied smile on his face once this was all over and done with. Normally when he ran, the speed of his body was balanced by a mind that hung back, tried to predict reactions and consequences.

Where had that mind gone? Had thinking too much worn it out?

He knew what he'd find in the CID room, and he found it: a dark, dank, mouldering atmosphere, devoid of hope, that made the well-lit second-floor office, with its contemporary furnishings, feel more like an airless stone-walled dungeon several miles underground. DI Giles Proust, who stood by the window with his back to the room, unwilling to look as if he might be waiting for anybody, could bring the subterranean dungeon vibe to any space that contained him simply by being in a bad mood.

Every dungeon needs chains, and Simon could see the invisible ones wrapped around DS Sam Kombothekra and DC Colin Sellers as they sat tensely at the conference table on one side of the room. Both of them gave Simon a look as he walked in – the same look, though Sam and Sellers were as different as it was possible for two men to be, a look that said, *What the fuck are you playing at, making him incandescent in advance?* Everyone knew the score: if you had something to tell the Snowman, something he didn't already know and might not like – and, since he didn't like anything, this was the broadest of categories – you approached him tentatively, stammering your willingness to reveal all immediately and take his inevitable abuse as your deserved punishment for not having told him the crucial information sooner, before you knew it yourself. What you didn't do was ring him as he was leaving work and already half an hour late for his supper, order him to stay put for an urgent meeting and refuse to say any more than that over the phone, as if you were the boss and he the underling.

That was the score. Simon knew it as well as Sam and Sellers did. He wanted to laugh at the stupidity of anyone who had imagined he'd put up with it indefinitely. He stood in the doorway, staring at Proust's rigid back. Real snowmen melted; not Proust. He generated his own ice from within.

No one said anything. Sam sighed. Eventually Sellers said, 'Waterhouse is here, sir.'

'He knows I'm here.' A challenge. Proust would ignore it.

'Shall I try Gibbs on his mobile, see where he's got to?' Sellers asked.

'DC Gibbs won't be joining us,' said Proust, still facing the window. For a second, Simon wondered if the inspector was about to hijack his meeting. Could Proust know already? How?

'Who would like to guess what Waterhouse has done with Gibbs? Has he promoted him to Chief Constable, do we think? Fired him?'

Simon relaxed. The Snowman wasn't one step ahead; he was flexing his sarcasm, the strongest muscle in his body.

'Dressed him as a black and white minstrel and sent him to wait in the wings?'

A grin passed across Sellers' face, but he couldn't hold it. The room's humour-neutralising atmosphere of clenched fury was too strong.

'There must be a reason why Gibbs is the only one of us not here, so let's have your most imaginative suggestions.' Proust turned to face his audience, taking care to look only at Sam and Sellers. 'Sergeant? Detective? For once, I'm inviting wild speculation. Thanks to Waterhouse, we have been forced to unlock our cramped conscious-nesses and enter a dimension in which anything is possible.' Every word pulsed with controlled outrage, as if the Snowman alone comprehended the doom that awaited them all. 'In our exhilaration, we have forgotten that – naming no names, and sparing finer feelings – some things ought not to be possible.' Finally, Proust looked at Simon – a look that made no bones about assigning him to that special category.

'Gibbs is interviewing a woman called Amber Hewerdine,' Simon said. 'I need to join him, soon as I can. I want the chance to question her myself. You're not going to like how this happened,' Simon looked at Proust as he spoke, 'but you'd be crazy if you didn't like the result, which is the first lead we've had so far on Katharine Allen.'

'Are we sitting comfortably?' Proust muttered, turning back to the window. 'Then let him begin.'

'Amber Hewerdine, thirty-four, lives on Clavering Road in Rawndesley, works for Rawndesley City Council in the licensing department. She made an appointment for three o'clock today to see a hypnotherapist called Ginny Saxon in Great Holling. I don't know what Hewerdine went to see her about – Saxon's refusing to tell me – but while she was there, waiting outside, she met Charlie. Charlie also had an appointment with Saxon, for two o'clock. She wants to quit smoking, a couple of people have told her hypno-therapy worked for them . . .' Simon wanted to say more – that it was a practical, rational solution to a common problem – but he stopped himself. Having done his best to assure Charlie that there was no need for her to be embarrassed, no reason for secrecy, Simon was determined not to feel embarrassed himself.

'Saxon was running an hour late, which seemed to be a problem for Hewerdine, so Charlie offered to switch appointments. She was happy to delay hers. She wasn't sure she wanted to go through with it anyway. She and Hewerdine had a brief conversation outside Saxon's house. While they were talking, Charlie was sitting in her car with an open notebook on her lap. Hewerdine might or might not have seen what was in the notebook.' Simon produced it from the inside jacket pocket he'd forced it into, and slapped it down on the table, so that the Snowman would hear what he was missing by turning his back on the room.

The gesture had no effect. As if he were conducting a recorded interview with a suspect, Simon said loudly and clearly, 'DC Waterhouse is taking a blue leather soft-backed notebook out of his pocket and putting it on the table. He's opening the notebook at the relevant page, the page Amber Hewerdine could have seen. Written on it are the words we all know: "Kind, Cruel, Kind of Cruel". In black ink, laid out like a list.' The notebook wouldn't stay open at first. Simon had to bend the covers right back. 'You all know Charlie's handwriting,' he said. 'Those of you who can be bothered to look can see it's her writing.'

Sam Kombothekra's eyes widened. There was an urgent question in them for Simon, one he couldn't answer. *I don't know why.* He thought he'd heard some people – he didn't know who, where, when – describe the way he felt as 'demob happy'. Except that in his case it was inappropriate; he wasn't leaving, not by choice at any rate, and was well aware that the fall-out from his new uninhibited, unedited approach might start to rain down on him any time now. On all of them. He tried to communicate this to Sam with a tiny shrug: *I'm not handing in my notice. I haven't been told I've got less than a month to live, or that Proust has. I'm doing it this way because it's the best way to do it.*

'Charlie took some work to the nearest pub, to kill an hour,' he went on. 'At four o'clock, when she went back to Ginny Saxon's, she met Hewerdine coming out. She said Hewerdine seemed a bit spaced out – in her own little world, as if stuff was preying on her mind. She told Charlie she'd seen what was in her notebook and asked her to confirm that the words "Kind, Cruel, Kind of Cruel" were there. Charlie told her they weren't, which was both true and untrue.'

'A factual impossibility,' Proust contributed sourly.

'Hewerdine couldn't have seen what she thought she'd seen,' Simon told him. 'Here's the crucial point: at three o'clock, when Charlie had the notebook open in the car – the only chance Hewerdine had to see it – the words *weren't* there, not all of them.'

Sellers opened his mouth, but Simon didn't need to hear his question in order to answer it. 'Charlie couldn't be more certain: when she and Hewerdine had their first conversation, at three o'clock, she'd written "Kind" and "Cruel", nothing else. About half an hour later, in the pub, with Hewerdine nowhere in sight, she went back to that page in her notebook and wrote "Kind of Cruel". Why? What was she thinking she'd achieve? Same as we've all thought: that staring at the words might help, might bring something to mind. It didn't work for her any more than it did for us. The words meant nothing to her beyond their obvious meanings, and she had the impression that it was the same for Hewerdine, who said to her, "I'm not asking you to tell me what it means, only to confirm that I could have seen those words in your notebook."'

Every time he stopped for breath, he risked interruption; he wasn't finished yet, not by a long way. 'Tell me if you think I'm leaping to conclusions, but it seems likely to me that seeing "Kind" and "Cruel" in Charlie's notebook sparked off an association that already existed in Hewerdine's mind between those words and "Kind of Cruel". She also mentioned to Charlie that she thought she'd seen the words written like a list on lined paper. Charlie wondered what I'm hoping you're all wondering now: did Hewerdine see the sheet of paper that was torn from the pad we found at Katharine Allen's flat, before or after it was torn off?'

Irritated by his colleagues' non-reaction, Simon allowed his impatience to erupt; it didn't count as losing your cool if you let it happen. 'Can you see how lucky we are to have this fall into our lap? I'll make a bet with each and every one of you – for as much as you want, name your price – that Amber Hewerdine didn't kill Katharine Allen and that she's going to lead us to the person who did.'

Slowly, Proust started to turn. *On the turn, like rancid milk.* 'By sheer chance . . .' the inspector began, his words as light as the footsteps of a ballet dancer. Simon saw Sam Kombothekra flinch at the grotesque disparity between the gently tripping voice and the scorn-contorted face. 'By sheer chance, the unfavourably married Mrs Simon Waterhouse, outside the premises of a hypno-quack in Great Holling, happens to run into a woman connected to the Katharine Allen murder.' Proust raised an index finger in the air. 'A woman who is thoughtful enough to reveal this connection, unprompted.' He shook his head, smiled. His cheeks were mottled with mauve patches; it was odd to think that his blood was red and warm like everyone else's. 'That's not luck. That's a coincidence so staggeringly improbable that I'm going to stick my neck out and say it didn't happen. Sergeant Kombothekra and DC Sellers would do well to extend their respective necks in a similar direction, if they care about their careers.'

Proust walked towards Simon slowly enough to make clear his disgust at the prospect of arriving at his destination. 'You don't, evidently,' he said. 'You let it be known – with no explanation or apology, as if it might have nothing to do with you – that Sergeant Zailer is familiar with a sequence of words that she has no right to be familiar with. An apathetic confession-by-omission: we infer from your story that you've breached the Data Protection Act – the Official Secrets Act, too, if we want to be pedantic about it . . .'

'Charlie's not just my wife,' said Simon. 'She's a police officer.'

'Barely, these days, from what I hear.' Proust snapped. 'Isn't she part of the team that's been leased out to some crackpot feelgood think-tank and charged with discouraging the inhabitants of the

Culver Valley from committing suicide? That's work for unpaid shoulders-to-cry-on, not for the police, even if idiots in police uniforms are doing it.' Turning to Sam and Sellers, Proust said, 'Does anyone but me think it's noteworthy that Sergeant Zailer's professional interest in suicide followed hot on the heels of her marrying Waterhouse?'

It was like having the whole of Hell in the office with you, Simon thought. 'Charlie used to work with us, and she's a better detective than most of the people in this room,' he said. 'I don't care what the Data Protection Act says. We all know there's no good reason why I shouldn't discuss Katharine Allen with Charlie, and it's lucky I did. If I hadn't, we wouldn't have got this lead. What are you talking about, it didn't happen? Are you saying Charlie's lying?'

The room filled with the sound of everyone breathing too loudly. If Simon had been asked to guess with his eyes closed, he'd have said twenty people hiding from a predator. *Or leaping off the top of a mountain.* There was something enlivening about refusing to be intimidated by an objectively intimidating person. Simon was surfing the crest of an adrenaline wave; he hoped it wasn't affecting his judgement.

'Let's not malign poor Sergeant Zailer, in her absence,' said Proust. 'Why would she lie? Mistakes have always been her speciality, even when she was on the right side of her sell-by date, and she must have made one in this case. The Hewerdine person saw the words in the notebook – *all* the words, together, at the same time. There's no connection between the Hewerdine woman and Katharine Allen's murder.'

Simon had foreseen that the Snowman's response would be grudging and unhelpful, but he hadn't predicted outright denial. He stood his ground. 'Charlie's sure. When Hewerdine saw the notebook, there was no "Kind of Cruel" on the page, only "Kind" and "Cruel". If you want to talk about staggering improbability, how about the likelihood of improbable things happening every second of every day? How likely was it that you'd be born – you, Giles Proust, exactly as you are? Or any of us. How *likely* was it that the four of us would end up working together?' Simon had to shout louder than he wanted to because he was shouting for everyone: all the people who had ever wanted to scream in the Snowman's face but hadn't dared do it. He was their representative.

'The four of us working together?' Proust said tightly. 'Is that what you'd call it? Not three of us trapped in an enclosed space with a delirious zealot?'

Simon forced himself to wait a few seconds before speaking. 'Is it really all that unlikely that a woman who lives in Rawndesley might be connected in some way to a murder that happened in Spilling, twenty minutes away? Or that that woman would bump into Charlie in Great Holling, near where they both live?'

Nobody said anything. Nobody would. Whenever the Snowman pointedly refused to answer a direct question, it meant that everyone else present was forbidden to respond; it was one of the many unwritten rules they had all grown used to.

'Amber Hewerdine saw the words "Kind" and "Cruel" in Charlie's notebook, and she made a connection,' Simon persisted. 'She asked Charlie about it because it mattered to her. Something about those words bothered her. She wanted to look at the notebook. Charlie said no, but that wasn't good enough for Hewerdine. Charlie left her car unlocked and the notebook on the passenger seat when she went in for her hypnosis appointment, wanting to test how determined Hewerdine was to get her hands on it. She soon found out: very. She came out a few minutes later, found Hewerdine sitting in her car reading it.'

'Seriously?' said Sellers. 'Cheeky cow.'

'Why did it matter to her so much to know if those words were in the notebook?' Sam asked.

'Ginny Saxon answered that question for me about twenty minutes ago on the phone,' Simon told him. 'During their session together, she asked Hewerdine for a memory . . .'

'A *memory*?' said Proust. 'That's how it works, is it? In a café, you ask for a serviette; in a hypnotherapy clinic, you ask for a memory?'

Simon couldn't help noticing that the Snowman's mood seemed to have improved. Did he enjoy watching Simon lose control and rant? Had he notched it up as a victory? 'Hewerdine didn't respond at first. Then, according to Saxon, she said "Kind, Cruel, Kind of Cruel". Saxon asked her to repeat it because it sounded odd and she thought she might have misheard. It's not the kind of thing her clients normally say when she asks them to describe the first memory that comes to mind.'

'I hope they normally tell her to mind her own business,' said Proust.

'Here's the strange part: Hewerdine repeated the phrase, then asked Saxon what it meant. Saxon said she had no idea and asked Hewerdine the same question, at which point Hewerdine denied that the phrase had originated with her. She claimed Saxon had said it first and asked her to repeat it. When Saxon denied this, Hewerdine threw a fit, called her a liar, refused to pay her for the session and stormed out.'

'And bumped into Charlie?' said Sam.

Simon nodded.

Sam chewed his lip, thinking. 'So . . . Hewerdine thought Saxon had said the magic words *and* that Charlie had written them in her notebook?' He frowned. 'Why wouldn't that seem as implausible to her as it does to me?'

'Haven't you been paying attention, Sergeant? Waterhouse has just explained to us the logical flaw in our finding anything implausible ever again. This evening heralds the dawning of a new era: the age of unqualified credulity.'

'I can't work out what Hewerdine was thinking,' Simon told Sam. 'That's why I'm keen to talk to her.' He gestured towards the door.

'Is that your way of asking permission to leave?' said Proust. 'Leave away. Next time, save yourself the trouble by neither arriving in the first place nor arranging a meeting to arrive at. I know you're opposed on principle to taking anything I say seriously, but on the off-chance that you might make an exception in this case: this Hewerdine person is a dead end. Until we know what the words mean, or what they are, we can't know how many people they might mean something to. What if they're a jingle from a well-known advert? What if they're the catchphrase of a cartoon character from a children's television programme?'

'We've searched and searched and got nowhere – nothing on the internet, no one who's heard of "Kind, Cruel, Kind of Cruel" in any context,' Simon reminded him.

'That doesn't prove there aren't ten thousand people for whom the phrase has significance,' said Proust, in the sort of menacingly patient voice that was designed to make Simon wonder if he really wanted to go on giving his DI cause to be patient. 'It proves only that we haven't found any of them yet. You're assuming our mystery words link only a handful of people: a murder victim, a killer, and your Hewerdine woman conveniently in the middle. I'm telling you – and being dismissed by your gargantuan arrogance – that those words might link a million people. Or they might link only fourteen people in a bland and harmless way that has nothing to do with murder.'

Proust walked up to Simon and knocked on his forehead as if it were a door. 'We don't know that the imprint of those words on the pad in Katharine Allen's flat has anything to do with her death.' The inspector looked to Sam and Sellers for support. 'Well? Do we? We found other words at her flat too – the list on the fridge, to take one example: "Renew parking permit, Christmas Amazon order" and the rest. If Waterhouse had bumped into a woman this afternoon who'd told him she needed to renew her parking permit, would he have sent his homunculus Gibbs to wait outside her house with a lassoo in his hand and an evil glint in his eye?' Proust snorted his appreciation of his own joke. 'It's laughable, Waterhouse – and by "it", I mean "you".'

'I'm not going to argue with you, sir,' said Simon wearily. *Sir?* Where had that come from? He hadn't called Proust 'sir' for years. 'I'm not going to argue with a position you've adopted just to piss me off. You know, I know, we all know: "Kind, Cruel, Kind of Cruel" is a sufficiently unusual collection of words for us to take this seriously.'

'If you're so keen to talk to the Hewerdine woman, why have Gibbs pick her up?' Proust snapped. 'Why have him start the interview on his own? Have you devised a special training programme for him that the rest of us aren't privy to? The Simon Waterhouse Diploma in Self-Indulgent Coincidence-based Policing and General Mania?'

Simon saw Sellers trying not to laugh. 'I asked Gibbs to bring her in to buy me a bit of time,' he said. 'I wanted to grill Charlie on the details, talk to Ginny Saxon, talk to you . . .' He knew he had to take the plunge, but was putting it off as long as he could. 'You need to know something about Gibbs. I'm going to tell him I told you, but . . . it's easier for me to do it if he's not here.'

'You've made a star chart for him,' Proust pre-empted. 'Every time he stuffs his career prospects further down the pan by running errands for you instead of completing the tasks assigned to him by Sergeant Kombothekra, he's awarded a gold star. Once he's earned ten, he gets to drive your mother to church and—'

'Making a lot of jokes, aren't you?' Simon cut him off. 'Pity you're too mean-spirited to acknowledge the cause of your new good mood: the lead I've brought you.'

'The lead Sergeant Zailer brought you,' the Snowman corrected him.

Simon sighed. Talking to Proust was like trying to force a car to start, over and over again, when that car had already been crushed to a metal cube. 'It's likely we're going to be putting Charlie's note-book into evidence,' he directed his words at Sam. '*I* think it's likely, anyway. So, you're all going to end up seeing what else is in the notebook, besides those five words.' Simon pointed to them. 'Rather than have you stumble across it, I'll tell you: it's letters. From Charlie to her sister Olivia, not written to be sent.' Simon stared down at the table. 'Written to give her anger an outlet.'

Proust made for the notebook like a bird of prey.

'Are they still at loggerheads?' asked Sam, who believed that harmonious relationships were both desirable and possible.

Sellers was taking a sudden interest in the view from the window: the Guildhall across the road that was having work done to its exterior. It was covered in scaffolding and blue plastic sheeting. *He knows*, thought Simon.

'Gibbs and Olivia are . . . having a thing. It's been going on since the night of our wedding.'

Colin Sellers shook his head, looked angry. Simon had exposed a man who was cheating on his wife, and, in doing so, breached the only principle Sellers held dear.

'Would this be the same Gibbs whose wife is expecting twins next April?' The speed with which Proust asked convinced Simon he'd known too. Sam hadn't; that much was obvious from his face. 'Gibbs and Olivia Zailer. So my star chart guess wasn't too far off the mark – he does your bidding and gets his very own Zailer sister. Can I refer to a booby prize without it being mistaken for smut?'

'I've just told you the only thing you'd find out from reading the letters in Charlie's notebook,' said Simon. 'So now you don't need to read them, and I'd appreciate it, and Charlie would definitely appreciate it, if you didn't.'

Sam Kombothekra nodded.

'None of my business,' said Sellers.

'Theoretically, we might find out more than the bare facts from reading the notebook.' Proust made a show of flicking through its pages. 'We might find out, in great detail, how betrayed Sergeant Zailer feels, her reasons for feeling that way, and how good she is at holding a grudge. Among other things. I wonder if we'd find out anything about you, Waterhouse.'

'I'm going to interview Amber Hewerdine,' said Simon, on his way out of the room.

Proust's voice came from behind him. 'Not unsupervised. I'll join you.'

'You?' Simon stopped. Turned. 'You want to interview a witness?'

'No. I couldn't care less about your witness. She isn't going to tell me anything useful.' Proust dropped the notebook on the table with deliberate carelessness. 'I want to watch you conduct an interview, Waterhouse. Do you know what I'd really like to do? I'd like to watch clips from all your filmed interviews, back to back: the frustrating ones, the dull ones, the half-hearted ones where you're going through the motions. Nostalgia's always been a weakness of mine, and today I'm feeling nostalgic about your career as a police detective. What say you treat us all to one final display of your investigative prowess and figure out why that might be?'

~

'This is a photograph of Katharine at her graduation,' Gibbs told the angry woman across the table from him. Her resentment of him was making him feel claustrophobic in the small interview room, with its custard-yellow walls and its window that offered a sick-joke view of an internal neon-lit corridor. Or perhaps it was his resentment of her. He'd decided he couldn't stand her when she'd told him that he had to pretend to be a feather-duster salesman for the benefit of her children. *A fucking feather-duster salesman.* Why would anyone do something as stupid as that for a living? 'Katharine was murdered in her flat in Spilling, on 2 November. She was twenty-six.'

'How many times are you going to tell me that?' Amber Hewerdine aimed her grey eyes at him like a weapon. 'Surely I know everything I need to know about her by now? She was twenty-six, a primary school teacher, unmarried, lived alone, grew up in Norfolk . . .'

'In a village called Pulham Market,' Gibbs supplied a new piece of information.

'Oh, well. That changes *everything*,' Amber extended her voice in a sarcastic drawl. 'Katharine Allen from Pulham Market? *That* Katharine Allen? Why didn't you say so? I've known *that* Katharine Allen for years. When you asked me if the name meant anything to me, I assumed you were asking if I knew a Katharine Allen who *wasn't* from Pulham Market in Norfolk.'

'The more I tell you about her, however irrelevant it seems, the more likely we are to find a connection between the two of you,' said Gibbs.

'I'll ask you for the twenty-fourth time: what makes you so sure there is one?'

'You know the flats in the Corn Exchange building? Katharine had one of those. A duplex – top floor and second floor down. She had part of the dome for her bedroom.' Gibbs swung his legs round, put his feet up on the table. 'I'm not sure I'd like to live right in the centre of town,' he said. 'Might be noisy.'

'I doubt it. Haven't they rolled out a nine o'clock bedtime across all of Spilling and Silsford and the villages in between? Or is that just what those of us who live in Rawndesley like to think?'

'The reason I mention Katharine's bedroom, in the dome, is because that's where she was killed. Multiple blows to the back of the head. With this.' Gibbs pushed another photograph across the table.

Seeing that a response was expected, Amber said flatly, 'It's a metal pole.'

'Katharine used it to open and close her bedroom window. It was too high to reach. The pole hung from a hook on the wall.'

Amber swallowed a yawn, allowed her eyes to close for a second.

'Sorry if I'm boring you.' Gibbs shoved another photograph at her, one he'd taken care to conceal until now. 'Someone took the pole off its hook when Katharine had her back turned, came up behind Katharine, and attacked her with it. Savagely. This is what Katharine's head looked like afterwards. She was hit more than twenty times.'

Amber recoiled. 'Do I need to know all this? Or see *that*? Can you put it away?' Her skin looked paler, blotchy. She covered her mouth with her hand.

'I was starting to wonder if murder's maybe no big deal to you,' said Gibbs.

'Why?' she said angrily. 'Because I'm tired? Because I'm not crying, like sensitive women are supposed to? I haven't slept properly for eighteen months. I'm likely to fall asleep at any time, unless I'm in bed with hours of night stretching out in front of me, in which case I'm guaranteed to stay awake. And, yes, the murder of a woman I don't know is less of a big deal to me than the murder of someone I know and care about would be. And, just so's you know, you can say the name "Katharine" five hundred times if you want to, but it's not going to make me feel any closer to her than I would if you called her "Ms Allen" or "the victim".'

'She was known as Kat,' said Gibbs. 'That's what her mates called her, and her colleagues.'

Amber took a deep breath, closed her eyes again. 'Obviously I care that a woman's been murdered, in the abstract way that people care about the deaths of strangers. Obviously I think it's not ideal that there's someone out there who thinks it's okay to . . . do *that* to somebody else's head.'

'I don't expect you to cry,' said Gibbs. 'I expect you to be scared. Most people, guilty or innocent, would be scared to be threatened with arrest in connection with a murder.'

Amber looked at him as if he was an idiot. 'Why would I be scared? I had nothing to do with it and I know nothing about it.'

'Sometimes, if the police think a witness is lying, that person ends up facing charges.'

'Usually only if they *are* lying. Or if it's the seventies and they're Irish.'

The fear had to be there, under the bravado. 'I can tell you one thing for nothing,' said Gibbs. 'If the press find out we're even talking to you, unless you make some adjustments to your manner and your attitude, the whole country's going to decide you're guilty before it gets as far as formal charges – even if it never does. You're the sort of woman public opinion loves to hate.'

She laughed at this. 'What – skinny, gobby and defensive? With a difference, though, you've got to admit.' What was this? Was she flirting with him? Still smiling, she said, 'I have an irresistible abrasive charm that wins people over pretty much whenever I want it to. The only reason you don't like me is because I don't care whether you like me or not. Ask me why I don't care.'

Gibbs said nothing. Waited.

'I don't care because I think you're an idiot,' Amber told him, enunciating the words carefully. 'You want to know who killed Katharine Allen. I'm trying to give you what little help I can. Listen, and I'll try again. I don't know, but I'm guessing that she was killed by someone who knew her and either disliked her, or stood to gain in some way from her death. In case you're too dense to recognise it, that's a description of someone who isn't me. And yet, weirdly, you seem to think I can help you beyond pointing out those obvious facts, which has to mean you know something I don't. I've worked out, because I have a higher than average IQ, that it must be something to do with that fucking woman and her notebook.' She sighed heavily. 'Can't you see that the only way forward is for you to *tell* me whatever it is you're not telling me?'

It was a funny thing Gibbs had noticed about women: they really wanted you to talk to them, yet did everything in their power to make you not want to.

'Oh, what, end of conversation?' Amber's voice vibrated with scorn. 'Good idea. *Great* idea. If you're not going to say anything else, then neither am I – because there's nothing else I *can* say until something changes, until I'm given some new information that I *don't have.*'

'You're a witness, maybe a suspect,' Gibbs told her. 'We're not two detectives working together.'

'Right.' She shook her head, stood up. 'That's right. You're one detective, getting nowhere. And I'm a pissed off, knackered, under-used resource that wants to go home now, if that's okay with you?'

'Under-used resource?'

'If you'd tell me what's going on, I might actually be able to help you. Have you thought of that? Have you thought that maybe you want power more than you want help?'

The door opened. Waterhouse. And Proust. What the fuck was he doing in an interview room?

'Thank God,' Amber said, as if she'd radioed for back-up and it had arrived. Was she a nutter who got a kick out of pretending to be a detective? The more she said, the less Gibbs trusted her. He had no trouble imagining her taking a pole to someone else's head and loving every second of it.

'I'm DC Simon Waterhouse. This is DI Giles Proust.'

'I'm Amber Hewerdine, and I'm on my way home unless I can talk to somebody who isn't *him*.' She pointed at Gibbs.

'Why's that?' Waterhouse asked.

'We're getting nowhere. All he's done is tell me he hates me and so do all his friends.'

'He hasn't said that,' Waterhouse contradicted her.

'He's said the official police equivalent.' Without waiting for anyone to ask her a question, Amber launched into a description of her interview with Gibbs so far. The level of detail was incredible. Did she have a photographic memory? Gibbs gave Waterhouse a nod to indicate that what she'd said was accurate: an almost exact verbal transcript.

'I think there's been a bit of a misunderstanding,' Waterhouse said.

'No, there hasn't!' Amber snapped at him. 'I gave him every chance to understand . . .'

'Give *me* a chance to explain what I mean.' A polite order. 'If you're willing to stick around for a bit, I think we might get somewhere.' He indicated that she should sit.

She remained standing, turned to Proust. 'What the fuck's your problem?' she demanded.

'Do you want to calm down?' said Gibbs. 'DI Proust didn't say or do anything.'

'Apart from stare at me with his radioactive eyes, as if he thinks I'm subhuman.'

'He doesn't think that,' said Waterhouse. 'He always looks like that. I could wheel Mother Teresa of Calcutta into the room, and he'd look at her in exactly the same way.'

Gibbs wondered if he and Waterhouse were going to lose their jobs over this. Waterhouse seemed keen to be shot of his. Either that or he'd turned psychotic. Gibbs was sure his wife Debbie would kick him out if he got himself sacked through his own stupidity; her mother wanted her to leave him anyway, and Debbie usually listened to her mother. Gibbs was nearly sure that Debbie leaving him was what he wanted.

Didn't Mother Teresa die years ago?

'Are you familiar with the concept of percentiles?' Waterhouse asked Amber.

She nodded.

'I talk to a lot of people – suspects, witnesses, victims and perpetrators of crimes. Civilians, other police officers. Without wanting to do them down, most of them haven't got very good communication skills. You'd be surprised how poor even most intelligent people's communication skills are.'

'No, I wouldn't,' Amber told him. She went back to her chair, sat down.

'One fact leaps out from what you've just told us about what you and DC Gibbs have said to one another so far: you're an unusually good communicator. I'd put you in the top 0.1 per cent. Because you're an excellent communicator, you believe in the power of communication to resolve things. If only everyone would rise to your high level, there's nothing that can't be sorted out. Right?' Waterhouse sat on the edge of the table, blocking Amber's view of Gibbs, and his of her.

'Depends on the circumstances,' she said. 'In the case of two strangers trying to fill in factual gaps, yes. If it's something emotionally complicated, sometimes it's better not to communicate too effectively, in case people get hurt, but that doesn't apply here. I'm happy to upset DC Gibbs in the good cause of finding out what the hell's going on, and I'm sure he feels the same way about me.'

'So let's give it a try, your way,' said Waterhouse.

Was he really going to . . . ? He was. He'd already launched in. Gibbs enjoyed watching Proust's face as Waterhouse debriefed Amber Hewerdine as if she were a new addition to CID. *Crazy*. Even if he knew beyond the smallest flicker of a doubt that she'd had no involvement in Katharine Allen's murder . . . He must have absolute confidence in her innocence, Gibbs realised, or he wouldn't be doing this. *He must have inherited a fortune out of the blue or have a getaway car waiting outside, or he wouldn't be doing it in front of Proust.*

'Until today, we had no leads. Nothing,' he was saying to Amber. 'No one saw anything. The forensics led nowhere. We've dug around in every corner of her life and we're none the wiser. All Katharine's friends, colleagues and acquaintances have either been conclusively eliminated or we can find no reason to think they might have wanted to harm her. She was an ordinary, law-abiding young woman with nothing in her personal or professional life that would point to a reason to kill her. In a situation like that, detectives get desperate – they latch onto anything, anything at all, that seems unusual, rather than admit they've come away empty-handed. We latched onto the one detail that raised a question. In Katharine's living room, we found an imprint of five words on a lined A4 notepad: Kind, Cruel, Kind of Cruel.'

'An imprint? So not the actual words? Someone had written the words, then torn off the page?' Quick off the mark, Gibbs conceded. Maybe she should join CID. She could have his job, once Proust had fired him.

Waterhouse stood up, turned to Gibbs. 'Got the photos?' he asked.

Gibbs found them and slid them across the table.

Amber stared at them for close to a minute, pushing her hair behind her ears on both sides. If her expression was anything to go by, she seemed to find these pictures more disturbing than the photograph of Katharine Allen's battered head. 'I don't understand,' she said. 'How did you know . . . did the woman whose notebook I looked at ring the police about me, and then you made the connection?' Something flashed in her eyes, a mixture of impatience and superiority. 'You need to talk to her.'

Gibbs heard the silent part even if no one else did: *you bunch of morons*. He was going to enjoy this. 'She's a police officer,' he said. 'Sergeant Charlotte Zailer.'

'Writing those words on assorted pieces of paper and staring at them is our collective new hobby,' Waterhouse took over. 'We keep hoping something'll occur to us. Nothing has. The reason you're here, and here so quickly, isn't because you saw those words in Sergeant Zailer's notebook. It's because you can't possibly have seen them, even if you think you did.'

'I saw them,' Amber insisted. 'When I broke into her car.'

'Yeah, then you saw them. But you asked Sergeant Zailer if you could have seen the words earlier, at three o'clock. Right?'

Amber nodded.

'You couldn't have,' Waterhouse told her. 'You probably saw the words "Kind" and "Cruel", but that was all she'd written at that point. You turning up interrupted her flow. She talked to you briefly, then you went in to see Ginny Saxon. Later, Sergeant Zailer went back to that page in her notebook and finished what she'd started. That's when she wrote "Kind of Cruel".'

Gibbs was expecting Amber to lose her temper – to call Waterhouse a liar, and, by extension, Charlie. He was surprised when she simply nodded.

'I spoke to Ginny Saxon, Amber. She told me that you said those words to her – "Kind, Cruel, Kind of Cruel" – and then accused her of having said them first.'

'Which she didn't,' Amber said.

'She *didn't*?'

'I don't think so, no. I was convinced she had at the time, because the words meant nothing to me. I didn't recognise them, so I couldn't see why I'd have said them. Which won't make sense to you, unless any of you have ever been hypnotised. Have you?' She looked at each of them in turn. When her eyes landed on the Snowman, Gibbs thought he knew what she was thinking: that if he had been hypnotised, he ought to go back and demand that the hypnotist reverse the effect.

'Look, why don't I tell you what I think happened to me this afternoon?' Amber suggested, closing her eyes again. She sounded weary. 'See if you can make any more sense of it than I can. I went to Ginny Saxon for help with my insomnia. She went through this . . . I don't know, she said all this stuff which was meant to hypnotise me. It wasn't much different from a relaxation mantra, as far as I could tell. She asked me to tell her about a memory, any memory. I rejected the first one that came to mind because . . . well, it doesn't matter why, I just rejected it. My mind was on that: not wanting to say the first thing that had occurred to me, but wondering if I ought to, and if not, what should I do instead? While all this was whirling around in my mind, I just . . . heard myself say it:

"Kind, Cruel, Kind of Cruel". I thought, "Hey? Where the hell did that come from? What does it mean?" Ginny asked me to repeat it, so I did, and I must have . . . I suppose I convinced myself she *must* have said it first because . . . well, I've told you why. Because it meant nothing to me.'

'Go on,' Waterhouse said.

'I'm not sure if I was hypnotised, but I was . . . different from how I usually am. Something weird had happened to me. My mind was kind of trapped inside itself, on overdrive. I had no sense of perspective. I accused Ginny of lying, left in a rage, and walked into Sergeant Zailer. As soon as I saw her, I thought, "Oh, my God." I remembered the notebook, that I'd seen her writing in it, and suddenly my certainty that Ginny had said those words just vanished and I seemed to . . . *know* that I'd seen them in Sergeant Zailer's notebook. I asked her about it, she denied it . . .'

'And you decided to settle the matter once and for all by helping yourself to the contents of her car,' said Proust.

'I didn't steal anything,' Amber snapped at him. Her tone and the speed with which she turned back to Waterhouse and Gibbs made it clear that she regarded the Snowman as by far the least important person in the room. In spite of himself, Gibbs was starting to like her.

He could still see her as a killer, though. That hadn't changed.

'I haven't told you the strangest part.' Amber looked worried. 'While I was talking to Sergeant Zailer, outside Ginny's house, I had this weird sense of . . .' She broke off, frustrated. 'It's hard to describe.'

'Try,' Waterhouse urged.

'Like a split in my mind, as if I had two minds, both seeming to know contradictory things.'

Proust let out a sigh that lingered in the room long after it had ceased to be audible.

'Part of me *knew* I'd seen those words in Sergeant Zailer's notebook. I *had*. I remembered seeing them. Another part of me could see this really clear image of . . .'

'What? Image of what?'

'She can't answer the perishing question while you're still asking it, Waterhouse.'

'Of a page torn off that notepad.' Amber pointed at the photographs. 'An A4 sheet, with blue lines and a pink line separating the margin – like that. With "Kind, Cruel, Kind of Cruel" written on it, exactly like that imprint, like a list. Same capitalisation, even: all the "K"s and "C"s upper case. Except it wasn't an imprint, it was the words themselves, in black ink. I could see it in my mind, clearly. And I knew it couldn't be Sergeant Zailer's notebook, because that was much smaller than A4, but I also knew I'd seen the words in her notebook.' She stopped. 'I realise there are contradictions in what I'm saying, but I can't help that. There were, and are, contradictions in my head. Part of me still thinks Ginny Saxon put the words in my mouth.'

Gibbs and Waterhouse exchanged a look.

'I've never been inside any of the flats in the Corn Exchange building. I didn't know Katharine Allen.' Amber looked up at Waterhouse. 'What does "Kind, Cruel, Kind of Cruel" mean? Do you know?'

'No idea,' Waterhouse said through gritted teeth. Gibbs knew he saw it as an admission of his own failure, that after a month he still didn't know.

'Not "Cruel to be Kind",' said Amber.

'What do you mean?' Gibbs asked.

'That's the obvious phrase that the words "kind" and "cruel" bring to mind. Cruel to be kind means something, but "Kind of Cruel"? What's that?'

'I think we've established that none of us knows what it means,' said Proust. 'Before we delve any further into the dark art of hypnosis or the splitting of minds, shall we cover the basics? Where were you on Tuesday 2 November, between 11 a.m. and 1 p.m.?'

Even unsettled as she now was, Amber was quick. She was already flicking through her diary. 'I can't remember, but I'll have been at work if it was a Tuesday. I'll be able to tell you in a— Oh.' She slammed the diary shut, as if she'd seen something unpleasant in it.

'What?' Waterhouse heard her surprise and pounced on it.

'I was going to say I'll be able to tell you in a minute what meet-ings I had, if any, but it turns out I wasn't at work.' She sighed. 'I was on one of those driver awareness courses you lot seem to like so much. You know – someone goes two miles an hour over the speed limit at night when no one's around, and next thing they know they have to waste a day of their life listening to a boring windbag setting stupid puzzles: if Driver A falls asleep and stalls on the motorway, and Driver B behind him crashes into him and dies, who is responsible for Driver B's death?'

'You didn't have to go on the course,' said Proust. 'You could have taken a fine and points on your licence instead. What you can't do is break the law and get away with it. I'm sorry if that annoys you. Gibbs, give her something to write on and with. Write down where the course was, please. Will someone be able to confirm that you attended?'

'Yes and no,' said Amber. 'We were asked to bring our driving licences for ID, so it'll be recorded on some form somewhere that I was there, but I'm not sure anyone'll actually remember me. I can't remember any faces, not this long afterwards.'

'What do you remember about the day?' Waterhouse asked.

'It was mind-numbingly dull. Full of arse-lickers promising to change their driving habits as of that moment.' Seeing that he'd been hoping for more, Amber said, 'You want me to tell you some-thing that proves I was there and not killing Katharine Allen? Something memorable?'

Gibbs watched her internal struggle with interest. She didn't want to tell them, whatever it was. Would she succeed in forcing herself?

'There was a man there called Ed, in his late sixties. I don't remember any of the others' names, only his. When the windbag guy in charge asked us if any of us had personal experience of a traffic accident – us or someone we knew – about five people put their hands up. There were twenty of us altogether. Windbag asked for details. Most weren't serious. Ed's was. He told us that his daughter had been killed in a car crash in the early seventies, and

67

that he'd been driving when it happened. It was pretty awful. No one knew what to say. I think he said it was before there were seatbelts in the backs of cars, but I'm not sure. His daughter wasn't wearing a seatbelt, anyway, whether one was there or not. Ed collided with a driver who came out of nowhere and his daughter went headfirst through the windscreen and was killed. Louise – I think that was her name. Or Lucy. No, I think it was Louise.'

'Louise or Lucy,' Proust summarised impatiently. 'Let's wrap this up. DC Gibbs, would you arrange transport home for the various parts of Ms Hewerdine's mind and their warring hypotheses?'

Gibbs' nod was a lie. He wouldn't, because he didn't need to. Anticipating that Proust would want Amber Hewerdine sent home prematurely because he wasn't the one who'd given the order for her to be brought in, Waterhouse had arranged for Charlie to be waiting in her car in the car park to offer a lift and continue the interview more informally. Would the Snowman see her on his way out of the building and work it out?

Did it matter? Gibbs and Waterhouse would both be getting their marching orders anyway.

As if he'd read Gibbs' mind, Proust said, 'Waterhouse, I'll see you in my office at nine o'clock on Thursday morning – I'm not in tomorrow. I'll see you at nine fifteen, Gibbs.'

'What's wrong with now, sir?' said Gibbs, keen to have it over and done with.

'I'm tired now. Thursday, nine fifteen, after I've seen Waterhouse at nine. That clear enough for you, second time round? Should I issue you both with brightly coloured rubber wristbands, like they do at public swimming pools?'

The Snowman left the room, slamming the door behind him.

'I'm going to have nightmares about that man,' Amber Hewerdine said.

One way to approach a mystery is to try to solve it. If that doesn't work, another fruitful approach is to look and see if there's a second, more fathomable mystery hiding behind the mystery you can't solve. Often there is, and that's your way in.

Anything aiming to achieve invisibility hides behind the visible. We can go even further and say that invisible things hide behind their own visible equivalents, because they provide the most effective cover. Let me prove the point using an absurd analogy: you might move your bread bin and expect to see breadcrumbs on the pantry shelf behind it, but you wouldn't move it and expect to see another bread bin behind it.

That's why it is always wise, where difficult human situations are concerned, to look for the motive behind the motive, the guilt behind the guilt, the lie behind the lie, the secret behind the secret, the duty behind the duty – you can substitute any number of loaded abstract nouns and the formula will still work.

And bear this in mind too: a mystery that's impossible to crack, like Little Orchard, can afford to be visible. Unless Jo and Neil break their silence on the matter, which seems unlikely, no one will ever find out what happened that night. It is impossible to guess; all speculative scenarios seem equally improbable – which of course is the same as saying that all seem equally feasible. But what about a mystery that would be relatively easy to solve, if people knew of its existence, because there are only a handful of possible answers? That mystery is more vulnerable. It is a poor defenceless creature whose only hope of survival is to go unnoticed until all the relevant people have stopped caring.

Most organisms are desperate to survive in their present forms. Why should mysteries be any different? Yes – the more I think about that idea, the more I like it. Let's come back to it later.

Is it wishful thinking to assume that people will stop caring? Not at all. The hunger to know doesn't last forever. It's rather like a piece of elastic – our solution-seeking impulse stretches and stretches, and then suddenly, stretched too far, it snaps and loses all tension. This can happen remarkably quickly, unless certain conditions apply: if the stakes are incredibly high, if there is injustice involved, if finding or not finding a solution affects our status in the eyes of the world or in our own eyes, or – probably the most significant factor when it comes to extending the human solution-seeking impulse – if we think there is a chance that we will find out; if we can see an investigative way forward, for example.

I hope I've said enough by now to bring the mystery behind the mystery of Little Orchard into focus.

No?

Why is Amber the only person still obsessing, years later, about what Jo and Neil were so determined to hide? Why does she still care? That's the true mystery behind the mystery of Little Orchard.

The stakes are not high: Jo and Neil and their two boys returned unharmed. They have been, or have seemed, fine ever since.

Does Amber believe she will find out the truth one day? On the contrary: it makes her angry to think that will never happen. And that's another clue: people get angry when their status is threatened, when they feel they have been downgraded, or treated unfairly. But where is the unfairness?

Does Amber believe that someone else knows, someone less important than her, less deserving of the information? Or is there another reason why she feels she has a right to be told this very private thing that Jo clearly wants to keep to herself? Is she simply nosey and spoilt, heedless of boundaries?

Could it be that Jo owes her a secret?

3

Tuesday 30 November 2010

I am in Sergeant Zailer's car. Again. By invitation, this time. She has been asked to drive me home, and I can't understand why. If I were in charge of the investigation into Katharine Allen's murder, I'd have kept us there in that horrible yellow room until we made some progress.

I'd have stayed up all night if necessary, listening as I fast-forwarded verbally through my entire life – everywhere I've ever been, everyone I've ever met – in the hope of homing in on the moment that contained my sighting of that piece of paper.

Kind, Cruel, Kind of Cruel.

Wherever I saw it, it can't have been in a vacuum. I must have seen it *somewhere*, so why isn't that somewhere part of the memory? If my mind could only connect the image of that lined page to a background or setting, surely then everything would click into place. I'd be able to make a link between the physical surroundings and a person, or people.

I'd know who murdered Katharine Allen.

No. I wouldn't. Even if the page I saw was the same one that was torn from the pad in her flat, there's no reason to think it had anything to do with her death.

I screw my eyes shut, try to see the sheet of paper lying on a table or a desk, sticking out of an envelope file, Blu-Tacked to a fridge, Sellotaped to a wall. It's no use; none of those backdrops fits – or, rather, none fits better or worse than any of the others. The page hangs in blackness in my memory, unanchored.

'Stop trying,' says Sergeant Zailer. 'According to you-know-who, trying to remember is counterproductive. Just let whatever wants to rise to the surface come, and if nothing comes, that's fine.'

'Ginny Saxon? She said that to you?'

'Uh-huh.' Her light tone doesn't fool me; she wishes I didn't know that she went to a hypnotherapist for help, even though she knows I did too.

'Unless the detectives I spoke to were lying, I'm their only lead,' I tell her. 'So it's not really fine at all, is it, if I never manage to work it out? I'll spend the rest of my life wondering whether a murderer who belongs in prison is swanning around feeling smug thanks to my crap memory.'

I wait for her to tell me that I won't be responsible for whatever happens or doesn't happen, but all she does is grin. I'm disappointed and relieved. If she enjoys listening to me beat myself up, there's plenty more where that came from; I could keep her entertained for weeks. I seem to spend half my life arguing with well-meaning people like Luke, like my team at work, who want me to go easy on myself and don't seem to realise that I can't. If I were to let myself off the hook whenever I felt like it, where would that leave my assessments of other people? I can't think well of everyone I meet. Too many of them are annoying idiots, or worse. Since I don't believe in nepotism, it's only fair to judge myself as harshly as I would a stranger.

It makes sense to me, anyway.

'What's wrong with trying to remember?' I ask. 'You might not succeed, but more things rise to the surface if you poke around in the water than if you don't.'

'Apparently not. According to Ginny, concerted effort repels genuine memories. Something to do with our conscious mind scaring away what we store in our unconscious, forcing all the repressed stuff to bury itself even more deeply.' Sergeant Zailer turns to me, taking her eyes off the road. 'Does that sound right to you?'

I don't have to think about it for very long. 'No. Only if you believe in the unconscious as a kind of psychological detention centre: a self-aware storage facility with a built-in parole board deciding what to keep in and what to let out. If a brain surgeon sliced open your brain, or mine, would he be able to point to your unconscious and say, there it is, between the pituitary gland and the . . . patella?'

'I think the patella's your kneecap,' Sergeant Zailer says apologetically, as if this might upset me.

'Does the unconscious actually exist? Do buried memories exist, like moth-eaten clothes locked in a wardrobe that no one knows are there?' I probably ought to stop ranting at her if I want to be driven all the way home. *Sod it.* 'Let's say tomorrow I remember where I saw that piece of paper. Remembering is a mental process that creates new thoughts, thoughts about experiences we had in the past. That's not the same as saying that my memory of the page with those words on it is stored inside me *now*, in a container called "my unconscious" that I can't break into, waiting to be pulled out.'

Sergeant Zailer smiles again. 'Mind if I smoke?' she says, opening her window.

I shake my head.

She lights one, exhales into the night. 'How cold is it?' she asks. 'What?'

'Outside, in here. Is it cold? Warm? Has my opening the window had any effect on the temperature in the car?'

I don't know what she means. Then it occurs to me that she must mean exactly what she says; there's nothing else those words can mean.

'I don't know,' I say, a fraction of a second before I realise that the window's not just a little bit open; she's slid it all the way down. The car is full of smoke anyway, so she might as well not have bothered. My body chooses this moment to remind me of its existence by starting to shake. Sensations overwhelm me, all of them unpleasant. I'm starving hungry. My limbs, digits and eye-sockets ache. I'm exhausted, more so than usual. I feel as if someone's implanted my brain in the body of a seventy-year-old.

What does Sergeant Zailer see when she looks at me? A scraped-out hollow shell? I have no idea whether I look better or worse than I feel.

As we drive out of Spilling on the Rawndesley Road, everyone we pass seems to flaunt their delight in being warmer than I am: cyclists in fleeces, well-wrapped pedestrians. I can tell even in the dark that they're rosy-cheeked and glowing, bundled up in their chunky wool hats and scarves, their fur-lined boots. 'Can you close the window?' I say, as the penetrating cold makes straight for my bones.

Sergeant Zailer presses the button and it slides up. 'I was wondering how long it'd take you to notice you were freezing,' she says. 'I've got a theory. I've known you less than a day, but you strike me as an obsessive person. A brooder.' Seeing that I'm about to object, she says, 'I'm married to someone exactly like you. Actually, I'm married to Simon Waterhouse.'

'Good choice,' I say, on autopilot. I spot the flaw in my logic too late to take it back. 'Sorry,' I mutter. 'That was a stupid thing to say.'

'Don't apologise. Stupid or not, I liked the sound of it.'

What does she think I meant? That I find him attractive? I don't, but it wouldn't do any good to say so and would probably offend her. I meant that Waterhouse was a more appealing prospect than Gibbs or that poisonous ghoul Proust. I forgot for a second that Sergeant Zailer's choice of husband was unlikely to have been limited to the three detectives I met today.

Luke thinks I ought to talk to our GP about my impaired brain function, though he never calls it that in case it offends me. He gets really upset about it sometimes. 'Just ask her to put you in a chemically induced coma for twelve hours, so that your synapses or whatever have a chance to reboot,' he says, or something similar. I'm never sure if he's joking. A coma can't be the same as sleep, from a restorative point of view – though I have to admit, it sounds pretty good. Maybe I ought to chuck myself under a lorry.

There can't be many people who find the idea of a coma appealing. I wish that made me feel special in a good way.

'Amber.' Sergeant Zailer clicks her fingers in front of my face. The cigarette's in her other hand; for a second, neither hand is on the steering wheel. I try not to think of Ed's daughter Louise shattering the windscreen. I wish I'd kept their story to myself; I have no right to know it, and shouldn't have repeated it.

Maybe not sleeping is my punishment. For everything.

'Amber! You've drifted off into your own little world again. Simon does it all the time. He also wouldn't have noticed that the window was right down and the car had turned into Siberia. He lives inside his head, barely notices the world around him. Which makes me wonder . . .'

I wait for her to carry on. Am I supposed to guess?

'Are you a nostalgic person?' she asks me eventually.

A bizarre question for a bizarre day. 'Isn't everyone? I don't spend a lot of time thinking about the past, if that's what you mean.' *It would upset me too much.*

The day I met Luke, the joke he made that turned serious when I told him what a brilliant idea it was. Him wanting to chicken out, me egging him on.

A good secret. Before I let the bad one happen.

'Tell me,' says Sergeant Zailer. How does she know there's anything to tell?

'I was thinking about the first time I met my husband.'

'I like how-I-met-my-husband stories,' she says encouragingly. Stubbing her cigarette out in the car's ashtray, she lights another one. I'm going to stink by the time I get home.

'Luke's a stonemason. He was working on a terraced house in Rawndesley, putting in a new bay window. I was renting the ground-floor flat of the house next door. One day I was on my way out to work, and I overheard Luke having a screaming row with my neighbour, the woman he was working for. She was the one doing the screaming – hysterical. He was trying to get her to calm down.' *Good training for being married to me.* 'I couldn't make sense of it: she kept yelling at him that she couldn't give him the go-ahead if she didn't know what it was he wanted to do, that he needed to be clearer.' What was her name? I've forgotten. Would Luke remember? To us, she's Trained Monkey. *If I'd wanted someone with no creativity or initiative to work on my house, I'd have hired a trained monkey*. That was her best line and it stuck in our minds.

'Luke was trying to explain the situation as clearly as he could. I'd got the gist by the time I'd locked my front door, but this woman was a cretin. Eventually, she snapped at Luke that she didn't have time to discuss it now and she'd talk to him later. She stormed off, swearing under her breath, leaving Luke and me to stare at one another. Luke . . .' I break off, smiling. This is my favourite part of the story. 'Luke turned to me and carried on with his impassioned justification speech. He barely paused for breath. Didn't introduce himself, didn't stop to wonder who I was. Never mind that I was nothing to do with anything. It was as if he thought, "Right, that woman's stomped off in a paddy, so I'll present my case to this one instead." He was totally in the right. He'd made her a new bay window, and wanted to check before he put it in whether she wanted any carvings on it. Some people do. Usually they want whatever was carved into the old, knackered stone to be replicated. Sometimes, even if there were no decorative carvings on the old one, people want them on the new one to make it look grander, or in some cases they want their initials carved on.'

'Their *initials*?' Sergeant Zailer sounds horrified. 'On a stone bay window?'

'People want all sorts of things,' I tell her. 'Once Luke was asked to carve lines from Beatles songs onto the windowsills of a Grade II listed house, one line for each sill. He refused.'

'People are barking,' Sergeant Zailer mutters.

'Anyway, this horrible woman didn't want anything carved on her new window, but she misunderstood Luke, decided he was trying to tell her she ought to. She asked him what he was thinking of specifically, and, since he wasn't thinking of anything, and nor should he have had to . . .' I close my eyes. 'You get the idea.'

'I hope you forgave him on her behalf.'

'I told him she was an evil witch in serious need of a comeuppance. Her new window was fitted complete with a carving she knows nothing about. It's on the underside of the sill. She'll never see it, not unless she lies flat on her back under the window and looks up.'

I'm surprised by how much Sergeant Zailer seems to like my punch-line. I have that weird sense, though I'm not performing, of having won over my audience. 'What was the carving?' she asks.

'"This house belongs to a . . ." and then a very rude word. The rudest. In tiny letters.'

She laughs. 'Excellent.'

'We based it on the bookplate model,' I can't resist adding. 'You know: "This book belongs to . . ." Like you put in your books when you're a kid.'

'I'd love to see it. I wouldn't mind lying flat on my back under a window. I've done stranger things. What's the address?'

Is she serious? She's too keen; it puts me off. I've given her the story she wanted – now it's my turn to ask for something. Might as well strike while I'm popular. 'I'd like to look at the files, any notes you've got. Katharine Allen's murder.'

This time, when Sergeant Zailer laughs, it's a different sound altogether.

'Can you make copies for me? I won't show them to anyone. Not even Luke.'

'You're serious, aren't you?' She shakes her head. 'Bookplate model: this plan belongs to a highly unrealistic person.'

'I know you can't do it officially. But unofficially, could you?'

'Why would I want to copy confidential case files for you?'

'I need to know more about her. If there's a connection between her and me, I might see something that leaps out: the name of a friend, something that overlaps with—'

'Sorry,' Sergeant Zailer cuts me off. She sounds tired. I've infected her with my exhaustion. 'Look, it's great that you want to help, but . . . it's not your job to find the link, if there is one. It's Simon's job, and his colleagues'. I'm sure he'll be pestering you soon for every microscopic detail of your life so that he can cross-check it against what they know about Katharine Allen, but . . .'

'I get it,' I say, turning off the charm, aware that some might say I never turned it on. 'I'm an inferior, not an equal. I get to tell everything and ask nothing.'

'That's right,' Sergeant Zailer snaps. 'You're not police, there's this awkward document called the Data Protection Act, and both those things are exclusively my fault.' She sighs.

I miss her good mood. 'You said you had a theory,' I remind her. Has she decided that talking to me is risky? That I'm the type it's better to say nothing to, in case I ask for everything? She'd be right: I am that type. I don't care whose job it is to find the connection between me and Katharine Allen. However informative and cooperative I am when the police interview me, I will always know more about my life and history than Simon Waterhouse will. I need to see the names of everyone they've interviewed, every note they've made, every photograph they've taken – all the things they can't show me in case my alibi's a lie and I killed Katharine Allen myself.

If I were a detective and I really wanted answers, I'd risk it.

'Simon's nostalgic,' Sergeant Zailer says. 'He's never in the moment. Always somewhere else in his mind – another place, another time. A theory about whatever case he's working on that takes him out of space and time altogether. What he doesn't give a crap about is right here, right now. He's willing to make the present moment horrendous for everyone in it for the sake of understanding the past in the future. I was just thinking, if *he'd* seen the words you saw on a piece of paper and couldn't remember the context, I'd probably think it was because he'd been locked in his own little world at the time.' She turns to face me. 'Maybe you're the same. Maybe you were obsessing about something else when you saw the words, and you can't picture the rest of the scene because you were there in body only.'

Something flashes and dissolves in my mind. A fraction of a second later, no traces are left, apart from a vague sense of movement quickly swallowed by stillness. The first stage of remembering, or nothing? Probably nothing, I decide. Naïve to assume that a memory would lay itself bare in stages, like a stripper.

What do I obsess about? Sharon's death. What's going to happen about Dinah and Nonie. Little Orchard. Sleep. What I need to tell Luke but can't.

Was I brooding about one of those things when I saw a page with 'Kind, Cruel, Kind of Cruel' written on it? If so, that hardly helps to narrow it down.

'Ginny made an interesting point about nostalgia,' Sergeant Zailer tells me. We're nearly in Rawndesley; more car horn beeps here than in Spilling, more impatient people. The smell is different too, especially here on the purely functional side of town: exhaust fumes, takeaways. 'She said nostalgic people yearn for the past for a good reason – because they missed it, they weren't fully there when they should have been, when it was the present. They deprive themselves of the "now" experiences that are rightfully theirs. Then they feel cheated and try to recapture what they missed, and miss more of the present in the process. It's a vicious circle.'

'Too neat, too formulaic,' I say dismissively. 'Has to be made up, like the conscious/unconscious mind stuff. Did she share any other impressive theories?'

Sergeant Zailer smiles. 'A few.' She pulls another Marlboro Light out of the packet, lights it.

'You didn't spend the whole session talking about me, then – the strange woman you found in your car.'

'No offence, but at seventy quid an hour . . .'

'What did you go and see her about?'

'Giving up smoking.' Sergeant Zailer pretends to be shocked by the sight of a cigarette between her fingers. 'Shit!' she says. 'I guess it didn't work, and that's why I have to go back next week. No, to be fair, she covered herself, gave us both a get-out. She told me I wasn't ready to stop yet. For the time being, I've got her official permission to light up whenever I feel like it.' She sounds pleased. 'Before she can give me the hypno-suggestion that'll send the craving packing, I need at least twelve sessions of hypno-analysis.'

'That's eight hundred and forty quid,' I say. 'The "at least" sounds expensive too.' Ginny's the criminal Sergeant Zailer should have been keeping her eye on this afternoon, not me.

'Apparently I don't smoke because I enjoy it, as I've always thought.'

'Death wish?' I suggest.

'Compensation. Ginny says there's something weighing heavily on the negative side. That's why I need to treat myself all the time. The fags are my treats, and for as long as they do the job of making up for whatever's wrong, I'm going to continue to smoke them. Why wouldn't I? I'm not going to give up something I like in exchange for nothing. That'd be irrational.'

'How about the treat of not dying young?' I say.

She shakes her head. 'Avoiding illness in the future's too abstract, Ginny says. It's not a concrete perk to put in place of the fags, so it has no effect. Want to know why I'm telling you all this?'

It hadn't occurred to me to wonder. Why must openness always be justified, when withholding everything that matters is taken as standard – polite, almost? I'm the odd one out, surrounded on all sides by people who spend their days trying to say as little as possible. *People like Jo.*

I want to be told the truth and I want to be able to tell it.

'Ginny said I shouldn't talk about our sessions or even think about them in between,' says Sergeant Zailer. 'I'm rebelling. I hate doing what I'm told. Viewed alongside my compensatory smoking, it all adds up to a picture of someone whose needs weren't met in early childhood.' She laughs. 'I kind of agree with you – it's probably all bollocks. We'll both get fleeced and be no healthier or happier. Why did you go for hypnosis, if it's not too personal a question?'

'I don't sleep.'

She nods. 'Because you're repressing a painful memory,' she says in an overly earnest voice. Her grin makes it clear she's impersonating Ginny.

'No, I'm not. Trust me, my painful memories are real extroverts. It's the next road on the right.'

'Ah, but what about your *guilty* memories, the ones that make you squirm with shame whenever you think about them?' She sounds jarringly upbeat, given the subject matter. Did Ginny persuade her that suffering is fun?

'Still no repression,' I say. 'All my guilty memories clock in and out, every day. There's no subterfuge involved. I wish there were. Anywhere here's fine. That's my house – the one lit up like a pumpkin at Halloween.' Nonie's scared of the dark, and claims the house is too. She sleeps with her desk lamp on and can't walk past an unlit room without 'turning its light on to cheer it up'.

I wonder if Dinah will still be up. Neither of the girls has a set bedtime. Nonie always asks to go up to bed between seven thirty and eight; with Dinah, some nights it's eight, some nights she's still holding court at ten.

'So,' Sergeant Zailer says as she pulls over. 'What have you got to feel guilty about?'

Of course. Silly of me to think we've been talking for talking's sake. To Sergeant Zailer, I'm an object she's been charged with interrogating, nothing more.

I get to tell everything and ask nothing.

'I don't feel guilty about anything,' I say as I get out of the car. 'Everything bad that's ever happened to me is someone else's fault.'

~

Luke's standing in the hall when I walk in; he must have heard the car pull up. He chuckles at the sight of me as I take off my coat and hang it on a peg. I've been questioned in connection with a murder, and he's laughing. Can anything make this man anxious? 'You look like someone in need of a glass of wine,' he tells me.

'A glass?' He might as well have said 'thimble'. 'Fill the biggest saucepan we've got with Sauvignon Blanc and give me a straw.' I remove a second layer of clothing: my jumper. One of the things I love about our house is that it's always warm, despite looking as if it wouldn't be. I like the cosiness almost as much as the defiance of expectation.

'That bad?' Luke asks.

'Worse. I'm going to faint if I don't eat something.'

'There's loads of chilli left. I'll heat some up for you.' He heads for the kitchen and starts moving around energetically. I follow him, hoping to be able to make it as far as the nearest chair, so that I can slump at the kitchen table. 'Girls in bed?'

'Yup. Dinah fell asleep on the sofa at half six. I had to carry her upstairs.'

I raise my eyebrows in disbelief, which takes more effort than it should. The heat from the hot-plate, which Luke tends to leave on in winter to create an Aga-like effect, is making me feel drowsy, too heavy to move even the lightest parts of my body.

'She had a stressful day. I'm under orders to tell you all about it.' He hands me an extra-large pottery mug full of cold white wine: a compromise.

'What happened?' I ask, not because I'm keen to immerse myself in the details of Dinah's latest spat with Mrs Truscott, but because there are only two other things Luke and I are likely to talk about tonight, and I can't face either of them: my abduction by the police, and the letter from Social Services that's lying on the table in front of me, poking out of what's left of its envelope. It isn't there by accident. This is Luke's way of saying we need to talk about our least favourite subject. I wasn't here when he opened the letter, but I can see him in my mind, ripping into the envelope, fearless.

If I were the brave one and he the coward, would I force him to confront it? Read the letter aloud to him if he wouldn't read it himself?

'Did you know Dinah's been writing a play?' he asks, stirring the chilli.

'No.' *Knowing things is too tiring*. The thought is so out of character for me, it shocks me. I need food. 'That'll be hot enough if it's been on the hot-plate since teatime,' I tell Luke. 'And even if it isn't, I want it now.'

'*Hector and His Ten Sisters*. It's about an eight-year-old boy whose mother forces him to wear pink. She's so exhausted from looking after her eleven children that she can't face buying different clothes for each one, or different outfits for schooldays and weekends – too much effort. So she decides they all have to wear the same clothes every day, like a uniform, and since ten of her eleven kids are pink-obsessed girls, the mother figures it'd make sense for that to be the colour of the uniform.' Luke's standing with his back to me, but I can hear the smile in his voice. 'Hector has no choice but to go along with it, and pretty soon none of his mates'll talk to him or play football with him—'

'What's this got to do with Mrs Truscott?' I cut him off. Another time, I'd love to hear all about Hector and his sisters. Just not now.

Luke bangs down a bowl of chilli in front of me and hands me a fork. I lean away from the rising steam and manage not to ask if there's enough for me to have seconds, and thirds. He would tell me to eat my firsts first and see how I feel after that. Sometimes he reminds me that I live in a developed country, about fifty footsteps away from a Chinese takeaway, an Indian restaurant, a Co-op and a Farmers' Outlet shop; I'm unlikely to fall victim to a food shortage.

'Dinah showed the play to Miss Emerson, who said it was the best thing any child of any age at the school had written, ever.'

I can't help smiling at this. Dinah has a tendency to magnify any compliment she receives. Luke's ex-squaddie workmate Zac once told her her hair looked nice, and she thought nothing of amending that to, 'He's travelled all over the world and never seen anyone with hair as beautiful as mine, not in any country.'

'Miss Emerson suggested putting on the play at school. She asked Dinah's permission to show it to Mrs Truscott . . .'

'Oh, God,' I mutter, my mouth full. This is my favourite kind of meal: full of eye-wateringly strong red chillis that Luke will have added only once he and the girls were sure they'd had enough. I'm a masochist. I love food that makes me cry and sweat.

'Mrs Truscott said she didn't think it was suitable. Why?' He refills my wine mug. 'Because there's no reason why boys shouldn't wear pink, and we mustn't reinforce gender stereotypes or give the impression that having sisters is a terrible thing.'

I groan. Is it selfish to wish that nothing problematic, nothing requiring any thought or action on my part, would ever happen at school? When I meet Dinah and Nonie off the bus and ask them how their day was, the answer I'm desperate to hear is, 'Great fun and highly educative, though at the same time absolutely unremarkable and therefore in no need of further discussion.'

'When did all this happen? Why didn't Dinah say anything?'

'She wanted to deal with it on her own, and she did. Admirably or deviously or both, depending on your point of view. She agreed with Mrs Truscott that there was nothing wrong with boys wearing pink, and said that was exactly the point her play was trying to make: that if Hector's friends hadn't teased him, he wouldn't have had to take drastic action and there'd have been no tragic end for the ten sisters. They mock Hector mercilessly for wearing pink clothes and get horribly punished. Mrs Truscott fell for it, said Dinah's play could be part of the Christmas show, as long as she didn't allow it to interfere with her schoolwork or anyone else's. Dinah set up auditions, even formed a casting committee so that all decisions could be shown to be fair. I think that might have been Nonie's idea. Nonie was on the committee, anyway. Miss Emerson helped out with the admin, scripts went home with individual lines highlighted . . .'

'I can't believe Dinah didn't tell us.'

'She didn't want to invite us to her drama premiere until she knew it wasn't going to fall through.' Luke pours himself a glass of wine and brings it over to the table. I see from his face that he's angry. 'Which it did, pretty much straight away. One kid's mum rang up and said her daughter had come home sobbing because she hadn't got one of the "sister" parts and her two best friends had; another kid's dad stormed into Mrs Truscott's office complaining about the disgusting script his son had brought home, full of cruelty and torture and likely to provoke a pandemic of sister-hatred.'

'Torture? Teasing someone for wearing pink? It's hardly *The Killer Inside Me*.'

'You didn't let me get to the end of story,' Luke says. 'People get rolled in mud, pushed into fishponds against their will . . .'

'That ought to happen more often in real life.'

84

'One girl was so upset not to be given even a minor part that her mother threatened to take her out of the school and home-educate her. You can guess the upshot: Mrs Truscott told Dinah the play was causing too much trouble, and suddenly it was all off. Dinah was upset and she overreacted. She accused Mrs Truscott of being a coward with no principles.'

I have to tread a fine line here. Luke is worried, understandably. This means I must under no circumstances blurt out, 'Ha! Spot on!' I have a horrible feeling my face is giving the game away.

'I'm glad you're enjoying this, because there's more. Dinah told Mrs Truscott that a good leader needs to be strong and fair. They'd learned about it in history the day before. Strong as in not giving in to pressure from idiots. Fair as in not breaking promises you made last week. On being told she was a rubbish head and an even worse human being, Mrs Truscott apparently said very little, apart from that she was going to ring us and speak to us about what had happened.'

'Which she hasn't. Has she? Did you check the messages?'

'Of course she hasn't! She's putting it off, terrified of being told the same or worse by you.' Luke gives me a stern look. 'Which wouldn't do any good, Amber, however true it might be. There's no need for you to do anything, all right? I've dealt with it.'

I make a non-committal noise, unconvinced. Normally, things that have been dealt with by other people are precisely the ones in most urgent need of my interference.

'Dinah and I made a deal,' says Luke. 'She's going to apologise to Truscott first thing tomorrow. Hopefully Truscott won't then feel the need to . . . do anything more. I *think* I also persuaded Dinah to ask if she can have a go at writing another play for the Christmas show, one a bit less—'

'Fuck that!' I'm full of chilli and wide awake, ready to fight all night. 'What, a play about kittens and lambs cuddling each other, with nice little bows round their cute necks?'

'You know, you said that in a really menacing way.' Luke grins at me. 'There's no way I'm going to see *that* play. I'm scared. Those kittens and lambs, they're evil.'

'Dinah and Nonie's days at that school are numbered.' I've warned him before; he doesn't think I mean it.

'No, they're not,' he says, infuriatingly calm. 'It's a good school.'

It's the school Sharon chose for them. That's not what Luke said, but it's what I heard. 'A good school with a spineless head,' I say stubbornly. 'As our leaving letter will make clear. Or maybe I'll spray-paint it on her office door, so she can't hide it and carry on pretending everyone loves her.'

'Good plan.' Luke nods. 'Why don't you really stick it to her by making a dog's breakfast of the girls' education? Could you speak any French or Spanish when you were eight? I couldn't. Did you know there was a difference between simple and complex Chinese? I didn't. Dinah and Nonie *do*. Nonie told me the other day that Jackson Pollock was an abstract expressionist artist, and what that meant.'

'What did you tell the girls?' I ask, reaching for the wine bottle. 'About this afternoon, where I was.'

'I said you had to go back to work for an urgent meeting. They didn't believe me.'

'I'm not surprised. As lies go, it's a pretty boring one.'

'So let's hear the interesting truth,' Luke says. 'What happened?'

I fall easily into my usual pattern of telling him almost the whole story. I even tell him that Katharine Allen was murdered on Tuesday 2 November.

I say nothing about my driver awareness course, the one I didn't attend, having taken place on the same day.

~

Fifteen minutes later Luke goes up to bed, and I am pitched into the stretch of evening I dread most: the hour between ten thirty and eleven thirty, when I'm left alone to face yet another sleepless night. Eighteen months ago, when I first stopped sleeping, I assumed that the surges of crushing panic that accompanied my insomnia would prove to be temporary: either I would learn to sleep again, or I'd get used to not sleeping – psychologically and emotionally, it would get easier. It hasn't, and I no longer kid myself that it will. The censorious voice in my head starts up the second Luke kisses me goodnight and leaves the room.

This is when and how normal people go to bed. They go upstairs, without fear, and change into their pyjamas. They don't break into a sweat, their hearts don't beat as if they're about to explode, they don't suddenly find that they need to empty their bladders every ten minutes. They brush their teeth, yawn, roll into bed, maybe read a couple of pages of a book, eyelids drooping. Then they turn out the light and go to sleep. Why can't you do that? What's wrong with you?

Escalating exhaustion isn't the worst thing about not sleeping, not by a long way. The loneliness is worse, and the distorted perception it brings with it. People often look surprised when I tell them this, shocked when I compare prolonged insomnia to solitary confinement in prison. Your mind starts to gnaw away at itself like a deranged rat, I explain helpfully. I've had plenty of time to work on an appropriate metaphor – I might as well use it, even if it does make whoever I'm talking to sidle away, remembering somewhere urgent they needed to be ten minutes ago.

Don't think about how many minutes and seconds there are between now and six thirty tomorrow morning. Don't go and sit in front of the clock in the dining room so that you can count them off as they pass.

I stay where I am – where Luke reluctantly left me, cross-legged on the sofa – and wrap my arms around myself for protection, but the feelings I'm hoping to ward off come anyway: piercing isolation, the usual guilt accompanied by the conviction that this anguish is my punishment, disgust at my own freakishness, terror that's not attached to anything in particular, which makes it all the more frightening. As always, I want to beg Luke to come back downstairs. He won't be asleep yet, won't even be in bed. As always, I stop myself, try instead to concentrate on fighting the voice.

What if tonight's worse? What if I don't get any sleep at all, not even twenty minutes here and there? What if that becomes the new pattern? What if I get so tired I can't do my job any more? We wouldn't be able to pay the mortgage.

I haul myself up off the sofa and walk slowly to the dining room, concentrating on my footsteps, willing each one to take longer than it possibly can. I stop on the threshold, look at the clock. Ten thirty-five. I go back to the sofa in the lounge, lie down. Close my eyes.

I used to go to bed when Luke did, even knowing I wouldn't sleep; that was our tactic at first. We were both sure it was the best way. Every night, we'd review our policy and agree on it all over again. It became a ritual. Luke would hand me whatever book was lying on my bedside table and say, 'Do what you used to do. Read for a bit, then turn out the light, close your eyes, keep them closed, and see what happens. Even if you don't sleep, you can lie still and relax, get a bit of rest. And if you do happen to fall asleep – well, you're in the right place, aren't you?'

'Exactly,' I'd say. My answers tended to be short. I was too afraid of what the night had in store for me by this point, with my head actually on the pillow, to hold up my end of a normal conversation. Luke once told me that I looked as if I was standing in front of a firing squad, except I was horizontal.

The policy changed once we spotted the glaring flaw in our plan: I was incapable of lying still. My agitated shuffling and wriggling kept waking Luke up. He didn't mind; he would happily have rolled over and tuned back into whatever dream I'd interrupted, except that, desperate for company after too many dark hours of silent, churning misery, I would block his route back to sleep by snapping, 'I've had my eyes closed for four hours, I'm not relaxed, and, as you might be able to tell, I'm still awake. What do you propose I do now?'

Luke was too wary of upsetting me to suggest I move into another room; after six months of wrecking his nights as well as my own, I suggested it myself. The previous owners of our house had turned the attic into a long, triangular guest bedroom with an en-suite shower room at one end, so I moved up there for a while. And then, three months ago, I decided enough was enough and moved out of that room too. Time to get tough with myself, I thought: someone who doesn't sleep doesn't deserve a bedroom. *If you want a bedroom, let's see you earn it.* Since then, I've camped on various sofas – in the lounge, in Luke's home office, in the girls' playroom. Sometimes, if Luke's made a fire, I lie down on the rug in front of the still-glowing coals, hoping the warmth might help to loosen the knots in my mind. Now and then I used to curl up on the floor beside Dinah's bed, but Nonie put a stop to that. I told her there was no chance of my being able to fall asleep on her floor even for ten minutes, not with the light on all night. Her response left no room for negotiation: if I couldn't sleep next to her bed, then I mustn't sleep next to Dinah's either. Both or neither – anything else wouldn't be fair.

Once I dozed for half an hour in the bath, which I'd filled with cushions, and woke up with an agonising crick in my neck. Occasionally I go outside and try to lose consciousness in the car. I no longer own any pyjamas or nighties; I threw them all away a couple of months ago. Luke tried to talk me out of it, but I needed to do it. It was too depressing to see them every time I opened my wardrobe, sitting there in a smug, neatly folded, pastel-coloured pile.

I sit up, open my eyes. My eyelids hurt; I must have been pressing them shut too hard.

Do something useful. You've got a whole night to get through – another one. Do some ironing. Check the girls' homework diaries.

Jo once told me I ought to make the most of what she called my 'extra time' at night, use it to accomplish something: learn a language, take up painting. I pretended to think it was a great suggestion, then cried for an hour after she'd left.

Do anything. Open the front door and start screaming.

I think of the letter from Social Services on the kitchen table, and my heart leaps. In no other circumstances would it be an appealing prospect, but at this precise moment it's my best chance of not going mad. Reading it now will upset me exactly as much as reading it in the middle of the day would, which is what I want: a source of worry and misery that isn't night-specific.

I go to the kitchen, sit down at the table – facing away from the time display on the microwave that would like to remind me that it's ten thirty-eight – and pull the letter out of its envelope. A post-card falls out too, lands face-down – a typical Ingrid card, from some art gallery or other: a painting of a group of nuns sitting in a garden, under the trees. I pick it up, read it first. 'Don't be downcast,' it says. 'School fees threat <u>clearly</u> not in girls' best interests. All grist to our mill. M has shot herself in foot! We will win!'

I sigh. Ingrid, our social worker, has been competing with Luke for the Counterfactual Optimism Cup for several months now, unchallenged by me. I've given up trying to force them both to face the truth, which is that we might or might not win and there's no way of predicting which way it will go.

I read the formal letter. It tells me what I'd already worked out from Ingrid's card: Marianne is threatening to stop paying the girls' school fees if Luke and I are allowed to adopt them. *So what*? We'll pay the fees ourselves if we have to, somehow. I'll forge myself a certificate and work nights as a hypnotherapist – might as well, since I'm awake anyway. I'll charge people eight hundred and forty quid for the privilege of sharing their memories with me.

Dinah and Nonie love their school. How can that bitch Marianne threaten to deprive them of it, knowing what they've lost already? I guess the clue's in her name – the 'that bitch' part.

If Luke were here, he would quote back to me my own words about the girls' days at the school being numbered. He doesn't understand that I have two categories: things I enjoy saying I hate and bitch about endlessly, and things I really hate, like Marianne, which I try not to think or talk about at all if I can help it.

Apart from the unexpected school fees detail, the letter from Social Services contains only the information Luke and I were expecting: Marianne has lodged an official objection. 'I just don't think it's right – you're not the girls' parents,' is the only thing she's ever been willing to say to us on the subject. 'They're Sharon's children, not yours.' We have tried to point out that Dinah and Nonie will always be Sharon's children whether or not Luke and

I adopt them, and that not already being the parents of the children you're hoping to adopt is actually a pre-requisite condition rather than a barrier, but all she does is look past us and shake her head mechanically and too fast, as if someone's wound a key in her back.

I don't think I would ever kill anyone or arrange to have someone killed – not unless Dinah's or Nonie's life was at stake – but I would love, love, love it if Marianne Lendrim dropped dead tomorrow. She needn't wait that long, in fact; tonight would do just as well. I should probably feel guilty for wishing her out of existence, but I don't. My job as Dinah and Nonie's guardian is to deprive them of harmful things: first their only surviving grandparent, later alcohol, drugs, tattoos and piercings they'll regret, gap years in unsafe countries.

I slip the letter and Ingrid's card into my handbag and leave the empty torn envelope on the kitchen table for Luke to see in the morning. It's easier to do that than to say, 'I read the letter', less likely to lead to a conversation we'd both find unbearable.

Having sullied my mind with thoughts of Marianne, I need to cleanse it, to be close to Dinah and Nonie and see their sleeping faces. I spend a lot of time in their rooms at night, just watching them sleep, monitoring the effect it has on my mood: an instant injection of joy. When they're awake and we're together, it's more complicated. We're usually talking, and I'm worrying that I will fail them a little more with every word that comes out of my mouth.

I tiptoe upstairs, past Luke's bedroom – the one that also used to be mine – and his home office. As I climb the shorter flight of stairs up to the second floor, I think about the beautiful staircase Ginny asked me to imagine. *Your perfect staircase has ten steps. As you descend, I want you to see yourself drifting down into calm, and into relaxation . . .*

I stop at the top of the stairs outside Nonie's room, registering the anomaly for the first time. Ten steps, Ginny said. Definitely ten. Yet she counted me out of hypnosis with a brisk one-two-three-four-five. No mention of the staircase at the end of the session. What happened to it? If a ten-step staircase is the route to the place of total calm and relaxation, then surely it's the route out as well?

It's a tiny detail, but that's what's so annoying. How hard would it have been for Ginny to complete the metaphor, to say, *And now, as I count to ten, you're going to ascend the steps of your staircase one by one, with each step taking you out of peace and tranquillity and back to the shitty real world*?

If I were a hypnotherapist, I'd be good at my job and take care to get my imagery right. I *am* good at my job. I might only be Licensing Manager for the city council, as Jo would be the first to point out, but I'm brilliant at what I do, and if I couldn't do it brilliantly, I would do something else. It doesn't seem to bother most people that they spend eight hours a day five days a week engaged in an activity that they're average to rubbish at. I find myself thinking this, or a version of it, constantly. Luke says it's because I'm permanently knackered and cranky. In restaurants, I hiss at him, '*All* the chef needs to do is cook nice food – that's *it*, that's all that's required of him, that's the thing he's chosen to devote his life to. And what does he do? Cooks stuff that tastes like shit and serves it cold!'

All Ginny had to do to keep things logical and symmetrical was walk me back up my imaginary staircase. All DC Gibbs had to do was be open with me, and I would have been open with him. Sergeant Zailer too. It seems like hours ago now, but I think I was enjoying talking to her before she made it obvious that the whole conversation, from her point of view, had been a lead-up to a trap.

What do you feel guilty about?

Why did she ask for the address of the house with the rude carving on the underside of the windowsill? To test me? Easy way to check if I'm a liar and a fantasist?

Simon Waterhouse treated me like a human being. He made a sacrifice: relinquished his right to suspect me long before he could have known I had nothing to do with Katharine Allen's death, when we'd exchanged no more than a few words. Within seconds of meeting, we'd left our fixed roles behind and were simply two people pooling our knowledge to work something out.

Gibbs' and Proust's body language screamed disapproval; probably they thought Waterhouse unprofessional for trusting me when he had every reason not to, but if he'd been more circumspect and treated me less like an ally, would I feel I owed it to him, now, to tell him the whole truth? To try as hard as I can to remember where I saw that piece of paper?

I don't think so.

How long have I been standing here, outside Nonie's door? No more than a minute, perhaps, but it all counts; every second takes me closer to morning and the moment when I'll be part of a family again, no longer a writhing brain in a tense body, haunting ordinary people's nights with my wakefulness.

The girls' floor smells of floral-scented fabric conditioner. I wash their sheets once a week without fail; when I told Jo this, she laughed and said, 'Washing bedding once a week is *normal*, Amber. It's not something to boast about.'

I lean into Nonie's room to check on her. As always, she's curled on her side like a back-to-front question mark, with her mouth slightly open and her duvet tucked neatly under her right arm. On one side of her head lies the fat encyclopedia we bought her for her birthday, and on the other, lined up against the wall, a row of cuddly toys: a bear, a unicorn, a rabbit, a panda, a stocky owl that bears more than a passing resemblance to a darts player I've seen on TV, though I can't remember his name.

Nonie's room is full of line-ups: on her desk, her shelves, a few on the carpet. It doesn't matter what the object is as long as she can get her hands on enough of them to stand them in a row: pairs of paper glasses with 3-D lenses in them from the cinema, small bottles of bubble bath and shower gel, rings with coloured pieces of glass standing in for jewels, badges, marbles, hair bobbles, pots of lip balm. Nonie's lips are always chapped.

Tears fill my eyes, bringing with them the usual confusion, reminding me that love can be harder on the system than hate. There must be a connection between the two – between my loving Dinah and Nonie so much and the uncontrollable rage that often wells up inside me for no apparent reason. Before Sharon died, I didn't feel as strongly as I do now in either direction, positive or negative.

I tiptoe over to the bed and kiss Nonie on the cheek before making my way to Dinah's room. Slightly harder to see what's going on in here, with the light off, but my eyes soon adjust. Dinah's duvet is in a bunch at her feet, as if she made a point of kicking seven shades out of it before falling asleep. Her mouth is wide open. It occurs to me that Dinah and Nonie are the only people in the world whose sound sleep I don't begrudge. I'm glad they sleep well. I would willingly never shut my eyes again if I could guarantee them unbroken nights forever, full of peaceful dreams.

You're glad they're here. You can't imagine life without them – not a life worth living, anyway. That must mean, in a way, that you're glad Sharon's dead. How can it not mean that?

Easily.

Would you bring Sharon back if you could, knowing Dinah and Nonie would go back to her?

I ask myself this question every night. My answer is always the same: *yes, of course*. I can't stop checking, though. I need to prove to myself, constantly, that I am not evil, however screwed up and guilty I might be. *That's right, folks. Hang around with Amber Hewerdine at night and you're guaranteed hours of endless fun.*

Dinah doesn't care what her room looks like, as long as she never runs out of wall-space to stick up scraps of paper with Sellotape. Nothing counts for her unless and until she's written it down. On my way to give her a kiss, I notice a long, jagged-edged strip stuck to one of her curtains. I pull back the other one to let in more light from the street lamp outside, and realise I'm looking at a cast list. There's a pen sticking out from beneath Dinah's pillow that wasn't there yesterday.

This is new – today's work. I frown, puzzled. Is the play on or off? Luke and Mrs Truscott think it's off; does Dinah know better? Is she relying on me to save the day? Is that why she's stuck the cast list to her curtain, where I can't fail to notice it?

'HECTOR AND HIS TEN SISTERS,' she's written in capitals.

'CHARACTERS AND ACTORS. Hector: Thaddeus Morrison, Hector's mother: Miss Emerson'. I smile. Dinah didn't want to be in Miss Emerson's class, but it hasn't worked out too badly for her; Mr Cornforth wouldn't have been nearly as willing a slave.

I look at the names of the other characters: Rosie, Pinky, Strawby, Cherry, Seashell, Sunset, Candy, Berry, Flossy and Taramasalata. Hector's pink-obsessed sisters, presumably. Their obsession has spread to their names.

As I lean down to kiss Dinah's cheek, I freeze. *What if . . .*

No, there's no reason to think that.

Yes. There is.

I'm excited, and I don't know if I should be. Am I going to wake Luke?

I ought to make myself a cup of tea first and drink it, take the time to check that I think it's worth interrupting his night for this, but I'm too impatient.

I run downstairs, into a room that feels thick with sleep in a way that Dinah and Nonie's rooms didn't. 'Luke. Wake up.' A whisper and an order at the same time.

No response. I shake him. He opens his eyes. 'What's the matter?'

'What if they were headings? "Kind, Cruel, Kind of Cruel" – the first letter of every word was a capital apart from the "o" of "of". Kind-with-a-capital-K of Cruel-with-a-capital-C. Remember when I was telling you, I said why would you write it that way unless they were titles, or names? I didn't think of headings, but with the line spaces in between . . . What if whoever wrote it was planning to fill in those spaces with . . . something? Names of people, maybe.' What else could it be? Actions – that's the only other thing I can think of. I could divide my own behaviour into kind acts, cruel ones, those that fell somewhere in between.

I never would, though. *Nobody would.*

Luke pulls himself up, leans back against the headboard, rubs his eyes. 'Yeah,' he agrees, a shade too enthusiastically. I bristle. He's said one word, and already he sounds like a man doing his best in difficult circumstances. 'They could have been headings. But . . .'

'I realise it's a crap one, as eureka moments go, but it's still some-thing, isn't it?' I say defensively. 'I should tell the police.'

'It's the middle of the night, Amber,' Luke says gently. 'I need to sleep. Mention it to the police if you want, but . . . to be honest, if you've thought of it, I'm sure they have too.'

'That's right, sorry, I forgot – all minds generate the same thoughts, don't they? That's why Einstein wasn't the only person to come up with the . . . the . . .' *Oh, for God's sake.*

'Theory of relativity?' Luke suggests, grinning sleepily.

'Yeah. That's why all his friends and neighbours in Berlin came up with the very same theory at exactly the same time.'

'Berlin?'

'Wrong?'

'Munich, Zurich. Einstein moved around.'

There's no reason why I should know that. I hated all the science subjects at school, and Maths; I gave them up as soon as I could. My degree was in History of Art. Einstein's lucky to get a mention from me at all, frankly.

'Headings are normally underlined,' I say. 'The cops wouldn't necessarily make the connection. I didn't, until I saw Dinah's cast list. She's put her headings in capitals instead of underlining them.'

Luke looks unconvinced. I'm scared of the conversation ending, of being alone again. 'I might as well tell the police,' I say. 'I'll be talking to them tomorrow anyway.' And feeling like an idiot when they tell me it couldn't matter less whether the words I saw were three headings or not; what might matter is where I saw them – the part I can't remember and have no theories about.

'They want to talk to you again tomorrow?'

'Other way round.' I might as well rehearse my confession. 'I lied to them. Second of November, the day Katharine Allen was killed – it was the same day I was meant to go on that DriveTech course. They asked me where I was between 11 a.m. and 1 p.m.'

'What? You didn't tell me that.' No more drowsy voice; Luke is wide awake. *Amber 1, Sleep 0.* 'What did you say to them?'

'I told them I was on the course. They asked if anyone could verify that I'd been there. I said no one was likely to remember my face, but I had to take my driving licence as ID and it'll be on record somewhere that I attended.'

Luke frowns as he thinks it over. 'Yeah,' he says eventually. 'And if they check it out, that's what they'll find. You didn't kill Katharine Allen, you don't know who did, so it's a white lie. You're not crazy enough to tell them the truth, right?'

I smile, appreciating his non-prejudicial phrasing of the question. 'I have to. You won't talk me out of it, so don't bother. I know it'll make no difference, I *know* I'll have to tell Jo I've told the police, and she'll be furious . . .'

'Furious?' Luke looks around the room at his imaginary audience, the crowds that only he can see, all of them on his side and waving their banners to that effect. 'Amber, wake up! You and Jo committed a *crime*. One of you did, anyway. I'm not sure which one.'

'I think we both did, technically.'

'You could go to prison!'

'Hey – remember how good you are at not yelling at me? I'm trying to do the right thing, for once. It probably doesn't suit me, but I'd appreciate it if you'd at least try to be full of admiration.' Luke is right: I could end up with a criminal record, if not behind bars. Except that isn't what's going to happen. Simon Waterhouse will keep it to himself if I ask him to. *Won't he?* How can I be sure that he'll protect me, that he isn't a team player?

With those particular team-mates, what intelligent person would be?

'You said yourself: you're the only lead they've got in a murder case.' Luke struggles to sound unemotional. Like most men, deep down he believes that only illogical arguments can be put forward by anyone in the grip of a strong feeling. 'If you stroll down to the nick and calmly admit to being a liar . . .'

'I've got an alibi! Okay, it's not the alibi I gave them . . .'

'Why do they need to know that? You've got an alibi. That's all that matters. You were somewhere else when Katharine Allen was killed.' Luke groans. 'I'm wasting my breath, aren't I?'

'No,' I tell him. 'It helps to hear you say all this, helps to convince me that you're probably right.'

Luke throws up his hands. 'Then . . . ?'

'Telling Simon Waterhouse the truth might land me and Jo in the shit, and it won't help the police to find Katharine Allen's killer – true, and so what? It's a murder investigation, Luke. The police are going to be asking a lot of people a lot of questions, and for each one they'll want an answer that isn't a lie. I can understand why that's important to them. Can't you? They want *all* the information, not most of it, not just the bits people don't mind sharing with them. Who am I to decide that they need this fact but not that fact? I don't have an overview of the case. I don't even know where I saw those words written down. It's their case, not mine. I'm a link in their chain, whether I like it or not. If I don't tell them the whole truth, I'll be prioritising my own selfish desire to stay out of trouble over their need to investigate Katharine Allen's murder in the way that they'd ideally like to: not held back and misdirected by made-up stories.'

Luke sighs. 'I just can't see how it could make a difference,' he mutters. 'Jo'll hit the roof, Neil'll go mental . . . What?'

I've grabbed his hand. Something has unlocked inside my brain. At first I don't trust it. Two eureka moments in one night? Is it because I was hypnotised today, for the first time? Maybe what I told Sergeant Zailer was wrong, and there is a container in my mind called the unconscious; maybe, thanks to Ginny, the lid's a little looser than it was this time yesterday.

'Amber? What is it?'

'The headings,' I say. 'I made a connection: one piece of paper, another piece of paper.'

'Don't know what you're talking about.'

'You have one thought, it leads on to another thought, linked to the first one. Free association. Shrinks use it all the time. Don't they?' If they do, I've no idea how I know they do, or why I'm asking Luke, who knows less about psychotherapeutic techniques than I do. Straightforward facts are Luke's speciality, the kind that win you points in pub quizzes: the dates of famous battles, the highest mountain, where Einstein lived. 'Except it's not so free, because nothing's free-floating, everything's bound up with something else,' I go on, talking mainly to myself. 'With Ginny, when I said, "Kind, Cruel, Kind of Cruel" without knowing I'd said it or what it meant, I was thinking about Little Orchard. That's what was in my mind, immediately before I said those words.'

Luke closes his eyes. 'Amber, there's no reason to think—'

'Yes, there is.' I don't care about reason, only about what my instincts are telling me. 'What if that's it? What if I saw it at Little Orchard?'

But we've walked ourselves around Little Orchard how many times? And we can't find the page with 'Kind, Cruel, Kind of Cruel' written on it. We can't bring up a memory of having seen it in any of the bedrooms or bathrooms, in either of the two lounges, in the kitchen, dining room, games room or library. Not being ones to give up easily, we've been thorough in our examination of all the least obvious places: the utility room, the walk-in pantry, the wine cellar. We've imagined lifting jars of chutney and bottles of Vanish stain remover, but it's got us nowhere. One bedroom – the one shared by Jo's mother and sister, Hilary and Kirsty – has its own attached dressing room, a small windowless room lined with cupboards on both sides. We've opened them, all of them, and failed to find our piece of paper.

We've lifted broken slabs of paving in the garden, looked into the necks of earthenware pots and into a hole in a tree trunk that's big enough to force a small female hand into – just. We've trailed our fingers through cold pond-water, checked the two outbuildings at least three times each: a hexagonal wooden summerhouse full of dusty garden furniture and a collapsed table-tennis table, and a detached double garage containing lots of matching kitchen units and a few car tyres, though no cars. Really, detectives searching the place couldn't have done a more thorough job in person than we have using only memory. Would they have spotted that there was an electric blanket on the bed in the master bedroom, Jo and Neil's room, and been canny enough to pull it back in case there was something underneath? We did. There was nothing, only a mattress.

We've been back to Little Orchard again and again and found nothing.

The normal response, at this point – and I'm attaching no positive value judgement to the word 'normal' here, I'm using it only to mean 'most common' – the normal response would be to give up and assume that, wherever Amber saw the words 'Kind, Cruel, Kind of Cruel', it wasn't at Little Orchard.

That isn't Amber's response, and I'm pleased it isn't. I'm delighted that Amber's reaction to her memory not finding what it thought it would find is much more interesting than that, because it's the interesting, weird things that really help us. The details that seem to make no sense at all are the ones that, once we understand their significance, make sense of everything and tell us all we need to know.

Amber will not budge from her certainty that Little Orchard is where she saw those unexplainable words. Why is she so sure? Because Little Orchard was what she was thinking about – lying in the same reclining chair she's lying in now, with her feet up on that same footstool – immediately before she said, 'Kind, Cruel, Kind of Cruel' and accused me of having said it first. And, yes, sometimes one thought does lead on to another for a reason, because there's a link between the two, but it's just as common for the brain to flit randomly from one topic to another and for there to be no connection. I've told Amber this and it makes her impatient. In her case, she insists, there *is* a link, it isn't random.

How does she know there's a connection if she can't say what it is? She can't or won't answer that question. She is sure that she didn't see the Kind of Cruel page in any of the rooms we keep trawling, on our memory tours. It definitely wasn't in any of the places we've searched, double-searched and triple-searched. Several times, I have asked the obvious question: then why do we keep looking? I never get an answer, so maybe Amber doesn't know why. Or maybe she knows, but because the answer appears to be impossible, she's too embarrassed to say it. Remember: embarrassment, guilt, shame and humiliation are the most disabling emotions we can feel, far more detrimental to our wellbeing even than hatred or extreme unhappiness, which are other-focused and therefore easier on our sense of self.

There was only one part of Little Orchard that Amber didn't see: the locked study on the half-landing between the first and second floors. Locked, presumably, because the owners' private possessions were in there. It's not uncommon, if you rent a holiday house, to find a locked room or two, and not unreasonable for the owners of Little Orchard to be willing to make some of their home available to paying strangers – the vast majority of it – and yet maintain a degree of privacy in the form of one locked study that probably contains all kinds of private documents: bank statements, wills, important work files.

I don't think it's unreasonable, anyway. Amber seems to, though she never quite comes out and says so. I wonder why I hear anger in her voice whenever she refers to 'the locked room'. She says it sarcastically, with audible inverted commas around it. Is she angry with herself, perhaps? She knows the locked study is the only room in which she categorically cannot have seen the elusive sheet of blue-lined paper. The door remained locked throughout her stay at Little Orchard and she never went in there. Yet she's certain she didn't see the piece of paper in any other part of the house, or anywhere else in the grounds, and equally certain that Little Orchard is where she saw it.

So, two possibilities, as far as I can see. One: Amber *did* go into the locked study, and knows what she saw in there, but doesn't want to admit it. Unlikely, I think. Her need to find out where she saw those words strikes me as genuine.

Second possibility: against all logic, she's got it into her head that the piece of paper we're looking for must be inside that locked room at Little Orchard. But if that's where it is, then she didn't see it, end of story. Unless she's psychic or telepathic – neither of which she would believe in – she can't have had a vision of the inside of the study. Plus, Katharine Allen's notepad bore the imprint of those words a month ago, in 2010. How likely is it that the words were written and the page torn off before Christmas 2003, which was when Amber was at Little Orchard?

Amber knows all this, and has tried to give herself a good talking-to, I would guess, and it makes no difference: her instincts keep screaming at her, 'It's in the locked room'. She won't admit it, especially not to the police, because it makes no sense, and she's frightened to find her beliefs making so little sense. She wouldn't admit it to me if we were alone, even though I represent all things nonsensical as far as she's concerned.

It doesn't matter if she never admits it. That's not what I'm about, forcing people to admit to things they're ashamed of. This isn't a show trial. Though

I'd love it if I could encourage more people to feel less ashamed of their irrationality and be more tolerant of what they perceive to be the rubbish clogging up their minds. Every crazy superstitious belief has a purpose and can be reformatted and turned into something wonderful and liberating. Whenever you're scared, it means you're getting somewhere, or you have the chance of getting somewhere, if only you'd take it, if you don't let your fear shut it down. Scared without an obvious cause, I mean, not scared because you're in the sea and a huge shark's swimming in your direction.

So . . . Amber isn't denying any of what I'm saying, despite being someone who loves an argument more than anything else, so I'm going to risk making two more observations. She's presented us with a truly impossible mystery. If she saw the piece of paper at Little Orchard, then she can't have seen it in the one room she didn't go into. That's simply not possible. And yet she's sure she saw it in none of the rooms she *did* go into, and she's unwilling to accept that she didn't see it at Little Orchard at all but somewhere else.

Why might Amber want to tie us all up – including herself, especially herself – in the knots of an impossible riddle?

Earlier, I mentioned the way one mystery might hide behind another: a vulnerable, easily solved mystery sheltering in the shadow of one that's tougher and more resilient. I presented a theory, which attracted neither agreement nor disagreement: that the important question is why it matters so much to Amber that she still doesn't know why Jo's branch of the family disappeared and then reappeared. I suggested a few possible ways into answering the question, only to have it seamlessly replaced with a new and far more dramatic one. I'm not saying Amber did any of this deliberately or knowingly, but I'd be surprised if her unconscious mind doesn't know very well that the words 'locked room' act as a pretty powerful attention magnet.

The impossible mystery behind the impossible mystery. Impossible in very different ways, though: one impossible of content, the other of form. The mystery we mustn't allow anyone to solve because it would cause too much pain and suffering all round, hiding behind the one we can't solve because there is literally no solution, not unless the terms and conditions have been incorrectly presented. Still, we beaver away at trying to crack it, hoping we'll be clever enough to find a way of making it all come good, making the impossible possible. We'd feel Godlike if only we could do that. And we forget all about the unglamorous simple-to-solve mystery hiding in the shadows that offers us no psychic visions and no locked rooms. Who needs more pain and suffering in their life?

You need to tackle all the questions you want to answer least, Amber – one by one. That's the only way to make the impossible riddles in your life disappear.

Let's start with an easy one. How did you know there was an electric blanket on Jo and Neil's bed at Little Orchard? And paper drawer liners in the drawers in Hilary and Kirsty's dressing room, and a bowl full of cotton wool balls in Pam and Quentin's en-suite shower room?

Do I need to go on? A hole in a tree trunk in the garden, a grey plastic cutlery divider in one of the kitchen units in the garage? Katharine Allen was still alive in 2003, and you weren't an insomniac. You had no idea you would one day consult a hypnotherapist who would ask you to go over every inch of Little Orchard in your memory in search of a sheet of A4 paper that might prove to be an important part of a murder investigation.

You weren't making those details up, were you? They were genuine memories, vivid ones. If you deny it, I won't believe you. I could see the concentration on your face, and how much it mattered to you to get the particulars right.

You were remembering searching the house and garden for real.

What were you looking for?

4

1/12/2010

Sam Kombothekra was in Proust's office, sitting at a desk and in a chair that wasn't his. He'd never done it before, even on days when Proust was guaranteed not to come in. Sam hadn't known until he'd tried the door today that the Snowman was in the habit of leaving his small glass-walled cubicle unlocked; it had never occurred to him to wonder. Unless it wasn't a habit; maybe Proust had found yesterday so stressful that he forgot, but Sam didn't think so. More likely he assumed his office needed no lock – the fear he'd instilled over the years would be sufficient to keep people out.

On the desk in front of Sam was his DI's new 'World's Greatest Grandad' mug: red with white lettering and a picture of an old man with goofy teeth and a pink strawberry-shaped nose. Were the manufacturers trying to suggest that all grandads were alcoholics, or only the jolly ones? This mug was bigger and uglier than its predecessor, which the Snowman had hurled at Simon Waterhouse's head a couple of years ago. Simon had moved out of the way and the mug had smashed against a filing cabinet. Sam would have put money on Proust having bought this replacement for himself. His grandchildren were well into their teens and bound to hate him by now.

Sam watched as Gibbs walked into the CID room and did a double-take when he looked through the window of Proust's office and saw where his sergeant was sitting. *Yes, I'm in the wrong place*, Sam thought. *I've been in the wrong place for a long time*. Tomorrow, everything would change. Gibbs and Simon would be out of a job and Sam would have handed in his resignation. What would Colin Sellers do? These days, Sam felt as if he hardly knew Sellers, who had become secretive and withdrawn since the break-up of his extra-marital relationship with a woman called Suki. Sam had never met her, but he'd seen photos he wished he hadn't – photos he couldn't believe anyone would think of taking, let alone showing to colleagues. As Sam's wife Kate had been quick to point out, Sellers seemed to have got it the wrong way round: recklessly open while he was cheating on his wife, bragging about his long-running affair to anyone at work who would listen, then suddenly cagey when it was all over and he had nothing to hide. Nothing Sam knew of, anyway.

Gibbs came in without knocking. 'There's something you need to know, assuming we're pursuing the Amber Hewerdine angle.'

'We are,' said Sam. He'd lain awake most of last night wondering how he would handle work today. Proust was sure to insist he worked out his notice, knowing it was the last thing he'd want to do, but in every way that mattered, today was Sam's last day. He was determined to make it count. He would leave all other cases on hold for the next few hours and focus only on Katharine Allen's murder.

Which meant pursuing the Amber Hewerdine angle. Not because he was scared of Simon's anger if he didn't, or to prove anything to Proust, but because it was the obvious way forward. Simon had handled it badly, but he was right: Amber Hewerdine was an important lead, and they weren't exactly spoilt for choice. Sam couldn't remember ever having had so little to go on.

'When I went to Hewerdine's house to bring her in, she had her two daughters with her,' said Gibbs. 'First thing she did was warn me off letting them find out I'm police. She said it like it was a dirty word. Her attitude fucked me off, and it only occurred to me in the middle of the night to ask a question I should have asked straight away: why would she care if her daughters saw her talking to a detective? Hardly suggests innocence.'

'They're not her daughters,' Sam told him. It had the effect he hoped it would. He noticed, because his words usually made so little impact. Simon and the Snowman were the show-stealers.

'You're joking. Who are they, then? She called them "my girls".'

'Dinah and Oenone Lendrim.'

'In-own-y? What the fuck kind of name's that?'

'Greek mythological.' Sam smiled, knowing Gibbs would assume he knew this because his father was Greek. 'She's Nonie for all practical purposes. She and her sister Dinah are the children of Sharon Lendrim.'

'Am I supposed to recognise the name?' Gibbs asked.

'I thought you might,' said Sam. 'Don't worry, I didn't either. Sharon Lendrim was murdered on 22 November 2008. In Rawndesley. Unsolved.'

'And Amber Hewerdine's got her kids?' Gibbs shook his head as he processed the new information. 'This is . . . I don't know what, but it's something. Does Waterhouse know?'

Sam wasn't surprised by the question. Simon, in spite of his rudeness and unpredictability, was and would always be the human intelligence system into which all pieces of relevant information needed to be fed. Gibbs worshipped him. Sam believed Proust did too, in a funny sort of way. Nothing counted for anything until Simon knew about it; there was no point thinking about a problem unless Simon was thinking about it simultaneously, pulling your thoughts along with his. Sam had kidded himself for years that it wasn't the case, and he'd grown tired of the lie. He was Simon's superior in rank only. He'd be better off doing something completely different.

'He's not answering his phone,' Sam told Gibbs. 'I've left him a message. And . . . I need to get out of here.' He stood up, wondering what had possessed him. What was he doing in Proust's doom-box? 'Fancy a pint at the Brown Cow?'

'Sounds good,' said Gibbs. 'I'll leave Sellers a message. Where is he, d'you know?'

More than once in the past few months, Sam had been ignorant of the whereabouts of every single member of his team. 'I sent him to talk to Ginny Saxon. Probably a waste of time.'

'Don't know till you try, do you?'

Gibbs marched ahead as they left the building. He was a surly sod, but recently he'd started to offer Sam regular words of encouragement. *You tried your best, sarge. Good thinking, mate.* Colin Sellers was the same, and Simon. As if Sam were a shy new recruit with a confidence deficit. Which, come to think of it, was how he felt most of the time.

'No point me asking where Waterhouse is,' Gibbs said as they stood at the bar waiting for their pints amid the suits and ties and loud voices.

'There might be,' Sam told him. 'Not that I've heard from him, but I can guess.'

'Amber Hewerdine?'

'No, I don't think so. I rang her at work this morning.'

'Dark horse, aren't you?' Gibbs sounded surprised.

'I'm a DS. I'm supposed to make decisions and act on them.'

Gibbs looked momentarily confused. 'So what did she say?'

'Simon rang her first thing, asked to meet up. She gave him the brush-off. That's not how she put it, but it's the impression I got – before she gave me the brush-off too.'

'She was happy enough to talk to Waterhouse last night,' said Gibbs. 'He had a job persuading her to leave.'

'Too busy at work, too many meetings, it'll have to wait till tomorrow – that's what she said.'

'So if Waterhouse isn't with her, where is he?'

They picked up their drinks and made their way to the nearest free table. Gibbs pulled over a third chair, from which Sam inferred that he was expecting Sellers to join them. Gibbs was more relaxed in Sellers' presence than out of it. Sam wasn't close to either of them – he wasn't close to anyone at work – but he knew he'd miss his team more than he'd ever enjoyed working with them.

The Brown Cow had recently been renovated again. The walls were covered in wood panelling, painted a colour Sam's wife Kate called 'teal', while the old wood floor had been replaced with a red, blue and white tartan carpet. The landlord liked to change the look every couple of years, and the current flavour seemed to be trendy Scottish hunting lodge. The only constant was a large oil painting of a brown cow that had been there forever. There would be an outcry if anyone tried to take it down – a genteel, Spilling kind of outcry – and quite right too. Sam had grown fond of the cow, which kept its intelligent eye on you wherever you sat, and had proved over the years to be a good listener. Better than Simon, Sellers or Gibbs. Sometimes, when he was having trouble getting through to his DCs, Sam imagined he was talking to the cow instead and found he was able to express himself more clearly.

'Simon'll be thinking what you thought,' he said to Gibbs. 'How come Amber's avoiding him suddenly, after being so helpful last night? Was he wrong to trust her and tell her as much as he did?'

'I can answer that,' Gibbs muttered.

'He'll want to check her alibi for 2 November. That's where he is: working his way through everyone who was on that driver awareness course, or as many of them as he can. It won't be good enough for him to see a tick in a box next to her name. He'll want to find some-one who remembers her face, and can tell him if she was there for the whole day, or if she nipped out for half an hour at any point between eleven and one. Driving time from Rawndesley Road Conference Centre to Kat Allen's flat can't be more than five minutes.'

Sam raised his glass. 'Να σκάσουν οι εχθροί μας,' he said, before taking a sip. Gibbs wouldn't appreciate the irony of the Greek toast, which meant, 'May our enemies burst with envy'. Sam had no enemies, and as far as he was aware no one had ever envied him.

'The Conference Centre?' said Gibbs. 'That's where the course was?'

Sam nodded. 'Amber said there were twenty there, right? Twenty speeding drivers?'

'If you call a couple of miles over the limit speeding, yeah,' said Gibbs.

'More than enough people to take up Simon's whole day.' Sam sighed. 'He can't risk coming into work. Someone like me might ask him how he feels about getting fired, puncture his denial. I wouldn't be surprised if he didn't turn up tomorrow at nine for the official sacking ceremony.'

'He'll turn up,' said Gibbs.

'Will he? I thought he'd ring me when he got my message about Sharon Lendrim. I made a point of withholding most of the story, give him an incentive to get in touch.' Sam shrugged. 'I've heard nothing from him.'

'Don't take it personally. Tell me instead, if you can be bothered.'

Sam was shocked. 'It's my job to be bothered.' *A job I soon won't have.*

'Look, we both know what's going to happen tomorrow morning,' said Gibbs. 'To Waterhouse at nine and to me at nine fifteen. I just thought . . .'

'It's not tomorrow yet,' said Sam, feeling panicky. 'It's still today, and you still work for me.'

'All right, no need to pull rank.'

Sam laughed. 'Most DSs pull rank several times a day, every day. If I'd done it more often, maybe we wouldn't be in the mess we're in now.' Gibbs stared at him for a few seconds, then turned back to his pint.

What do you expect him to say? Don't blame yourself, there's nothing you could have done? Of course Sam wanted to tell Gibbs about Sharon Lendrim's murder; of all the conversations they might have today, it promised to be the easiest.

'All I know at this stage is what DS Ursula Shearer from Rawndesley's told me. Sharon Lendrim lived in Rawndesley, on Monson Street. She was a single mum with two kids, worked at the hospital as a diabetic dietician.'

'Kids have the same father?' Gibbs asked.

'No one knows, but there were no dads in the picture at any point. Sharon's mother Marianne told the police she was sure Sharon had used a sperm bank, or a donation from a gay friend – to spite her, because she knew Marianne would be against both. According to DS Shearer, spite's the only reasonable reaction to Marianne Lendrim.'

'Did they alibi her?' Gibbs asked.

'They did. She was in Venice staying in a friend's apartment on 22 November 2008, so whoever poured petrol through Sharon's letterbox at ten past one in the morning and chucked a match in after it, it can't have been Marianne.'

Gibbs frowned. 'That's what happened?'

'Sharon was asleep in bed, died from the fumes.'

'What about her daughters?'

'This is the interesting part. As soon as the blaze took hold, neighbours noticed it and called it in. When the fire service arrived, they found Sharon dead inside the house and the girls' beds empty. They'd been expecting to find the two sisters the neighbours had told them lived in the house, a five-year-old and a six-year-old.'

'In Venice with Wicked Grandma?' Gibbs guessed.

'No,' said Sam. 'Nothing so normal. While their mother was dying alone at home, Dinah and Nonie Lendrim were at the pub.'

～

Charlie was keeping a list of all the ways in which her quality of life was blighted by her sister Olivia's affair with Chris Gibbs. Sometimes she forgot what number she was up to. The new addition that had just occurred to her – that she'd been unable to suggest she and Liv meet in the Brown Cow, her favourite pub in the world, in case Gibbs was in there – was either number twenty-six or twenty-seven.

Charlie could have gone upmarket with her choice of an alternative meeting place, or picked somewhere in the same league as the Brown Cow, but she'd plumped instead for the Web & Grub, a small, smelly internet café overlooking the Winstanley Estate that shared its premises with a minicab firm and served no hot food. The sum total of today's bounty was five sandwiches standing in a forlorn line on the counter between the till and the home-made cardboard tip box: two tuna mayo and three cheese ploughmans, all in triangular plastic packets. Hot drinks were served in Styrofoam cups; for those who preferred something cold, there were bottles of water and cartons of orange juice and Ribena in a large humming fridge, the glass door of which was covered with greasy finger smears and half-peeled-off stickers. On the phone, Olivia hadn't said a word about the choice of venue, which was how Charlie knew she'd taken the point: it was her fault that they were missing out on the Brown Cow's spinach and asparagus crepe, its chorizo and red lentil casserole, its Sausage Alsacienne.

No booze at the Web & Grub either. A pint of strong lager would have helped Charlie get through this meeting, her and Liv's first in months. Did she have time to nip to the offie next door, buy a can and drink it before Liv arrived?

Too late; here she was. As she walked over, she waved frantically and tearfully, as if from a rapidly departing ocean liner. The joyful expression on her face hardened something in Charlie. In her sister's shoes, if their roles had been reversed, Charlie would have taken Liv's forgiveness as an insult, found it more offensive than the months of silence.

Who the fuck are you to forgive me, when I did nothing wrong in the first place?

Charlie wondered how she could still be so angry, when the voice in her head was manifestly on Olivia's side. She'd said nothing on the phone about forgiveness, deliberately. All she'd done was ask if she and Liv could meet.

Don't tell her she's lost weight and looks fantastic. She'll know you know why that is. Might as well write 'CHRIS GIBBS' in capitals on the table between you.

Liv sat down, clutching her strange cow-skin handbag to her chest like body armour. Its stiff handles obstructed Charlie's view of her face. Their curved shape brought bridges to mind: building them, burning them.

'This feels so weird. I thought I might never see you again. Did you think that too?' Liv gabbled. 'No, course you didn't. You knew you could talk to me whenever you wanted to. God, I'm actually shaking! For some reason this feels like a clandestine meeting. Must be the unsalubrious surroundings. Not that I'm complaining,' she added quickly, holding up both hands in a gesture of surrender, as if Charlie was aiming a gun at her heart.

Don't say, 'If you want to talk about unsalubrious . . .'

'I'd have met you anywhere. I'd have met you in a caravan.' Eyes wide, Liv stared at Charlie, gripping the handles of her bag with both hands. She shuddered.

Charlie nodded to indicate she'd got the message: Liv was desperate to make peace. She'd once told Charlie she hated caravans so much that even the word made her feel sick; she tried to avoid hearing it or saying it. At first Charlie had thought this was an affectation – she'd been on the same family holidays as Liv every year, in their parents' mobile home, and suffered no adverse effects – but her sister's consistency over decades had made her think again. As phobias went, it was a bizarre one. Charlie wondered what Ginny Saxon would have to say about it.

'Do you want to get something to eat?' she asked Liv.

'Do you?'

'I don't think I'm hungry.'

'Me neither. So let's have lunch with no food.' Liv giggled. 'Like in *Dallas*. Remember how they used to sit down to enormous delicious meals, then have a huge row and all storm off?'

Don't tell her she's way too obvious, shamelessly invoking happy childhood memories. So you both loved Dallas; *so what?*

'I don't mean *we're* going to have a huge row. Of course we aren't.' Liv looked terrified. 'I'm so pleased to see you, I wouldn't fall out with you even if you . . .'

Asked you to swear that you've shared bodily fluids with Chris Gibbs for the last time?

'I can't think of anything.' Liv shrugged. 'My mind's gone blank. I'm too scared of you. You'd better do the talking.' The hands went up again. 'Not that I'm saying you're scary. Shit, now I sound passive aggressive, like I'm saying one thing when I mean another. I'm honestly not.'

'I've been seeing a hypnotherapist,' Charlie announced. It was easier to come out with it while Liv was wittering. Except she wasn't any more, which meant that the rest of what Charlie had to say, the follow-through, had the pressure of attentive silence to contend with. 'Well, I've seen her once, but I'll probably go again. It's for my smoking. To help me give up. It seems to work for loads of people, so I thought I'd try it. It's no big deal, and I wouldn't have mentioned it, except . . .'

'You wanted an excuse to get in touch with me?' Liv suggested hopefully.

Charlie inhaled, held the air in her lungs for as long as she could, imagined it was nicotine. 'Turns out I picked the wrong woman to go to for help,' she said eventually. 'I don't want to get into the details, but it seems there's a connection, or possible connection, between my . . .' Charlie couldn't bring herself to say 'therapist'. 'Between this hypnotist woman and a case Simon's on at the moment.' Hypnotist, therapist – Charlie wasn't sure which sounded worse.

'Which case?' said Liv. 'Not Kat Allen?'

All the necessary defences shot up within seconds. No effort was required; Charlie barely felt a thing. She was getting better at this. Her soul, after years of practice, was accustomed to adopting the brace position.

Of course, Liv would know all about Katharine Allen's murder, via Gibbs. *Kat*. As if she'd known her all her life. Liv being Liv, she saw no reason to keep quiet; why not ram home her invasion of Charlie's world instead? People deflected attention from their own crippling selfishness in a variety of ways, Charlie had noticed. Liv's way was to hide behind a mask of naïve childlike enthusiasm.

'Simon had to be upfront at work about my connection with this . . . woman – Ginny, she's called – and I didn't want you hearing about it from anyone else.'

It wasn't as hard as she'd feared it might be to parrot Simon's words as if she believed them herself. Olivia didn't need to know that Charlie loathed Simon at the moment, or that her loathing of him did nothing to diminish her love for him, which made her resent him even more.

He hadn't needed to humiliate her by taking her notebook into work, where anyone who wanted to, including Gibbs, would be able to read her undignified, unsendable letters to Olivia. Charlie had begged him, in tears, to tear out and take in only the relevant page, the Kind of Cruel page. When that failed, she shifted the focus of her begging: couldn't he see sense and spend five minutes or half an hour, or however long it took, constructing, with Charlie's help, an acceptable lie that would allow him to tell his team everything they needed to know without endangering his job?

No, he couldn't. Or, rather, he wouldn't. 'I'm sick of things being complicated,' he said. 'I've got some new information. Other people need to know it. I shouldn't have to start second-guessing, planning, scheming, worrying how to protect my job, myself or anyone else. All that's a waste of my energy. If anyone doesn't like the truth, that's their problem. Sometimes I don't like it either, but there's no point pretending we don't all have to live with it.'

Charlie was better than most at facing the truth – she figured she must be, or else why did she feel miserable so much of the time? – but she'd have liked, if at all possible, to keep certain truths private: her visit to a hypnotherapist, the emotional letters she'd written in the naïve belief that no one but her would ever see them. Frantic, she'd blurted out a series of desperate suggestions she hadn't had time to think through: Simon could give her a chance to talk to Ginny Saxon again, persuade her to ring the police, say nothing about Charlie, but claim to be worried by something sinister a client had said under hypnosis. A bit far-fetched, perhaps, but Charlie thought she could have persuaded Ginny to go along with it, in the interests of client confidentiality and helping to progress a murder case.

Simon hadn't been willing to discuss it. 'I'm going in, I'm taking the notebook, I'm telling it straight – that's what *I'm* doing. Other people can tie themselves in knots if they want to, sack me if they want to, tell themselves I don't give a shit about their feelings if they want to. None of that's down to me.'

Later, it had occurred to Charlie that her plan wouldn't have worked anyway. If Sam or Gibbs or Sellers had interviewed Amber Hewerdine, they would soon have found out about Ginny Saxon's other client, the smoker with the notebook.

'You invited me here to tell me you're having hypnotherapy?' said Liv. 'Not because you've missed me, or you want to put the past behind us and go back to how things were, or . . .' She stopped, looked down at the table. 'Sorry, I don't mean to put words into your mouth.'

Charlie was busy trying to stop them spilling out.

Don't say you'd love to go back to the way things were before she fell into bed with Gibbs.

Don't point out that the past is somewhat larger than the unpleasant experiences she'd like to leave behind, that it also includes things she's eager to hang on to – one in particular that she's keen to have spill over into the present.

Don't demand to know how she has the gall to use language – words with fixed meanings – in such a dishonest, self-serving way.

Charlie thought about Amber Hewerdine, her intolerance of anything that had even the faintest whiff of bullshit about it. Ginny Saxon must have had the afternoon from hell yesterday, with first Amber and then Charlie to contend with; surely most people who went to her for help were more gullible and asked fewer tricky questions.

Are you wishing Amber Hewerdine was your sister, a woman you've met twice and barely know? Pathetic.

'I'm happy to talk to you about whatever you want,' Liv said. 'I just . . . assumed we were going to talk about me and Chris, that's all.'

'If you want to talk about Gibbs in the way you'd talk about any other boyfriend – *your* other boyfriend, for example – that's fine by me. If you'd rather not mention him, also fine. What we're not going to discuss, ever, is the rights and wrongs of anything – whether or not you've fucked me over, whether I've overreacted . . .'

'The contentious stuff,' Liv summarised.

Charlie nodded.

'But . . .'

'Problem?'

Liv sighed. 'It's a bit odd, isn't it? How can we sort anything out if we don't—'

'Sorting out's not going to be possible,' Charlie said briskly, mentally flicking through the dozens of vicious accusations she might hurl at her sister, given the chance. 'The only thing I can think of that might work is if we pretend everything's normal and there was never an issue. I'm willing to try it if you are.'

Liv looked worried. 'Can I ask something, just to clarify?'

'Everything's clear.'

'Not to me it isn't. You say I can talk about Chris as I would any other boyfriend, but you don't really mean it, do you? How will you feel if I ring you in a complete state on the day his and Debbie's twins are born?'

Maybe she hadn't made herself clear after all. 'How I would *feel* is irrelevant. That's the part we wouldn't talk about and you won't ask about if you've got any sense. What I'd *say* is the same as I'd say if you were seeing a man I didn't know whose wife had just given birth to twins: if it upsets you that much, end it, unless ending it would upset you more.'

'I'll feel too guilty to mention Chris's name *ever*,' Liv said moodily. 'You know I will. How can I have a conversation and leave my feelings out of it? I'm not a robot.'

Charlie wanted to groan and rest her head on the table. Was she going to have to draw up a contract, complete with sub-clauses and restrictive covenants? 'You can talk about your feelings all you like, as long as it's not your feelings about me and *my* feelings.'

'So, for the sake of argument . . .'

'We won't be having any arguments,' Charlie said firmly.

'. . . it's okay for me to say, "I stayed up all night weeping because I have to marry Dom and I can't marry Chris," but not okay for me to ask if you've forgiven me or if you ever will?'

'By George, she's got it,' Charlie quoted *My Fair Lady*, another favourite thing from her and Olivia's childhood.

Liv shook her head, looked irritated. 'All right, then. I agree to your ridiculous terms. God, you've only been married to Simon four months and already he's got you talking as if feelings are some kind of disgusting waste product. Please, for your own good, don't talk to me about it if you don't want to, but please try and feel some emotion while you still can, before Simon roboticises you entirely. Because that's what's happening, Char.' Liv's voice shook. 'He's trying to turn you into a . . . a blank space, so that he can live with you without feeling threatened.'

Charlie smiled. 'Oh well,' she said. 'To go back to the theoretical example you just gave: it makes no odds to me whether you do or don't, but you ought to realise that you don't *have* to marry Dom.'

Liv started to cry. 'You got a tissue?' she whispered.

'Blank spaces don't need tissues,' Charlie told her. 'We're dry, dry, dry.'

'How can you bear this, Char?'

'Ginny would say because I learned in early childhood to block out my emotional responses. Did you know that unprocessed traumatic memories are stored in a different part of the brain from the rest of our experience?'

'Ginny?' Liv asked.

'My hypno woman. Apparently I'm one of the most emotionally dissociative people she's ever met.'

'Is that what your new rules are about?' Liv asked. '"One of" isn't good enough for you, you're going for the gold medal?'

'Yeah,' Charlie played along. 'Just wait till Ginny hears about this conversation – she'll have to agree I've blown the competition right out of the water.'

'It's *so* not you to go and see a hypnotherapist. You've never said anything about wanting to give up smoking.'

'Ginny says I'm not ready to give up yet. While we both wait for me to be ready, I have a feeling I might learn a thing or two. Like, did you know that some people repress painful memories so that they're not conscious of the memory being there at all until they recall it under hypnosis, whereas other people have accurate *factual* memories – they know every detail of what happened – but they shut out the feelings that ought to go with the events? I'm that kind, the second kind. It obviously makes more sense to be the second kind.'

'Charlie . . .'

'The other lot, Group A, they never know when they're going to be blindsided by something they suddenly remember. We're cleverer and more devious. We tell ourselves we can't be repressing anything, because, look, we know everything there is to know about ourselves, all the facts. *And* we feel like shit all the time anyway, and we're proud of it, so there can't be any bad feelings we're repressing, right?'

'It's Simon, isn't it?' Liv said. 'That's why you're seeing this woman. It's all for him.'

Charlie snorted. 'Yeah, it's Simon's idea. Doesn't it sound exactly like him to suggest consulting a hypnotist? Alternative therapies are never far from his mind, as you know.'

'He's told you he doesn't like you smoking, hasn't he?' Liv persisted.

'No. He doesn't care. He's used to it.'

'He's worried about your health, now that you're officially his. He's trying to protect his investment. He doesn't want to spend his retirement nursing a wife with emphysema and an amputated leg.'

'*With* an amputated leg? I think, if you have your leg amputated, you don't hang around with it afterwards. I could be wrong. You definitely are. The hypnotherapy was my idea. And of all the men who might end up with a crippled wife who can't breathe, Simon would handle it better than most. There's nothing he likes more than the tragic symbolism of making huge sacrifices.'

'Sex!' Olivia announced, banging her fist on the table in triumph. The taxi-drivers huddled around the buzzing fridge interrupted their half-Polish, half-English banter to look over. 'Sex, not death.'

Charlie nodded. 'It's a winning campaign slogan. I'd vote for you.'

'Simon's using your smoking as an excuse for why he won't sleep with you. *That's* why you needed to meet me suddenly and tell me about your hypnotherapy that's purely for the purpose of helping you to stop smoking, which you want to do *only* for health reasons. It's plausible. Lots of people would fall for it. You weren't sure I would, though. You know I know how much you love your fags, how little you care about long-term consequences. You couldn't risk Chris telling me when you weren't there to monitor my reaction, could you? You needed to see for yourself if I was going to fall for it.'

'All true,' Charlie said. 'You're wrong about the sex, though.'

Olivia looked affronted. 'I'm *not* wrong,' she said petulantly.

'Look, believe me, I know how painful it is when you have to ditch a theory that fits perfectly. Simon using my smoking to avoid sex – it's a great idea, one that deserves to be true. Unfortunately, it isn't. Simon's never said anything about my dirty habit, positive or negative. It's never occurred to him to try to use it as a way of avoiding sex. He doesn't need to.' Charlie laughed. 'We're talking about a world expert on intimacy-avoidance here. You think he couldn't avoid sex with a *non*-smoker? His methods are effective across the board. They aren't nicotine-dependent.'

'So if it's not what I think it is, what is it?' Liv asked. 'Why are you seeing a hypnotherapist?'

Charlie gave it some thought. Then she said, 'I can't answer that question. You'll have to ask my Hidden Observer – the part of me that's in charge of storing information that on some level I need to know, but that mustn't be allowed to reach my conscious mind.'

Olivia reached into her handbag and pulled out her diary. 'When are you next free?' she asked.

'Why?' said Charlie.

'I'd like us to meet up again, as soon as possible. Talk.'

'We're talking now.'

'Yeah, and it's not working for me,' Liv said, standing up, open diary in hand. 'Email me a date. I'll be there, wherever and whenever you say. Hopefully next time I'll enjoy it more.'

'Not much chance of that,' Charlie muttered as her sister ran for cover.

~

'While the fire crew was trying to tackle the blaze at Sharon's house, the landlord of the local pub, the Four Fountains on Wight Street, was ringing the police,' said Sam. 'Dinah and Nonie Lendrim had walked into his pub wearing only their pyjamas, shivering and holding hands.'

'Are you trying to give me the creeps?' Gibbs said.

'Landlord's name was Terry Bond. He was staying open late that night. He had a special licence for a live event, an open mic comedy night. He was pretty surprised to see two little kids walk in, and even more surprised when they told him what had just happened to them. They'd been woken by a firefighter in uniform: helmet, protective mask, the works. Dragged them out of their beds, down the stairs, out of the house. According to both girls, this person said only two things to them the whole time: "Fire", and then, "Run", once he or she had got them outside onto the pavement.'

'He or she?' Gibbs said. 'They couldn't say if it was a man or a woman?'

'Dinah was sure it was a man. Nonie reckoned a woman. Eventually DS Shearer and her team stopped asking. The girls were getting more and more disturbed by their inability to agree and started shaking every time a detective went anywhere near them. Both changed their tune a few times, to make the other feel better. It was useless, Shearer said. Which is a shame because, whoever was behind that mask, man or woman, that's who murdered Sharon Lendrim.'

Gibbs waited, not quite as patiently as he would have if it had been Simon explaining.

'Dinah did as she was told and ran towards the main road,' Sam said. 'Nonie hung back, worried about her mum. She saw the person wearing the fireman's uniform run back to the house, and then Dinah yelled at her, "Come on, Nonie, run."'

'As you would, if you'd been given the order by an adult supposedly trying to save your life,' said Gibbs.

Sam nodded. 'The uniform would have been enough to do the

trick. People wearing firemen's uniforms save lives. They're heroes. Everyone knows that, even kids of six and five. Nonie assumed the firefighter was heading back into the house to get Sharon out. Her sister was telling her to run, so she ran.'

'Leaving the killer to, what? Lock the front door, throw petrol through the letterbox and set it alight? Fire-starter, not firefighter.'

'Right. A fire-starter with a front door key, so probably someone Sharon knew. Someone evil enough to coldly take a life, but who also cared enough to save Sharon's daughters.'

'I doubt Sharon was cold when she died.' Gibbs frowned. 'Unusual for an arsonist with a grudge to shift the kids out of the way first. Normally they don't give a shit. As long as they get their target, the whole family can burn for all they care – it's part of the punishment.'

'Not in this case. This killer's twisted enough to imagine her principles are intact because she left the two girls alive. She took a big risk to save them: let herself be seen, spoke to them. Mask or no mask, Dinah and Nonie might have provided the police with a detail that would have given her away.'

'Why "her"? Say "him" if it could be either.'

Sam grinned; he'd seen the objection coming. 'The proper non-sexist approach is to alternate, if you're unsure of the gender. And that's not why I said "she". If I had to guess, I'd go for Sharon Lendrim's murderer being a woman, for two reasons. Most arsonists – the ones who don't give a monkey's if spouses, babies, grannies die too – they're men. This one saved two girls. It's the sort of thing a woman might do.'

'There are plenty of men out there who'd eat a bullet before they'd burn two kids to death. I'm one of them, you're another. Is your second reason any better?'

'Dinah and Nonie were disorientated,' said Sam. 'It's the middle of the night, there's a stranger in their bedroom in a firefighter's uniform and mask. I think, all other things being equal, they'd both assume it was a man. It's a job people associate with men. For Nonie to say it was a woman . . .'

'Whereas for Dinah to say it was a man, she could have just assumed it was?' Gibbs shook his head. 'But they both heard his voice. Her voice, whatever.'

'Ursula Shearer agrees with you,' Sam told him. 'Just as likely to be either, she reckons.'

'Wonder what Waterhouse'd say.'

Sam sighed and pressed on. 'One thing the girls are unanimous about, though it only occurred to them later when they were questioned: they didn't see fire or smell smoke as they were leaving the house. And Nonie didn't see anything when she looked back. The only reason they had for thinking their home was burning down was the uniformed firefighter saying, "Fire" and dragging them out of their beds.'

'Because there was no fire, at that point,' Gibbs muttered.

'The girls ran as far as the BP garage on the junction of Spilling Road and Ineson Way, but it was closed – it's not twenty-four hours. That's when they thought of the Four Fountains. They knew it was still open, that Terry Bond had a special licence for that night. Well, Dinah did.'

'A six-year-old who knows the closing time of the local pub?' Gibbs slurped a sip of his pint. 'I don't get it. Why didn't they run to a neighbour's house?'

'They couldn't explain. Ursula Shearer thinks it's the way their mother's murderer said, "Run". Urgently, as in "Run and keep running, get the hell out of here, don't look back". Not "Nip next door". Also . . . Dinah mentioned to more than one of Shearer's DCs that she didn't want to wake anyone who was sleeping, not if she didn't have to.'

'A considerate six-year-old who knows the closing time of the local pub?' said Gibbs. 'I don't buy it. Could she and her sister have offed the mother?'

'Not outside of a horror film, no.'

'Some people's lives *are* horror films.'

'There's a less creepy explanation, thank God,' said Sam. 'There was quite a history between Sharon Lendrim and the Four Fountains.

In June 2008, Terry Bond applied to the council to change the terms of his licence. He wanted to stay open later on Thursdays, Fridays and Saturdays – one thirty instead of eleven thirty – so that he could host regular open mic nights.'

'Amber Hewerdine's Licensing Manager for the city council,' Gibbs muttered under his breath.

'Well spotted,' said Sam. 'Keep that detail in mind. It's important.'

'I'd never have guessed,' said Gibbs sarcastically.

'Terry Bond didn't want to have to apply for a special licence every time he wanted to put on a comedy night. He was more ambitious, wanted to make the Four Fountains the number one venue for live comedy in the Culver Valley. A group of concerned locals opposed the extension to the pub's licence. They argued that later hours would mean more drunks making more noise late at night, more damage to property, more litter.' Sam would have been on their side, if the pub had been in his neighbourhood. 'They had a strong case: the pub's in a primarily residential area, it used to be a family home, it's surrounded on all sides by family homes. You get the idea. The head of the local residents' association did a recce and established that Sharon Lendrim's back garden backed onto the pub's car park, with only a low fence separating the two. This woman – bit of a puritan, by all accounts – persuaded Sharon that an extension to the pub's hours would be a disaster for her, especially with two young children. Sharon panicked and joined the campaign against the licence extension. Within a couple of weeks, she was in charge of it – a very vocal and articulate champion of the cause, whose best friend since school just happened to be the city council Licensing Manager. Dinah and Nonie knew all about it. There were posters and papers all over their house, residents' association members traipsing in and out.'

'Killjoys,' said Gibbs. 'Sitting quietly in their houses not drinking. Freaks.'

'The killjoys were delighted that their spokeswoman just happened to be Amber Hewerdine's best mate, until they found out that Amber, far from being willing to use her influence to help her friend, did the very opposite: told Sharon she was being ridiculous, paranoid and unreasonable. The two of them fell out for a few weeks, didn't speak. Meanwhile, Terry Bond, not quite understanding why all this trouble was coming his way, withdrew his application. The last thing he wanted was to be hated by all his neighbours. He wasn't Sharon Lendrim's biggest fan, as you can imagine, and she wasn't his. When she was murdered, twelve people contacted Ursula Shearer's team to say that he must have been behind it. Only one person contacted them to say that Terry Bond definitely wasn't Sharon's killer.'

'Amber Hewerdine,' Gibbs guessed.

'After Bond withdrew his application, Amber rang Sharon and asked if they could meet, try to sort things out. Sharon agreed, mainly because Dinah and Nonie adored Amber and were missing her. A lunch was arranged, at which Amber told Sharon a few things about the residents' association that Sharon hadn't previously been willing to listen to – that basically they opposed anything and every-thing they could. Objecting to things was their hobby. They'd protested about an Indian restaurant opening nearby, a French bistro, even an art gallery, on the grounds that it would serve wine at its private views which would lead to drunks staggering out onto the pavement armed with dangerously sharp-cornered framed pictures. Seriously, I'm not joking. They disapproved of anyone having fun, wanted everybody to sit at home in silence drinking water, or at least that was Amber Hewerdine's take on it. Not dissim-ilar to yours.' Sam smiled.

'Amber presented Sharon with a challenge: to go with her to one of Terry Bond's specially licensed comedy nights and see how she felt afterwards. According to the statement Amber made after Sharon's murder, Sharon agreed to go along out of guilt. She was worried Amber was right: that she'd been tricked by a load of Nimbys into panicking when there was nothing to panic about, and destroyed a harmless pub landlord's dreams in the process.'

'I've yet to meet a harmless pub landlord, but carry on,' said

Gibbs. 'Or shall I do the honours? Sharon had the best night of her life, she and Terry Bond got on like a—'

'Choose another metaphor,' Sam advised.

'Is that what happened?'

'Amber says yes. She says Sharon loved everything about the Four Fountains, loved the comedians on the bill that night . . .'

'I hate comedians,' said Gibbs. 'They're not funny.'

'. . . remembered that no noise from the pub had ever disturbed her or her daughters, even on special licence nights when it was open till 3 a.m., sometimes. Terry Bond told her why she'd never been bothered by noise. When he'd taken over the Four Fountains, he'd installed new double-glazed acoustic glass windows, sound-proofed his walls, he didn't allow any of his punters to go out into the beer garden after 9 p.m., he'd put up signs all over the beer garden saying that anyone who disturbed the peace would get turfed out and barred . . .'

'He wanted Sharon Lendrim on his side.'

'According to Amber Hewerdine, he got her,' said Sam. 'She told him to put in another application. This time she'd support him and even speak in his favour at the licensing hearing, as a convert. Bond was delighted, understandably. He gave Sharon a free ticket to the pub's next comedy night, told her he'd even treat her to a babysitter for the girls, promised to erect a high fence and plant a line of conifers at the bottom of his beer garden, give her house a bit of extra protection.' Sam realised he'd barely touched his drink. That'd explain the thirst, then. He downed it in two, aware that downing it in one sounded better, even if you were only saying it to yourself. 'The next comedy night at the Four Fountains was 22 November 2008,' he said. 'The night Sharon died. She had a great time, accord-ing to Bond. And his teenage daughter, who babysat for Dinah and Nonie. Sharon stayed at the pub until eleven, then went home to bed. Dinah was still up, chatting away to Bond's daughter. She went to bed when Sharon did, at eleven thirty. Before that, she'd heard the sitter say to Sharon, "You're back early." Sharon jokingly replied, "This isn't early. I'd have liked to stay for the rest, but I'm way too old to stay up all night." That's how Dinah knew the pub would still be open, when she and Nonie were running and needed somewhere to go – not because she's a psychopathic freak-child who hangs around in bars in the early hours.'

'So the girls not wanting to wake the neighbours . . .' Gibbs began.

'Might have had something to do with hearing countless members of the residents' association bitching about inconsiderate people who don't care if they disrupt hard-working taxpayers' sleep,' Sam finished his sentence for him.

'So Bond had no motive to torch Sharon's house,' said Gibbs.

'Not if what he, his daughter, Dinah Lendrim, Nonie Lendrim and Amber Hewerdine say is true, no,' Sam agreed. 'Trouble is, no one else knew about Sharon's change of heart or her deal with Bond.'

'Five people's not enough?'

'Normally it would be, if twelve people weren't saying the opposite: that Terry Bond hated Sharon Lendrim, that she'd never have changed her tune about the extension to the pub's opening hours, that it must have been a revenge killing contracted by Bond. By the time Sharon was murdered, Bond had put in a fresh application to the council's licensing department and the residents' association were swinging into action again to fight it. Amber Hewerdine told Ursula Shearer that Sharon was scared to come clean and tell her Nimby followers she'd switched sides. She'd been putting it off . . . and then she was killed.'

'And it looked as if Bond wanted her out of the way so he'd stand a chance of winning second time round,' said Gibbs. 'None of this answers how come Amber Hewerdine's got Sharon Lendrim's kids.'

'Sharon made a will naming Amber as guardian in the event of her death. She was anxious that her girls shouldn't go to Marianne, their grandmother and only living blood relation. Now Amber and Luke are trying to adopt them. Marianne's dead against it, Ursula Shearer says. Social Services have interviewed her about both of them, Marianne and Amber. They wanted her take on the possible adoption and Marianne's objections to it, since she knows everyone involved.'

'And?' Gibbs asked.

'Ursula likes Amber and trusts her,' said Sam. 'Thinks she's brilliant for the girls, her husband Luke too. Though she did say she can be a handful and likes to tell people how to do their jobs. Nothing Ursula can say will convince Amber that Sharon wasn't murdered by one of the residents' association members.'

Gibbs spluttered as his beer went down the wrong way. 'The puritans?'

'It's rubbish, Ursula says. The Nimbys have all been alibied. Amber knows it, but she's sticking with her theory. Every so often she rings Ursula and tries again to persuade her: someone killed Sharon to blacken Terry Bond's reputation. Maybe no one could prove Bond was behind it, but suspicion's a powerful force. It might have been enough to ensure the licensing committee turned down any request Bond made for an extension in the future. If that was Sharon's killer's aim, it worked in a way. When Bond heard Sharon had been murdered, he was devastated and withdrew his application immediately. He agreed with Amber's theory – the only person who did – and blamed himself: decided it was his application to the council that had caused all the trouble. You can imagine how he'd have tortured himself.'

Sam had been able to tell, listening to her story, that Ursula Shearer felt sorry for Bond. It had prompted him to ask her if Bond was still landlord of the Four Fountains. He told Gibbs the answer. 'The pub never hosted another comedy event after the night Sharon died. In 2009, Bond and his daughter moved away. They live in Cornwall now.'

'We shouldn't be here,' said Gibbs. 'We should be checking Ursula Shearer's case notes on Sharon Lendrim against ours on Kat Allen, see if they've got any more in common than we know about.'

'Ursula's copying everything and sending it over,' said Sam. 'My prediction is that, aside from Amber Hewerdine, there'll be no overlap.'

'You're already wrong,' Gibbs told him. 'Both are unsolvable. We can't find anyone who disliked Katharine Allen, never mind wanted her dead. Two years after the event, no one's banged up for Sharon Lendrim's murder, DS Shearer's satisfied it wasn't Terry Bond or any of the puritans. Has she got unprovable theories, suspects no shit'll stick to? Anyone she's got a dodgy feeling about?'

He was right. Sam hadn't thought of it, and he should have. Simon would have.

'She's got no one in the frame at all, has she?' said Gibbs. 'Neither have we, for Katharine Allen.'

Sam nodded. It didn't necessarily mean anything.

Yes, it does. There's never nothing. Never. Except now, when there's nothing twice.

The only time you found nothing in a victim's life to explain their murder was when it was a stranger sex attack. Neither Sharon Lendrim nor Kat Allen had been interfered with sexually.

'Two murders with no loose ends trailing from what we can see,' Gibbs went on. 'In both cases, there's no solution that makes sense, but there's nothing that doesn't make sense either. A murderer who wanted to kill two people without anyone being able to guess why, in either case. Someone whose brain takes nothing and turns it into something, maybe. To everyone else, the reason for killing would appear irrational or nonexistent.'

Sam had to admit it was a valid point. Some motives made sense across the board, and were out there in the world for all to see, like a very public row between a landlord and a residents' association; others were written on the world in invisible ink, existing only in the embargoed stories their owners repeated endlessly to themselves but never to anyone else. Unless Sam had misunderstood, Gibbs had in mind a killer who would only kill if he were sure there was no chance of the reason being suspected by anybody.

He or she. Someone private, tidy, careful.

Sam knew what Gibbs was going to say before he said it.

'Amber Hewerdine killed them both. Don't ask me to prove it – I haven't got time. I'm getting sacked tomorrow, remember?'

∼

'I wish I could be more helpful,' Edward Ormston said to Simon, adjusting his glasses and the angle of the photograph in his hand. The two of them sat side by side on tall stools pulled up to the breakfast bar in Ormston's kitchen in Combingham, drinking tea. Simon was trying not to be distracted by the sight of Ormston's Wellington-boot-clad wife playing with two red setter dogs in the back garden. Dogs needed to be walked regularly, Simon knew that, but he'd never seen anyone cavort with them in the way this woman was, laughing and leaping around. When he left, would Ormston bang on the window and yell, 'Pack it in, will you? You look like a fucking idiot!' Unlikely; he seemed a kind man with a gentle voice and no hard edges, which made him an alien being as far as Simon was concerned.

'No, I'm sorry,' said Ormston. 'I couldn't tell you if she was there or not. I don't remember anyone's face from the course. If you think you're not going to see people again, you don't bother to file away their images for future reference, do you? I don't, anyway. They were nineteen strangers, twenty if you count the teacher. I beg your pardon, the facilitator.' Ormston smiled. 'Everyone seems to be a facilitator of something or other nowadays, don't they? There were no facilitators when I was your age.'

'Her name's Amber Hewerdine,' said Simon. 'She works for the city council, in the Licensing department. She's got a husband called Luke who's a stonemason, and two kids.' Thinking of the message Sam had left on his voicemail, Simon added, 'They're not her kids – she's their legal guardian, since their mum died. Amber and Luke want to adopt them, but they haven't yet.'

'How awful – the death of their mother, I mean. Sorry, I don't quite understand . . .' Ormston was too polite to ask outright why Simon was telling him a stranger's life story.

'I was wondering if any of those details might jog your memory. Her family situation's unusual . . . Obviously none of it's ringing any bells.' Simon tried to keep the disappointment out of his voice. Ormston was the last person on his list to try; all the other people on Amber Hewerdine's DriveTech course he'd either interviewed in person or over the phone, or abandoned as being uncontactable, for the time being at least. Nobody he'd spoken to remembered Amber's face, though all had stressed this didn't mean she wasn't there. Too much time had passed; they had all seen and forgotten many faces since 2 November. Simon had left Ormston till last, figuring he was the 'Ed' Amber had mentioned, the one who had survived the car smash that had killed his daughter. *Louise or Lucy*. There was a framed photograph on the kitchen wall of a blonde-haired toddler. Was that her?

'We didn't exchange names or personal details,' Ormston said. 'There was very little chat of any kind, even during the breaks. People kept their heads down, communicated with the outside world via their mobile phones. None of us really wanted to be there. We were all mildly embarrassed and wanted to get it over with and get out of there as quickly as we could.'

'Amber remembered you. She called you "Ed".'

'Ah. I think I can explain that. Perhaps I can help you a little after all.' He smiled. 'You see, the facilitator asked me my name, in front of the group. I'm Ed to anybody that knows me – never Edward – so that was what I said. Everyone in the room heard me say it. I'd have preferred it if he hadn't drawn attention to me by asking for my name and no one else's, but I didn't hold it against him. I understood why he'd done it. It was his rather clumsy way of trying to relate to me as a human being, once his relating to me as a course participant had landed him in what he felt was an awkward situation. And to be fair, I'd already drawn attention to myself.'

'You'd told the group about your daughter dying,' Simon said.

Ormston's eyebrows shot up. 'You know about that?'

'Amber mentioned it.'

'Bless her,' said Ormston.

Simon wondered if he was religious. Then he wondered why he'd never heard his own devoutly Catholic parents bless anybody. He had always assumed they excelled at being godly, though they were incompetent in every other area of life; perhaps he'd been wrong and they were rubbish even at being religious. That, Simon realised, would leave them with no redeeming features. It was a depressing thought.

'Is that your daughter?' He gestured towards the framed picture on the wall.

'Yes. Louise. Isn't she beautiful?'

'It must be unbearable to lose a child.'

'Nothing is unbearable,' said Ormston, staring at the photograph. 'That I can promise you. We bear everything. What choice do we have?'

'This has nothing to do with my case, but . . . why did you tell them? On the course, about Louise's death. You could have kept quiet. No one would have known.'

Ormston nodded. 'I considered it. I thought that very thing to myself: there's no need to tell them. Then I thought, why shouldn't I tell them? It was the true answer to a question I'd been asked. I wouldn't have volunteered it, had we not been asked specifically if any of us had personal experience of a traffic accident, but I didn't see why I should go to the trouble of concealing it, either.'

Simon understood completely; it was how he'd felt when Charlie had told him about meeting Amber Hewerdine outside Ginny Saxon's clinic and begged him to waste time making up unnecessary lies. 'Telling the truth might not be the best thing for the people having to hear it,' he said, 'but it's usually the best thing for the teller.'

'Couldn't agree more,' said Ormston. 'And do you want to know something that hardly anyone knows?'

Simon imagined what he would say next, in an ideal world: *Do you want to know who murdered Kat Allen? What the words 'Kind, Cruel, Kind of Cruel' mean?*

'When you do what's best for you, you always end up astonished to discover that it's best for everyone else too. Not many people realise that; I didn't for a long time. We all imagine that if we're upfront about what we want and need, we'll meet with resistance and end up having to fight our corner, maybe a fight we can't win. In fact, it's forcing ourselves to do what we imagine will be best for others that leads to trouble and conflict.'

Simon wasn't convinced, but he didn't feel able to disagree, when Ormston had so recently agreed with him. All he knew was that his mind felt lighter since he'd decided that being straightforward and direct was best for him – better, even, than having a job, or else he wouldn't have risked it.

'Hold on a second,' said Ormston, narrowing his eyes to a squint. 'Amber. Do you know, I think there was an Amber. Yes.' He nodded. 'The facilitator asked how many of us were amber gamblers at traffic lights. I'm fairly sure one woman said something about her name being Amber. I think she was the one who gave the big speech. She had a cut-glass voice, I seem to remember, like a royal. And . . . an unusual turn of phrase. There was a general exchange of raised eyebrows when she started to speak.'

Simon frowned. Amber Hewerdine's accent was pure Culver Valley. 'What speech?' he asked.

'About road deaths being unavoidable in the modern world, and if we really wanted people not to die on our roads we should scrap cars altogether. I'm paraphrasing – she put it more colourfully and eccentrically than that. Since no one wanted to abolish cars, she said, we should all stop complaining.' Ormston chuckled. 'Everyone seemed terribly worried I'd be upset, but I wasn't. There was something satisfyingly death-defying about her point of view. She was against speed cameras and driver awareness courses, against speed bumps, against twenty-mile-an-hour zones. No one should base their driver behaviour on fear and worst-case-scenario thinking, she said. Whenever you get into a car, you might die, so you might as well accept it and drive happily, as fast as you like, free of fear and guilt. I think that was her philosophy.'

Ormston glanced out of the window. In the garden, his wife had calmed down, even if the two dogs hadn't; she was throwing sticks for them to fetch and return to her. 'I can't say I agreed with her that more deaths was a price worth paying for more freedom, but I admired her nerve,' he said.

'Could this woman have absented herself from the course at any point during the day?' Simon asked.

Ormston shook his head. 'We were all there for the duration. Even the lunch break, we all stayed in the room, apart from people nipping to the loo.'

'Is this her – Amber, the woman who made the speech?' Simon passed Ormston another photograph. This one came from the *Rawndesley Evening News*. Amber stood between two city councillors, smiling. The caption read, 'Council Officials Welcome Introduction of Cumulative Impact Zone in East Rawndesley'.

'You remember so much of what she said. Are you sure you don't remember her face?'

'No, I don't,' said Ormston. 'I'm sorry, but you wouldn't want me to pretend, would you? I don't recognise that face at all.'

So. The answer is 'the key', and the answer is the key. I'm not repeating myself. I'm saying that the answer 'the key' is the key. We can view each new answer as a key to a locked door barring our way. Sometimes we open one locked door and find ourselves standing in front of another, which means that we need to hunt for the next key. Often we find ourselves coming up against door after door after door. When that happens, as I suspect it will here, it's both a bad sign and a good sign: our journey is likely to be considerably more frustrating, but, if we can get past the obstacles that block our path, the prize could be substantial. It stands to reason: the more precious the object, the greater the protection.

Why did Amber ransack Little Orchard from top to bottom? Because she was looking for the key to the locked room, as she's just told us. She *thinks* she also told us why she was looking for the key, what happened when she found it, and what that proves. In case that one sketchy story didn't offer enough proof of her conclusion to satisfy us, and knowing, on one level, that her determination to utter as few words as possible is as unhelpful to her as it is to us, she backed it up with several subsidiary stories, all equally sketchy and pared down to essentials – all, as she sees it, providing further proof.

Of what, though? That Jo is a bad person? Amber suspects that the sum total of her stories doesn't even come close to disproving Jo's essential goodness, of which Amber reminded me more than once this morning, in the interests of fairness: Jo is a devoted mother to her two boys, a loving wife to her husband Neil, a wonderful daughter and sister. Her mother Hilary and her entirely dependent sister Kirsty spend nearly every day at her house. She cooks most of their meals, even gives them food parcels to take home, knowing it's the only way they'll eat properly. Hilary, a single mother, ground down from years of looking after a severely handicapped child twenty-four hours a day, would not be able to cope if Jo didn't feed her and boost her morale constantly. Jo's brother Ritchie has never had a job. He is what some would call a layabout, but Jo doesn't judge him, and regularly reminds Hilary of all the reasons to think well of him: he's clever, creative, kind, loyal, and one day he will find his passion and realise what he wants to do with his life, as long as those close to him continue to believe in him. Jo gives Ritchie money whenever he needs it, and Neil doesn't protest about this. Presumably, as one of the chief beneficiaries of her family-conquers-all policy, he knows better than to question it.

Jo is as devoted a daughter-in-law as she is a daughter. When Neil's mother Pam died of liver cancer, Jo saw straight away that her father-in-law, Quentin, would not be able to manage on his own, and moved him into her home. Sabina, nanny to William and Barney, is part of the family too. She is also in Jo's house all the time, being fed, being looked after. She makes no distinction between her working day and the rest of her life, and leaves Jo's side only to go home and sleep, by the sound of it.

Is Amber part of this big, warm, Jo-centred family? She ought to be. She's married to Neil's brother, Luke. Yet she speaks as a non-beneficiary, as an outsider. Why? Because of the stories she's told us, that prove . . . what?

Let me talk us through them, adding a few observations of my own and filling in the missing details using intelligent guesswork, based on things Amber has said in this session and also this morning when we were alone together. If you're going to tell a story, you might as well tell it properly, bring it to life. That's what I'm going to try to do, and I'm willing to bet I'll end up with as much truth in my stories as I would if I were describing events about which I believed I had objective knowledge. Amber, forget these are your stories and just listen. Remember, a story is not a memory; a memory is not a story. Each story contains memories, but the interpretations and analyses we impose on events come later. Those can't be called memories.

Boxing Day 2003. Jo, Neil and their two sons have returned unharmed. Jo has gathered everyone together, announced that everything is fine, but refused to explain why she and her husband and children disappeared from the family gathering and, in doing so, turned Christmas, a day that should have been happy and celebratory, into a traumatic ordeal for all those close to them. Everyone, on the face of it at least, accepts the lack of explanation, and goes along with Jo's idea that Boxing Day should become the Christmas Day that never was. So, first there is the present-opening and the chaos of torn wrapping paper everywhere, and then there's a festive turkey dinner for eleven people to be cooked – by Jo alone. Amber now believes that her sister-in-law had a brilliant, devious idea while she was putting together that lavish meal, insisting she needed no help from anyone and could work far more efficiently if she had Little Orchard's substantial kitchen entirely to herself: look as if you're slaving away for the common good, and no one will suspect you of burying yourself under a mountain of hard slog in order to avoid potentially problematic conversations. Amber is convinced that this has been Jo's policy ever since.

While Jo is busy assembling the perfect Christmas feast, what is everyone else doing? Neil is upstairs having what everyone is calling 'a nap', though he's been asleep for so long, it seems to Amber that what he's actually doing is trying to cram a whole night into the daytime, which probably means he didn't get any sleep the previous two nights. Luke is sitting in a corner with a notepad and pen, making some last-minute alterations to his Christmas Day quiz. His father, Quentin, is boring Ritchie with one of his interminable, labyrinthine stories – this time focusing on a septic tank, and several unsuccessful attempts to install it – from which Ritchie has no idea how to escape. Sabina is trying everything she can to stop Barney crying, walking him around, joggling him up and down, lying him flat on his back.

Hilary hovers nearby, giving unwanted advice. She tells Sabina that Jo ought to see sense and forget about breast-feeding. Barney has only just been fed, and he's hungry again; that must be why he's crying. Breast-fed babies are hungry and dissatisfied, Hilary says. They scream all the time and never sleep – ask any midwife, any health visitor. Never mind what they're supposed to say, the official line; ask them what they really think, off the record. Sabina says it's Jo's decision and that Hilary is arguing with the wrong person. As it happens, Sabina agrees with Hilary. She has looked after dozens of babies, and there's no doubt in her mind that the bottle-fed ones are more contented, better sleepers. Their mothers are happier and more relaxed because they can delegate the job of feeding to others when they need a break. Sabina has said all this to Jo, she tells Hilary, but Jo wants her son to have the best possible start in life, food-wise, and health professionals are unanimous about what that is, so Sabina is putting her own views to one side and supporting Jo's decision. What else can she do?

Hilary isn't satisfied. From her bag, she produces a baby's bottle in a sealed plastic bag and a carton of formula milk. Jo isn't here now, she says – she's busy cooking. Let me give Barney this, she says. I've done it before. Jo knew nothing about it, and it made such a difference. He was like a different baby that day, hardly cried at all. Pam puts her foot down. Nothing must be done to Barney without Jo's consent. Whatever we might think, she says, it's Jo's decision. She makes no mention of Neil, her son and Barney's father. His views on how his son ought to be fed are irrelevant.

A quiet, relatively polite row ensues between the two grandmothers. Pam is normally quiet and compliant, and Hilary is put out. Life is hard enough, she argues, for everybody. Why make it harder by letting a child go hungry? Kirsty, unused to seeing her mother angry, starts to make distressed noises and sway from side to side. Five-year-old William is upset by the noise and runs away from it. Amber goes after him. She catches up with him in the garden. He tells her he is frightened of Kirsty, whom he describes as being like 'a big monster'. Amber doesn't know what to say to this, and asks if William has ever told his parents about his fear of Kirsty. Yes, he says, and Mummy said he mustn't be scared of her. She's his aunt, she's family. She loves him and he must love her, even though she's different. It's not her fault. William asks Amber not to tell Jo what he said, or that he ran away from Kirsty.

This makes Amber angry. Jo shouldn't tell William how he ought to feel; she should understand that a five-year-old is obviously going to be alarmed by someone like Kirsty, who is clearly an adult and yet doesn't behave like one. How dare Jo make William feel he has to keep his fear secret? To cheer him up, Amber suggests they play a game, a sort of hide-and-seek: hunting for the key to Little Orchard's locked study. William is hugely excited by this idea, and so they begin their search, speculating as they go about what

138

might be inside the forbidden room. No one asks what they're doing as they wander all over the house, in and out of bedrooms. By the time dinner is served, they've searched everywhere apart from the kitchen, the utility room, and Jo and Neil's bedroom and en-suite bathroom, which they can't get in to because Neil is first napping and then showering and getting ready for Christmas dinner.

After the meal, Luke's quiz is the next thing on the agenda. Amber and William do not take part. They continue with their secret game, telling everyone they hope to have a surprise to present later in the day. Is Amber aware that she wants her own secret, since Jo has one she's not sharing? Does she have moral scruples about violating the privacy of Little Orchard's owners, should she be lucky and find the key? No and no would be my guess. Consciously, Amber is worried only about *not* finding the key, wondering if she was crazy to embark on this hunt that's surely doomed to failure. What if she never finds it? William will be desperately disappointed.

No need to panic: close examination of the kitchen reveals a key on a long string, hanging from a nail sticking out of the back of a pine dresser. That must be it, Amber tells William as soon as she spots it dangling in the gap between the dresser and the wall. Why else would anyone keep a key in such an inaccessible place? Amber hurts her back as she struggles to shift the dresser so that she can reach the key. It's too heavy for her to lift alone, strictly speaking, but she perseveres because – like Jo earlier, and in the same room, the kitchen – she doesn't want help. She wants to prove she can do everything herself.

William, overcome by excitement, runs to the lounge and interrupts Luke's quiz with his triumphant announcement: he and Amber have found the key to the locked room. Amber declares her intention to use it, and have a nosey around – who wants to come too? A deliberately provocative invitation: daring the others to stop her. If Amber wasn't so resentful of the silence surrounding Jo and Neil's disappearance, would she have behaved differently? I think so. I think it's no coincidence that she created an opportunity to stage a protest against metaphorical if not actual 'no entry' signs and things being kept from her.

Jo is furious. She demands Amber hand over the key to her immediately. She's responsible for the house, she is quick to point out. She and Neil were the ones who rented it from the owners and are therefore its trusted guardians. Amber tells her to lighten up. It's not as if they're going to do any damage to the study. They're just going to have a look and see what's in there. It's the harmless conclusion to the harmless game Amber and William have been playing. Luke, Ritchie and Sabina are tempted, infected by Amber's enthusiasm, and William's. They all agree that it can't do any harm; jokes are made – cryptically, to protect William – about sex toys and cannabis plants. Quentin doesn't care. He is only interested in his own concerns, and the contents of Little Orchard's locked room can't possibly affect him. Pam thinks they should put the key back and says so, as firmly as she said before that Barney shouldn't be given the formula milk; this prompts Hilary, immediately, to say that a quick peek won't hurt, just to make William happy.

Amber suggests a vote, knowing she will win. Jo puts her foot down. She is furious, nearly crying with anger. She quickly disabuses Amber of the idea that any sort of democratic principle can be applied; she and Neil paid the full cost of the rental, as well as the deposit, which makes them the only two people entitled to a say in the matter. Neil agrees: unlocking the study is out of the question. No one speculates that the key Amber found might belong to a different door; they all assume it's the right one. Jo tells Amber, in front of all the others, that the whole idea – the hunt-the-key game and involving William in it – was totally, utterly immoral and that she ought to be ashamed of herself.

Amber refuses to feel ashamed. She still believes it would do no harm to have a quick look inside the room – that most people would, if they found themselves in a similar position, just as most people eavesdrop on juicy conversations and look over strangers' shoulders to read the text messages they're composing whenever they can. On some level, she argues, the owners of Little Orchard must know this.

Jo says she would never eavesdrop, or try to read somebody's private correspondence.

Amber says she would never tell anybody when to feel ashamed, or congratulate herself on being a better person than anyone else.

Amber gives the key back to Jo.

5

Wednesday 1 December 2010

'Seventy-three? Seventy! Seventy-six?' Nonie fires numbers at me, her voice trembling with anguish.

'Stop panicking,' I tell her, wishing she was in the passenger seat next to me and could see my face, knowing she's wishing the same thing. Nonie is a victim of her own scrupulous fairness policy: when, she, Dinah and I are in the car together, she and Dinah must both sit in the back, even though they would both love to sit in the front. Dinah has suggested they take turns, but Nonie won't allow it. Since none of us knows how many car journeys there will be in total, in the whole of our life together, we can't be sure that it won't be an odd number. Someone might end up having an extra turn.

'I can't do it! I don't understand! Seventy-seven?'

'No. Sorry,' I say. Are desperation and panting part of most people's Maths homework routines? I try to catch Nonie's eye in the rear-view mirror. I've always been able to soothe her with my eyes quicker than with words.

'Seventy-five!'

I hate Wednesdays. On Wednesday afternoons I'm not free; I am bound by a tradition I would dearly love to put an end to: I pick the girls up from school and we go for supper at the house known by everybody as 'Jo's', though Neil, William, Barney and Quentin live in it too. Also on Wednesdays, Nonie has Maths last thing in the afternoon, the lesson that never fails to convince her that she's the stupidest person on the planet.

'There's no point shouting out random answers, Nones.' I fiddle with the controls on the dashboard. I was foolish enough to let Luke persuade me to buy a better, newer car than I felt comfortable with, given our precarious finances, and have never understood its various knobs and dials. The complicated multi-arrowed air-current diagrams indicate that it offers a range of heating options, but I've never had time to work out what's what, so I press whichever buttons take my fancy and never remember what sequence of actions led to the desired result, on the rare occasions that I'm lucky enough to get it. Today, I'm unlucky. Instead of warmth evenly distributed throughout the car, I get a suffocating faceful of scorched air. I decide I'd rather freeze. I envy the girls the winter coats I bought them that look like inflatable air-beds with sleeves.

'Even if you hit on the right answer, you won't understand why it's right,' I tell Nonie. 'If you'd just calm down and let me explain . . .'

'What did Mrs Truscott say?' Dinah asks.

'Hang on, Dinah, let me finish.'

'You'll never finish. Nonie will talk about how she doesn't understand anything in Maths *forever*.'

'It's all right for you! You're brilliant at Maths. I'm rubbish at it. I'll always be rubbish.'

'It's seventy-four, *obviously*. Sixty-six plus eight: seventy-four. What did Mrs Truscott say, Amber?'

'Don't *tell* me!'

'Dinah, *don't*—'

'I already have. What did Mrs Truscott—?'

'Don't cry, Nones, it doesn't matter.' She needs to see me smiling at her. Trying not to think about Ed from my missed DriveTech course and his dead daughter, I take my eyes off the road ahead and turn in my seat so that Nonie can see my face. Hopefully there's a reassuring expression on it and not one of abject terror. It's myself I'm telling as much as I'm telling her not to panic and not to cry. I don't know how to pay enough attention to both girls at the same time; it's a riddle I can't solve. I'm sure there must be an answer, one a parent would know instinctively, but I'm not a parent and never will be – not a proper one. I'd like to give each of the girls all my attention all the time, but that's not possible, and neither one will ever wait. Dinah is too demanding and Nonie too worried.

I hate Maths for what it's doing to her. I'd like to kick its spiteful teeth in. I always suspected it was a noxious pile of pointlessness, and now I have proof of its vileness in the amount of misery it's causing this lovely, hard-working child whose happiness is my responsibility. Surely if I can bring about the un-banning of Dinah's play, I can arrange for Maths to be eliminated from the curriculum for good? Obviously some people need to study it, the ones who are going to go on to be mathematicians and scientists, but there are others – like me, like Nonie – who equally obviously don't need to bother with it because we're never going to get very far and we'll always find it the dullest thing in the world on account of it having no people in it.

Luke has forbidden me to air these philistine views in Nonie's presence. While I secretly wonder who I might be able to sleep with in order to secure for her the decent Maths GCSE grade she'll need in order to get into a sixth-form college to study proper subjects like English Lit and History and Psychology, subjects with people in them, Luke continues to believe that one day, with the right help, everything will click into place and Nonie will tap into her innate mathematical abilities, so long dormant. I don't believe this for a minute, but I'd hate to think that my endless pessimism might limit her life chances, so I lie.

'There's no need to be scared of Maths, Nonie.' *Yes, there is. There's every reason to be scared of a thing you hate and can't get away from.* 'I can give you another sum to do – and Dinah, please don't tell her this time. Let me try to explain the method to her. Nones, once you understand the thought process involved . . .'

'I'll never understand it,' Nonie says quietly. 'There's no point. Can we listen to Lady Gaga?'

'Tell me about Mrs Truscott first,' Dinah insists.

'I've already told you.' I reach behind me, give Nonie's knee a supportive squeeze. I ought not to let Dinah steamroller over her sister, but I sense that Nonie is secretly hoping I won't object to the change of subject. 'Your play's back on.'

'But what did you say? How did you persuade her?'

'Can we listen to Lady Gaga, Amber?'

I grit my teeth. We're not even halfway to Jo's house yet. There's a limit to how many loud, pounding songs I can cope with, hot on the heels of a Maths meltdown. My secret rule is no music before we pass the Chinese supermarket on the junction of Valley Road and Hopelea Street. If Dinah and Nonie would only learn to love Dar Williams or Martha Wainwright, I'd happily let them listen all the way from school to Jo's.

'Amber? Can we?'

'Tell me what Mrs Truscott said!'

'In a minute, Nones.' I risk taking both hands off the wheel for a second and blow on them in a vain attempt to warm them up. 'I just . . . I don't know, Dinah, I don't remember every word of the conversation. I told her how much the play meant to you . . .'

'You're lying. I can always tell when you're lying.'

'Even when I've got my back to you? That's not fair.'

'What's not fair?' Nonie asks, alarmed in case an injustice snuck past her and she missed it.

'Dinah knowing I'm lying.'

'Why isn't it fair?'

'Because I'm a grown-up. I've been one for ages. I've earned the right to get away with more than I seem to be able to.' When I'm not lying, I'm being too honest. I know that later I will have to explain to Nonie what I meant by this remark, once I've finished explaining the whole of Maths to her.

'What did you threaten her with?' says Dinah, who will not be diverted. 'She wouldn't have backed down unless you scared her more than she was already scared of the parents who complained.'

'Is that how you see me, as someone who lies and threatens and intimidates people?'

'Yes.' After a pause, Dinah says, 'Maybe it's not a good idea for you and Luke to adopt us.'

'Don't say that!' Nonie wails. Wonderful; she's in tears again. 'It *is* a good idea. It's the *best* idea.'

I'm not sure if my heart is still beating. The car continues to move forward; that has to be a positive sign.

'If you adopt us, you'll become a parent,' Dinah clarifies. 'You'll stop doing all the best things you do, like frightening Mrs Truscott. You're always laughing at the stupid things our friends' parents do and say, all their stupid parenty rules. You'll become as stupid as them.'

Relief pours through me, flooding every inch of me. 'I won't become parenty. I promise.' *If the adoption is approved, if Marianne doesn't ruin everything.*

'So what did you do? To Mrs Truscott?'

'Amber, is seventeen plus three twenty?' Nonie asks.

'Yes, it is. Well done.' This is what she always does, and it makes me ache with love for her. Afraid she's a disappointment to us all because she couldn't answer the harder question, she asks herself an easier one and answers it correctly, to prove that she's not a total waste of space. To Dinah I say, 'You guessed right. I threatened her, and she caved.'

Excited gasps from the backseat. I can't help grinning.

'What did you say you'd do?' Dinah snaps, unable to contain her eagerness to know. 'Did you nearly hit her?'

'No. It's really dull. You'll be disappointed,' I warn her. 'I tried to persuade her first, told her it wasn't fair to promise you could put on your play and then take it back, but she just kept saying it was unfortunate and couldn't be helped, as if it had nothing to do with her. So I pointed out that whenever there's a concert or panto at school, she's there handing out wine and sherry to the parents with a big smile on her face and receiving completely unrelated voluntary "donations" to school funds that just happen to be about the same price as a glass of wine, or two, or four, if Dr and Mrs Doubly-Barrelly have brought Granny and Grandad along.'

'That's really clever,' says Dinah. Unusually for her, she sounds humble. Full of admiration. I ought to feel guilty, but I'm chuffed to bits.

'I don't understand,' says Nonie.

'School's not allowed to sell alcohol,' Dinah tells her. 'You need a special licence from Amber's work and school hasn't got one. Mrs Truscott's been selling it, but pretending she hasn't been, and Amber threatened to have her arrested if—'

'Well, not quite,' I chip in. 'I just told her that, as Licensing Manager for the council . . . To be honest, that was all I needed to say. Like all the best threats, mine was implied, not overtly stated.' *Shit*. It's not ideal that I said that out loud. I clear my throat. 'Threatening people is wrong, nearly always, but so is . . . alcohol pushing. If you drink too much alcohol you can get addicted to it and even die. Okay, who wants some Lady Gaga?' I say brightly.

'I need to understand my Maths homework first,' says Nonie, nervous now that her wish looks likely to be granted. 'Ask me a sum.'

I imagine groaning loudly – a long roar, like a lion's – until the urge to groan passes. 'Okay. But, please, *please*, try not to get upset, whatever happens.'

'You mean when I get it wrong?'

'No.' *Yes*. 'That is not what I mean. What's fifty-eight plus five?' Am I reinforcing her belief that she doesn't deserve to listen to music until she's completed a gruelling intellectual obstacle course? Should my motto, as her guardian, be melodic pornography first, Maths later?

Nonie's panic is instant. 'I don't know! Fifty-three? No! Sixty-one? Sixty!'

'Calm down, Nonie. Listen. Fifty-eight plus *two* is sixty, isn't it? So . . .'

'I know that! Fifty-eight plus two is sixty, fifty-eight plus one is fifty-nine. See? I can do it as long as it doesn't go over the next ten!' The sound of her hyperventilating fills the car. It makes me want to open my window and risk losing my nose to frostbite.

'Nones,' I say evenly. 'I can teach you what to do, other than panic, if it does go over the next—'

'Fifty-two! Fifty-three!'

'Don't, like, *explode*,' Dinah contributes helpfully.

'Nonie, I can't do this if you just keep shouting numbers at me, love.'

'It's fifty-three!' she shrieks, triumphant suddenly. 'Fifty-eight plus two is fifty, plus another three to make the five . . .'

'She's counting on her fingers,' says Dinah. 'It's supposed to be *mental* arithmetic.'

'Fifty-three,' Nonie insists. 'Isn't it, Amber?'

'Well, actually, you've done pretty well,' I start to say.

'Pretty well?' Dinah queries. 'It's *sixty*-three. Fifty-eight plus two isn't fifty, it's sixty.'

'Oh, no! I *hate* it! I'll *never* get an answer right!' Nonie sobs.

'Yes, you will, Nones. You did brilliantly.' I give her leg another squeeze. 'You used the right technique. You understood how to do it, that's the most important thing. You got fifty and sixty mixed up, but so what?' *They're close enough, in the grand scheme of things. Do we really have to split hairs?* 'I know you *meant* sixty.'

'It's lucky you're not a Maths teacher,' Dinah tells me.

I manage not to say that I would rather spend my days monitoring the behaviour of slugs than teaching Maths, and award myself a point for restraint and maturity.

'Amber does teach Maths,' says Nonie. 'She teaches it to me.'

There are more empty crisp packets than usual blowing around the pavement outside the Chinese supermarket, as well as a couple of empty lager cans and the contents of several car ashtrays near the kerb. Living with Dinah has made me more sensitive to this sort of sight. There's no way she won't notice. *One, two, three . . .*

'Look at that,' she says. 'It's disgusting. People who drop litter should be put in prison. They should have their cells filled with piles of rubbish, so high that they can't stick their heads above the pile, and they have to breathe in the horrid smell forever.'

'You can't do that to people, whatever they've done,' says Nonie. 'Can you, Amber?'

I switch on the car stereo without asking the girls whether they still want music or not, and turn the volume up higher than I'm normally able to tolerate. I don't even like Lady Gaga, except as a way of ending conversations, when I'm too drained to talk any more. I should have tried this technique with Simon Waterhouse when he tried to insist on seeing me today. *I'm sorry, I'm far too busy. Now let me drown out all your follow-up questions with 'Bad Romance'.*

I wasn't prepared to talk to him without first warning Jo; it wouldn't have been fair to her. Jo probably gets better behaviour from me than anyone else I know: more consideration, more tact. I can never decide if this is sensible self-preservation on my part or a foolish waste of my thoughtfulness, given the way I feel about her. It benefits me as much as it does her if I deprive her of reasons to attack me, but sometimes she lays into me anyway, which forces me to notice my incessant pandering to her, and its futility, and then I become enraged to no effect whatsoever.

Why didn't I decide it was more important to be fair to Simon Waterhouse, who has only ever treated me well? Why does it still matter to me to prove to Jo that I'm a better person than she thinks I am?

'What's "Kind, Cruel, Kind of Cruel"?' Dinah asks in the short gap between two songs.

I turn off the stereo. 'Where did you hear that?'

'Nowhere.'

I pull in to the kerb, slam my foot down on the brake. 'Dinah, don't mess me around. This is important. Where did you—'

'I didn't *hear* it anywhere. I saw it written down.'

'Where? When?' *It can't be this easy, surely.*

'This morning. On yesterday's telly page. You wrote it. It was your handwriting.'

My whole body sags. I must look like an airbag with a puncture, slowly deflating. 'Right,' I say. 'Sorry, I . . . I misunderstood. I was just doodling.'

'A doodle's a picture, not words,' says Nonie.

'But why did you write those words?' asks Dinah. 'Where did you get them from?'

'I don't know. I was just mucking around, I suppose.'

'Why did you say it was important? Why are those words important?'

'Dinah, stop!' Nonie begs.

'They're not, they're—'

'You're lying again.'

'Dinah, please.' I try to sound authoritative.

'Please don't make you admit that you're lying? Why don't you just say you'd rather not tell me?'

It's either a way out or a trap. I'm desperate enough to try it. 'I'd rather not tell you.'

'Okay.' I can't see Dinah's shrug of acceptance, but I can hear it. *Brilliant. Lies and reconciliation: the way forward.*

'Is Kirsty going to be at Jo's?' Nonie asks.

'Probably. With Hilary.'

'Amber?'

'Mm?'

'What's wrong with Kirsty? How did she get like that?'

'I don't know, Nones. I can't really ask.' *I tried it once, tactfully, and got savaged.*

'I'm glad Nonie's my sister,' says Dinah. 'I'd hate to have a sister like Kirsty. I wouldn't be able to love her. You can't love someone who's like that.'

'Dinah! That's—' I break off. I was going to say that it was a terrible thing to say, but perhaps it's more terrible to make an eight-year-old feel guilty for expressing her feelings. 'Jo loves Kirsty very much,' I say instead. 'And if you and Nonie had a sister like Kirsty, I'm sure you *would* love her, actually, because—'

'I wouldn't,' Dinah insists. 'I wouldn't let myself. When someone's like Kirsty and can't talk, you can't tell if they're a nice person or a mean person. What if you love them and all the time they're mean and horrible, but the meanness is locked inside, so you don't know?'

I struggle to hide my shock. 'It's not like that, Dines. Kirsty isn't nice or not nice in the way most people are. Her mind's never developed enough for her to be one or the other. Mentally, she's almost like . . . well, she's like a baby.'

'How can you say that if you don't know what's wrong with her? How do you know she isn't the kindest or cruellest person in the world, but because she can't say anything, no one ever finds out?'

'Some babies seem quite mean,' says Nonie. 'The ones who scream angrily. I know all babies cry, but some do sad crying. I think those are the nice ones.'

If Sharon were here, would she know how to deal with this barrage of bizarre theories from her daughters? I close my eyes. *Don't go there. Focus on something else: the litter, the complicated symbols on the dashboard.* I can't let myself think about Sharon; I need to arrive at Jo's with my defences intact.

What's fifty-eight plus sixty-three?

'Amber!'

Dinah's voice brings me back. I must have fallen asleep for a few seconds. It would be nice to be able to say I feel refreshed, but it wouldn't be true. Rather, it's as if someone's pumped a heavy fog into my brain. I sigh and start up the engine. I ought be delivering a lecture about the innate value of all human beings as I drive, but I don't have the energy. Instead, I make the girls swear not to mention our conversation about Kirsty to Jo. Ever.

～

'Hello, hello! Come in!' Jo holds the door open for us, a big smile on her face. Today is a cloud-hair day, which means she didn't bother to apply what she calls her 'special stuff' this morning to make each individual curl stand out. I look at her and see a woman who is so obviously welcoming and kind-hearted that it's almost embarrassing to remember how often I've suspected otherwise. This is always my first reaction. Something about the sudden sight of her encourages my brain to play tricks on itself.

She's wearing faded jeans with rips in the knees and a tight orange T-shirt with a scoop neck, beaming at us as if we've made her day by turning up. 'Hi, sweetie, how are you? Hi, Nones – did you survive Wednesday Maths? Amber, you look knackered, hon. If you need to close your eyes for ten minutes, you're welcome to use mine and Neil's bed. No one'll bother you if you go in there. I'll make you up a hot water bottle if you want.'

I need to close my eyes for ten years. 'I'm fine, thanks.' Of course someone would bother me. No one could succeed in remaining alone in a room in Jo's house for more than thirty seconds. There are too many people wandering around, always. I can hear Quentin, Sabina and William talking in the background, all at the same time. Beneath the voices is an uneven galloping sound I've heard many times before: Kirsty running across the upstairs landing with Hilary following close behind.

'Sure?' Jo asks.

'It's very tempting. I wouldn't sleep, though, and then I'd feel worse.'

'Poor you. It must be awful.'

I force a smile, think about the time she asked me impatiently if I'd ever wondered whether maybe I just wasn't tired enough, wasn't working hard enough during the day, and that was why I wasn't able to fall asleep.

This is what I do. When she's nice to me, I remember all the wounds she has unwittingly inflicted over the years. When she's chilly and insensitive, her long list of good deeds is what clamours for my attention. I struggle to perceive her in the round and never quite succeed. All I know is that she's not at all like me. It would be too easy to explain the difference between us by saying that she's more changeable than I am, or that she doesn't hold grudges and I do. I know other weirdos – Luke, for example – who are able to forgive, forget and move on, but with Jo it's as if she's pressed some kind of internal delete button and anything she doesn't want to think about, like Little Orchard, is wiped from the record as if it never existed, enabling her to grin at me like an ecstatic idiot who remembers nothing.

'Earth to Amber, as Barney would say!'

Did she ask me a question? 'I'm fine, Jo, really.' It's too early in our visit for me to start thinking analytically. I haven't even taken off my coat, and nothing has happened so far that requires analysis. *Act like a normal visitor. Ask for a cup of tea.*

'You must be gasping for a brew,' Jo says, on cue. In this house, whatever you want or need is offered before you have the chance to ask for it. It's strangely disempowering.

God, I'm a petty bitch. How can anyone stand me? Maybe no one can.

Sharon could stand you. The bitchier you were, the more she laughed. That's why you were so much kinder around her. You knew there was no point bitching – she'd only keep liking you anyway, stubborn cow that she was.

'Reading your face, I'd say you've had a rough day,' Jo says. 'Tell you what, you can have one of my new posh teabags – each one individually wrapped in its own packet inside the box. There's classy for you.'

'It's no more than I expect,' I say mock-grandly, and she laughs on her way back to the kitchen, a room she will not be parted from for longer than five minutes at a time.

Dinah and Nonie have disappeared behind the closed door of the dining room with William and Barney, leaving their puffy air-bed coats on the hall floor. I gather them up, take mine off and try to hang all three on the pegs on the wall. As usual, I fail. Everyone who lives in or near Rawndesley has at some point popped round to Jo's, hung up a jacket, cagoule, duffel or mac here, left without it, and never returned to collect it. I once stood where I'm standing now and listened as Neil, in a tone of mild surprise, went through the coats one by one. 'That's Mrs Boyd's from across the road, and . . . oh, yeah, this is Sabina's mum's, from when she came over from Italy, and I think Jo said this one belongs to someone from Sabina's Pilates class.'

Jo is a very different sort of homemaker to me – not that I'd ever describe myself in those terms. I organise my home for the benefit of the people who live in it: me, Luke, Dinah and Nonie. Jo runs hers for the greater good of mankind. I still can't quite believe she let Quentin have William's bedroom when Pam died. William and Barney now share the tiny box room that's barely big enough for one child.

I dump our coats on the nearest chair, head for the kitchen and nearly trip over Neil, emerging from the downstairs loo with his phone clamped to his ear. 'That doesn't come into it,' he says. 'You know how it works: you tender for a job, you quote an all-in price. If it takes you longer than you thought it would, you don't get to come back and ask for more money. You suck it up.' He makes rude gestures at his phone for my benefit. There's a crash from upstairs. We both look up, see the ceiling shake. Neil eyes the door of the downstairs loo as if he's considering going back in there.

I wasn't expecting him to be here. I don't normally see him when I come round on Wednesdays; he usually works late. Isn't it a bit inconsiderate of him to come home when there's obviously no room for him in his house? I watch from the narrow hall as he starts to climb the stairs, then, after another thud and a cry of 'Kirsty!' from Hilary, thinks better of it and comes back down. He has nowhere to take his argumentative phone call; Jo is in the kitchen, calling out for me to join her, Quentin and Sabina are talking in the lounge, the children are making a racket in the dining room.

I remember asking Neil what he did, when Luke first introduced me to him and Jo. 'I've got my own little company,' he said affectionately, as if he was talking about a poodle or a hamster. 'We make window films.'

'What, like *Rear Window* by Alfred Hitchcock?' I said. It was a stupid joke.

'No-o-o,' said Jo with exaggerated patience, rolling her eyes at Neil conspiratorially. 'Alfred Hitchcock made *Rear Window* by Alfred Hitchcock. We've never heard that one before, have we, Neil?'

When I asked Luke about it later, he admitted he hadn't noticed Neil's puzzled expression, the way he'd looked at Jo when she'd said that, his answer to her supposed-to-be-rhetorical question: 'No, I don't think we have heard it before. You're a true original, Amber.'

'Amber? Do you want this tea or not?' Jo yells.

'Coming!'

'*Ciao*, Amber!' Sabina calls out.

'Is that Amber?' Quentin sounds surprised. Didn't he hear the doorbell, or Jo inviting us in, or William and Barney demanding to know when we were arriving, as I know they must have at least seventeen times?

'I don't think I've told Amber about my run-in with Harold Sargent,' Quentin announces, as if this is good news for us all. 'I don't think I've told Luke, come to think of it. Course, Harold's thinking about having one of those stair-lifts installed now, but I said to him, I said, "They only work on some staircases, you know. Might not work on yours." '

Oh, God, please someone or something distract him before he comes looking for me, armed with one of his long, pointless anecdotes. He hasn't told me about his run-in with Harold Sargent and nor should he, because I have absolutely no idea who Harold Sargent is. Even when I start out knowing who and what Quentin is talking about, within ten seconds I'm lost. His stories are so dull that my mind drifts off, and when I realise I've been AWOL and tune back in, the cast of characters has often changed entirely: instead of Margaret Dawson and the railings outside the station, he's talking about someone called Kevin's bad attitude, and the dangers of failing to fibre-glass the insides of septic tanks. Quentin and Pam had a septic tank about twenty years ago, when they lived in the middle of nowhere between Combingham and Silsford, and Quentin is still obsessed with the damn things.

'I think Amber is too tired now to talk,' I hear Sabina say. *Thank you, thank you.* 'You know she doesn't sleep.'

I smile at this. Sabina is well aware that Quentin doesn't know anything about me, despite my having been attached to his son for nearly a decade, which is why she's telling him. One of his stranger characteristics is that he can be relied upon to know nothing about the people in close proximity to him at any given time, while simultaneously knowing all the tiny, tedious details of the lives of everyone the people around him have never heard of or met. If he bumped into Harold Sargent on the street, he would find himself suddenly full of information about the minutiae of my life, all the better to bore poor Harold with.

'Why don't you tell me instead? I would *love* to hear the story,' Sabina says convincingly. She's an angel. 'Should I make you a cup of tea first?' Although perfectly able-bodied and afflicted by no disability, Quentin cannot perform even the smallest domestic task, and no one ever suggests that he might. The closest he ever came, one Christmas at my house when everyone but him was helping with the Christmas dinner preparations, was to say, 'I'm sorry I'm not helping.' Pam giggled as if it was the silliest idea in the world, and said, 'That's all right, darling. No one expects you to.'

She was more frightened for Quentin than for herself when she was dying. 'He can't do the simplest things, Amber,' she whispered to me once. 'Can't fend for himself at all, and it's too late for him to learn now.' *Why?* I wanted to scream. *Boiling an egg is no harder now than it was fifty years ago.* 'It's my fault,' Pam said. 'I enjoyed looking after him. And he worked so hard . . .' If she hadn't been sick, I might have argued with her. Until he retired, Quentin managed the Lighting and Mirrors department at Remmicks; how punishing can it have been? I'm sure I could sell lights and mirrors to people five days a week and still manage to put a slice of bread in the toaster at the weekend.

Raised voices are coming from the dining room. 'No, listen,' says William. 'I'm older than Dinah, Dinah's older than Nonie, Nonie's older than Barney, so . . .'

'Do "more beautiful than",' Dinah orders. 'I'm . . . oh, no, that's the same, isn't it? Do "is keeping a secret from".'

I have no idea what they're talking about, but I can't help wondering if Dinah's thinking about secrets because of me.

Why don't you just say you'd rather not tell me?

'Amber? Your posh tea's going cold!' Jo bellows as if the hall is miles from the kitchen. Nothing is far enough away from anything else in this house. It's one of the things I can't stand about the place, and there are plenty of others. The small square multi-coloured tiles on the kitchen walls give me eye-ache. I'm generally in favour of colour, but here it's abused. Each room is painted a different cheerful primary, like a nursery, and stuffed full of too-large, too-grand furniture, most of it antique and unsuited to a house that was built in 1995. You can't take a step without falling over a heavy carved mahogany sideboard or an ornate walnut desk. Occasional tables jut out at odd angles to ensure that nobody can walk in a straight line. The kitchen has an oversized breakfast bar that protrudes into the middle of the room, surrounded by six high stools. Jo always orders me to sit on one, so that I can chat to her while she gets supper ready, and then she has to squeeze around me, muttering, 'Sorry, if I could just move you slightly to one side . . .' There is no side of the breakfast bar where I might sit and not need to be moved. If I sit on the window side, I'm in the way of the fridge; at the curved end, I'm blocking the dishwasher; on the hall side, I'm pressed up against the door to the pantry.

Kirsty is still making a racket upstairs. I hear Hilary trying to soothe her, much as I tried to soothe Nonie in the car. 'Hi, Hilary,' I call up to her. 'Need a hand?'

Neil brushes past me on his way to the front door, phone still at his ear. He opens the door and steps out on to the pavement. 'Right, I can hear you now,' he says. He might have been furious with the guy he's speaking to a minute or so ago, but he sounds suddenly upbeat, and I understand why: the restful hum of traffic from the road is a relief.

'No, ta, we're fine!' Hilary calls down the stairs. 'We'll be down in a sec.'

Neil pulls the door shut behind him.

I find Jo in the kitchen, leafing through the local paper. She could have brought my tea out to me instead of letting it go cold, but she prefers it if I pay court to her in the place of her choosing.

I'm over-analysing again.

'Have a high-chair,' she says. It's what she calls the breakfast bar stools. *Because she wants to turn everyone into her child.*

Oh, give it a rest, for God's sake.

'Sabina just saved me from one of Quentin's interminable narratives,' I whisper.

'She's brilliant with him. She's more of a nanny to him than to the boys these days.'

I make the agreeing noise I reserve for occasions when I disagree with Jo; it's very similar to the noise I make when I agree with her, only quieter and less wholehearted. Whether Jo is aware of it or not, Sabina has never been a nanny to the boys, though that has been her job title from the start. As far as I can tell, her role here is indulged-older-daughter-cum-publicist-to-Jo. Jo has always tended to William and Barney's every need while Sabina watches, awe-struck, and provides moral support, irrespective of the morality of what is being supported. When William hit another boy at play-group, Sabina agreed with Jo that it was the other boy's fault for provoking him. She celebrates, vocally, all Jo's child-rearing deci-sions, and offers visitors a running commentary on what a wonderful mother Jo is, in between going for runs and massages and to English language lessons, which Jo always couches in terms of poor Sabina desperately needing a break.

Sabina is a skilful handler of both Quentin and Jo because they're adults; it's only children that she doesn't have the first clue what to do with and is slightly afraid of. Luke and I have laughed till we've cried about the idea of her deciding to train to be a nanny. Still, the joke's on us; Sabina must have known what we would never have believed: that there are people out there keen to spend their money on the illusion of childcare.

I've often wondered if Sabina truly likes Jo, deep down – though not as often as I've wondered if Neil likes Jo.

The posh tea is delicious. 'Mm. Why don't I have heavenly things like this in my house?' I say.

'Count yourself lucky. You don't have Quentin in your house,' Jo whispers, grinning.

'I do, believe me.'

'You *do* have Quentin living in your house? Funny, I could have sworn he lives here.'

I laugh for longer than the joke deserves, falling easily into what Sharon used to call my 'SONS' routine: being the source of narcis-sistic supply that Jo needs me to be. In her spare time, inspired by having Marianne as a mother, Sharon read every book about dysfunctional parenting that she could get her hands on. Her house was full of chunky volumes with titles like *Toxic Parents: Overcoming*

Their Hurtful Legacy and Reclaiming Your Life, which she refused to hide when Marianne visited.

Sharon and Jo never met, though for years Jo kept saying Sharon sounded like 'a hoot' and she'd love to meet her, and Sharon got to hear plenty about Jo's antics from me, so they probably knew each other about as well as two people who had never met could.

I couldn't introduce them. It's my own fault that I couldn't, and it makes me feel sick when I think about it. One moment of recklessness . . . This is the dark core of everything I hold against Jo and against myself: that I was stupid enough to give her the power to destroy me and Luke, to destroy me and Sharon . . .

'I'm making the simplest, loveliest supper in the world.' Jo's voice brings me back to the present. 'Even a non-cook like you could manage it: linguine with basil, tomatoes, mozzarella and olive oil stirred in – that's it, all there is to it!'

'So basically Insalata Tricolore with pasta?'

'Yup. With a sliver or two of red chilli, black pepper and Parmesan. Why didn't I think of it years ago? Quentin won't eat it – leaves in it, no meat, not hot enough, yada yada. I made him a shepherd's pie this morning.'

'You're a saint,' I tell her.

She turns to face me. 'I meant what I said before. You should count yourself lucky. Sabina helps a lot, but . . . sometimes I still fantasise about putting a pillow over his face.' She claps her hand over her mouth. 'Sorry, that's a terrible thing to say.'

'No, it's not. It's wholly understandable. It'd only be terrible if you did it.'

Dinah comes tearing into the room. 'Amber, William's been teaching us the difference between transitive and intransitive relationships. Can I tell you?'

'Not that again!' says Jo. 'The child's obsessed.'

William has a tendency to develop strange fixations. He seems older, more serious, more pedantic every time I meet him. Barney, in contrast, is regressing: a few weeks ago he ditched his normal voice and started to speak like a lisping toddler. He's kept it up ever since. Jo thinks it's cute, but it drives me mad.

'You don't know the difference, do you?' Dinah gloats.

I don't. My education was sadly lacking, evidently.

William, Nonie and Barney appear in the doorway.

'William learned it at school, along with a gazillion other things, but for some reason, this is the one that stuck,' says Jo.

'A transitive relationship is like "is younger than",' Dinah explains. 'If I'm younger than William, and Nonie's younger than me, then Nonie's also younger than William. An *in*transitive relationship is like "is cross with". If I'm cross with you and you're cross with Luke, that doesn't mean I'm cross with Luke, does it? I might not be.'

'Very clever,' I say. Why did no one ever teach me that?

'Let's go and put more things on our lists!' says Nonie.

'We're making lists of transitive and intransitive verbs,' William tells me. His tone implies I'm a dullard who cannot hope to keep up. I wonder if he has any friends at school.

'Whap aboup, "Wikes pizza"?' Barney suggests, in his new baby patois.

'No, that's—'

'That's almost perfectly right, Barney. You just need to add a bit more.' Jo flashes a warning look at William. 'You could have "Likes pizza *more than*". Well done, Barn! Clever you!'

Dinah shoots a disbelieving look in my direction. I think about Nonie's Maths homework and feel compromised.

Once the children have withdrawn, Jo says, 'William's teacher's a genius. Seriously. A *proper* genius who spent years refusing to get a job because he was unwilling to do anything but read and think. His life story's fascinating. He lives on a boat.'

Of course he does. In the abstract, people who live on boats annoy me, though I liked the only boat-dweller I've ever met, a man I used to work with at the council.

'Jo, about Quentin . . . I know I said you're a saint, and you are, but . . . you know you don't have to be one, don't you? If it gets too unbearable having him here . . .'

Jo stops chopping basil. She lays down her knife and stands with her back to me, stiff and still. 'What are you saying?'

I feel something harsh and hostile creeping towards me; its invisibility renders it all the more menacing. How have I cocked this up? I'm sticking up for Jo, a tactic that can normally be relied on to go down well.

Whatever you say now will be wrong. And you won't know why. And you'll feel victimised and relieved at the same time, relieved to be able to say to yourself, 'This is it, this is what happens, and it does happen. Look, it's happening now.'

'What point are you making, exactly?' Jo asks again, in the voice I find hard to believe I haven't exaggerated in my mind when I'm not listening to it.

Second-guessing isn't going to work. My best chance is honesty. 'Ignore me,' I say. 'I know you're way too good a daughter-in-law to turf him out. It's my guilt talking. Luke and I ought to take him off your hands now and then, but we don't because the thought of having him to stay . . .' I shudder. 'I suppose I self-servingly thought I'd help instead by suggesting you send him packing. The more I see you suffering with him, the worse it makes me feel. And let's face it, there's nothing wrong with him apart from . . . everything that's wrong with him. Why can't he live on his own, or try and meet a boring widow who'd be willing to take him in?'

Jo turns to face me. 'I don't expect you to share him,' she says, moving back in the direction of normal temperature speech. 'You've got your hands full with Dinah and Nonie. But I can't evict him, Amber. How can I? He'd be lost on his own, utterly lost.'

She folds her hands, watching me carefully. Why? Why isn't she getting on with chopping stuff up? 'Wouldn't he?' she says, when I say nothing. 'Admit it.'

Honesty worked for me once; it's worth trying again. 'Yes, he'd be lost, initially, but . . . that's his problem, Jo. He's in possession of his faculties and able to get himself a life if he wants to, even at his age. I freely admit I might be a selfish cow, but for me the right to enjoy one's own life – own and *only* – trumps duty to others every time. I took Dinah and Nonie in because I wanted to. I love having them; they enhance my life. I'd never in a million years allow Quentin to move in.'

'Yes, you would. If Luke was an only child, if it was a choice between having Quentin live with you or—'

'Jo, seriously. Under no circumstances whatsoever would I agree to live under the same roof as Quentin Utting.'

'Well . . .' She considers what I've said. 'Luke certainly doesn't feel that way. And if you do, you deserve to die miserable and alone, with no one to love and look after you.' She turns away, cuts open another packet of mozzarella. The cheese rolls out onto the work-top like a squashed wet golf ball.

~

You deserve to die miserable. And alone. With no one to love and look after you.

Damn. No one heard it but me. *Damn, damn, damn.*

'I don't think that is what I deserve,' I say matter-of-factly, trying to ignore the sensation that I have poison inside me. 'If I'm unbear-able to be around when I'm old, then, okay, fair enough, but if I make the people close to me feel good rather than like hanging themselves from the nearest coat peg, then I think I'll deserve *not* to die miserable and alone.' I do this only with Jo: speak as if I'm representing myself at the Old Bailey.

'Shall we drop it?' she says tightly, her eyes fixed on her pile of basil.

Luke certainly doesn't feel that way.

Yes, he does. Luke would hate to have Quentin living with us as much as I would. More. Luke has never spoken to Jo about his feelings. She's a liar, and I want to tell her that I know it. Dropping it is the opposite of what I want to do.

'I don't think believing that no one should sacrifice their own wellbeing for the sake of someone else should automatically dis-qualify me from—'

'You can't let anything go, can you, ever?' Jo snaps, smacking her chopping board with the packet of linguine she's holding in her hand. 'You can't just . . . move on. You have to keep goading me . . .'

I hear a moan from behind me: Kirsty with damp hair, in pyjamas and a dressing gown, and Hilary in jeans and a shirt that's covered in wet patches. I'm pathetically pleased to see them, and have to bite back the urge to say to Hilary, 'How much of that did you hear?'

'Hi, guys,' I say instead. 'You okay? Nice bath, Kirsty?' Jo once asked me if it had ever occurred to me that I never asked her younger sister any questions about herself, so now I always do. *So what if she can't answer? It's not for your sake, it's for hers. How would you feel if no one ever asked you how you were or what you'd been up to?*

Hilary and Kirsty often stay the night at Jo's; the lounge has two sofa-beds which Jo bought in order to encourage this to happen, at around the same time that she turned an under-stairs cupboard and part of her and Neil's previously decent-sized bedroom into two minuscule shower rooms in order to have enough bathrooms for all comers.

'I think Kirsty and I are going to head off, love,' Hilary tells Jo. 'I can't get her to settle, and . . .'

And our own large house containing our comfortable beds is only three minutes' drive from here?

'Oh, what a shame!' says Jo. 'What's up, Kirsty? Are you tired?'

'We'll see you tomorrow,' says Hilary. 'I think she is tired, yes. We spent a lot of last night wandering around the house, didn't we, Kirsty?'

Did Jo object to my views about Quentin on Hilary's behalf, because Hilary has sacrificed most of her life for Kirsty? But that wasn't what I meant. Hilary adores Kirsty; she doesn't regard it as a sacrifice, doesn't resent it. Like Jo, Hilary is a looker-after, and Kirsty is her beloved daughter and genuinely helpless. Kirsty doesn't bang on about Harold Sargent and septic tanks. It's totally different.

I'm doing it again: defending myself even though no one's listening.

'Right,' says Jo, once Hilary and Kirsty have gone. 'I think it's time to crack open a bottle of wine. What d'you reckon?' She smiles at me.

I don't know what craziness has got into me, but I hear myself say, 'Year Zero again, is it? I was hoping you'd stay angry for a bit longer, so that I can say something else you're not going to like. I've become involved, bizarrely, in a police investigation.' Even as I say it, my connection with violent death doesn't strike me as the most remarkable thing: what's more shocking is that, for the first time ever, I have openly mentioned the officially cancelled past in Jo's presence. I wonder if she's thinking the same thing. Is she aware of her history-erasing streak? Maybe it's all in my mind.

I tell her as little about Katharine Allen's murder as I can get away with, and finish with a cheap trick: I add that of course she'll be able to understand why I have to tell the police that she attended my DriveTech course on my behalf, pretending to be me.

She is aghast – scared more than angry. 'You can't tell them! Amber, how can you . . .' She shakes her head. 'I did you a favour, one I should never have agreed to. The whole thing was wrong. I seem to remember making that point at the time. You should have gone on that course yourself.'

Yes, I should have. Instead, I threw myself on the mercy of the only merciless person I know – and that was just a month ago. How recently did I stop being such a complete idiot? What if I still am one? That's a scary thought.

'Instead, you betrayed Sharon by—'

'Oh, no!' This I am not having. I'm on my feet. 'I never betrayed Sharon. And if you thought it was wrong, you should have said "no", simple as that.'

'I wanted to help you, wrong or not! I'm not judgemental like you. I care about people. And now you're going to turn me in to the cops? Thanks a lot!'

Another thing wrong with Jo's kitchen: it has no door to outside. 'I need some air,' I tell her. 'I'm going for a walk round the block. I won't be more than ten minutes. You can start your next Year Zero from when I get back.'

I don't bother with my coat; all I want is to get out. As I walk, I try to work out why I didn't take Dinah and Nonie and leave for good. Why did I promise to go back? Why did I suggest yet another artificially clean slate, as if pretending nothing bad ever happened is a policy I approve of?

'Amber?' I turn and see Neil behind me, mobile phone in hand. 'Are you okay?'

Right back at you, Neil. How can you be okay, married to her?

'Can I ask you something?' I say.

'Sure.'

'Feel free to tell me to mind my own business, but . . . that Christmas we all went away together. Why did you, Jo and the boys disappear? What happened?'

I did it. I asked the question and nothing horrendous happened. Yet. A bark of a laugh escapes from my mouth; it sounds odd even to me. 'Sorry,' I say. 'It's just that I've wanted to ask for years. I was always too scared.'

'Me too,' Neil says awkwardly, looking down at his feet as he stamps them to keep warm. I can't feel the cold; my anger is heating me from the inside. 'Scared, I mean.'

'What . . .' I fall silent. I know what he's going to say, and it shocks me that I haven't thought of it as a possibility – not once, not even fleetingly. 'You don't know why you disappeared, do you?'

Neil shakes his head. 'I went to bed before Jo that night, remember? Next thing I know, she's shaking me awake, telling me we have to get the boys and go. When I asked why, she—' He breaks off. 'I feel bad telling you this.'

'It's not as if you're giving me privileged information,' I say, trying to make him feel better. 'We're both as unprivileged as each other.'

'We sat in the car. That's all we did, all night. Near Blantyre Park in Spilling. I don't know why there. That's where Jo told me to go, to Spilling. We sat there, fed William crisps and pop to cheer him up. He and Barney were both tired. Crying. I kept asking why, what the plan was. Jo wouldn't say anything. She wouldn't let me drive us home to Rawndesley, wouldn't let me phone and let you all know we were okay. She got really angry with me when I said anything, so . . . I stopped asking questions.' Neil shrugs. 'Stupid, really. I'm not proud of it, but . . . Jo's Jo. The boys fell asleep eventually. I nodded off in the driver's seat. When Jo woke me it was morning. She told me to drive up north. Manchester or Leeds, she said, a big city. We went to Manchester, spent most of Christmas Day and night in a hotel. Jo woke me again in the middle of the night and said we had to go back to Little Orchard. I never understood any of it. It was crazy.'

Nearly as crazy as staying married to an unpredictable, unstable . . . What? What is Jo, exactly?

'Have you asked her about it since?'

Neil lets out a low whistle, wide-eyed. 'Course not. Whatever it is, she made it clear enough that night that she didn't want to talk about it.'

'It was a beautiful house, Little Orchard,' I say. It's unbelievable, absolutely incredible to me that I'm saying its name out loud, to Neil of all people. 'Have you got the owner's details?' *And now I'm saying something insane that I haven't thought through properly.* 'Luke and I were thinking we might—'

'You can't. It's not available for hire any more. Jo tried to book it again, for us and some friends, but it's been rented out long-term.'

I wonder if whoever's renting it has seen the words 'Kind, Cruel, Kind of Cruel' written on a lined sheet of A4 paper recently.

Pretending not to have noticed the fear on Neil's face, I ask if I can have the owner's details anyway.

~

There are some advantages to never sleeping. If you want to do something and not be seen doing it, you have plenty of opportunity. Tonight, for the first time since my insomnia started, I was impatient for Luke to go to bed, for what I think of as 'my' part of the night to start.

And now it's quarter past midnight and I'm staring at a calendar on a computer screen, with two blankets wrapped round me (because I don't allow myself to have the heating or a fire going at night, however cold it is – another punishment for my failure to sleep), wondering why Neil bothered to lie to me about Little Orchard when he must have known how easily I could catch him out. Did he think I'd take his word for it when he told me the house was no longer available for short-term lets, that he and Jo had binned the owner's contact details?

I'm not sure why I didn't take his word for it. I didn't expect to find anything interesting when I typed 'Little Orchard, Cobham, Surrey' into the Google search box, but here it is on a website called My Home For Hire, and this calendar, with its blue date squares to indicate availability and orange ones for dates already booked, seems to know nothing about a permanent or semi-permanent tenant. According to the 'Check Availability' page on the screen in front of me, I can book Little Orchard any time between now and a week on Friday, any time between the following Monday and 20 December. Between and after those dates it's booked. I look at the prices: £5,950 for a week, or £1,000 a night, as long as I commit to staying a minimum of two nights. The owner can be contacted at littleorchardcobham@yahoo.co.uk.

I enter my own email address in the box provided and type 'Booking Enquiry' in the subject box. I compose a message, asking if I might book Little Orchard for the weekend of 17 to 19 December, and mentioning that I was one of a party that stayed in the house in December 2003. I add a couple of lines about how much I enjoyed my first stay, how I've wanted to go back to Little Orchard ever since, especially with my two girls, who I know would love it.

I read my message through. The last part embarrasses me. It strikes a false note; I'm trying too hard. I delete the gushy bits, press send and sit back in my chair, readjusting my blankets. I have no idea, at this point, whether I am willing to spend two thousand pounds we can't afford on a return visit to Little Orchard.

For what purpose? To look for some words on a piece of paper, words you have no good reason to believe you'll find there? Luke will think I'm crazy. He'll worry about me.

Either Neil flat-out lied to me, or his intelligence is out of date. Perhaps someone rented the house for the whole of last year, and now they're gone. Neil didn't say when Jo had tried to book Little Orchard again for them and their friends.

Which friends? Neil and Jo haven't got any. They spend all their free time with family.

He lied to me.

Why? Why would he fear the prospect of Luke and me going back there? If he thought Jo would be averse to the idea, that would be enough of a reason, but why would he think that? Why would Jo care? Could it have something to do with the key to the locked room?

Keeping me out of Little Orchard's study mattered to Jo. That argument is the only time I've seen her physically shake. I remember thinking then that, even for Jo, this level of outrage and disgust was over the top. What if I was wrong? What if it wasn't disgust at my lack of scruples, but fear, the same fear I saw on Neil's face a few hours ago?

Of what, though? Did Jo and Neil use that key before I thought of looking for it? Did they lock something in Little Orchard's study while we were there? Was it something to do with Jo's reason for wanting to vanish with Neil and the boys in the middle of the night?

The computer makes a pinging noise: a new email. I open it. It's signed Veronique Coudert. French, obviously. 'Dear Ms Hewerdine, Thank you for your enquiry. Unfortunately, I am not offering Little Orchard to visitors for the foreseeable future as I am now living in the house myself with my family. I am sorry to be the bearer of disappointing news, and I wish you luck in finding an alternative property for your weekend in December.'

I chew my lip. So, not a long-term rental, then; the owner has moved back in.

Except that she can't have, because there are bookings on the availability calendar for December.

Why would a woman I've never met lie to me? Why would Neil? Unless Veronique Coudert lied to him too. Or unless the availability calendar is wrong, out of date. *Which?* I'm too exhausted to be able to distinguish between the ideas I ought to pay attention to and those I should discard.

A loud noise like a slap sends a jolt through my body. It came from downstairs and sounded like a pile of post hitting the hall floor. Have we been assigned an insomniac postman?

I make my way downstairs, still trying and failing to make sense of what's just happened. If Little Orchard was no longer available for hire, it would surely be the easiest thing in the world to have it removed from the My Home For Hire website. Why wouldn't Veronique Coudert take care of that, to save herself the bother of having to reply to endless emails like mine? Unless the house *is* still available, to everyone but me. Or everyone but me, Jo, Neil . . .

I stop on the landing outside Luke's room, shivering from the cold. We had to give our names in 2003. Jo had a form. She'd filled in all our names and we all had to sign. Hilary held Kirsty's hand and together they planted a squiggle in the right box. It was some sort of official document. My name was on there, and my signature. As names go, Amber Hewerdine is a memorable one.

Why wouldn't Veronique Coudert want any of us to go back to her house?

Could we have done something wrong seven years ago, something I know nothing about? If Jo and Neil did unlock the study door, did the owners find out somehow? Perhaps Jo filled in a Guest Satisfaction Feedback Form and, under 'Other Comments', wrote that one of her party, the utterly unprincipled Amber Hewerdine, had been in favour of sneaking a look at the forbidden room, and that she, wonderful morally upright Jo, had put her foot down.

Yeah, right. I'm too tired to work out at what point my sensible speculations drifted over the border into the realm of pure fantasy.

There's a large brown padded envelope lying on the hall floor directly beneath the letterbox, bent in the middle from where it's been rammed through. I open it, pull out a few sheets of white A4 covered in small print, and a scrap of paper with extravagant loopy handwriting all over it. 'Dear Amber, Sorry if I pissed you off before. I did genuinely enjoy talking to you, and, believe me, I don't feel that way about most people. I've been assured by someone who (infuriatingly) is hardly ever wrong that you shouldn't be a suspect even though technically you are, so here's some information about the Katharine Allen case that I'm not supposed to give you. It would infuriate the infuriating person if he knew I had, even though, in certain moods, he could easily decide to do it himself – it's only me that's not allowed to. If anything strikes you as important, please get back to me and no one else about it, and please destroy these notes once you've read them. Charlie Zailer.' She's written her phone number beneath her name.

It's an odd note. The infuriating person must be Simon Waterhouse. *Her husband.* Why tell me anything, even the tiniest detail, about their relationship? I read the note again and decide she must be drunk and/or so lonely that she's past caring. In the months after Sharon's death, I said all kinds of inappropriately intimate, emotional things to strangers; it makes me cringe to think of it now, the way I seized upon people I hardly knew and tried to stuff them into the gaping hole of Sharon's absence.

I take the printed pages upstairs and sit down in front of the computer again. A mad impulse to send Veronique Coudert another email seizes me. I decide to act on it, before common sense has a chance to exert its killjoy influence. What harm can it do? Worst case scenario, a French woman I'm never going to meet will decide I'm bonkers – so what?

'Dear Veronique,' I type. 'Thanks for your reply. Do the words "Kind, Cruel, Kind of Cruel" mean anything to you? Or the name Katharine (Kat) Allen? Yours, Amber Hewerdine.' My heart racing, I press 'Send'. Then I turn my attention to Charlie's notes.

They're disappointing. It's not her fault; it's mine, for expecting something significant to leap out at me. I read everything through twice and find no point of overlap between Katharine Allen's life and mine. She was born in Pulham Market, where her apparently happily married parents still live. She has two sisters, one married with two children and living in Belize and the other single with a baby and living in Norwich. Katharine worked as a primary school teacher at Meadowcroft School in Spilling. She and her boyfriend, Luke, were on the point of moving in together when she was murdered. Luke has a solid alibi and was never a suspect.

Kat Allen's boyfriend shares a Christian name with my husband. I decide that doesn't count as overlap.

A new email from Veronique Coudert appears in my inbox. I click to open it. It says, 'Dear Ms Hewerdine, Please do not respond to this message. Yours, Mme Coudert'.

Two middle-of-the-night emails, two instant responses. *Odd*. She can't possibly have been sitting at her computer waiting for me, a complete stranger, to contact her. *Unless Neil warned her* . . . No, that's ridiculous.

I chew the inside of my lip, thinking. Please do not respond to what? There's nothing to respond to. And she's switched from Veronique to Madame; pushing me away.

I sniff the air, imagining I can smell something bad: more lies. It's possible to lie incredibly subtly, I realise, by referring to the absence of a message as a message.

She didn't answer my questions. She could have, but she chose not to.

Because they were intrusive and inappropriate.

I sigh, turn my attention back to the notes in front of me. Katharine Allen was popular at work: her pupils and fellow teachers liked her a lot. She was friendly, helpful, a team player . . .

Reading all this for the third time is getting me nowhere. The only mildly attention-grabbing fact here is that Kat Allen, as a child, acted in three television dramas. Though 'acted' might be putting it a bit strongly, since she was four, five and six when she played her three roles: 'shy girl on bus' in *Bubblegum Breakdown*, 'second drowning girl' in *Washed Clean Away* and 'Lily-Anne' in *The Dollface Diaries*. Her two sisters had brief stints as child stars too. It's clear that whichever detective made these notes did not find the Allen sisters' dramatic backgrounds to be either interesting or relevant.

There's a funny smell in the house; I'm not imagining it. And an odd noise, too, coming from downstairs. I drag myself out of my chair to go and investigate, and fail to yawn because the muscles around my mouth are too weary. I need to lie down on a floor somewhere and close my eyes. I think I've set a record tonight: I can't remember having felt quite as tired as I do now at any point in the last eighteen months. With luck, I might black out for a whole hour, which hardly ever happens.

I feel the heat as I approach, before I see it. Then there's the colour, stronger than I've seen in my house before, and more mobile, flaring and trembling.

I interpret what I'm seeing and I think, 'Oh. That.' I am not panicking. I don't think I am panicking. Our hall is on fire. Waves of horror flow towards me but they don't touch me, though I am trapped in the circle they make. I can hear screams that no one is screaming. *Move.* Everything has gone into slow-motion.

The flames have already climbed to the top of both walls, like a deadly species of ivy, golden and flickering. Through the smoke, I see something that looks like metal on the floor by the letterbox. I can't tell what it is. *Move. Now.*

This is my fault. I took the batteries out of all our smoke alarms. They kept going off when Luke cooked, and each time, no matter what we said, Dinah and Nonie started shaking and crying hysterically, insisting there must be a fire somewhere in the house.

Did Sharon's killer do this?

Mustn't think about that now. I know exactly what to do. I turn away from the blaze, walk upstairs, wake Luke, tell him to keep calm. Through a sort of filter, I become aware that he is not calm, that I am better at keeping calm than he is. He immediately starts to cough. I am only coughing occasionally. I tell him the girls are safe: they're above us, on the next floor up. I tell him to open the window on the landing outside Nonie's bedroom. From there, we can climb out and it's just a small drop down onto the flat roof of the two-storey extension the previous owners added to the house. I pick up Luke's mobile, put it in his hands, say that as soon as he's opened the window he must ring for help.

I run upstairs and wake the girls, whispering reassurances. From their point of view, it must seem as if my sole reason for waking them is to tell them that everything is going to be fine, and nothing to do with anything bad happening. I'm telling the truth: I believe everything will be okay, and that's why I'm not scared. I'm shocked, but not afraid – that's what I'm telling myself. *Not scared. Not scared.* I've worked it out: the only way we won't be fine is if the flames climb all the way up the stairs to the second landing before we get out of that window, and they won't. When I last saw them – the flames – they were up to the top of the walls but still only halfway along, halfway into the space between the front door and the beginning of the stairs. As I guide a silent Nonie and an outraged Dinah into their dressing gowns and slippers, I make sure not to use the word 'fire'.

Luke is waiting for us by the window. He helps the girls to climb out and tries to help me too, but I make him go first. I have to be last, have to risk myself and no one else. Nonie is coughing. If I knew who had started the fire I would kill them, no question, for making her cough like that.

Some time later – I have no idea how long – we are sitting at the far end of the extension's roof, dangling our feet off the edge, waiting to hear the sound of a fire engine. We shiver from the cold and cling to one another. It's ridiculous that our house is ablaze behind us and we're still freezing.

'Will we be able to fix the house?' Nonie asks.

'The house doesn't matter,' I say. 'We're all that matters.'

Dinah bursts into tears, covers her face with her hands. 'It's my fault. This is my fault.'

'Of course it isn't,' I say.

'It is. I made you buy this house. You bought it because I said I loved it.'

'And because *we* loved it.'

'But you wouldn't have bought it if I'd said I *didn't* like it, and I loved it for a bad reason. I thought it looked like the sort of house a really famous person might have used to live in, and I want to be famous.'

Luke and I exchange a look that fails to deliver a unanimous verdict on which of us is best qualified to deal with this.

'I wanted a house that could have a plaque on it one day saying, "Dinah Lendrim lived here from 2009 to . . ." whenever I moved out,' Dinah sobs. 'I've seen them on houses in London, when Mum used to take us, and they're always tall old-looking houses like this one. Like number 10 Downing Street. Remember that bungalow we looked at, with the beautiful garden? I loved that house really, but I pretended I hated it because you never see a house like that with a famous person plaque on it!'

Luke says something in response: the right thing, hopefully. I can't concentrate. Why are the fire brigade taking so long? Maybe they aren't; maybe we've only been out here for a few seconds. If you're outside sitting on a roof, several metres from the burning house behind you, is there any way the fire or the smoke can get you? At what point ought we to jump off? *Not yet.* The ceilings of our old plaque-worthy townhouse are high. I'm not risking the girls breaking bones unless and until I have to.

From the front, our house looks very similar to number 10 Downing Street. Why has this never occurred to me before?

'If we'd bought that bungalow, this wouldn't have happened.'

'Yes, it would,' Nonie corrects her older sister, something she doesn't dare do often. 'Whoever it is that started the fire, it isn't the house they want to burn. If we were in the bungalow, they'd have set fire to the bungalow. Wouldn't they, Amber?'

I hug her tightly.

'Amber?'

'Mm?'

'Last time . . . when Mum died, the bad person who started the fire made sure that me and Dinah were safely out of the house.'

Oh, God, please don't let her ask what she's about to ask.

'Why didn't they do that this time?'

Last time, this time, next time. For most seven-year-olds, having someone set fire to their house would be, at most, a one-off event. Something black and hard is growing inside me. It might be a hunger for revenge.

Luke says, 'We don't know that anyone started this fire. It could have been an accident.'

No, it couldn't.

'Amber? Do you think Granny Marianne set fire to our house?' Nonie asks.

'Don't be stupid,' says Dinah.

'Why's it stupid? She was always mean to Mum, and she never wants to see us. She doesn't even ring up any more.'

'Your grandmother didn't start the fire,' I say.

Why? Because she couldn't have started the last one? Does it have to be the same person?

'We shouldn't have taken the batteries out of the smoke alarms,' says Luke.

'We've got a human smoke alarm.' I point to myself. *One that spends all night moving from room to room, checking everything's okay, just in case.*

'Amber?'

'Yes, Nones?

'I'd hate to be famous. Sometimes at school when people ask me what Nonie's short for, if I can't be bothered saying Oenone and explaining that it's Greek, I say it's short for Anonymous. Can I change my name to Anonymous, before people at school find out it's not true?'

I hear a siren in the distance. It's coming closer. I start to cry.

If something happens once, we might not pay much attention to it. If it happens twice or more, we start to see a pattern. The human psyche loves patterns so much that it does its best to find them whenever it can, even sometimes seeing ones that aren't there.

The row about the key to the locked study at Little Orchard was part of a pattern: Jo has a long history of thinking herself more virtuous than other people and claiming the moral high ground whenever she can. Once when Amber asked if Kirsty's condition had a name – if she was born that way or had had some kind of accident – Jo demanded to know why Amber felt it was an acceptable question to ask. Does anyone ever ask you what made you the way you are? she said. She didn't give Amber any answers, except to say that there was nothing *wrong* with Kirsty. She was just different, and everyone loved her exactly as she was. Amber had taken care not to use the word 'wrong', knowing it would upset Jo; she had phrased her question as sensitively as possible, yet Jo had heard the unspoken insensitive version and responded to that.

Amber knows not to give Jo a hello kiss, as she is in the habit of doing with most people she's close to. She tried it once in the very early days of her and Luke's relationship, and Jo burst out laughing and backed away, saying, 'Don't kiss me. I won't be able to keep a straight face.' When Amber asked what she meant, Jo said, 'That whole pretentious mwa-mwa thing. Sorry, I'm a northerner – I just can't do it.' Amber must have been taken aback. Hurt, too, I would imagine. For many people, it's not pretentious at all to kiss someone hello. It's simply an expression of affection, and no one likes to have their affection rejected. Neil, who witnessed the exchange, might have been aware of Amber's embarrassment. Perhaps that was why he decided to shift the focus and tease Jo. 'Northern girls will only kiss you if there's something in it for them,' Neil told Amber. 'Preferably a good seeing-to, marriage and two children, in that order.' Did Amber hope Jo would be hurt? If so, she must have been disappointed when Jo just shrugged and said, 'I'm not a tactile person.'

Later, when Amber told Luke what had happened, he agreed that it was true, Jo wasn't tactile, though he'd never thought about it before. 'She always hangs back when the kiss-greeting stuff's going on, makes sure she's not in the firing line.' Did this corroboration from Luke that it was nothing personal take the sting out of the incident for Amber? Clearly not, or she wouldn't today, years later, think it worth mentioning. Hanging back is one thing, she might have thought, but if you screw up and someone gets close enough to lean forward and try to kiss you hello, surely you should let them get on with it, however uncomfortable you feel, if the alternative is to embarrass and reject them.

And Jo's policy is inconsistent. Amber has walked into Jo's lounge and found her sitting on the sofa with William and Barney on either side of her, giving them both a big cuddle. Seeing Amber there, Jo sprang up immediately, almost pushing the boys away as if she'd been caught doing something shameful. Maybe if that hadn't happened, Amber would have forgotten about the earlier incident. Maybe that's what reactivated it in her mind: concrete evidence that Jo doesn't mind kissing people in general, only Amber in particular.

If this is what Amber believes, I think she's wrong. Children who have been victims of physical, sexual or emotional abuse often grow up to be non-tactile adults. Often the sole exception they're willing to make is for their children.

Jo's thoughtlessness is a recurring theme for Amber, and particularly wounding, I would guess, because Jo has proven herself time and time again to be capable of its opposite; there's no doubt she knows how to be considerate when she wants to be.

Shortly after Amber and Luke got married, Jo asked Amber if she planned to give up her job when she had her first baby. Amber said no: she couldn't bear the thought of giving up her career. Jo, who had been a speech therapist until she had William and stopped working, laughed at this quite openly. Assuming Amber's recall is accurate, Jo's response was to say, 'Anyone'd think you were a Hollywood actress or a

Nobel-Prize-winning scientist. You're a licensing officer for the council, for God's sake.' In fact, Amber wasn't *a* licensing officer, she was *the* Licensing Officer for Rawndesley city council – she didn't, of course, point this out. Nor did she tell Jo that it was possible to love and take pride in a job that, from its title, didn't sound particularly glamorous. I'm assuming Jo decided to end the conversation there, secure in her assumption that Amber was wrong to prize her professional identity so highly. What she ought to have done was say, 'Oh, I'm sorry, how ignorant of me. Tell me about your job. What do you love about it?'

When Amber told Jo about her promotion from Licensing Officer to Licensing Manager, Jo said, 'Aren't those just different names for the same job? I still don't understand what it is you do all day.' When Amber tried, not for the first time, to describe the ins and outs of her work, Jo interrupted her and changed the subject.

Once, before Barney was born, Amber and Luke went away for the weekend with Jo, Neil and William. On the Friday evening, Amber had a bath immediately before going to bed. The next morning, when Jo asked her if she'd had a good night's sleep, Amber replied that she had and that she'd known she would when she got into bed. 'I always sleep well on the rare nights that I and my bedding are spotlessly clean at the same time. Not that it happens very often,' she joked. Luke and Neil laughed. Jo wrinkled her nose and said, 'Yuck! That's disgusting. Did you really need to tell us that?'

Generally, Jo seems to feel free to question Amber's ethics and behaviour whenever it suits her. She tried to interfere in Amber's wedding plans, leading Amber to tell Luke she'd always wanted to elope abroad to get married, which was a lie. After Sharon died, when Amber told Jo that she and Luke were planning to buy a bigger house that could more easily accommodate four people, Jo was dead set against the plan and seemed unaware that it was none of her business. She accused Amber of being selfish, putting her own needs before Dinah and Nonie's.

Amber was confused. Her main reason for wanting a bigger house was so that the girls wouldn't have to share the only spare bedroom she and Luke had at the time. Amber made the mistake of admitting to Jo that a secondary consideration was that she herself might feel the need for space, both physical and psychological, once Dinah and Nonie moved in. Jo tutted and said, 'The size of your house is neither here nor there. What those poor kids need is stability. They've always known you and Luke in that house. Don't you think they've got enough change and trauma to deal with, without you adding to it?' When Amber pointed out that Dinah and Nonie were excited about helping to choose the new house, Jo shook her head dismissively and said, 'There's no point talking to you. You'll think what you want to think, whatever I say.'

Point or not, that conversation wasn't followed by a change of policy on Jo's part. She continued to criticise Amber's actions and decisions, particularly with regard to the girls, and regularly expressed the view that it was 'wrong' for Amber and Luke to have guardianship of them. 'They should be with their grandmother,' she doggedly insisted whenever the subject came up. 'You and Luke might be fond of them, but you're not family. It can't be the same.' On being reminded that Marianne Lendrim, though opposed to the idea of adoption, was perfectly happy for her granddaughters to live with Amber and Luke and had said it would be impossible for her to have them live or even stay the occasional night with her, Jo's response was to sigh heavily and say, 'Well, of course she's going to say that, isn't she? If I were in her shoes, I'd also minimise contact, protect myself. She knows that one day Dinah and Nonie are going to be old enough to be told that their dead mother made a will that said she'd rather her daughters were brought up by any old heroin addict or paedophile than by their own grandmother.'

Does any or all of this explain why Amber resents Jo as much as she does? I think there's something else, something she's not telling us.

Amber?

6

2/12/2010

'Waterhouse!' Proust sounded pleased to see him. 'I wasn't sure you'd present yourself at the appointed hour, but here you are: nine o'clock on the nose. Shut the door behind you, please.'

'Six words. That's all it takes.'

'I beg your pardon?'

'"Waterhouse, you're sacked. Gibbs, you're sacked." Say it and get on with what matters. Someone tried to kill Amber Hewerdine and her family last night. They'll try again. Next time they might succeed.'

Proust looked to his left, then his right. 'Gibbs? You're hallucinat-ing, Waterhouse. Have a seat.' He gestured towards the only one in his office.

'That's your chair.'

'Am I using it at the moment? If I'm offering it to you and not sitting in it myself, how can there be a problem?'

Simon walked around the inspector's desk and sat down. He felt foolish, as if he was trying to impersonate a DI, indulging an embar-rassing ego-boosting delusion in public. *First point to the Snowman.* Soon it would be game, set and match.

'I'm afraid I have more than six words for you, but let me suggest another time-saving ruse. How about you don't interrupt me every ten seconds?'

Simon nodded.

'Instant agreement. That means you imagine it'll be easy for you.' Proust smiled as he paced the floor. 'You're not afraid of me any more, Waterhouse. You always have been – until very recently you were – but no longer.'

Was this item one on the agenda, or preamble? Did it matter?

'There was never any need for you to be, and I always wondered why you were. There's nothing so terrifying about me, is there? I speak my mind, and I don't suffer fools – which would be particularly problematic for you, I can see that – but still . . . why the fear? Nobody else is frightened of me. Anyone would think I was some sort of tyrannical bully.'

'Anyone would,' Simon agreed.

'I'm sure you'd be the first to admit that I treat people fairly, you included. I bend over backwards to be fair to you.' Proust shook his head. The puzzled look on his face appeared to be genuine. To which was he a great loss, Simon wondered: the acting profession or the specially-reserved-for-extreme-cases penthouse padded cell at the local nuthouse?

'I've always put your fear of me down to some peculiar deficiency in you. One among many.' The Snowman lunged across his desk to grab his new World's Greatest Grandad mug. Simon flinched, remembering having its predecessor hurled at his head. 'I'll admit, there have been occasions when I've found your phobia useful as a means of controlling you, and times when it's irritated me beyond measure because it interferes with your ability to listen to the many sound arguments I put forward, each and every working day. Either way, you can hardly blame me for noticing my new team member: Brave New Waterhouse. Brave and confused. You have no idea why your fear of me might have quit its post and strolled off into the sunset, hand in hand with your fear of unemployment. Well? Have you?'

No.

'I'll tell you why.' Proust leaned in over the desk. His breath smelled of hot stewed tea. 'Something new and daunting has entered your life. So petrified are you of it that, suddenly, all your trifling fears of old have been put into perspective: your doddery DI, your frail ageing parents. Have you been standing up to your mother as well? Refusing to drink the blood of the Virgin Mary or whatever it is that she and her oddball cult get up to, unfazed by recent proof that the whole outfit's nothing more than a cover for a global epidemic of sexual perversion . . .' Proust stopped. Frowned. 'I've lost my thread,' he said.

'You were insulting my mother.'

'I was not!'

A fist banging down on a desk, shaking it; tea sloshing in the air, spattering the floor. Simon was unmoved by the special effects; he'd seen it all before. He was trying to get his head round the Snowman's battle tactics, struggling not to be impressed. *Challenge an opinion and the holder of that opinion might put forward a counter-argument; contradict an uncontestable fact and, chances are, your audience will slink off in confusion to question their own sanity.*

'Act your age for once in your life, Waterhouse!' Proust snapped. 'Don't try to turn this into a slanging match. I'm trying to help you, believe it or not.'

Tough choice, but I'll go for 'not'.

Proust exhaled slowly. 'Your disrespect used to spill out in spite of your best efforts; now, suddenly, you're sloshing it around like a tramp urinating on a . . .'

Another unscheduled break. Simon was unwilling to help a second time by suggesting things a tramp might piss on.

'Pathetic, Waterhouse. That's not me talking, it's your inner voice. I'd attempt the accent, only I don't speak low self-esteem. It's a language I've never needed to learn.'

Simon weighed up his options. What was to stop him walking out? He was waiting for one thing only: to be told he was fired. Was it better to be fired at close range than remotely, from a distance? Simon couldn't see how; still, he planned to sit tight until he heard the words.

'Any idea what this new source of terror in your life might be?'

'There isn't anything.'

Proust laughed. 'What, not even Charlie Zailer? Wedlock, Waterhouse. Hear that second syllable: *lock*. You're trapped. You can't get divorced. That would involve admitting you made a mistake, which you're congenitally incapable of doing. Yet you're cripplingly afraid of the demands marriage is bound to make, demands you're too inadequate to respond to. Blown everything else out of the water, hasn't it? If you stumbled upon a ticking bomb, you might sit down on it and put your feet up. No other fear can touch you now that you're grappling with the big one.'

'If I disagree, will it spoil your fun?' Simon asked.

'If you disagree, it'll prompt me to wonder, and not for the first time, how a person can live for more than forty years without self-knowledge and fail to notice its absence. There's not a drop of the stuff in you, Waterhouse; this is my attempt at a much-needed transfusion.'

'Your need's greater than mine, as evidenced by your fantasy that you're a suitable donor,' said Simon. Did that make sense? In his head it did. His words echoed in the silence that followed.

'Insult me all you like,' Proust said eventually. 'You won't convince me that your judgement is the trustworthy ally it used to be. Do you honestly believe Sergeant Zailer went for hypnosis because she wants to give up the bifters? Smoking is one of the few pleasures in her miserable life. Aren't you itching to know what she's really up to? I promise you, however much money flows from your and Zailer's joint bank account into the tasselled purse of a tinpot wizard in Great Holling, it's not going to solve the problem, whatever it is. And if you happen to know what it is already, or if you take my advice and find out, please don't enlighten me. There are limits.'

'Apparently there aren't.'

Proust spun round, his face a mess of pink and white patches. 'You think I want to kick you off the job? You're wrong. Cast your mind back over the toxic wastelands of our many years together. I've had any number of opportunities to get shot of you. What did I do? Let them roll on by, each and every one.'

That was true. *That and nothing else.*

'Trouble is, whether I want to lose you or not, I don't have much choice. You've made it compulsory. If I were to let you carry on, business as usual, how would that look to the rest of the team? I'd be the DI who let an out-of-control DC trample all over him

– everyone'd get to hear about it. I'd lose the respect of every single person in this nick, right down to the canteen staff and the cleaners.'

'Culture shock might not be as bad as you anticipate,' Simon muttered. He could cope with the abuse; what he couldn't handle was the Snowman telling him he didn't want to lose him.

That wasn't what he said. Stop hearing things he isn't saying.

'It's not about culture shock!' Proust slammed his mug down on the windowsill and rubbed the sides of his skull with white-tipped fingers. Simon watched, inferred from the body language that the inspector cared about something. Since that thing was neither Simon nor basic human decency, it was hard to imagine what it might be. 'It's about hanging on to my own perishing job! It's about having the gumption to recognise when one of my DCs crosses over from being a good bet to being a liability, and having the courage to point it out.'

'You've never said I was a good bet.'

'If I had, I'd have been wrong eventually if not straight away, which is why I didn't bother. Listen to me, Waterhouse. Let me sit down, will you?' Was the inspector asking permission? Something in his tone suggested an awareness that Simon was the younger and stronger of the two of them.

This isn't a heart to heart, Simon told himself, trying not to notice his own thickening discomfort. *This is me getting sacked.*

They swapped places. Simon hoped that, once Proust was seated, normal interaction between them might resume. Then he realised what a twisted hope that was, and that getting out of here while he was still halfway sane might be the best thing for him, whether he wanted to go or not.

'Look at you: oblivious to your own decline,' Proust declaimed from the comfort of his chair. If Simon had been waiting to hear a charge that he'd be able to refute with conviction, this was surely it. He felt as if he'd spent his whole life witnessing his own decline, aware that his inner resources were depleting, and there was nothing he could do to halt the process.

'You have nothing that gives your life meaning apart from this – quite literally nothing – yet you recklessly endanger your career, allowing yourself to believe the loss of it wouldn't bother you. And for what? For the fun of being rude to me in front of your pals? You could have got the result you wanted, and risked nothing, by passing on Sergeant Zailer's information about Ms Hewerdine to DS Kombothekra. You'd have ended up in an interview room with Hewerdine eventually—'

'Someone set fire to her house last night,' Simon interrupted. 'If I'd followed the proper channels, we'd still be doing background checks.'

'I asked you not to interrupt me.'

'If Amber hadn't got her husband and the two girls out in time . . .'

'Which she did.'

'. . . she could have been dead by now, before I'd had a chance to ask her anything at all.'

Proust's eyes narrowed. 'Once a person's been interviewed by you, they can die happy – is that what you're saying?' He shook his head, made a church and steeple out of his hands. 'Why do I bother, Waterhouse? Can you tell me that? You know so much. Why don't you tell me why I bother trying to help you?'

'Feel free to stop bothering at your earliest convenience,' Simon said.

'Open your ears and switch on your brain!' the Snowman bellowed, lurching up out of his seat as if it had pushed him from underneath. 'You've singled Amber Hewerdine out for special consideration. Why? For no good reason, you assume she didn't kill Kat Allen, when she's the only person we can link to the murder scene, albeit indirectly. Unless you're looking to put a lined A4 notepad in the frame, Hewerdine's all we've got! You insist her alibi's sound, when everyone you've spoken to who was on that perishing course says they don't remember her face! You tell us we ought to trust her, having listened to her brag about her lack of respect for the law. She expects to be able to drive at whatever speed suits her, and finds it inconvenient to have to pay the price when she—'

'Oh, come on. Everybody—'

'Not everybody! Not me. I don't speed, and if I did and I got caught, I'd accept my punishment. Amber Hewerdine's best friend dies in an arson attack – Hewerdine ends up with her daughters. I think we can call that a capital gain. Consensus at the time fingered a local pub landlord—'

'Not everyone thought that. Only—'

'Interrupt me one more time, Waterhouse, and I really will have your job.'

Did that mean what Simon thought it meant?

'Hewerdine makes a big show of coming forward to help the police.' Proust picked up speed as he ranted. 'She disagrees about Terry Bond, doesn't blame him for the fire. She's Sharon Lendrim's best friend since childhood. She's in a unique position in relation to the crime, knows something no one else does . . . Is any of this sounding familiar? Think of Sergeant Zailer's notebook. How many innocent people have you met who manage to be in a unique position in relation to two murders?'

Nothing irritated Simon more than the Snowman making a good point.

'Hewerdine claims that Bond and Sharon Lendrim were the best of friends when Lendrim died. They'd had a little-publicised reconciliation . . .'

'Sharon's daughters knew they'd resolved their differences. So did Terry Bond's daughter, according to Sam's contact.'

'Sergeant Kombothekra's *contact* is Ursula Shearer. She couldn't find a killer on a Cluedo board, even if you stuffed her head into the secret envelope.' Proust ran his tongue over his lower lip. 'I'm not saying Terry Bond or any of his henchmen started the fire. Amber Hewerdine did. She must have. She was the only one to gain from it: she got Sharon's girls.'

'Makes no sense,' said Simon. 'If her aim was to divert suspicion from herself, why not let everyone think Bond did it? Why come forward and say she thinks it's someone from the residents' association? It's a pretty unlikely—'

'For crying out loud, Waterhouse, I shouldn't have to explain this to you! Pretty unlikely wins people over. It wins over idiots like you! Pretty unlikely makes an ambitious DC or DS want to prove his superiority by demonstrating his ability to think outside the box. Hewerdine's a consummate actress. She comes forward with a theory that's not quite as obvious as what everyone else is saying, and gets to look not only helpful but clever too: an original thinker. She flatters her way into the inner circle of detectives by showing that she's on their level, she can think like one of them – exactly the tactic she tried with us. Gibbs and I saw through it; you lapped it up. She worms her way in, and she's able to keep track. Now she's set fire to her own house, and she's confident she'll know if and when we start to zero in on her, because her best buddy Waterhouse will tell her everything she needs to know.'

'Why burn her own house down?' Simon asked.

An overflowing look from Proust.

'If you're one of the victims, you can't be the perpetrator?' *What are you doing, dickhead? If he's got something to say, let him say it himself. Too late.*

'Ms Hewerdine is a victim of special distinction,' said Proust. 'The only one to survive, along with her nearest and dearest. Katharine Allen didn't survive. Neither did Sharon Lendrim.'

Three crimes: two arson attacks, one in 2008 and one last night, and one bludgeoning a month ago. Same perpetrator? If so, why change the method for the second killing, then revert to arson for Amber Hewerdine? Katharine Allen's murder didn't fit the pattern.

'Don't forget that Ms Hewerdine's house is still standing,' said Proust. 'A bit of redecorating in the hallway, a new front door . . .'

'She's guilty of nothing,' Simon told him. 'You're barking up the wrong tree. If you were right, that'd have to mean she staged her meeting with Charlie outside Ginny Saxon's clinic. It's impossible. She'd have to have known Charlie would write "Kind, Cruel" in her notebook. How could she know that?'

Proust reached for a pile of papers, waved them in the air. 'The

Wizard of Great Holling told Sellers that Hewerdine referred to the prospect of her entire family dying as "a bonus".'

'She made a joke.' *And you're shaking the wrong papers at me; those are expenses forms, not Sellers' interview with Ginny Saxon.*

'Why did Hewerdine go and see Saxon in the first place? Insomnia!' The Snowman said it triumphantly, as if inability to sleep and responsibility for two murders were much of a muchness. 'What keeps people awake at night? Guilt. You heard Hewerdine talking about her mind splitting in two. You didn't take that as paving the way for a diminished responsibility defence, in case she loses control of us and we end up charging her?'

'No, I didn't,' said Simon. 'I heard a woman trying to describe an unusual experience she'd had. Unusual and disturbing.'

'No, that was Sergeant Zailer, the morning after your wedding night,' Proust snapped. 'Amber Hewerdine's a lunatic – one who likes to play dress-up detectives. She's a criminal. We know this; it's not up for debate. She ran off without paying Ginny Saxon, she invaded Sergeant Zailer's car without permission . . .' Proust continued to dry-spit for a few seconds after his words had run out.

He was right. In the absence of other suspects, it made no sense to be convinced of Amber Hewerdine's innocence. In different circumstances, Simon might have tried to unconvince himself.

'Anything else you want to say before the others come in?' Proust asked.

The others? Simon had been under the impression that Gibbs was booked in next; he didn't know anything about anyone else.

He still hadn't been fired. He wondered why not.

'Let them in, then,' said the Snowman.

~

Sam Kombothekra looked at his watch. Eleven minutes past nine. He'd given up trying to work, knowing he wouldn't be able to concentrate. The Snowman no longer wanted to see only Gibbs in his office at quarter past; he'd extended his invitation to include all of them. Sam glanced over at Sellers, who was laughing at something on Twitter, working his way through a packet of Maltesers. Hadn't it occurred to him that a mass sacking might be on the cards? Sellers was like a big kid, oblivious to the concerns of the adults around him. Gibbs' apparent lack of nerves made more sense. He must have made peace with the possibility that he'd lose his job when he decided to go rogue and follow Simon's orders instead of the ones that came from Proust via Sam. There was something Zen about Gibbs, Sam decided, then wondered what the word meant. It was a branch of Buddhism, he knew that; was it also an adjective?

As the only apprehensive person in the room, Sam wondered if he was being paranoid. Perhaps there was nothing to worry about. He and Sellers had done nothing wrong; it was hard to see how Proust could get rid of them, or why he'd want to today, when surely even he could see that what he needed was a solid team working on the new information that might lead to the closing of three cases.

Or might not. Sam was anxious to know which it would be, needed to try for the better result. Where had this right-man-for-the-job feeling come from? Part of the problem was never knowing which world he lived in: the one defined by Simon or the one defined by Proust. On Tuesday and yesterday, Proust's had been in the ascendant for Sam. Now, after Amber Hewerdine's house fire, Simon's was. It made Sam want to stay – made him want, above all, not to be forced to go. He prayed the Snowman wasn't about to take the choice away from him.

The door of Proust's office opened. Nobody came out. Sam saw Simon hovering, sensed his uncertainty about whether to stay or go. 'Come on,' he said to Sellers and Gibbs. 'Let's get it over with.' He led the way, his mind full of images of soldiers going over the top to face an onslaught of bullets. This was one thing he wouldn't miss: the despondent march towards an enclosed space in which nothing good was ever waiting for anybody.

'Progress on the arson attack?' the Snowman barked at him as he walked in. 'Or, failing that, on anything?'

'Last night's fire at the Hewerdine house has been confirmed as arson . . .' Sam began.

'Progress on the arson attack beyond stating the obvious fact that it was an arson attack?' Proust fired back. He took his eyes off Sam and moved them along the line. The four of them always stood in a line in his office, like skittles waiting to be felled by a rolling ball.

'Fire chief reckons it was intended to look deliberate,' Gibbs said. 'Fire-starter pushed a can of inflammable liquid accelerant through the letterbox.'

'He might just have been getting rid of it,' said Sellers.

'Through the letterbox? Wouldn't it be more likely he'd drop it outside the—'

'Progress, I asked for, not squabbling. Anything else?'

'Amber Hewerdine's keen to speak to Simon as soon as possible,' said Sam.

'I hope you've armed her with a stick, Sergeant.'

'Sir?'

'So that she can fight off the competition. Do you know what she wants to talk to Waterhouse about?'

'She wouldn't say much to me, but—'

'I can see her point. Why bother? If you had something important to say, would you waste time saying it to you, Sergeant?'

Here we go. 'Depends who else there was to say it to, sir.'

'Who else?' Proust intoned rhetorically, tilting his head back. 'Who else indeed. I think you've hit upon the problem there, Sergeant. There's no one else, no one of any value. This *team* is a decaying organism. Sellers, when did you last make a significant contribution to anything, apart from the canteen's cash-register? DC Gibbs, you've chosen the dark side, for reasons too chilling for a sensitive chap like myself to want to speculate about. You've joined the ranks of the dead souls. Waterhouse, King of the Dead Souls – the less said about you the better, especially since I've spent the last fifteen minutes saying it in a dozen different ways, none of which you heard. And Sergeant Kombothekra, the worst of a bad bunch.'

Sam tried not to show his surprise. *The worst*. It wasn't a label he'd ever associated with himself, any more than 'the best' was.

'Let's revisit some of your best lines, shall we, Sergeant? What did you say or do when Waterhouse took it upon himself to have a suspect brought in for interview without your knowledge or mine? What did you say when you found out he'd shared confidential case information with his wife? Nothing. Not a word. You're his sergeant. What makes you think you can sit back and leave the disciplining of him to me? Never mind taking the lead, you don't even speak up in a supportive capacity!'

Sellers was sweating. Sam could feel the heat coming off him.

'Don't expect shows of support from any of us,' Simon said quietly. 'You won't get any. Nobody supports you.'

Proust nodded as if he both wanted and had anticipated the response. 'You've all known me long enough to know my strengths and weaknesses,' he said. 'You prefer, uncharitably, to dwell on the weaknesses. Of course you do. I'm your DI. Everybody needs a punch-bag, and I'm yours. I accept it. Most of the time, I don't complain. Which is why I don't expect to hear a word of complaint from any of you now . . .' – the Snowman shook his index finger at them – '. . . because I'm about to demonstrate how fair and flexible I am, and it's going to clash with your blinkered image of me.'

Sam found it oddly comforting that they'd reached this stage already: the make-sure-not-to-catch-anyone's-eye stage, during which the inspector sang his own praises. It always followed the how-do-I-hate-you-let-me-count-the-ways stage, and signalled that Proust was at least halfway through his latest horror show.

'This morning, I was going to initiate disciplinary proceedings against DC Gibbs and DC Waterhouse – proceedings that would have resulted in their immediate suspension and their not quite so immediate but equally certain dismissal. Then I heard about the events of last night, and changed my mind. Waterhouse told us on Tuesday that Amber Hewerdine was of interest to us in connection with Katharine Allen's murder. Turns out he was right. We know more now than we knew then. I hope I don't have to spell out for you why we now have three crimes that we need to be thinking about instead of one. Sharon Lendrim's death and last night's attack on the Hewerdine house were both arson, Hewerdine and Lendrim were friends, Lendrim's daughters were in both fire-targeted houses, though removed before the attack from one and not from the other, which is interesting. Amber Hewerdine is linked to Katharine Allen's murder scene by her certainty that she's seen the words "Kind, Cruel, Kind of Cruel" on a sheet of paper that sounds as if it came from the notepad in Allen's flat. What do we think about a link or lack of one between Lendrim's death and Katharine Allen's?'

'Amber Hewerdine's the link,' said Simon. 'Whoever killed Lendrim killed Allen. We need to find out who knew we'd interviewed Hewerdine in connection with Allen's murder. Someone who knew decided to warn Hewerdine off helping us, and the warning doubled as a confession. Last night's arson had a clear message for Hewerdine: "I killed Sharon, I killed Katharine Allen, and I'll kill you if you don't keep your mouth shut."'

'Possible.' Proust nodded. 'There's another possibility: our arsonist didn't know anything about Hewerdine talking to us, and has never heard of Katharine Allen. The timing of the attack on Hewerdine's house is purely coincidental.'

'I don't believe that,' said Simon.

'I don't either,' said the Snowman. 'Which leaves us with the question of why Katharine Allen was beaten to death with a window pole and not . . .' He stopped, rubbed his index finger along his upper lip. It looked like a moving pink moustache. 'Setting fire to a flat would be a different proposition from setting fire to a house. No darkness means no invisibility. Our man might have decided he wouldn't feel comfortable standing in a well-lit corridor dripping liquid accelerant through the letterbox.'

'Or he knew he'd be able to talk his way into Kat Allen's flat, whereas he knew Sharon Lendrim and Amber Hewerdine wouldn't let him in,' said Simon.

'There's no "he",' Gibbs said. 'Hewerdine killed Lendrim and Kat Allen, and set fire to her own house. Do we know that anything went *through* the letterbox? Could it have been done from inside? Even if it couldn't, Hewerdine could have stood outside, poured the stuff into the house, then gone back in, closed the door and set fire to it.'

'Well, Sergeant Kombothekra? Are you going to answer Gibbs' question?'

'All we've been told definitely at this stage is arson. I'll need to ask more specifically if the fire could have been started from inside the house.'

'You will, won't you?' Proust agreed. 'You'll also need to rake through everything Ursula Shearer's got on the Lendrim murder. Identify any gaps. Expect to find plenty. Someone who wasn't a fireman was wandering around in a fireman's uniform – where did it come from?'

'I'm meeting DS Shearer this morning, sir. I'll ask her to bring me up to speed.'

'Good. You and she are professional soulmates. I'm sure you'll get on very well. Waterhouse, I want you—'

'It could have been a fireman,' Simon interrupted. 'We know it wasn't one from the Culver Valley; that's all we know. What about neighbouring counties?'

'Sellers, contact the fire services in Tokyo, Tahiti and Echo Island, which I hear is privately owned by the Disney family. Waterhouse, I want you focusing on Amber Hewerdine and nothing else. If Gibbs is right, you might see your way to—'

'He isn't,' said Simon.

'—persuading her to confess. That would make all our lives easier.'

'We can do that by ruling out Amber Hewerdine as a suspect.'

'Give me one good reason,' the Snowman snapped.

'Because she's obviously innocent,' said Simon.

All right, confession time. Amber's right: I lied. There was no row at Little Orchard between the two grandmothers about whether or not baby Barney ought to be given formula milk against his mother's wishes. I made it up, start to finish. I've no idea why I picked that subject for Hilary and Pam's imaginary argument; I might just as easily have said they bickered about Tony Blair's decision to go to war in Iraq. I have no idea whether Jo breast-fed or bottle-fed her children, nor what Sabina's views on the subject are, nor Pam's, nor Hilary's. The incident was pure invention on my part, so you can scratch it from the record and forget it entirely.

Or can you? I hope you're both experiencing a certain amount of confusion right now as you struggle to delete this fictional incident from your understanding of what happened at Little Orchard. Something inside you is saying, 'Hang on, I'm not sure I can forget it all that easily. I've been told it happened, after all.' Even Amber, who was there and knows for certain that it didn't happen – who protested when I claimed it did – is fighting against a sense that it can't have come from nowhere; this phantom, this non-event, must have some significance, if only in my mind.

Picture this scene, from every TV drama you've ever watched: the prosecuting barrister tells the jury, 'The defendant was heard yelling, "I'm the most dangerous murderer in town and proud of it. Check out my blood-soaked T-shirt!"' The defence barrister leaps to her feet and says, 'Objection, Your Honour, that's hearsay.' 'Sustained,' says the judge. 'The jury will disregard that last statement.' Does the jury disregard the statement? Of course not. The opposite happens: the hearsay lodges in the jurors' minds more powerfully than any other piece of evidence, because it's been officially banned. By disallowing it, the judge has tapped into an archetype that we are all aware of deep in our bones. What gets banned? Dangerous truths get banned. Banned information must therefore be true information.

My made-up row between Pam and Hilary isn't anything as respectable as hearsay. It's a downright lie. As its inventor, I can promise you that it has no relevance whatsoever. The fact that you're both finding it hard to erase proves that once you turn something into any kind of story – and I laid it on pretty thick with the detail – you make it real, you turn it into an object, albeit a conceptual object. If it's a lie, then it's both real and false, which is confusing. This is how lies and liars flourish in the world. We believe them because we would prefer not to be confused.

I wouldn't normally lie about the life experiences of one of my clients, particularly in the presence of the police. It was unprofessional of me to do so, but Amber is determined to say as little as possible, so my aim was partly to compel her to participate in what we're trying to achieve here, and partly to try and win her over with the boldness of my impropriety. Simon, you might not know why Amber respects you more than any of your colleagues, but I do, because she's told me: she admires your willingness to be unprofessional in a good cause. In Amber's mind, professional behaviour is a crutch for mediocre dullards to lean on. Truly intelligent people realise that hiding behind a professional role will inevitably involve a certain amount of counter-intuitive, inauthentic behaviour, and to get the best results from people, we must be our true selves in their company.

My true self was getting desperate to break the stalemate, and is delighted that we've had a breakthrough moment. This is what's so great about hypnotherapy: nothing can happen and nothing can happen, and you feel as if you're getting nowhere, and then suddenly a new memory comes up.

I knew Amber would contradict my lie. I also knew she wouldn't be able to speak authoritatively about what didn't happen at Little Orchard without remembering what did and remembering it powerfully. Simon, if I asked you to tell me what you did yesterday evening, you might say, 'I watched TV.' You'd be on memory autopilot, if you like. You could say those words without the memory being particularly vivid. But if I then challenged you, if I said, 'No, you didn't – you went ballroom dancing,' your truth-seeking instinct would rebel, and your memories, the weapons you would need to argue against me, would assert themselves more strongly: watching the news while drinking a cup of tea, feeling a bit chilly because the heating had gone off an hour before . . .

My lie forced Amber's memory to get its act together, and now we have more raw data to work with, so let's look at it. On Christmas Eve, when Neil said he was going to bed, Jo told him she wasn't coming with him. She stayed downstairs with her mother, sister and brother while Neil, Amber and Luke went upstairs. That much we knew already. The extra detail we can now add is that Jo, Hilary and Ritchie all looked preoccupied. They had something they wanted to discuss, or were in the middle of discussing – something important. It was obvious from all three of their faces that they were keen to be alone so that they could get on with talking about it, whatever it was. Amber might not be able to believe that it's taken her this long to remember what she now knows to be a key feature of that Christmas-Eve-going-to-bed scene, but I have no trouble believing it. We fail to remember things for a number of reasons: repression, denial and distraction are the most common ones. People often confuse repression with denial, but they're vastly different from one another: in repression, we genuinely have no idea that something happened. From the point of view of our conscious mind, it's as if it never happened, until such time as hypnotherapy or something else coaxes our subconscious into cracking open and yielding it up – crude, inaccurate metaphor, but you get the gist. Amber might have seen the piece of paper with 'Kind, Cruel, Kind of Cruel' on it at Little Orchard, and repressed the memory.

Denial's different: it's more like having a stain on your shirt sleeve that upsets you. You pull your jumper over it so that it doesn't show and almost but not quite forget that it's there. Distraction is when you don't remember something you otherwise would because your attention is elsewhere; something else is in sharp focus in the foreground, causing you to neglect the background. Perhaps Amber saw the words 'Kind, Cruel, Kind of Cruel' at Little Orchard but doesn't remember having seen them because they were the least noticeable part of a particular scene. If so, there's every reason to be hopeful. If she can suddenly remember Jo, Hilary and Ritchie having been secretive and preoccupied on Christmas Eve, she may yet remember any number of crucial details.

Amber didn't remember the strained, conspiratorial atmosphere between Jo, her mother and her brother until now because of a distraction: the stand-out feature of the episode was Neil's reaction to Jo's failure to go upstairs with him. He was disappointed, confused, irritated, and he let it show. Amber noticed because it was so unusual: generally, no one openly expresses dissatisfaction with Jo's behaviour. Jo cannot be questioned, challenged, criticised at all; everyone is scared of her, and rightly so.

The secret behind the secret. There is something badly wrong with Jo, something no one in the family knows about, not even Jo herself.

7

Thursday 2 December 2010

Charlie Zailer is looking at her watch when I arrive. There's an unopened can of 7UP on the table in front of her. Given where we are – a dingy internet café called Web & Grub, full of taxi-drivers, greasy surfaces and smudgy grey handwritten price labels – I wonder if she chose it for its air-tight container, as a health precaution. 'This won't take long,' I tell her.

She looks embarrassed. 'Take as long as you want.' She gestures for me to sit. I don't want to. I'm too full of nervous energy. 'Simon told me what happened last night,' she says. 'Are you okay?'

'Did you see anything?' *I'm not the one who needs to be answering questions.*

'No. If I had, I'd have told Simon. I saw nothing.'

She looks like someone who did not set fire to my house. I never thought she did, so there's no mental adjustment to make.

'I was the only person on the street when I posted that envelope. Did the fire destroy it?'

'No. I was awake. When I heard the fire, I was upstairs reading the notes.'

'You *heard* the fire?'

I nod. It bothers me that I can't describe the sound, apart from inaccurately.

'How long after?'

'I don't know. Maybe three quarters of an hour. I'd skimmed through the Katharine Allen notes twice before I went to look, but I don't know how long the fire had being going before I noticed it. Whoever did it could have got there ten minutes after you left.'

'Or before I arrived. If you were going to set fire to a house, would you do it straight away, soon as you got there? Or would you take your time, get your bearings first?'

'I'd get it over with and get myself out of there as quickly as I could.' I can see that she disagrees with me. 'You'd linger?'

'I'd want to familiarise myself with my surroundings. Unless I already knew them by heart.'

My legs shake. I lean my hands on the table to steady myself.

'Why don't you sit down?' she says.

Why don't I? Why am I kidding myself that I can nip in here, grab an easy answer and run to the police station with it, waving it in the air like a football scarf? *Yes, when I was outside your house last night, I saw a man who looked as if he might be called Neil loitering in the bushes with a box of matches in his hand.* She was never going to say that; I was stupid to hope she would.

My suspecting Neil makes no sense, not even to me. When I think about him in isolation, I know that he'd never set fire to anything, especially not a house with two children in it. It's only when I think about Jo that I start to wonder about Neil. Jo wouldn't do her dirty work herself if she didn't have to.

'Whoever started the fire could have been there when I was,' Charlie says. 'Could have watched me post that envelope through your letterbox.'

'Maybe you saw something you don't remember seeing,' I say, aware of how unlike myself I sound. If I had photographs of Jo and Neil on me now, would I show them to her, hoping to jog her memory? I like to think I wouldn't.

I wish I still had the luxury of being able to laugh at the idea of recovering buried memories.

First thing this morning I phoned Ginny Saxon and booked myself in for tomorrow, ten until one: three hours, without a break. Two hundred and ten pounds, plus the seventy I owe her from Tuesday's aborted session. She was resistant to the idea of spending more than an hour with me, until I explained that the urgency had more to do with murder and arson and less to do with me being a spoiled brat who can't manage on her hour-a-week ration like everyone else.

Kind, Cruel, Kind of Cruel. The memory of seeing those words is in me somewhere. It's only partially buried; I can see that piece of paper, the capital Ks and Cs . . .

'Are you . . . have you moved out?' Charlie asks.

'Temporarily.'

'Where to?'

My chest fills with something solid. It's difficult to speak when there's so much you're trying not to say. 'Extended family.' *It could be worse. You could be at Jo's.* 'I need to ask you a very big favour,' I blurt out. No point pretending it's trivial. It's the most important thing I've ever asked anyone to do for me.

And you're asking a stranger. Good plan.

'Why me?' Charlie Zailer asks. 'You hardly know me.'

I want to tell her that knowing people in the conventional sense means nothing. I know Luke, but I can't tell him about the worst thing I've ever done. I knew Sharon; I couldn't tell her either. I know Neil – we even share a fear of Jo – but I don't know if he's an ally or an enemy; I don't know if Veronique Coudert lied to us both about Little Orchard, or if Neil lied to me.

I'm pleased that Charlie asked *Why me?* instead of telling me how busy she is, how little she wants to get involved in my problems.

'Why did you give me the Katharine Allen notes after telling me you couldn't?'

She grins at the mention of her misdemeanour. 'I was pissed off with Simon. He took my notebook into work, the one you saw – waved it around in front of all his colleagues. I asked him not to, but he didn't listen. He never does. Ah, now I see why I've been chosen for the very big favour. You think you've got leverage. Any time you like, you can tell Simon I gave you those copied files.'

'I wouldn't do that.' I'm about to ask how she can think that I would. I stop myself in time. It's not the sort of question you can ask someone you've met three times.

'Make sure you don't,' she says. 'I want to use it myself at some point, to score a shock-point in an argument about who's better at screwing who over. What's the favour?'

I'm going to need to sit down for this. I choose the chair that looks least filthy.

'There's a house in Surrey called Little Orchard, a holiday let. I stayed there once, in 2003 . . .'

She holds up a hand. 'I know I said take as long as you want, but if we're starting seven years ago . . .'

'The background's not important,' I tell her. 'I want to book to stay there again. The house is advertised on a website called My Home For Hire. I emailed the owner last night. She said she wasn't renting the house out any more, but she was lying. She just doesn't want to let it to me, but . . . I need to go there again.' I'm trying to read the expression on Charlie's face. I'm hoping it's not disbelief.

'You want me to book it for you, under my name?'

I nod. 'I'll pay. It won't cost you anything.'

'I'm not encouraging you to do this, but, in theory . . . Couldn't you just book it using a made-up name?'

'Wouldn't work,' I say. 'At some point, money's going to have to change hands. Paying cash'd look too suspicious. I'd need a real bank account in a name that isn't mine, and . . . I don't have one.'

'So you thought of mine?' Charlie laughs. 'You're unbelievable.'

'All you need to do is transfer the money I'll have given you, make the arrangements for picking up the keys, find out any alarm codes . . .'

'Amber, stop. Even if I had time to drive back and forth to Surrey . . .'

'You won't have to. I've never met Veronique Coudert . . .'

'Who?'

'The owner. I've never met her. She doesn't know what I look like. I'll pick up the keys, pretending to be Charlie Zailer. None of it should put you out hardly at all.'

'And yet you described it as a very big favour.'

'It's . . . conceptually big,' I say. 'In practical terms, it's next to nothing.'

'I see. Conceptually huge because overwhelmingly bad and wrong, but I won't have to burn off too many calories.' She shakes her head. 'And the owner, this Coudert person, will agree to let the house to me because . . . I haven't been blacklisted?'

I can't bring myself to contradict her.

'Which means you have. Why?'

'I honestly have no idea,' I tell her.

'Can I be equally honest with you?' She sticks her little finger into the opening of her 7UP can and tries to lift it off the table. It falls back down with a thud. 'If you were asking this favour of your best friend, it'd be inappropriate, but for you to ask me, a police officer . . .'

'My best friend is dead. She was murdered,' I snap. 'Someone set fire to her house two years ago.'

Charlie nods. 'Simon told me. You must know plenty of people, Amber. Why are you asking me to do this? Why not Simon? What time are you seeing him?' She looks at her watch. I hate her for how much she knows, how much power she has when I have so little.

'Why . . .' I have to stop to clear my throat. 'Why would I ask Simon? He's . . . This isn't . . .' My inability to produce an intelligible sequence of words frightens me. Last night, for the first time since my insomnia began, I had no sleep at all.

'It's got nothing to do with Katharine Allen's death,' I tell Charlie.

'Hasn't it?'

'No.'

It's true. I don't know that Jo has done anything wrong, or that Neil has. I don't know that there's any connection between them and Little Orchard beyond their having stayed there once. I don't know that they hid anything in the locked study, or know what's hidden there. Maybe nothing is. Hidden and private are two different things.

'You're going to tell Simon about this conversation, aren't you?'

'Yes. He's my husband, and we both work for the police. If you thought you'd be able to persuade me to do your very big favour and keep it from him . . .'

'What about last night? The notes you gave me – you're happy to keep that from him.' Is she right? Have I been thinking of it as leverage? Tiredness is like a fog that has settled on my brain and obscured everything; I can no longer negotiate my way around safely. I have no idea what I'm doing, thinking or feeling.

'I *was* happy to keep it from him,' Charlie says. 'Now I'm thinking I'd better come clean about that too.' She sighs. 'Look, Amber, I was an idiot last night, and you're being one now. I know you haven't killed anybody. I'm as convinced of that as Simon is, but if you want to know what I really think . . .'

I don't. I never said I did.

She takes my silence as a sign that she should go on. 'Your wanting to book this Little Orchard place again is connected. To your friend's death, to Katharine Allen, to the fire last night. I don't know what the connection is. I don't think you're sure either. If you were you'd go to Simon, if you could guarantee you wouldn't end up looking stupid. I'm not him, but I'm connected to him. Whether you realise it or not, that's why you asked me. That and my track record for preposterous behaviour, for which I take full responsibility.'

She's smiling at me. I'm in no mood to be smiled at.

'Take it straight to Simon,' she says. 'I know it's not what you want to hear, but it's the best advice I can give you.'

~

I don't like taking advice. I am not good at switching off my own instincts, forcing myself to tune into someone else's. I know how wrong I can be. A hunch tells me that Charlie Zailer's judgement is less reliable than mine. I don't recognise myself in too many of the statements I hear her make about me. She told me I'd have approached Simon and not her if I was sure Little Orchard was connected to Katharine Allen's death, if I could guarantee I wouldn't look stupid.

Not true. Apart from Luke, Dinah and Nonie, I don't care what people think of me. If I mention to Simon a possible connection between Little Orchard and Katharine Allen's murder, I know what his next move will be. He would have no trouble getting into the locked study; if you're police and you're investigating a murder, you're allowed to break down the door.

Whatever's in that room, I want to see it before he does.

Why? Because you think you'll find out something about Jo and Neil? Because Neil is Luke's brother, and if he might have killed someone . . .

How can you even think it?

Neil has done nothing. Lack of sleep is turning me insane.

I haven't told Simon because there is no solid reason to think there's any link between Little Orchard and any murder, Katharine Allen's or Sharon's. A connection in my mind isn't the same thing as a connection in the real world.

He will find out anyway, as soon as he gets home tonight, probably. Let Charlie tell him; my throat is already raw and inflamed on one side from talking too much. I wonder if I'm getting ill. When I do, this is where I always feel it first: up near my tonsils.

If he's going to find out tonight, that gives me only this afternoon to do . . . what? I don't know how serious I am. Not serious enough to put into words what I might do.

I rub my neck as Simon looks over what he's written, checking he's got it all down. 'Are you going to have to tell anyone about the DriveTech course?' I ask him.

'I ought to. But . . . as long as I bear it in mind as we go along, I should be able to get away with keeping it to myself. I can't make you any promises, though. Sorry.' He looks up at me expectantly. 'Are you good for another half hour or so? I've got a few more questions.'

I'm not sure my eyes will stay open for much longer. I need to sleep. If Simon would only leave, I know I'd be able to black out for at least an hour, curled up on this lumpy floral sofa. I am not allowing myself to hope that I might sleep better here, at Hilary's house, than I do at home. I don't know where the idea came from, and I've been trying to push it out of my mind ever since I first became aware of it lurking.

Another detail I haven't shared with Simon: how Luke and the girls and I ended up here. I made sure to present our new living arrangements as unmysterious and self-explanatory: we're staying with our extended family. He hasn't queried it because it makes sense. What makes less sense is that, in spite of Hilary's house being easily large enough to accommodate six people, she and Kirsty have temporarily relocated to Jo and Neil's, which, as of today, is even more problematically not-big-enough-for-the-people-in-it than it was before.

It was the only way. I'm trying not to think about how it happened, because it terrifies me. It makes no sense; it made none while it was happening, and yet everyone present, including me, knew what was coming and greeted it as if it were an old familiar friend when it arrived. We are all so used to the madness; no one is thrown by it. As soon as we were alone, I said to Luke, 'This is beyond irrational.' 'I'm not complaining,' he said. 'We've got a big house all to ourselves for as long as we need it, and it's on the school bus route. Count yourself lucky we didn't end up at Jo's. Would have been a nightmare.'

That was when it hit me: we might all be used to it, but I am the only one who thinks of it as 'the madness'.

It should never have felt inevitable that we would end up at Jo's. It scares me that Luke doesn't see this as plainly as I do. She tried to insist we move in with them; it was the first thing out of her mouth, before 'Are you all okay?' We could have said, 'No, thank you.' Instead, we ummed and ahhed and tried tentatively to suggest that having us all descend on her might not be the best thing for her. We appealed to her self-interest and nothing else.

Because there is nothing else.

She told us not to be ridiculous, that she'd love to have us all to stay, and started talking about special beds that pull out of fat-armed chairs, with properly sprung mattresses. I wasn't really listening. I was trying to alter something in my brain in order to make it possible for me to say yes without wanting to die. Did I wonder how Luke felt, or was that later? I knew he wouldn't be keen on the cramped conditions at Jo's, or on living with his dad for the first time in twenty-five years, but was it any more than that for him? I couldn't face asking him how he feels about Jo, and still can't. He would want to know why I was asking, turn the question back on me.

Hilary saved us. She said, 'I've got a better idea, Jo. Why don't Kirsty and I move in here for a few weeks? You and Kirsty would be able to spend more time together, which would do wonders for both of you, and Amber, Luke and the girls could move into our house and—'

'Thank you,' I said before she'd finished. 'That would be so kind of you, Hilary. Are you sure you don't mind?' She didn't answer straight away. I worried I'd misunderstood, but how could I have? There had been nothing ambiguous about her suggestion. That's when I noticed that everyone was looking at Jo. Everyone: Luke, Neil, Hilary, Sabina, Quentin, Dinah and Nonie. William and Barney were upstairs asleep. Part of me was surprised Jo hadn't woken them too; the family meeting could have been better attended, the room fuller. Quentin, Hilary and Sabina had all been summoned from their beds for no reason that I could understand. Hilary had had to wake a neighbour to look after Kirsty while she went out. Ritchie, Jo's brother, had been invited but had pleaded illness. He had an upset stomach.

'Brilliant, Mum!' Jo grinned. 'Perfect. I can't believe I didn't think of it.'

Did Hilary sense that I was desperate not to stay at Jo's but too afraid to say so? Was she saving me, knowingly?

'Amber? Are you awake?' *Simon's voice.*

My eyelids are as heavy as concrete. I force them open. 'The answer to that question will always be yes. I don't have any other answers, apart from the ones I've already given you.'

'You're better at answering questions than anyone I've ever

interviewed,' Simon says gravely. 'That's why I've got more, because you've told me so much. Does that make sense?'

Yes. I'm too exhausted to try to formulate unnecessary words.

'Your sister-in-law, Johannah. Jo. You say you told her before she stood in for you on the DriveTech course that she had to remember all the details to tell you later. Why was it so important to you to have those details?'

'I was supposed to have been there. I knew what Jo and I were doing was . . . well, I don't think it was wrong, actually – I don't think it matters in the grand scheme of things if people lie about going on pointless courses that are a waste of everyone's time – but I knew it was illegal. Officially, it was supposed to be me on that course, and it wasn't, but at least if I knew exactly what had happened, if I could feel as if I'd been there . . .' I shake my head impatiently, sick of my longwinded justification. 'Self-deception is the short answer,' I say.

'And Jo, when you told her you wanted to know about the course in microscopic detail, she didn't query it, didn't wonder why?'

'No. I think she assumed I'd need something to say, in case people asked me how it went.'

Is he dissatisfied with my explanation? It's hard to tell. There's something critical about the set of his features even when he's dispensing praise.

'You described Jo as being "addicted to the moral high ground". Why would she agree to do something illegal that she herself thinks is wrong?'

'She's equally addicted to power. If she sacrifices her . . . moral purity as a massive favour to me, I owe her one.' I chew my lip, unhappy with my answer. It's true, but there's so much more to it than that. 'She's often vicious to me, but . . . quickly, almost like a subliminal flash of nastiness, over before I know it. And she's never quite horrible enough, or for long enough. I never feel I can prove it. I've started to wonder recently if it could be deliberate.'

'How do you mean?' Simon asks.

'A tactic. She reels you in by doing more for you than anyone could ever expect: sacrificing more, cooking more, saving you from all bad things. Then, when she's got you close enough and trusting again, she aims another killer jab at your soul.'

'Go on.'

Really? He must be a masochist.

I have official permission to say some of the things I spend my life trying not to say. 'She should either do what she can to help me, without trying to make me feel guilty, or not help me because it's against her principles. One or the other. I didn't ask her to go on the DriveTech course for me. She offered. I should have said no. I'd have lost my licence for a bit. So what? Some of the oldest points on it are due to come off soon anyway. Sorry, Jo, but you don't get to do the evil deed and still pass yourself off as the virtuous one. If it's so terribly wrong, don't do it unless what you really want is to be seen performing a grand gesture, so much greater a sacrifice because you *doubly* disapprove. You disapprove of my willingness to break the law by having you stand in for me on the course, and you disapprove of my reason for not going on it myself.' *Damn*. I seem to be yelling at Simon as if he were Jo. How embarrassing. 'Sorry,' I mutter under my breath.

Why do I find it easier to free-associate in a police interview than in a hypnotherapy clinic? Perhaps Simon Waterhouse can cure my insomnia.

'Carry on,' he says. I decide that he would make a good therapist. Not demanding that I design a staircase, that's the secret of his success.

'Jo got exactly what she wanted out of the situation. She got to bear the burden of my sin, like Jesus or something, and pass herself off as a saint. She wasn't doing it for me. She made that clear. I would have deserved everything I got. Dinah and Nonie were the innocents who couldn't be allowed to suffer . . .' – I make quote marks in the air with my fingers – '. . . "any more than they already have".'

'She said that?'

I nod, pleased that he thinks it worthy of special notice. Ever so subtly, Jo placed me in the same category as Sharon's murderer and portrayed herself as Dinah and Nonie's rescuer.

Simon is looking at me, waiting.

'I need to be able to drive the girls around,' I explain. 'To friends' houses, horse-riding, ice-skating . . . just about everything. For their sake, Jo allowed herself to be morally compromised. It's always for someone else's sake. A few years ago, I confided in her about something, asked her to keep it from Luke. Something I'd done.'

Why are you telling him this?

I'm not. Describing how Jo responded to the secret and revealing the secret are two different things.

'I didn't know Jo as well then as I do now, otherwise I'd never have told her. I was still dazzled by her good side. She agreed not to say anything – for Luke's sake, on that occasion. And I'm expected to be grateful to her for being willing to sacrifice her pristine moral integrity because she cares so much about whoever I'm currently failing. Sorry if none of this makes sense.'

'It makes sense.' Simon, writing in his notebook, shifts in the green wing-back chair. Torn threads of its fabric rest on his shoulder like skinny green fingers. Most of Hilary's furniture has an air of house-clearance-sale about it. She is too busy looking after Kirsty to think about furniture. In spite of its disrepair – cracked and flaking paint on the windows, pieces of coloured stained glass missing from the panel above the front door – it's a lovely house. *Especially when the alternative is Jo's.*

'You know what really gets me?' I say. 'Jo could have told Luke what I asked her not to tell him. What was stopping her? She kept saying *I* had to tell him, laid such a guilt trip on me about how she hated lying to him that it took me more than a year to notice that, hate it or not, she was doing it anyway. If not telling someone something they'd want to know counts as lying.' I sigh, close my eyes, force them open. 'When I said I wasn't going to tell Luke, ever, it was as if Jo didn't hear me. She just kept saying I had to tell him, and the reason she gave over and over again was herself: for as long as we were colluding to keep it from him, she was morally compromised.'

Simon is frowning. 'You say she kept quiet for Luke's sake, but if she tried to persuade you to tell him . . .'

'Yes, for his sake: he deserved to hear it from me, he deserved my confession. Translation: she wanted trouble for me that I couldn't accuse her of directly causing. That's why she didn't put her so-called principles into practice and tell Luke. Morally compromised! As if otherwise she wouldn't be, as if, without my murky secret staining her soul, she'd be free of sin! Funny that she doesn't seem to think being obnoxious to me whenever she feels like it affects her moral status at all.'

'Playing devil's advocate for a minute – didn't you put her in a difficult situation by confiding in her? If you knew she wouldn't be happy about participating in a deception . . .'

'I needed someone to talk to. I thought she was my friend.' I rub the hollows under my eyes with my fingers. They feel too deep, too tender. 'Isn't there something admirable about accepting that other people's messes have fuck all to do with you and resisting the urge to cast yourself in the leading role, as judge? Accepting that your thoughts and actions are ethically irrelevant, because it's not *your* dilemma, giving someone else's morality room to breathe, even if it's . . . questionable?'

She turned out to be right, though, didn't she? You told her it wouldn't matter, but it did.

I wonder if Jo felt morally compromised at Little Orchard, when she forced Neil out of bed in the middle of the night and refused to explain why they had to take William and Barney and disappear. I'd bet all the money I have that she didn't; since the need for secrecy originated with her rather than with me, wrongness can't have been involved.

'I don't suppose you want to tell me what this secret was?' Simon asks.

'I'd tell you if it were relevant to anything. Trust me, it isn't.'

'You said Jo disapproved of your reason for not going on the DriveTech course yourself?'

'I was planning to, until Terry Bond phoned me.' From one upsetting story to another, without a break. It would be rude to groan. None of this is Simon's fault.

'Terry Bond as in former landlord of the Four Fountains pub?'

I nod. 'He's in Truro now, but we talk from time to time. He rang to tell me his restaurant was finally open. He'd wanted to open months ago, but there were various setbacks. He'd organised a buffet lunch to celebrate, sort of like a launch party. He said he had to have me there or it wouldn't be worth doing. It was the same day as the DriveTech course and very short notice, but . . . I couldn't say no. I didn't want to say no.'

Simon waits for me to go on.

'He needed me there.' I would probably be crying if my eyes had any moisture left in them, if lack of sleep hadn't dried it all up. 'Because of everything that had happened with Sharon and because . . . I'm important to him in my own right. And for the sake of a bullshit driving course . . .'

'You're important to Terry Bond? Why?'

'I knew he wasn't a murderer. I convinced the police, in the end. Or, if you'd prefer Jo's version, I didn't know anything and was kidding myself: Terry might well have killed Sharon, and, since I can't claim to know that he didn't, I betrayed my best friend's memory by going to the opening of his restaurant.'

'So if I speak to Bond, he'll be able to alibi you?' Simon says.

'Yes. If you're willing to take the word of a former murder suspect.'

'Did you try to unbook the course, book yourself in for another date?'

'I'd already done that as many times as they let you.'

'So . . . what you told us about the man on the course called Ed, about his daughter dying in a road accident – Jo told you that?'

I nod.

'Did she mention that she sounded off about drivers' rights and freedom?'

'Jo?' I laugh. 'If someone on the course said that, it can't have

been her. She's a big fan of punishment for minor misdemeanours.'
Of course she is. Punishment is how self-proclaimed good people
get to hurt others and still look good.

Simon studies his notes. 'The woman calling herself Amber
said it. There was only one on the course.' He looks at me to
check I've understood. 'Cars are lethal machines, she said – if we
want them in our lives, we have to accept some road deaths.
What we shouldn't accept is that we must all drive unnaturally
slowly and think about death all the time, forced to worry about
speed cameras, fines; made to go on pointless courses. She didn't
tell you any of this?'

'No. Those aren't Jo's opinions. They're the opposite.'

'Maybe she was impersonating you not only in name,' Simon
suggests. 'Could she have thought those might be your views?'

A shiver makes my skin prickle. Then I think again. *Just because
it scares me doesn't mean it's true.* 'Yes, but . . . she wouldn't want
to air those views. Jo wants her opinions to be heard and no one
else's.'

'You're on record as saying that someone from the residents'
association murdered Sharon,' Simon changes the subject. 'Is that
what you really think?'

'I never said that. I said they *could* have, and I pointed out that,
since Sharon had switched her allegiance from them to Terry over
the issue of the pub's extended licence, they were the ones with the
motive, not him. It was fucking outrageous the way they queued
up to accuse him.'

But you never really believed one of them was a killer, did you?

'Amber? Are you all right?'

'Fine,' I lie. 'Tired, that's all.'

'Who do you think murdered Sharon?'

Nobody. Nobody.

I will not allow a name to come into my mind. I manage a shrug.

'Do you think it's the same person that torched your house last
night?'

Is he serious? How am I supposed to know that?

You know.

'Try not to worry,' Simon says, having done his best to worry me. 'There'll be a police presence here for the foreseeable future, as well as at Dinah and Nonie's school. All their teachers are aware of the situation.'

I manage to restrain myself from saying that I've seen the police presence outside Hilary's house, such as it is, and I'm not impressed: so far, it's been one young uniformed bobby with a shaving rash and a too-loud car radio.

'Just a couple more questions about Dinah and Nonie Lendrim,' Simon says, as if they're nothing to do with me, just two random girls who don't even share my surname. If the adoption goes through, Dinah and Nonie will still be Lendrim. Luke joked about adding both of our surnames to theirs. 'Triple-barrelling them', he called it. Dinah and Nonie Hewerdine-Utting-Lendrim. He asked me if I thought the double-barrellers at school would feel threatened. We laughed about it.

'Do you know who their father is, or fathers?' Simon asks.

'No. Neither did Sharon. She had artificial insemination, both times.'

He looks as if he's not quite sure what that means.

'She bought donor sperm from some private place. That's all I know. She made me swear not to tell anyone.' *I've no way of knowing she'd have wanted me to make an exception for you, but that's what I'm telling myself.*

'And Marianne, Sharon's mother – she's against the adoption, even though she doesn't want the girls herself and doesn't mind you and Luke being their legal guardians?'

I nod. 'It's only the adoption she wants to block.'

'Why?'

Because she's a vile witch. I try to formulate a more open-minded, informative answer. 'She doesn't see the need. Dinah and Nonie live with us already, we're their guardians . . . Marianne thinks that for us to become their parents would be denying Sharon's existence, pretending she was never their mother. It's rubbish!' I snap. 'Sharon will always be their mother. Luke and I would be their adoptive parents. It's different. It's not an either-or.'

'But . . . you said before, things'd be pretty much as they are now, in practical terms. Why does it matter so much to you and Luke to adopt them?'

'Are you asking if we're infertile? We're not.'

'No.' He looks surprised. 'That wasn't what I meant.'

I mumble an apology. Are most people embarrassed by their own idiocy as regularly as I am?

'It matters to us because it matters to Dinah and Nonie,' I tell him. 'They want a mum and dad.' Does he understand? Even if he does, his understanding is worthless if he can also see Marianne's point of view: that there's no need. *If there's no need, if nothing would change, why go through a legal battle that will serve no purpose other than to waste time and money, upset the girls, upset a poor elderly lady who has already lost her only daughter?* I take a deep breath, remind myself that Simon hasn't said any of this, nor do I have any reason to believe it's what he thinks.

I speak to him as if I'm addressing a press conference. People who issue statements to the press don't always tell the truth. They take what they wish was true and present it as fact. 'Dinah and Nonie want parents, and they're going to get them,' I say, as if no other outcome is possible.

I'm starting to get an inkling of why Amber might find it so hard to let go of the Little Orchard mystery. Because she is clever and, whether she's aware of it or not, highly intuitive, she alone in the extended family senses that there is something badly off-kilter about Jo. Neil, Hilary and Sabina probably think of Jo as sensitive – a little bossy and controlling, maybe – but only Amber perceives it as anything more sinister or dangerous than that. Yet Amber sees Jo regularly, and so from a factual point of view she knows that everything in Jo's life is above board. The only unknown is the unsolved puzzle: where did Jo go when she disappeared that Christmas? Why did she disappear? Why did she reappear?

The mystery behind the mystery; Amber is hoping that the answer to the more localised question might bring with it the answer to the one that constantly evades clear definition, and so can never be asked.

It doesn't have to work like that. We can do it the other way round. Let me prove it. Thanks to Amber's rather incredible powers of verbal historical re-enactment, I am now confident that I can solve the more elusive puzzle decisively, although I still have no idea where Jo, Neil and the boys disappeared to, or why.

Everything I've heard about Jo tells me that she's suffering from narcissistic personality disorder. She's a classic psychologically abusive narcissist. She fears aloneness so much that she stuffs her house full of as many people as possible; she's cruel and critical, doesn't allow others their points of view; she's self-contradictory. Amber, everything you've said about Jo being vicious one minute, then requiring you to participate in her pretence that her outburst never happened – that's textbook narcissistic personality disorder. You yourself told me that Sharon diagnosed it, though she probably only intended to make a joke when she referred to you as a source of narcissistic supply to Jo. Sharon knew all about dangerous narcissists from her experience with her own mother, of course. Narcissists unleash their venom on you when they're feeling bad, in the way that you or I might burp loudly if we had wind. Once the trapped air is released, we feel better: normal again. A narcissist feels no guilt and has no awareness that his or her unpleasant eruptions might adversely affect others.

Simon, you're looking uncomfortable. How can I diagnose a woman I've never met? Unfortunately, with narcissists, remote diagnosis is almost always the best you can do. Most of them hate and fear the idea of psychotherapy. They denigrate and ridicule it to anyone who will listen. They accuse therapists of being sick and depraved, filling their patients' heads with lies. Narcissists cause few psychological problems to themselves, being happy to deny the truth about their disorder forever and assume the world is to blame for everything that goes wrong for them. It's the husbands, wives, children and colleagues of narcissists that seek therapy in their thousands – literally – because of the suffering inflicted on them by the narcissists in their lives.

And before Amber points out that Jo is devoted to her children . . . Narcissists are, as long as those children reflect well on them and treat them as the font of all wisdom. As soon as the adorable accessories start to want to be a bit independent, or develop ideas of their own that aren't necessarily in accordance with the narcissist's views, God help them.

Let's bring this back to Christmas Eve at Little Orchard. Jo doesn't socialise with friends, and seems to have no interest in making any. Her preferred company is family: her family of origin, the family she's made with Neil, and in-laws like Amber and Luke. Chances are her family of origin is where she suffered whatever trauma caused her to become a narcissist, but because narcissism is all about repressing real pain and believing instead in a false, idealised version of one's self, life and history, Jo will have idealised her childhood, her mother, her siblings – perhaps to the point of worship, of believing they're perfect.

People who overvalue family – and someone with no friends has to fall into that category – almost always esteem the family they were born into more highly than the family they were instrumental in making. Easy to see why: their birth family was where the importance of family above all else was instilled in them, the notion of 'Everything you could possibly need and want is here within these walls, so there's no need to venture out.' The birth family, or whoever's in control of it, would be foolish to brainwash its children into believing that once they grow up and marry and have children of their own, that 'chosen' family will trump the pre-existing one. The opposite happens: to preserve its own strength and influence, the birth family instils in its children the belief that, while the chosen family is of course important because family is paramount, it's never going to be quite as important as the family of origin.

You must both have met women who ignore their husband's opinion but bow down to their father's? Men who force their young children to deny their own needs if those needs are inconvenient to Granny or Grandpa? Jo is a classic example, possibly the daughter of a narcissist herself. Does Hilary mind being needed by Kirsty for every tiny thing, or does she rely on that need to boost her own ego and make her feel important? Narcissists tend both to come from and to create families that overvalue family. They have to. Who would want to be friends with a person who behaves so appallingly and so erratically? Family members are easier to brainwash and find it harder to escape.

Amber, on the other hand, is only Jo's sister-in-law. She could easily escape. She could say to Luke this evening, 'Jo's a bitch. I don't want to see her any more.' Why doesn't she?

The mystery behind the mystery.

Neil, Jo's husband, has no idea why he was woken in the middle of the night on Christmas Eve 2003 and forced to leave the house in secret. He doesn't need to be told, does he? He's family, yes, but not blood. He's not a member of Jo's first family, the family that stayed in the lounge after everyone else went to bed to discuss something secret and important.

If anyone knows what made Jo decide that she, Neil and the boys needed to vanish that night, it's going to be Hilary, Jo's mum, or Ritchie, her brother. And whether they know or not, I'd put money on the vanishing act having been somehow caused by or linked to that private conversation in the lounge.

Are you all right, Simon? Do you want a glass of water?

8

2/12/2010

'Do you appreciate your parents?' Marianne Lendrim asked, as if she were the one conducting the interview. When she'd agreed to come in so willingly, Gibbs had assumed that willingness would extend to answering his questions. He'd been wrong. So far she'd done all the asking. His insistence that he wasn't able to tell her anything because the investigation was confidential didn't seem to put her off at all. This, about his parents, was the first thing she'd asked that he was able to answer.

'I get on all right with them,' he told her.

'Getting on with them is easy. Do you appreciate everything they've done for you?'

'Probably not as much as I should.' It was nothing personal. According to Olivia, Gibbs was insufficiently appreciative of most things. 'It's not your fault,' she'd told him. 'I blame your parents, even though I've never met them. The children of enthusiasts grow up to be enthusiasts. Did your parents ever point out beautiful things to you when you were little? Did they talk about beauty and joy, did they know how to have *fun*? A lot of people don't.'

Gibbs' mum and dad didn't talk much at all, and when they did, it was about nothing in particular. Just the usual shit, same as most people. Gibbs had more in common with his parents than he did with Olivia. Beauty and joy? No one he knew talked about them, and it was obvious why not. Even thinking about them felt wrong when you were sitting across a table from Marianne Lendrim, their diametric opposite. Her grey hair was plaited and wound into two Cumberland-sausage-style circles behind her ears. On either side of her nose, her cheeks drooped like two empty pink bags. Her expression was superior and critical, as if nothing she saw or heard suited her at all. Her clothes wouldn't have suited anyone: an expensive-looking red velvet skirt with a slit in the side and a visible silk lining, worn with black woolly tights and bulky black and grey trainers. Was she planning to sprint to Buckingham Palace for an audience with the Queen as soon as Gibbs had finished with her?

'If I were you, I'd start appreciating your ma and pa,' Marianne advised him. 'You don't want to die young, do you?'

'I didn't say I don't appreciate them. What's me dying got to do with it?'

'Children who don't appreciate their parents tend to die young. Sharon did.' Gibbs attributed the glee in her voice to her mistaken assumption that she'd shocked and scared him.

'Sharon died because someone set fire to her house,' he said. 'Was that someone you?'

'You know it wasn't,' Marianne barked at him. She got angry whenever he tried to steer the conversation. She wanted to hold forth without interruption. 'I was in Venice.'

'Did you have someone else set fire to Sharon's house on your behalf?'

'No, and if you're going to—'

'Then her dying can't be anything to do with her being unappreciative of you as a mother, unless I'm missing something,' Gibbs said.

A smug smile appeared between the two crumpled pink cheek-bags. 'Think of all the great writers and artists who died young: Kafka, Keats, Proust, almost any you care to name. Their biographies will tell you illness killed them, but what caused the illness?'

'Spoken to all their doctors, have you?'

'Instead of cherishing their parents and honouring them, they perceived them as problems. Obstacles. It stands to reason: if you feel ingratitude and resentment towards the people who gave you life, you're attacking the life force inside you. That's the cause of nearly all illness.'

Gibbs wished he had a job that didn't involve listening to so much crap. If he'd been sacked this morning, it would have been someone else's turn by now. He could have lived his whole life without meeting Marianne Lendrim.

'Think about the people you know. Who are the robust ones? Who are the ones always off work with a cold or a migraine? Healthy people respect and appreciate their parents. If you don't believe me, do your own research. You'll come and find me to tell me how right I was. You won't be the first, I can promise you that. If you're harbouring any kind of negativity towards your parents in your heart, your body will attack its own vital energy. It's just a matter of time.' A cunning look appeared on Marianne's face. 'This Katharine Allen person – how did *she* feel about her parents? She died young too.'

'There was no problem between Kat and her parents,' said Gibbs.

'So you say. You can't know that.'

'Kat Allen was beaten to death. It's hard to see how your theory could apply to her, or Sharon. Can negative attitudes start house fires? Can they bring metal poles crashing down on people's heads?'

Marianne threw him a pitying look. 'I'm not God. I don't know everything about the laws of cause and effect. What I do know is this: if you send jagged heartwaves out into the world, they end up coming back to you in ways you can't possibly anticipate.'

'So Sharon didn't appreciate you. Did you appreciate her?'

Marianne laughed as if the question was ridiculous. 'I was her mother. Mothers are supposed to love their daughters, not appreciate them. Daughters sacrifice nothing for their mothers, nothing at all. Appreciation and respect are what children owe their parents, and it's a one-way debt, just as the duty of care is one-way, parent to child.'

Gibbs was baffled.

'I never stopped loving Sharon,' Marianne told him. 'Though God knows, from any objective standpoint you'd have to say she was unloveable.'

'Where were you last night between midnight and 2 a.m. ?' Gibbs asked.

'In bed, asleep. I usually am, in the middle of the night.'

'Alone?'

'Yes.'

'Do you remember where you were on Tuesday 2 November?'

'I work on Tuesdays, as a volunteer at the infirmary,' said Marianne. 'I must have been there. I haven't taken any days off recently.'

'Katharine Allen was killed between 11 a.m. and 1 p.m. on Tuesday 2 November,' Gibbs told her. 'What did you do during your lunch hour on that day, do you remember?'

'Well, I didn't kill a girl I've never heard of, if that's what you're implying.' Marianne stared at him with contempt. 'I get a free lunch from the canteen when I volunteer, and that's where I always go, with my magazine and my crossword – ask anyone who works there.'

Gibbs planned to, though it was hard to summon enthusiasm for the idea when he already knew what he'd hear. Marianne Lendrim was telling the truth. She was right up there on the list of people Gibbs hoped never to meet again, but she hadn't murdered Kat Allen and she hadn't killed her daughter. Until a law was passed outlawing unpleasantness, there was nothing he could lock her up for or charge her with.

~

Having done the right thing and refused to do Amber Hewerdine's very big favour, Charlie saw no reason why she shouldn't visit the My Home For Hire website and have a look at the house Amber claimed was nothing to do with Katharine Allen's murder. Little Orchard. She typed the name into the search box, thinking that she didn't like it much. There was something falsely modest about it. 'An orchard? Yes, but only a teensy one.' There was no other reason for it to have that name, and anyone with an orchard at the bottom of their garden would do better to be honest and call their house Lucky Rich Git Manor. Or *Manoir*, since the owner, Veronique Coudert, was presumably French.

Why was nothing happening? The words 'Little Orchard' were still sitting in the search box; Charlie had forgotten to press enter.

She did so as the phone on her desk started to ring. It was Liv. 'Got a minute?' she asked Charlie cheerfully, as if no long silence had ever stretched between them.

If you're going to tell me you and Gibbs have finished, I've got all day. 'No. I'm working.'

'Liar. What are you really doing?'

Charlie made a face at the phone. 'What do you want, Liv?'

'This Sharon Lendrim woman who died in a fire, whose children—'

'You shouldn't know any of that,' Charlie cut her off, battling against the usual struggle-for-breath feeling that accompanied bad news.

'Neither should you,' said Liv. *And I'm going to tell.* If only she'd show her true colours and say that next, Charlie thought, it would be satisfying in a funny sort of way.

'True. I shouldn't know about it either.' *The difference is that I work for the police and you don't. And I'm married to Simon, not just shagging him while we wait for him to have twins and for me to marry someone else.*

'I was thinking: given that Kat Allen starred in some TV stuff when she was younger . . .'

'Liv, I'm not going to talk to you about a case that's nothing to do with either of us.'

'Fine.'

Charlie heard a loud click. She was suspicious. Since when was Olivia so easy to get rid of? This was the second time in a week that she'd ended a conversation, which was something the old Liv would never have done. Whatever the situation, she always wanted to carry on discussing it until you were slumped on the floor with blood trickling out of your ears.

No, Charlie wasn't going to allow herself to fall into that trap. There was no old Liv and no new Liv. Her sister was her sister, the same person she'd always been.

She can afford to end conversations now; she doesn't have to cling any more. She's in the middle of the action, whether you like it or not. There's no getting rid of her.

Now that this had occurred to Charlie, and now that she was looking at photographs of a wisteria-covered red-brick house that instantly, for some reason, made her think of an upmarket old people's home, she found she'd lost interest in Little Orchard. Liv's phone call had taken all the fun out of it.

You're supposed to be at work, not having fun. Specifically, Charlie was supposed to be drafting a document called 'Crisis Intervention in a Multi-Agency Environment: A Guide for Practitioners'. To say that it wasn't what she fancied doing this afternoon would have been putting it mildly.

She clicked on 'Check Availability'. There seemed to be some bookings, despite the house allegedly being no longer hireable. Had Veronique Coudert blacklisted Amber, as Amber suspected? Would there be any harm in Charlie putting it to the test? She could send an email, ask about availability. Would it matter, as long as she backed out before any money had to change hands? As long as she didn't tell Amber what she'd done, which she wouldn't?

She clicked on 'Contact the Owner', and drafted as short a message as possible, without even a 'Dear Sir or Madam' or a 'Yours faithfully'. She didn't want to waste any more time than she had to, so she stuck to the basics: was Little Orchard available for any of the weekends in January 2011? She pressed send, annoyed with herself for feeling guilty. The part of what Amber had wanted her to do that was wrong was the part she had no intention of doing: booking the house so that Amber could stay there in her name, without the owner's permission. Outrageous. A simple enquiry, on the other hand, was harmless.

Charlie wondered why she felt the need to keep telling herself that. She wondered what Simon would think. At what point would she tell him?

She sipped her cold tea, wishing it was hot, but not enough to do anything about it. One of three things would happen: Veronique Coudert wouldn't reply, or else she'd reply and say that the house was available, or she'd say that it wasn't.

Whatever she does, you'll have no idea what it means.

Charlie knew she should tell Simon straight away. Or Sam. The name Veronique Coudert did not feature in the Katharine Allen files, Charlie knew that, but it was possible Coudert was connected to the Sharon Lendrim case. Somewhere in Rawndesley nick there might be files full of her name. Or she could be bugger all to do with anything criminal. Which would mean that Amber Hewerdine had even more nerve than Charlie had credited her with, if she'd tried to enlist the help of a police sergeant simply because she was put out not to be able to rent the holiday home of her choice. *Cheeky cow*.

Why had Liv phoned? What had she been about to say? Something to do with Katharine Allen having acted in a few films as a child – why was that important? Phoning her sister back was out of the question. Charlie decided instead to re-read all the Katharine Allen notes, see if she could work out what it was that had drawn Liv's attention.

She had a new email, from littleorchardcobham@yahoo.co.uk. She clicked on 'Open Message' and saw that Amber had been right about having been blacklisted. The owner of Little Orchard, whose entirely un-French name Charlie did not recognise, was happy to let the house to Charlie, it seemed. So why not to Amber?

And if this woman whose email Charlie was looking at now was the owner of Little Orchard, as she claimed to be, who was Veronique Coudert?

~

Having said goodbye to Ursula Shearer and pushed a sandwich down his throat that he'd barely tasted, Sam's next task was to drive to Rawndesley and interview Ritchie Baker, brother of Amber Hewerdine's sister-in-law, Jo. Sam didn't know why this loosely related man should be of particular interest, but Simon had asked him to speak to Baker, ask him about last night, get a sense of what he was like as a person. Oh, and assess the state of his health insofar as that was possible, given Sam's lack of medical qualifications. That part, the least achievable of the stated aims, had been thrown in at the end, almost as an afterthought. 'I'll tackle the rest of the clan myself,' Simon had said grimly, and Sam hadn't been able to help picturing Simon, with a snarl on his face similar to the one that often resided there, knocking one family member after another to the ground.

Ought he to worry about following orders from Simon when, as skipper, he was the one who was supposed to manage workloads and assign tasks? If Simon thought Ritchie Baker ought to be interviewed, he was likely to be right. Sam was determined not to let Proust's continual undermining of him do any more damage to his confidence than it had already. Part of being a good team leader was recognising your team members' strengths and giving them the opportunity to excel. That was what Sam's wife Kate thought, anyway; she'd been horrified to hear that Sam had been on the point of resigning when he'd believed Simon and Gibbs would be going. 'You know, in an emergency, you could live without Simon Waterhouse,' she'd said.

Sam heard a female voice call out his name as he approached his car in the car park. He turned and saw Olivia Zailer, Charlie's sister. Sam hadn't recognised her at first. She'd lost weight. The coat she was wearing had the most sticky-out cuffs and collar Sam had ever seen. Her shiny pink lipstick was almost fluorescent; her hair, piled in a sort of tower on her head, was more shades of blonde than Sam would have believed possible. Not a lot of people who turned up at the nick looked like this, as if they might be expecting the arrival of a film crew at any moment. 'Have you got time for a quick chat?' Olivia asked.

'I haven't really. Sorry.'

'Less than a minute, less than thirty seconds. Promise, promise!' She beamed encouragement at him. What was she doing sleeping with Chris Gibbs? Sam decided now wasn't the time for him to be wondering about the unlikeliness of them as a couple; it might show on his face.

'Quickly, then,' he said.

'Whoever set fire to Sharon Lendrim's house . . .'

'Whoa, hang on a second. I can't talk to you about that, Olivia. Neither should Gibbs be talking—'

'He hasn't said a word to Debbie. She knows nothing.'

Was Sam supposed to find this reassuring?

'Oh, come on, Sam! Are you going to stand there should-and-shouldn'ting me, or do you want to hear what I've got to say?'

It was clear what Sam needed to do in order to fulfil his professional obligations: end this conversation and tell Proust that Gibbs had breached confidentiality. What was the point? Proust already knew that Simon had shared privileged information with Charlie; he knew that Gibbs had acted without authorisation when he'd brought Amber Hewerdine in on Simon's say-so alone. If Sam told him about yet another of Gibbs' transgressions, would it make any difference to anything? Would Gibbs be punished? The longer Sam worked for the police, the more convinced he became that punishment did nobody any good, neither the authority that meted it out nor its recipient.

'I'd prefer to hear it from Gibbs, whatever it is,' he told Olivia. 'And if he hasn't got the sense not to talk to you about work, you should have the sense to stop him when he starts. I don't talk to Kate about cases I'm working on. Ever.'

'I haven't told Gibbs yet,' Olivia grinned as if she was describing an endearing feature of their courtship. 'I wanted to try it out on someone else first. I tried to talk to Charlie about it . . .'

'Another person whose case it isn't,' Sam pointed out.

'. . . but she didn't want to know, so I thought, "Who's *reasonable*? Who can see beyond the rules and the oughts and . . ." '

'All right, let's hear it.' He was going to cave in eventually; might as well save himself some time.

'Whoever led Sharon Lendrim's two children out of the house before they set fire to it was wearing a fireman's uniform, right?'

'I agreed to listen,' said Sam. 'I didn't agree to tell you anything.'

Olivia rolled her eyes. 'I *know* they were dressed as a fireman. I also know that Kat Allen was in a few films when she was a kid. Two questions: does anyone know where the fireman's uniform came from? And have you found a link between Kat Allen and Sharon Lendrim?'

Sam couldn't speak. Her audacity had rendered him mute. There was a reason, he thought, why Olivia Zailer wasn't a detective. Even if Sharon Lendrim and Kat Allen had been killed by the same person, there was no basis for thinking there must be another connection between them. If you're a killer and two people at different points in your life incite your murderous rage, and you kill them both, you might be the only thing linking one of them to the other; chances are you will be. Sam didn't say any of this. Nor did he tell Olivia that, no, he didn't know where the fireman's uniform had come from and neither did Ursula Shearer. Sam had listened incredulously to Ursula's description of her team's attempts to trace the uniform. They had trawled the Culver Valley thoroughly, but had looked no further, focusing nearly all of their investigative time and energy on trying to prove that Terry Bond wasn't as innocent as he appeared to be. Sam could see no basis for assuming that Sharon Lendrim's killer must have been local, or that he or she must have sourced the fireman's accessories locally. He had tried not to feel superior when it had occurred to him that Ursula Shearer had never lived anywhere but Rawndesley.

'Goodbye, Olivia,' he said firmly, unlocking his car and opening the door. It was freezing cold, apart from anything else.

'Hang on, I haven't finished.' She leaned forward, grabbed his arm. 'As an adult, Katharine Allen was a primary school teacher. As a child, she was an actress.'

'What are you playing at?' Something had sprung up in Sam that he didn't stand a chance of pushing down. He didn't want to, not this time. 'Who do you think you are? Grabbing hold of me, like I'm some kind of . . . None of this is any of your business, I can't discuss it with you, and if you can't see that, if you can't see or don't care that you're putting me in a difficult position . . . I'm supposed to be grateful that *Debbie* doesn't know? What planet are you on? Has it occurred to you that you might be putting two murder investigations in serious jeopardy by carrying on the way you are?' What was happening here? *I don't yell*, Sam thought. *Ever*. What had he said? How could she already be crying? Dread swelled inside him.

Who had heard? Someone could easily have been eavesdropping on his outburst. Gibbs, Simon, Proust – they were the ones Sam should be yelling at. Not Charlie Zailer's sister.

She had already started to walk away. Sam stared after her, rooted to the spot by a gut-curdling heaviness. He recognised it as guilt wound around with the remnants of his rage.

Olivia turned before she reached the road, and again Sam was shocked by the crying. From the state of her eyes, she had done considerably more of it than he'd have thought possible between her storming off a few seconds ago and now. How much worse was it to be yelled at by someone who was known for his politeness?

Sam knew he'd cocked up. It wasn't fair to lull people into a false sense of security by seeming oh-so-mild-and-approachable, and then lose his temper. 'Olivia, come back,' he called out. Hadn't she nearly died of cancer when she was younger?

'No, I won't come back! I'll *never* come back!' Olivia shouted at him across the car park. A group of young uniformed PCs, on their way out of the building, did their best to act naturally. Sam wished he was invisible. Did she have to make it sound like a bitter lover's tiff? This wasn't an I'll-never-come-back situation. Only seconds ago, Sam had been certain it was a Stop-accosting-me-outside-the-nick-like-a-nutter situation.

'I'm telling you nothing. Nothing! You shouldn't need me to tell you anyway. Katharine Allen was a child actress who became a primary school teacher. You're the big, important detective. You should be able to work it out for yourself.' She marched away down the street on her impossibly high heels.

Sam got himself into his car and out of sight as quickly as he could. What were the chances of his being able to concentrate on work now? *Zero.* He hoped Ritchie Baker wouldn't mind repeating his answers several times. *Katharine Allen was a child actress. Now she's a primary school teacher.*

What the hell could that mean that Sam didn't already know?

At last, an accusation! If I sound pleased, it's because I am. Accusations are always good news from a therapist's point of view. We take it as a sign that we've touched on a psychic nerve; we're getting too close to a painful source of fear, guilt or shame. Either that or a patient has a legitimate grievance against us. Let's try to work out which this is.

Amber's accusation is that I'm proceeding as if Kirsty is of no account, talking as if Jo, Hilary and Ritchie were the only people in that Christmas Eve scene who mattered; Kirsty might as well have been a cushion, from the way I told it. It's worth bearing in mind that Amber had a similar accusation levelled at her by Jo, when Jo decided that Amber's failure to ask Kirsty questions she couldn't possibly answer was remiss and discriminatory. A ridiculous charge, and there was a fair amount of self-conscious absurdity in Amber's tone when she made her charge against me, as well as quite a lot of anger. She deliberately sent me a confusing signal.

As a joke? A parody of Jo's unreasonableness? Or does she really believe that my failure to mention Kirsty as one of the four participants in what she calls 'the Christmas Eve conspiracy' is proof that I am prejudiced against disabled people?

From everything I've been told about her, my guess is that Kirsty has a mental age of no more than two. Perhaps younger, since two-year-olds can usually speak a little. They can express their own emotions and pick up on the emotional states of others. Kirsty cannot speak at all, or respond to what is said to her.

I don't know. I'm no expert on mental disability, but I'd have thought it was fairly safe to assume that Kirsty didn't understand anything of the private conversation that took place on Christmas Eve after everyone else had gone to bed, and therefore she cannot really be said to have been party to it, though she was physically present. This doesn't make her a cushion; it's simply a realistic assessment of her likely involvement.

However, in one sense, Amber's right: because Kirsty is mentally handicapped and cannot be in possession of any information that might help us here, I discounted her. I haven't focused on her in the same way that I've focused on all the other characters in the Little Orchard drama. Now that she's been placed right in front of my nose, so to speak, I'm starting to have all kinds of interesting ideas about her. You've talked about her a lot, Amber – constant references to her. I didn't notice. Prejudiced as I am, I assumed a mentally handicapped woman couldn't be important.

At Little Orchard, William told you he found Kirsty scary and asked you not to tell Jo. To cheer him up, you suggested a game: hunt the secret key. The study's locked door annoyed you. I'm guessing that long before you found the key and had the big row about whether to use it or not, you and Jo discussed the locked room, maybe when you all first arrived and were looking round the house for the first time. You made a joke, perhaps, about wanting to get into the study and have a nosey, and Jo reproached you. Yes? Okay, and then on Boxing Day, after the disappearance and reappearance of Jo, Neil and the boys, after Jo had invoked the need to respect privacy once again – hers, this time – you'd had enough. Stuff privacy; you wanted answers. I can completely understand why you were determined to find that key, and how important it must have been to you. Which is why I wonder: why bring William into it? Five-year-old boys aren't known for their unobtrusiveness, or for their discretion. With William involved, Jo was more likely to find out what you were up to and try to stop you.

You're not that selfish, though. You knew the hide-and-seek opportunity would be huge fun for William and so you took the risk. Not because you wanted to cheer him up, as you claimed, or not only because of that. You also wanted to reward him for admitting to being scared of Kirsty.

You were very keen to tell me, last time we met, about Dinah's take on Kirsty: that it's impossible to tell if she's nice or horrible. You explained to Dinah that those considerations don't apply when a person is as severely disabled as Kirsty is, but Dinah wasn't convinced. She said that, since

Kirsty can't speak, nobody can prove that she isn't the nicest or nastiest person in the world. Dinah felt justified in being suspicious of Kirsty, and remaining so.

You said twice if not three times that you could have been much firmer with Dinah than you were and pointed out to her that what she was saying was inaccurate, that it would be unfair of her to hold that view about a helpless, harmless woman. Why didn't you say any of that? Don't you think it's important to instil compassionate beliefs in children and correct their misunderstandings?

Let me move into the third person, because this isn't an attack. I'm just asking questions. Amber explained why she didn't challenge Dinah: after years of putting up with Jo, she dislikes the practice of telling other people what they ought to think and how they ought to feel. Also, she holds Dinah and Nonie dearer than any principle. She didn't want Dinah to feel guilty for having made what might seem to an eight-year-old to be a logical assumption.

I'm not convinced. It's possible to explain to a child that she's wrong without making that child feel guilty. You say it without anger or reproach, you say, 'I can understand why you might have thought that. It's an easy mistake to make.'

Looking at these two incidents together – suggesting the hide-and-seek game to William immediately after he'd expressed his forbidden fear of Kirsty, and failing to tackle Dinah's misunderstanding of the implications of Kirsty's disability – it seems pretty clear to me that Amber identified with both William and Dinah when they made these comments. My guess is that Amber herself has forbidden thoughts about Kirsty, ones she feels guilty about.

It's unlikely that she would be scared of her, like William is. She wouldn't suspect Kirsty of being mutely evil, like Dinah does. What, then?

Incidentally, Amber has referred to Jo describing her brother Ritchie as the baby of the family, but she hasn't said anything about whether Jo or Kirsty is the older sister. I'd bet a thousand pounds – not that I *have* a thousand pounds – that Kirsty's the middle child, born two, three, maybe four years after Jo. Narcissistic personality disorder is caused by emotional trauma, usually around the age of three: the shock of safety or love suddenly being ripped away, like a rug being pulled out from under you. When Kirsty was born, assuming she was born the way she is, there must have been a huge amount of emotional upheaval in the family. That trauma is likely to be at the root of Jo's narcissism.

Kirsty can't speak. She probably can't understand much either. She's so severely handicapped that there's a danger of people treating her as if she's a cushion, just something that's there in the room. Jo had a private conversation with her family of origin on Christmas Eve night, so private that her husband Neil wasn't party to it. Jo thinks it's normal and acceptable, at an extended family gathering, to conspire with one's mother, brother and sister against one's husband, whom one has sent to bed alone. She thinks it's acceptable to wake Neil in the middle of the night, demand that he join her in an escape without telling him what it is they're escaping from. Most women confide in their partners, but not Jo. Like all narcissists, she's a control freak. She knows what she wants to do, and can't allow any opinion of Neil's to prevent her from meeting her own needs.

Kirsty, on the other hand . . . Who could possibly be a better confidante, from Jo's point of view? She can't disagree, she can't spill the beans. Around Kirsty, Jo would feel no need to lie about anything, to hide anything.

I'm going to go out on a limb here: Amber didn't correct Dinah's misapprehensions about Kirsty because they're too similar to her own. Every time Amber looks into Kirsty's eyes she finds herself wondering, *What do you know? How do I know you haven't got all the information I want? All right, you can't talk, but who knows what goes on behind those eyes? I don't even know what's wrong with you.* And then Amber would feel guilty, because of course she knows Kirsty doesn't know anything.

Or maybe she looks at Kirsty and thinks, *You must have seen and heard things that, if only you were normal, you'd be able to understand and tell me about.* In which case, Amber would feel even more guilty. Imagine being resentful of poor Kirsty. What kind of terrible person would that make you? Imagine being jealous of Kirsty; what's wrong with you, that you're jealous of someone so much worse off than yourself?

But it's entirely understandable. Remember earlier I said Amber's desperation to know why Jo, Neil and the boys disappeared must have been kept alive all these years by something, some force? One of the possible explanations I suggested was that she might be convinced that someone else knows the truth, someone less deserving than her.

Kirsty is that person. It infuriates Amber that Kirsty might have the secret information stored somewhere in her damaged brain in the form of never-to-be-understood data that she's taken in through her eyes and ears, while she, Amber, who is more than capable of listening and understanding, is left out in the cold: an outsider who knows nothing.

I also said earlier that perhaps Amber believes Jo owes her a secret. Which would mean that, at some point before they went to Little Orchard, Amber told Jo a secret – a big one, is my guess. Narcissists spend much of the time selling themselves to others, being charming and seductive to reel you in, to make sure they've got you there, close by, for when they need someone to lash out at. Amber might easily have been fooled into thinking she could trust Jo, before she knew her well.

How she's suffered since. That's why she puts up with Jo's regular attacks: because Jo has something on her. That's what she can't bear to think about, and why she's putting all her energies into impossible mysteries, which are stacking up. Have you noticed? We've got two of them now. Kirsty can't know anything, yet Amber can't shake the suspicion that she does; Amber didn't see the words 'Kind, Cruel, Kind of Cruel' in the locked room or in any other room at Little Orchard, but she knows she saw them at Little Orchard.

As I said before, I'm not against impossible mysteries. Their impossibility doesn't make them nonsensical. On the contrary, they're highly meaningful. They're what's keeping you out of your own personal locked room, Amber, at the same time as offering you a way in. Their impossibility, and the extent to which it frustrates you, is your subconscious trying to signal to your conscious mind that it can't bear this much longer. Things need to come out.

9

Thursday 2 December 2010

'You said you'd tell us as soon as we were in the car,' says Dinah. 'We're in the car now, so you have to tell us.'

'I *want* to tell you, Dinah. I just didn't want to do it surrounded by teachers and . . . whooping posh girls dressed as tortoises and hares.'

'They were rehearsing for an *Aesop's Fables* assembly,' Nonie says. The inside of the car smells of chlorine. Today is the girls' swimming day; their hair is still wet.

'You never come and pick us up on a Thursday. We always come home on the bus.'

I realise what is so unusual about the way I feel: I have the energy I need for this conversation. As soon as Simon left me alone at Hilary's, I lay down on the sofa and clocked out of the waking world. I woke up two and a half hours later, at three o'clock, feeling clearer in my mind than I have for a year and a half, and knowing that I had to go to Little Orchard.

Have to. I have to go back.

'We're going to a house in Surrey,' I tell Dinah and Nonie. 'It'll be an adventure.' Snow is falling on the car. It started a few seconds ago, but it's the thin kind, the kind that isn't going to stop me. I'm not sure anything could, in my present mood. I would heave giant boulders out of my way if that was what I had to do to get to Little Orchard. I haven't given myself a chance to think about why. I don't care why.

'But there was only five minutes of school left to go,' Dinah protests. 'If you were going to pick us up early, why didn't you pick us up properly early, so that we could miss a whole lesson?'

'I came as soon as I could,' I say. *And I brought biscuits.*

'What house in Surrey and why?' Nonie wants to know, not unreasonably.

'It's called Little Orchard. It's a holiday home, like the one we went to in the summer, in Dorset. Luke and I stayed there once, years ago.'

'Are we going to stay there now?'

'Has it got a trampoline?' Dinah enquires warily, as if I'm bound to have overlooked this crucial consideration. 'Is Luke meeting us there later?'

'No, we're not staying there. I just need to check something with the owner.' *Who's unlikely to be there.* What do I plan to do if she isn't? Break in?

'We'll stop somewhere for a nice dinner on the way back.' I try to make it sound like fun, aware that I'm going to have to compensate the girls for four boring hours in the car.

'I can't miss school tomorrow,' Dinah says. 'It's the first proper *Hector and His Ten Sisters* rehearsal.'

'You'll be there,' I tell her.

A few seconds later, I become aware that whispering is taking place behind me – contentious, not collaborative. Dinah and Nonie need to learn how to mouth words silently. I listen to the tutting and hissing, imagining facial expressions and frantic hand gestures that I can't see. As always, I appreciate the girls' efforts on my behalf. It is usually me and not themselves that they're trying to protect when they carry on like this. Eventually Dinah blurts out, 'The cast list for *Hector* has changed. Two girls who were going to be Hector's sisters aren't any more. But it's okay, I've told them they can have even better parts in the next play I write. Even though I'm *never* going to write another one because it's so stressful. But they don't know that. Anyway, it's all arranged now and everyone's okay about it, so it's fine.'

I know spin when I hear it.

'You can't promise them main parts in a play you're never going to write.' Nonie sighs. 'I'll have to write it if you won't. I won't make it good. I'll just write any old thing, so that they can be in it.'

'Write the worst play you can,' Dinah advises. 'That's what they deserve, now that they're—'

'*Dinah!*' Nonie sounds scared.

'Now that they're what?' I ask.

'Nothing,' Dinah says firmly.

Am I going to insist she tells me? How bad can it be? Or perhaps the question I should be asking myself is: how convincingly could I pretend to be interested in the theatrical wranglings of eight-year-olds at the moment? *Not very*. I'll ask another time. Or maybe I won't. Maybe it's okay and not at all negligent of me to assume that Dinah has not been tying up unsatisfactory cast members in the PE changing rooms and beating them with skipping rope handles.

'What do you need to check at Little Orchard?' Nonie asks patiently. She wouldn't get impatient even if she had to ask me a thousand questions before I told her what she wanted to know.

'Why don't you ring the owner, or email him?' says Dinah. 'No one goes all the way to Surrey to check something. You're not telling us the truth. *Again*.'

'Dinah!' Nonie mutters.

'It's okay, Nones. She's right. You deserve to be told the truth.'

'At last!' says Dinah. 'She's going to stop treating us like stupid little kids.'

It's hard to know where to start. 'There's too much I don't understand,' I say. 'Someone set fire to our house. I don't know who or why . . .'

'And we don't know who set fire to our old house,' Nonie says matter-of-factly. 'Mum's house.' When she mentions Sharon, the sadness in her voice is more prominent. Before Sharon died, Nonie never sounded sad. Dinah has always been bossy, but there's a steeliness in her now that never used to be there. I blink away unhelpful tears. Thinking about how all of us have changed isn't going to bring Sharon back.

'I feel as if I don't know anything at the moment,' I try to explain to the girls. 'I need to find some answers. The more I know, the safer we'll all be.' I hope that this is true, and try not to think about how easily it could be the opposite of the truth.

'Aren't the police supposed to find the answers?' says Nonie.

'They're rubbish,' says Dinah. 'They've had two years to find out who killed Mum and they still don't know.'

This is a big step forward, and I know I have DC Colin Sellers to thank for it. He was heroic last night. Dinah and Nonie both liked him; he made them laugh, and didn't pressure them for information. For a long time, neither of them would say the word 'police'.

I think about Simon Waterhouse. I want to tell the girls that a better, cleverer detective is now taking an interest in what happened to Sharon, but I'm afraid to raise their hopes.

I carry on with my explanation, for my own benefit as much as theirs. 'This morning, I tried to book to stay at Little Orchard – I thought we could maybe go there for a weekend some time. The owner told me it wasn't available to rent any more, but I didn't believe her. She said she and her family were living there. I want to see if that's true. If it isn't, I want to know why she lied to me. The only thing I can think of is that maybe when we stayed there before, she wasn't happy about the way we left things, or . . . I don't know. But I want to try and find out.' I hope I'm not telling them too much. What would Luke think?

He'd think that racing off to Little Orchard was a crazy plan. Which is why you didn't ring him before you left, why you left a note instead, knowing you'd be in Surrey by the time he got back from work and found it.

'Oh, no,' Nonie mutters.

'What's up, Nones?'

'It'll be embarrassing. And horrible. I don't want you to have a fight with anyone.'

'What, with a horrible woman who lied and said we couldn't stay in her house?' says Dinah. '*I* want to have a fight with her.'

'Nobody's going to be having any fights,' I tell them, hoping it's a promise I can keep. What if Veronique Coudert objects to my turning up at her home without warning? She's unlikely to fling open the door and welcome me with open arms.

The snow is thickening, but still not settling. We're okay; the roads are grey, not white. I switched off the radio on the way to the girls' school, when a smug male voice told me not to make any unnecessary trips. I have never done anything more necessary than what I'm doing now. I wonder if this is how people who drown trying to save their dogs from icy water feel before they take the stupid risk that ends their lives, before I hear about them on the news and think, 'What idiots'.

'So . . . you want to find out why this woman doesn't want you to stay in her house again?' Nonie asks.

'Right.'

'But . . . so it hasn't got anything to do with the fire last night, or Mum dying?'

I open my mouth to confirm that there is no connection, and find I can't. The words and my tongue will not cooperate with one another. 'I can't answer that, Nones,' I say. 'I just don't know.'

'But how could it have anything to do with those things?' she persists.

How could it? How could it?

The answer has something to do with five words: 'Kind, Cruel, Kind of Cruel'. If I saw them at Little Orchard, and that's why I said them to Ginny immediately after I'd been thinking about Christmas 2003; if Katharine Allen's killer wrote them on a notepad in her flat before tearing off the page to take away; if my helping the police with their enquiries inspired someone to set fire to my house; if fire is the link between the attack on us last night and Sharon's murder . . .

Three words. Kind, Cruel, Kind of Cruel. It's three words, not five.

'Amber?' says Dinah.

'Mm?'

'Why did you write down "Kind, Cruel, Kind of Cruel"?'

A playwright and a mind-reader.

Can I explain without including Katharine Allen in the story? I don't want Dinah and Nonie to have another murder in their heads.

'Is it anything to do with us?' Nonie asks. 'If it is, you have to tell us.'

There's a lay-by a few metres ahead. I pull over, slotting my car between two parked lorries. When I turn, I see fear on both girls' faces and feel guilty for having shared so much of my uncertainty with them. *And now you're going to do it again.* I stretch out my hand to them. Nonie squeezes it. Dinah inspects it, but doesn't touch. 'It's absolutely nothing to do with you. I promise. There's nothing for you to worry about. Everything's going to be fine. "Kind, Cruel, Kind of Cruel" is something I remember seeing somewhere, but I can't remember where. I thought if I wrote it down and kept looking at it, it might jog my memory, but it hasn't. Not yet, anyway.'

'Is it important?' Nonie asks.

'She doesn't know,' Dinah says in an over-the-top bored voice. 'It might be.'

'Right. It might be,' I say. 'I'm sorry, Dines. I know it's frustrating. It's frustrating for me too.'

She turns away from me, stares out of the window at the cars blurring past at sixty miles an hour. 'Fine,' she says. 'Are we going to this Little Orchard place or not?'

~

There is no snow in Cobham, Surrey. It has rained, though; all the way from the motorway, the tree-lined roads and leafy lanes were heavy with moisture. Despite the cold, I opened the car window and breathed in wet air that smells different from the air in the Culver Valley.

Little Orchard has a new front door – dark red instead of black, with no stained glass panel set into the wood – but otherwise it looks the same as it did seven years ago. The difference is not in the house but in me. When I was here in 2003, I had no difficulty in accepting that both I and my surroundings were real, that we were part of the same scene. Today, I feel detached, as if I've been superimposed onto the landscape. No matter how many times I tell myself that I'm here, the knowledge refuses to sink in and become part of what I take for granted.

Here I am. Here we are.

Mine is not the only car on the gravel courtyard. There's a blue Honda Accord parked close to the side of the house.

'Is this it?' Nonie asks. 'It's massive. Why did you and Luke need such a big house to stay in? Did you come here with friends?'

I resist the urge to be honest and say that I have no idea who I came here with. A group of labelled faces: Jo, Neil, Hilary, Kirsty, Ritchie, Sabina, Pam, Quentin. What did I know about any of them in 2003? What do I know about them now?

'There's a trampoline!' In her enthusiasm, Dinah sounds like a child – unusually for her. 'It's one of those massive ones, like William and Barney's!'

'It looks like a Latin teacher's,' says Nonie.

'The trampoline?' Dinah sneers.

'No, the house. A kind, old Latin teacher could live here. He'd have a big study with a coal fire in it and he'd wear slippers, and call pupils into his study and talk to them about their Latin homework.'

'You're just describing Mr McAndrew from seniors,' Dinah says. 'He doesn't live here. How would he get to school?'

'I imagine him living in a house like this,' says Nonie. 'With a cat. Definitely not a dog.'

'Why not a dog?' I can't resist asking.

'It's a cat kind of house.'

'What's our house?' I ask.

'Burnt,' says Dinah.

'Not a pet house at all.'

'Good answer, Nones,' I say, relieved that I'm not preventing my home from being its true self by failing to fill it with terrapins or gerbils. 'Right, girls, I want you both to wait here. I'll be no more than—'

'No!' Dinah protests. 'You're not leaving us in the car, no way!'

'We could go on the trampoline,' Nonie suggests. 'We'd take our shoes off.'

'She's going to say no,' Dinah warns.

'I am. You can go on William and Barney's trampoline at the weekend, Nones, like you do every weekend.'

'But I want to go on *this* one.'

'Come on, you can come with me to the house, stretch your legs a bit.'

'And listen to the fight!' Dinah rubs her hands together in anticipation.

We step out of the car into the cold, damp night. It's six o'clock and as dark as any midnight. I brush crumbs off the girls' school uniforms, knowing they're there even though I can't see them. 'What are you going to say?' Nonie whispers as we approach Little Orchard's front door.

'Listen and you'll find out,' Dinah tells her, and I'm grateful to her for answering on my behalf. In my head, I am already talking to Veronique Coudert; I don't want to be distracted by any other conversation.

I ring the doorbell and wait. It's a big house. It might take her a while to get over to this side, if she's right at the back.

'If no one's in, we can go on the trampoline,' says Dinah.

'Someone's here,' I say. 'Whoever owns that car is here.' I point to the Accord.

'They might have left it there to make burglars think someone's at home when they're not,' says Nonie.

I ring the bell again, but I'm too impatient to wait. 'Let's try round the back,' I say. We used only the back door when we stayed in 2003. I don't remember any of us discussing why this was, but it must have come from somewhere. Perhaps Little Orchard is one of those houses where the front door is never used. Jo must have known this; Veronique Coudert must have told her.

By ringing the front door bell, have I signalled to whoever is inside that I am a stranger – someone who doesn't know Little Orchard well, someone not to be trusted?

Dinah and Nonie follow me round the back of the house. The sound of their footsteps on the gravel is comforting: soft irregular crunches behind me. Nothing here has changed. The garden is still multi-layered, a staircase shape, each step a perfectly rectangular lawn with a neat brick border. Lights are on in the kitchen and in one of the bedrooms.

My phone starts to ring in my coat pocket. *Shit*. It'll be Luke. I don't want to talk to him at the moment, but I know how worried he'll be if I don't answer. 'Hi,' I say. 'Now isn't a good time.'

'Amber, what's going on? You're taking the girls to Little Orchard? Why?'

'We're here now,' I tell him. 'Everything's absolutely fine. I'll talk to you later. Okay?'

Without waiting for an answer, I switch off my phone and toss it in my bag.

'He's not going to be satisfied with that,' Dinah says matter-of-factly.

'Probably not,' I agree.

I knock on Little Orchard's kitchen door. A black-haired middle-aged woman opens it. She's wearing a blue and green patterned cotton caftan over faded jeans, pink flip-flops on her feet. Wound around her right hand is a yellow duster streaked with grey. She looks anxious at first. Then she sees the girls and smiles. 'Hello,' she says. 'Can I help you?' Her accent isn't English.

'Veronique Coudert?'

'No. Who are you? I am not expecting tonight you come, anyone come. No one tell me. House is not ready.' She is flustered. Spanish, I guess, maybe Portuguese.

'I'm Amber Hewerdine. Is Veronique Coudert at home?' *Of course she isn't. How many owners of holiday rental properties turn up to watch their cleaners change the bedding and empty the bins after each group of guests leaves?* 'Or . . . can you tell me where I can find her?' If she says Paris, I might burst into tears. I've driven all the way from Rawndesley. My girls are standing behind me patiently, wishing they could bounce on a forbidden trampoline in the dark. *Please.* I'm praying that Little Orchard's cleaner can sense how disastrous it would be for me to have to go home with no new information.

'Veronique Coudert? Who is Veronique Coudert? I do not heard of her.'

'The owner of Little Orchard,' I say.

'No.' The cleaner shakes her head. 'I do not know this name. This is not the house of Veronique Coudert. You are sure in the right place?'

'This is Little Orchard,' I say, feeling unreal, aware of Nonie and Dinah behind me wanting to ask a hundred questions each. 'Are . . . is this your house?'

'No, I am the maid . . . ah, how you say? The cleaner. I am Orianna.'

'What's the name of the owner?'

She takes a step back as I lunge forward unintentionally. My need for answers is making me clumsy. Behind Orianna, Little Orchard's kitchen is the same as it was in 2003, except for the absence of Jo. I find myself staring at the wooden dresser. I can't see if the nail is still there, sticking out of the back, if the key to the locked study is hanging where it hung seven years ago.

I could push Orianna out of the way, and . . .

No. No, I couldn't. Is this why I brought the girls with me, so that I would have no choice but to behave responsibly? 'What's the owner's name?' I ask again.

'I . . . who are you? Why are you ask these questions?' Orianna continues to back away from me, though I'm standing still.

I tell her my name again. 'I want one answer and then I'll go,' I say. 'Who does this house belong to?'

'I like that you leave now, please,' she says.

'What harm will it do to tell me the owner's name?'

'I do not know you. I have never seen you before.' She shrugs. 'You come here, I do not expect it . . .'

'She's scared,' Nonie whispers.

Tough. 'You're saying the name Veronique Coudert means nothing to you?'

She shakes her head. 'I have to go, I am so sorry.' The door closes in my face. I listen as she turns the key in the lock.

'Do you still want to go on the trampoline?' I ask the girls. If Orianna doesn't like it, if she wants to get rid of us, all she has to do is answer my question. Or get the owner down here, even better.

'We can't,' says Nonie, as if she's the adult in charge of two children. 'It's not fair on that lady. She's scared of us. She wants us to go.'

I nod. 'All right, come on, then. Back to the car.' I am talking about moving without moving. I can't think about anything apart from the shock of what I've just heard. How can Orianna not know the name Veronique Coudert? It makes no sense.

Nonie elbows Dinah. '*Tell* her,' she says. 'You have to. I hate this.'

'Stop it! That hurt!'

'Hate what? Tell me what?'

'Or I will,' Nonie threatens.

'She said it might not be important!'

'Dinah, you'd better tell me,' I say, as a strange current of energy starts to move through my body. I think it's fear. I want to turn and run, but I can't. I'm with the only two people in the world that I would never, under any circumstances, run away from.

'Kind, Cruel, Kind of Cruel,' says Dinah matter-of-factly. 'It's no big deal, just . . . I know what it means.'

'What?' I grab hold of her, pull her towards me. My heart feels as if it's tumbling down a steep flight of stairs that has no bottom. 'What do you mean? You can't . . . how can you know what it means?'

'I'm the one who invented it,' she says.

Did you know that, in psychotherapeutic terms, the house is a metaphor for the self? Jo tries to cram people into her house and keep them there because she fears that, at her core, there's nothing but emptiness. Amber felt frustrated not to be able to fling open the door of Little Orchard's study and reveal its contents; she is someone who values truth and integrity, forced against her will into lying.

And Simon's feeling more uneasy by the second. He's dying to know if there's a shred of truth in anything I'm saying. We're not helped by the fact that Amber's choosing not to share with us an awful lot of important information. There are three things going on here: repression, denial and secrecy. Amber, just because there's plenty you're choosing not to tell doesn't mean you know all the facts yourself. Some of what we need to know is hidden inside you, and you have no idea it's there; some, you know it's there, but you're trying to pretend you don't. That's why you're so proud of whatever secrets you're keeping on a conscious level. You imagine that if you can keep those in, the other stuff doesn't stand a chance of coming out.

And yet you're here because there are things you want to know. Look, you've even brought a detective with you. I think you're asking yourself the wrong questions, and that's why the answers aren't coming. Ask yourself this: what am I terrified of finding? What am I not prepared to let out?

Last time we met, you asked if most of my clients' repressed memories tend to surface while they're here with me, or do clients arrive and say, 'Hey, some new memories have popped up since I last saw you!'? The way you phrased the question made it clear you found both options preposterous. I told you the truth: the overwhelming majority experience their breakthrough moments here, under hypnosis.

You were suspicious. You asked why that should be the case; surely a memory could spring up from the subconscious and enter the conscious mind at any time? I said yes, in theory, but a lot of repressed memories are painful. People know they're safe here. They know it consciously and subconsciously. Patients are more likely to release trauma in a safe supportive environment that exists expressly for that purpose than at home on their own, or on their way to the office in the morning.

When I said that, you looked at me in astonishment, and that told me something about you: that you can't imagine feeling safer in a relationship with me or any therapist than locked inside your own head, alone. You think keeping your secret or secrets is keeping you safe, but the opposite is true. However ashamed or guilty you feel, you will feel better if you let it out and deal with the consequences.

I don't blame you for not trusting me. People who have suffered years of abuse by a narcissist find it difficult to trust themselves and other people. As you've said yourself, most of the time you try to behave in the way Jo wants you to. To avoid attack, you focus only on Jo's needs when you're with her, which makes you a co-narcissist. You resent her for forcing you into this role, and you resent yourself for playing it, which makes you suspicious of both narcissistic and co-narcissistic tendencies.

Before you'll tell me what I want to know – and bear in mind, you're the only person suffering from your *not* telling me – you need me to pass certain tests. I have to prove to you that I'm not a narcissist like Jo, that I'll let you express your feelings and listen without judgement, and without telling you how you ought to feel. I hope I've proved that. It's not enough, though; I also have to prove that I'm not a co-narcissist – by challenging you, by not letting you get away with anything. Which is why my behaviour might seem erratic to you, because I'm trying to satisfy both those needs simultaneously: provoking one minute, empathising the next.

It's a risky strategy. If I confuse you, if you never know what behaviour to expect from me, there's a danger you'll mistake me for another Jo.

A therapist isn't meant to show her hand in this way. I shouldn't wave diagnoses at you like a big show-off, or let you lie there with your eyes closed and a self-satisfied smile on your face while I do all the work. I shouldn't share all my cunning tactics with you. So why am I doing both?

I'm trying to impress you. Simon impressed you the first time you met him, so much so that you're willing to put yourself through this ordeal to help him solve his murder case. If I can wow you with my psychoanalytical brilliance and convince you that I'm both worthy and potentially useful, the big neon sign in your mind that's flashing the words 'Mustn't tell Ginny' might switch itself off; you might tell me whatever it is you're withholding. Your subconscious would receive the signal that the warning sign had come down, which would make it more likely to—

What?

Amber? What is it? Have you remembered something?

10

2/12/2010

Simon was standing outside Jo and Neil Utting's house in Rawndesley when his phone started to vibrate in his pocket. He pulled it out, looked at the screen. Charlie. 'Make it quick,' he said. She'd probably only heard the 'quick' part; he'd started speaking as soon as he'd seen her name, knowing they weren't yet connected.

'Where are you?' she asked.

'Just about to interview Johannah Utting. Why?'

'I need to—' Charlie broke off. 'Who?'

Simon could have done without the suspicious tone, just as he could do without the snow that was landing on his head and the back of his neck. 'What do you want?'

'Who's Johannah Utting?' Charlie asked.

Simon closed his eyes, knowing what the next question would be: *Is she attractive?* It was what Charlie always said, whenever he mentioned a woman's name. *Pathetic.* And confusing. How was Simon supposed to know what attractive was? 'I've got to go,' he said. 'We'll talk later.' End of call, phone off, end of problem. *For the time being.*

Jo Utting was probably what most men would call attractive, though not in a way that Simon found appealing. He had always been slightly alarmed by very curly hair, especially on women. It made him think of dolls coming to life in horror films. Not that he could remember watching a film in which that happened. Jo Utting's hair was the curliest he'd ever seen, each strand a coiled yellow spring. Was there nothing she could do to straighten it?

Simon was ushered into the small red-brick terraced house by Jo and a foreign-sounding woman who told him with a grin that she was Sabina, as if he ought to have heard of her. He would have found it hard to describe the scene that he walked into – did find it hard, even in his head, where he was both raconteur and audience-who-already-knew-the-story. As a police officer, Simon had landed in many strange and unpleasant situations over the years, but never one quite like this.

An unfeasibly large number of people, some children, appeared all at once and all tried to engage him in vigorous conversation at the same time. None stopped trying when he or she noticed that everyone else was trying, assuming any individual noticed the others at all, which was by no means certain. Simon was trapped in a cloud of intolerable noise that promised never to end. He couldn't respond because he couldn't hear any of the questions. By the time he'd managed to absorb one in its entirety, he'd become aware that no one was in a position to listen to his answer; he was no longer the focus of interest. The various participants in this bizarre entanglement had turned their attention to one another instead and were making announcements over heads and between bodies about timetabling practicalities: what needed to be done, by whom, how long would it take. Simon heard himself mentioned frequently but was neither included in the discussion nor even glanced at occasionally as all present spoke at length and simultaneously about how they would fit in talking to him, given all the other things they had to do.

At the back of the hall – which seemed miles away, though it couldn't have been more than four or five feet – a tall, broad-shouldered man with a crew cut was yelling into his mobile phone about the price of etched glass. Although the subject did not interest him, Simon clung to the sound of that distinct voice for as long as he could, until it was swallowed up by the wider cacophony. He heard the word 'Pilates', knew he'd heard it before, wondered what it meant.

It was impossible to move beyond the hall into a room, or to express the need to do so. A few seconds later and Simon had lost sight of Jo Utting, the person he was keenest to talk to. She'd been standing right in front of him – he'd had the impression that she was at the centre of the scrum – and then suddenly she wasn't there any more. A large woman with limp, dark blonde hair who looked to be in her mid-thirties stood in a doorway staring at Simon, her mouth hanging open. She was wearing pyjamas with pink elephants on them. Simon registered that she was disabled. Behind her, he saw two thin unmade temporary-looking beds that reminded him of television news coverage of disasters, interviews with people who were living in sports centres because their homes had been flooded.

Or burned down ...

A short elderly man appeared beneath Simon's chin, demanding to know what was being done to save an important tree. A demolition order had been served on the tree, unfairly. It was the one on the corner of Heckencote Road and Great Holling Road. Was it fair to destroy a tree that was nearly a hundred years old so that yet another hotel could be built, which would only add to the traffic problem in Rawndesley? Talking over the old man was an even older-looking woman, insisting that Simon wasn't here to discuss trees. They both fell silent at the same time, as if they'd cancelled each other out.

At last, here was a gap into which Simon could insert a response if he so wished. The problem was that he had no idea who the elderly man was, or the woman. He also felt that his own identity was less solid than it had been when he'd arrived a few minutes ago. This kind of environment, a chaotic family home, was alien to him. He'd grown up in a quiet, guest-free house. Until he'd moved in with Charlie, he had never had a guest in his own house apart from Charlie, who was never invited and who, in any case, didn't count.

The European-sounding woman, Sabina, leaned over the old man to grab Simon's arm. 'No comment,' she shouted in his face. This confused Simon, who hadn't yet asked her anything. 'I'm not saying nothing without my lawyer here,' she went on in a pronounced Cockney accent. 'I know my rights. No comment.' She started to laugh, then said in her normal voice, 'I have always wanted to say that to a policeman. Don't worry, I am joking. It's busy here. We are very noisy, I'm sorry.'

Jo Utting's curly head appeared, protruding from the farthest visible doorway. 'William, Barney, get out of the way,' she said. 'Let DC Waterhouse through.'

William and Barney, Simon thought. Two people; from Jo's tone, probably the smallest two. There was no way he'd be able to get to the room that contained Jo if only two people moved, not without some heavy lifting of animate objects. At least four people needed to move.

Someone pushed him forward. 'I will deliver you to Jo,' said Sabina. How and when did she get behind him? 'In this house, you must push in.' Somehow, with her help, Simon made it through the crowd to the kitchen and Jo. The relief he felt was short-lived. He'd accepted Jo's offer of a cup of tea, and was on the point of asking if he could close the door so that he could hear himself think when an earnest-faced boy appeared in front of him. 'Do you know the difference between a transitive relationship and an intransitive relationship?'

'William, don't pester him,' Jo said, reaching for a mug. 'Why don't you and Barney go and play on the Wii for a bit?'

'It's okay,' Simon said. He didn't know the difference. The boy looked about twelve or thirteen. If there was something, anything, that he knew and Simon didn't, that situation needed to be rectified. 'Transitive and . . . ?'

'Intransitive.' William straightened his back like an army cadet.

'Go on, then, tell me.'

'The Queen is richer than my dad, my dad's richer than my uncle Luke . . .'

'William!' Jo rolled her eyes. 'Sorry,' she mouthed at Simon, blushing.

'. . . my uncle Luke's richer than me. That means the Queen's richer than me. It's a transitive relationship. But if the Queen was richer than someone who was richer than me, but the Queen *wasn't* richer than me, that would be an intransitive relationship. Except with richer it would always be transitive. Intransitive could be something like lives next door to—'

'All right, William, that's enough,' said Jo. 'I think DC Waterhouse gets the point. Go on, run along.'

Her son left the room with an air of disappointment, as if he'd had more to say and would now never have the chance. An odd boy, thought Simon.

He wanted to cheer when Jo walked over and closed the kitchen door, putting a barrier between the two of them and the noise. 'His dad *isn't* richer than his uncle Luke,' she said, as if it mattered to her. 'I think William assumes that anyone who runs his own business is Bill Gates, or something. I wish!'

'I need to ask you about last night,' Simon said.

'Not before I've asked you if what Amber's told me is true. You're not going to tell anyone she didn't go on that driver awareness course herself?'

'I'm going to do my best not to.'

'In that case . . .' – Jo let out a long breath – '. . . thank God. I've got two small children, a dependent father-in-law living with me permanently since his wife died of breast cancer, a severely mentally handicapped sister living with me temporarily, a mother who's getting on and not as strong as she used to be.'

'I'm hoping there'll be no need to bring up the DriveTech course,' Simon told her. *Two small children.* Was the strapping, articulate, approximately twelve-year-old William one of them? Simon wouldn't have described him as small. He also wouldn't have called Jo's accent 'cut glass', as Edward Ormston had. Educated, yes; upper middle class, yes, but not royal. Not aristocratic.

'People rely on me.' Jo handed Simon a cup of tea. 'I know what I did was wrong. I care about people too much, and take all their self-made problems onto my own shoulders.' She let out a bitter laugh. 'Everyone's always saying I'm helpful and self-sacrificing to a fault, but even I draw the line at being prosecuted!' She turned on Simon, as if in response to a threat he'd made. 'You can't punish me for caring enough to try to help people.'

I could, actually. 'Where were you last night between midnight and 2 a.m.?'

'In bed, asleep. You don't seriously think I'd set fire to Amber's house?'

'Will your husband be able to confirm your whereabouts?'

'He was asleep too. We all were.'

That was easy, then. If everybody had been asleep, that meant no one was in a position to confirm that everybody had been asleep. Any one of them apart from the kids, Jo included, could have got up and gone to Amber's house to start that fire. Risky. What if they didn't make it back before the news woke the rest of the family? Amber was known never to sleep. She could have noticed the fire much sooner than she did and phoned Jo's house within minutes, immediately after calling the fire brigade.

Who in this house would have taken that risk?

'Who is "we all"?' Simon asked. 'Who stayed here last night?'

'Me, Neil, William, Barney . . .'

'Your husband and sons?'

'Yes. And Quentin, my father-in-law.'

'Sabina? Is she a relative too?'

'She's the boys' nanny. No, she didn't stay the night. Neither did Mum and Kirsty. They went home round about six, six thirty-ish.'

'Before you served the evening meal?' Simon asked.

Jo turned a wounded look on him, as if he'd deliberately raised her hopes and then let her down. Was he reading too much into it? He reminded himself that they'd only just met. Nothing she did or said could put him in the wrong here. He was doing his job. 'You're taking a closer interest in the details of our daily life than I feel comfortable with,' she said eventually. 'You must know nobody here would set fire to Amber and Luke's house? God! We're their family. We're all they've got. Ask Amber if she thinks one of us might have done it. She'll laugh in your face. What does it matter when we had dinner, for God's sake?' Jo was looking not at Simon but at the cup of tea she'd given him. He half expected her to grab it back.

'Amber, Dinah and Nonie stayed for dinner, yes?' Simon continued evenly. 'Did Sabina stay too?'

'Yes,' said Jo in a clipped voice. 'She stayed all evening, went home about eleven. Why?'

'So the people at dinner were you, Neil, your two sons, Sabina, your father-in-law, Amber, Dinah and Nonie? Anyone else?'

'No.'

'And it was during dinner that Amber told everybody what happened when she went to see a hypnotherapist the day before – the police officer she met, with the notebook?'

'No,' Jo said sullenly. 'She didn't say anything about a notebook. She did her usual trick of saying as little as possible. All she told us was that she'd seen a hypnotherapist, and this had led to her getting mixed up in a murder investigation.'

'Did she tell you the name of the woman who was murdered?' Simon asked.

'Katharine Allen.'

'Did that name mean anything to you?'

'No.'

'Yet you've remembered it.'

A slowly released sigh from Jo. 'I've been Googling her all day, haven't I? As anyone would. Murder might be an everyday occurrence for you, but in our family it's quite unusual. Not that I'm saying my life's boring or anything, but . . .' She shrugged.

'So your mother, your sister and your brother were the only members of the family who didn't know that Amber had been questioned in connection with Katharine Allen's death?'

Jo frowned. 'No, they all know. Well, apart from Kirsty, my sister, who isn't capable of understanding things on that level.'

'They know now,' Simon clarified, 'but before the fire . . .'

'Even before the fire, Mum knew,' said Jo. 'I told her all about it when I rang her.'

'You rang her? When?'

'Last night, before I went to bed. I don't know exactly what time. Half eleven-ish? I ring her every night, to check she and Kirsty are okay and say goodnight. Even if I didn't, I'd have rung her last night to tell her about what had happened to Amber. I rang Ritchie too.'

'Why?'

'Isn't it obvious?' Jo asked.

'No.'

She filled the kettle with water, put it on again, selected a cup for herself. Simon noticed it was superior to the one she'd given him, which was chipped around the rim and covered with a tracery of cracks under the glazing.

'If something important happened to someone in your family, wouldn't you make sure everyone knew, soon as you could?'

'How often do you see your mother, sister and brother?' Simon countered with a question of his own.

'My brother every two or three days, I guess,' Jo said. 'I see Mum and Kirsty every day. It's hard for Mum, looking after Kirsty, and since none of us works, it makes sense for us to get together – someone to talk to, you know.' She smiled brightly; the expression remained fixed in place for too long, unmoving.

'If you don't work, why do you need a nanny?' She was presenting her account of her family as if it made sense, but it didn't, not to Simon. Seeing each other every day, ringing every night?

Jo laughed. 'Have you ever tried looking after two children on your tod? Neil's at work all day, Mum's busy with Kirsty . . . If I tried to do it all on my own, I'd go loopy. Not so much now, but certainly when the boys were little. Even now, Sabina supervises their homework while I make the dinner most nights. And one of us is normally dealing with Quentin too. Since Pam died of liver cancer – that's Neil's mum—'

'Breast cancer,' Simon corrected.

'Liver cancer.'

'You said breast cancer before.' Something was badly wrong here. Simon felt a shiver pass through him.

'No, I didn't. Are you telling me I don't know what my own mother-in-law died of? It was liver cancer. It was horrendous. Start to finish, it took five years to kill her, and now she's not suffering any more – good for her – but Neil and I are stuck looking after Quentin and feeling terrible if the thought ever crosses our mind that it would have been *so* much easier the other way round.' Jo's eyes were bright with tears. 'If Quentin had died first, if Pam had been the one to survive . . .' She flung out an arm towards the door, pointing. No more shiny smile. '*You* don't have to live with him every day. You didn't have to stand by and watch Pam die. I did, so don't tell me she died of breast cancer, as if you know more about it than I do.'

'When did she die?'

'January this year.'

Simon nodded. He found it interesting that Jo was choosing to present their disagreement as a diagnostic one. Clearly she knew better than he did what illness had killed her mother-in-law, so it made sense for her to pretend that their argument was one she could easily win. In the matter of what she had said earlier in the conversation – whether she had initially said liver cancer, as she claimed, or breast cancer, as Simon remembered – the two of them were evenly matched, each as likely as the other to be right or wrong.

'So you rang your mother twice last night? The second time after you'd heard about the fire?'

'Neil phoned her, immediately after Luke phoned and woke us up. I was in shock, couldn't think straight, but Neil knew I'd want Mum there, and Sabina. He phoned everyone – Ritchie too, but Ritchie couldn't come. He's got a stomach bug.'

'And someone woke Quentin, presumably?' Amber had said everyone but Kirsty, Ritchie, William and Barney had convened in Jo's lounge in the early hours of the morning.

'Neil woke his dad, yes.'

'Going back to dinner time . . .' Simon began.

'Pasta with mozzarella, basil, tomatoes and olive oil,' Jo snapped. 'Treacle tart for pudding. How interested can you be in an ordinary family supper, for God's sake? How's us talking about my dinner last night going to help you catch any murderers?'

'Were William and Barney there when Amber told everyone about Katharine Allen, and being interviewed by the police?'

'No. They and the girls had left the table. I knew Amber had something important to tell us, so I sent them off to play.'

Simon nodded, relieved that the family wasn't so abnormal as to discuss murder at the dinner table in front of children.

'About the DriveTech course . . .' he started to say.

'We've talked about that,' Jo said in a warning tone. 'You said you wouldn't bring it up again.'

No, I didn't.

'I need to know that I don't have to worry about . . . any kind of comeback,' said Jo. 'I want you to give me your word.'

'No comeback,' Simon promised. If he had to, he'd renege on it. For the time being, he was prepared to say whatever worked. He sensed that at any moment, if Jo didn't like what she heard, she might end the interview.

He forced a smile. She tried to match it, flattening her mouth into a line.

'One more question, then I'll be out of your hair,' he said. 'You told Amber about Edward Ormston – his daughter Louise, who died?'

Jo's face was a blank. 'Who?'

'Ed from the DriveTech course.'

'Oh.' Pink spots appeared on her cheeks. 'Ed, yes. Sorry, I just . . . without the context . . . I told Amber everything. She insisted. Not that either of us ever thought *this* would happen.'

'You didn't quite tell her everything,' said Simon.

'Yes, I did. What didn't I tell her?' A clear challenge: *name one thing I missed out.*

For the second time today, Simon described the speech made by the woman calling herself Amber: the hypocrisy of a society that overvalues cars but refuses to accept their downside.

Jo didn't say anything. She seemed to be still listening, long after Simon had finished. Was she waiting for him to say something else?

'Why didn't you tell Amber that you said all that?'

'I'm not sure I did say it.' Jo's shrug was offhand, as if nothing could matter less to her.

'Ed Ormston's sure you did. I believe him.'

'Well, then . . . Look, I don't remember, okay?' Jo rubbed her forehead. 'Maybe I said something, but it wasn't *that*, I wouldn't have come out with a load of nonsense like that. Ed's no spring chicken, is he? I had a bit of a rant, yes, but I don't remember the details.' She made a dismissive gesture with her hand. 'I was angry to have to be there, wasting a day, and I went off on one, I suppose. But if Ed thinks that's what I said, then he misunderstood me.'

'How, exactly?' Simon asked.

'I don't know! It was a month ago. Do you remember things you said a month ago?' Seeing that she'd given Simon pause, Jo pressed her point. 'You don't,' she said. 'No one does. We remember what other people say, not what we say ourselves.'

Like I remember you saying breast cancer first. Not liver cancer.

'You weren't impersonating Amber, then?' Simon said. 'Coming out with what you imagined to be her opinions, in her absence and as her stand-in?'

Jo's face twisted. 'You'd be better off asking her about impersonating me. Why do you think she's so desperate to adopt Dinah and Nonie?'

'For their sake. They want parents,' Simon repeated what Amber had told him.

'No. No! That's not what it's about, not at all. It's about Amber wanting to be me, like she always has. I'm the mother of two children, so she has to be. It's sick. *She's* sick.' Jo lunged towards Simon. He backed away, but all she seemed to want to do was peer into his cup. 'You need more tea,' she told him in a voice that was nothing like the one she'd been using a few seconds ago. 'You should have said.'

'I thought you said you cared about Amber,' Simon reminded her, since she had trouble recalling her own words.

'You think if someone's sick I shouldn't care about them? Then you're as sick as she is, sick in the head. I forgot to ask you if you take sugar. Do you?'

'No.'

'Good.' She flashed him another shiny smile. 'Because there's no sugar in the house.'

~

Olivia wiped her eyes and headed for the kitchen. Time to stop crying and make a cup of Lapsang Souchong. And to stop dwelling on what Sam Kombothekra had done wrong, tempting though it was to think about anything other than what she herself was doing wrong, every second of every day. Not that she spent all her waking hours with Chris Gibbs, but even when they weren't together, like now, her sinful state still applied; there was no shaking it off. Gibbs didn't seem to care that their relationship was unjustifiable and potentially disastrous for all involved. Whenever Olivia raised the subject, he said infuriating things like, 'That's just the way it is. There's no point wishing it wasn't.' He seemed unconcerned about his good or bad person status. Not that Olivia thought in those terms; it was a gross oversimplification.

She had never before met a man who took a keen interest in her but none in himself. He'd never said he loved her, but he'd told her once that he worshipped her. In isolation, that would be lovely, but Olivia found it disconcerting when she tried to reciprocate by complimenting him, only to have him stare at her, bemused, with a question in his eyes: *Who?* As if she was talking about someone he'd never met. He refused to put himself under the spotlight of his own thoughts, which, handily for him, meant that he was never able to explain or analyse his behaviour. He regularly referred to the future – a future in which he and Olivia were together, one that didn't include their respective partners or any children – but when Olivia asked how he thought this state of affairs might come into being, he shrugged, as if that part was nothing to do with him.

Something had to happen soon to change things, surely? He was about to become a father. How could that not turn everything on its head? Meanwhile, closer to home – *at* home – the prevailing assumption was that Olivia would shortly marry Dominic Lund, who was sitting in the next room, reading legal papers in front of the TV, unaware that his fiancée had been deceiving him for the past five months. I could make something happen, Olivia thought, but no matter how many times she repeated the idea to herself, she didn't believe it. She didn't feel she had either the power or the right to decide what course her life should take. Anything she might do could make things so much worse.

As a young woman, she had nearly died of an illness that was beyond her control. As it turned out, she'd survived, but other people, not her, had made that happen. Since then, Olivia had been unable to rid herself of the conviction that no action of hers could make any difference to anything. It didn't matter what she did. She wasn't a person the world noticed or cared about. Charlie was; Simon was. They only needed to blink and the universe rearranged itself around them. When Charlie had had an ill-advised affair a few years ago, it had been reported in every national newspaper.

Was that why Olivia was practising making people angry? To prove to herself that she could have an impact?

Dom appeared in the kitchen behind her, empty wine glass in hand. 'Are you going to tell me what you're crying about?' he said.

'I'm not any more.'

'Adjust the tense,' he said impatiently.

'Someone shouted at me when all I was doing was trying to help them,' Olivia told him.

Dom smirked as he reached for the wine bottle on the kitchen table. 'Hardly surprising. I've seen you try and help people.'

'Let me ask you something.'

'I'm busy, Liv.' Under his breath, he muttered, '. . . knew it was a mistake to come in here.'

'It won't take long. Please?' He wasn't the ideal audience, but he was the only one she had. Gibbs was the person she wanted to impress with her theory, but she'd ruined it by going to Sam first, not certain enough of the brilliance of her contribution to share it with Gibbs before she'd had feedback from an expert. And now that she would rather eat a bucket of toenails than tell Sam anything ever again, it meant she couldn't talk to Gibbs about it either. If he thought her hypothesis was strong enough, he'd share it with his team. Of course he would; how could he not? And if Sam looked into it and it turned out to be a dead end, it would only confirm his view of Olivia as a melodramatic idiot.

I could test it myself, she thought. No one needs to know. Unless I turn out to be right.

'What daft plot are you hatching?' Dom asked, twirling a strand of her hair round his finger.

'Why would someone who acted in three films as a child give up acting as an adult?' Olivia asked him.

'No money in acting for most people.'

'Right. So you do the sensible thing, become a primary school teacher.'

'Fuck all money in teaching,' Dom said.

'Acting's still your first love. You wouldn't forget all about it.'

'What are we talking about?' Dom asked between mouthfuls of red wine. His lips were stained burgundy. He had the most stainable lips of anyone Liv had ever known. Would anyone else notice that about him and appreciate how cute it was, if . . . No, she couldn't even think it. Leaving Dom was out of the question.

'Not all child actors are going to grow up loving acting,' he said. 'If their parents are pushy, they might grow to hate it. "Fuck off, Mum, I don't want to be in *Lassie 23: Return of the Stinking Mutt*. Can't I go to school like all my mates, be a normal kid?"'

Olivia hadn't thought of that.

'Then you'd get the ones who think they could have been contenders,' Dom went on, warming to the theme. 'The ones who pretend the day job's just paying the bills until they're spotted by Steven Spielberg.'

'What about the sane ones?' Olivia said. 'Not screwed up by pushy parents, or still holding out for Hollywood. The ones who know they're not star material, and who enjoy their day jobs, but . . . let's say they teach in a primary school . . .'

Dom frowned. 'Who is this ex-actor primary school teacher?'

'She was murdered.' Olivia knew he would assume any insider information came from Charlie.

'In Spilling? Then she's Simon Waterhouse's problem, not yours.'

'A primary school teacher who'd once been an actress would be keen on promoting drama within the school.' Liv tried not to cringe as she spoke her theory aloud. 'Wouldn't she? She might, that's all I'm saying. If she enjoyed acting when she was a kid, she might think it'd be fun for her pupils. And . . . where there's drama, there are costumes. If Kat Allen was the only teacher at her school who had ever been in films, perhaps she was in charge of drama at the school.' *Perhaps she got hold of a fireman's costume and wore it to set fire to Sharon Lendrim's house.* 'Maybe she arranged theatre trips for the kids she taught. Maybe she hired minibuses and took them to see pantos.'

'Not knowing what you're talking about, it's hard for me to get excited about that possibility.' Dom yawned.

'Theatres have wardrobe departments. She might have taken a group of them, shown them around, asked the wardrobe manager if the kids could try on the costumes, maybe borrow some.' Seeing Dom's face, Liv groaned. 'I just can't believe that being a child actor didn't have some kind of . . . lasting effect. Look, I'm making it sound more implausible and complicated, the more I say. Let's keep it simple, the chain of connections: acting, costumes, fireman costume.'

'*Fireman* costume?'

'It's complicated.' She couldn't be bothered to explain.

Dom turned away. 'Whatever you're doing, you don't need me for it,' he said, taking his wine back to the lounge.

Olivia knew she was getting carried away – something she did better than anyone of her acquaintance, even Simon Waterhouse – but this idea would drive her mad if she didn't attend to it. One phone call, that was all it would take. Or, if she was lucky and not a hundred miles wide of the mark, a series of phone calls. And some acting.

She'd do it first thing tomorrow.

~

Having satisfied himself that Ritchie Baker was too inert to do anything as labour-intensive as attempt to kill anybody, Sam asked the question Simon had sent by text message less than a minute ago, preceded by the word 'URGENT' in capitals. 'What did Pam Utting die of?'

'Liver cancer. Well, it started in her liver. They caught it early, thought they'd got it all, then it came back, spread everywhere. Look, do you mind if we don't talk about death and disease?' Ritchie laid a hand on his stomach. 'I feel really rough. I spent half of last night and most of today on the bog.'

Sam didn't doubt it. The flat stank. Opening some windows would have helped, but it was hardly the kind of thing a visitor could suggest. And it was cold outside – snowing. Sam was doing his best not to breathe through his nose, and sounding bunged up as a result. If Ritchie asked, he would pretend he had a cold, but Ritchie wasn't going to ask. Apparently happy to answer questions, he had so far contributed none of his own to the conversation. *The ideal interviewee*. Except that Ritchie's tame passivity was oddly contagious, and set the tone, somehow. If Sam wasn't careful, their dialogue would peter out into a companionable droopy-eyed silence.

The flat was bachelor-pad shabby and then some. Everything Sam could see that was made of any kind of material was creased or scrunched into ridges – the tea-towel hanging from the hook on the door, the duvet and bed sheet, Ritchie's scattered clothes – mainly black T-shirts with Celtic symbols on them and black jeans; a bath towel on the floor, the thin, bunched-up rugs that looked to have been dropped at random, their once-white fringes twisted into uneven grey clumps. A brightly coloured felt wall-hanging – children dancing around a well – was wrinkled, and hung at a funny angle instead of flat against the wall.

Apart from the bathroom, which Sam had no desire to inspect, Ritchie Baker lived in this one big rectangular room. Everything was here: sink, hob and kitchen units lined up beneath the windows, a bedroom corner clumsily marked out by two wardrobes at right angles to one another, an alcove with a computer in it that Sam could imagine Ritchie's landlord describing as a study area. At the other end of the room, a circle of armless chairs tried their best to ring-fence as much lounge as they could get away with. Sitting down anywhere but on Ritchie's bed beside Ritchie would have meant disturbing the arrangement of chairs, so Sam had opted to stand.

He wrote 'liver cancer' in his notebook. Would that be enough detail for Simon? *Assume not*. 'Thought they caught, hadn't, spread everywhere,' Sam added.

At one time, it would have bothered him that he didn't know who Pam Utting was, or why he was asking about her. Utting was the surname of Amber Hewerdine's husband, Luke, so presumably Pam was a relative of some kind. Luke's mother, perhaps. How, if at all, did she fit into the Kat Allen investigation? How did Ritchie Baker fit in, and his sister Johannah? All Sam knew was that he'd been working the murder of a young woman, and now suddenly he had connected murders and attempted murders coming at him from all sides. He was struggling to see them as leads in his original case, though Simon was adamant that was what they were. Sam felt distanced from Kat Allen's death by too much time and too many people; it couldn't be a good thing.

'I might have lied before without meaning to,' Ritchie said matter-of-factly, as if he didn't mind either way. 'Someone might be able to confirm I was here all last night: the woman in the flat below. If you're lucky, she might have been kept awake by me flushing the loo every half hour. I think her bed's directly underneath my bathroom.'

'If *you're* lucky, you mean.' Now that Ritchie had mentioned her, Sam would have to follow up on it. *Excuse me, madam, can you verify that your upstairs neighbour spent most of last night empty-ing his bowels?*

'While we're on the subject of whens and wheres, I don't suppose you'd be able to tell me what you were doing on 22 November 2008?' Sam asked.

'No idea. Sorry.'

'A woman called Sharon Lendrim was killed that night, not too far from here. Did you hear about it?'

'No, I don't think so.'

'You didn't know her, then?'

'No.'

'The name doesn't ring any bells?'

'Nope.'

'What about Katharine Allen?'

Ritchie shook his head. 'Sorry. No.'

'Do the words "Kind, Cruel, Kind of Cruel" mean anything to you?'

'You mean apart from kind meaning nice, and cruel meaning—'

'That's right.' Sam cut him off more forcefully than he'd meant to. 'Apart from that.'

'Then no,' said Ritchie. 'Sorry I'm not being much use to you.'

Either he was politely concealing his curiosity, or he had none.

'What about Tuesday 2 November. Do you remember what you were doing then, between eleven and one?' *Were you beating a primary school teacher to death with a metal pole?* Sam wished he knew why he was asking these questions of this particular man. Ritchie was related to Amber Hewerdine, sort of; he was one of the few people who had known yesterday that Amber had been interviewed by the police on Tuesday. Was that a good enough reason to be asking him about Kat Allen?

If you'd already asked everyone in Kat's life everything you could think of to ask, then, yes, Sam supposed it was.

'Sorry,' Ritchie said again. 'I don't really need to remember much, so I tend not to. I probably couldn't tell you what I did yesterday. I was ill yesterday, so I remember it for that reason, but if I wasn't, I mean.'

'What about checking your diary?' Sam suggested. Normally, he'd have assumed the person he was talking to would think of this on their own. He believed that Ritchie was doing his best, and that was the problem. A more imaginative person deliberately trying to mislead him would almost certainly have been more help. 'And if you've kept your diary from two years ago . . .'

'I don't have one. Never have. I don't work, and I don't see that many people – if I go out, I tend to go to Jo's. Or Mum's, sometimes, but usually Jo's.'

In other words, you don't have a life. Sam wondered if this alone was grounds for suspicion. 'You've never had any kind of diary, not even for appointments?' *You and your loved ones don't spend your evenings cross-checking to make sure that anything that's written in one person's diary is written in everybody's?* There were as many ways of living as there were people, Sam concluded, and his own wasn't necessarily the best.

'I tend not to prearrange things,' Ritchie said. 'I do what I feel like doing, as the mood takes me.'

All right, don't rub it in. 'What do you do when you stay in?' Sam asked, then regretted it. An image of Ritchie sitting on the lavatory with his black jeans round his skinny ankles had to be hastily banished. 'What are your interests? Are you looking for a job at the moment?' There were no books in the flat that Sam could see, no magazines, no CDs, music system, radio – nothing to indicate that Ritchie had much enthusiasm for anything. Or maybe everything was on his computer: films, music, even friends.

'There aren't that many jobs I'd want to do,' Ritchie said. 'I don't see any point in doing a job just for the sake of it, if I'm not passionate about it.'

'For money?' Sam suggested.

Ritchie looked vaguely confused, as if this was a consideration that would never have entered his head if Sam hadn't mentioned it. 'I'm lucky, I suppose. Jo and Neil kind of support me. Jo's brilliant. She sticks up for me when Mum has a go about me being lazy. I feel bad, because she and Neil haven't got much themselves, but Jo says they've got all they need and that's what family's for. Says she'd rather I took my time to decide what I want to do with my life than have me rush into the wrong kind of work and get trapped. That's happened to loads of people she knows.' Ritchie pushed his hair out of his eyes. 'It's too easy to carry on doing what you're doing, even if you don't like it.'

'Your mum disagrees with Jo?' Sam asked.

'Yeah.' Ritchie smiled. 'Mum's a typical mum, really. She wants me to achieve something so that it can count as an achievement for her, by proxy – that's what Jo reckons. Mum never had the chance to do anything much because of looking after Kirsty. I think she finds it hard seeing me having what looks to her like . . . well, like a pretty easy time of it, I guess. Jo's more like Mum in that sense: putting other people first, looking after them. Mum doesn't resent Jo like she does me. It's stupid, really. We all end up going round in circles: Mum sticking up for Jo, Jo sticking up for me . . .'

'Does your mother think you're exploiting Jo by letting her support you?' Sam asked, thinking that it would be understandable if she did. He wondered how Jo's husband Neil felt. Were there rows?

'Yeah.' Ritchie nodded. 'Some years back, Jo asked Mum to change her will, asked her to leave the house just to me, said she was more than happy to give up her share. She had a house already, she said. I'm the one who needs Mum's house when she dies, if I'm not going to be renting this dump forever.'

Sam avoided eye contact, concentrated on writing in his notebook. Was this the information Simon wanted? It certainly sounded as if it might be. Sam had given up asking himself how Simon was able to sniff out the presence of an as-yet-unheard story where no one else could. It wasn't one of Sam's strengths, but he had others. He was already feeling better about Olivia Zailer than he'd expected to. He'd yelled at her, but she'd asked for it. And so what if he didn't have the benefit of her ideas about Kat Allen's murder? Was he really going to start worrying that he wasn't privy to the speculations of every civilian who had nothing to do with his case? No. His strength, one Simon lacked, was the ability to look at a situation in a balanced way.

'Mum said her will was her business and she wasn't changing it,' Ritchie went on. 'She came out with some spiel about fairness: how parents have to treat all their children equally, no matter the circumstances, even if one's loaded and one's skint. Not that Jo's loaded, but . . . she's comfortable.'

'You disagree?' Sam asked. The more he heard about Ritchie Baker's mother, the more he approved of her.

'I wouldn't, normally,' said Ritchie. 'I always assumed Mum'd divide things equally between all of us. It wouldn't have occurred to me to want the house for myself if Jo hadn't had the idea. But she suggested it, she said it was what she wanted, and Mum still wouldn't. That's just pig-headed, isn't it? That's trying to make a point.'

Perhaps one that needed making, Sam thought. Never having met Jo Utting, he was finding Ritchie's version of her difficult to believe in. 'Your sister's really that selfless that she'd gift you her share of your mother's house?'

Ritchie smiled. 'Ask Jo if she's selfless,' he said. 'She'll piss herself laughing. She's got everything she could possibly want, she says. Nice husband with a successful business, nice house that they own outright, two beautiful kids, Sabina to help her with day-to-day stuff . . . All Jo wants is for me to be in as fortunate a position as she is. She says to me all the time, "Don't sell yourself short and get any old job just to please Mum. Hold out for something that matters."' Ritchie chuckled to himself. 'Tell you the truth, I think she likes it that I don't work. She likes it that she can ring me or pop round any time and I'm always here.'

He was genuinely fond of his sister, Sam thought, and not only for materialistic reasons. 'So your mother didn't change her will?'

'As far as I know she hasn't,' said Ritchie. 'We haven't discussed it again, for obvious . . . Oh.' He stopped. 'I guess the reasons won't be obvious to you, if you don't know.'

Sam waited.

'The day after Jo and Mum rowed about it the first time – the only time – something weird happened. Jo . . . kind of disappeared without telling anyone where she was going or why. With Neil and the boys. Oh, she came back, but only after they'd missed the whole of Christmas Day. No one's ever said anything, but I think Mum's always thought that their vanishing act had something to do with that argument on Christmas Eve about the will and the house.

Actually, it wouldn't surprise me if Mum *did* change her will after that, without saying anything to anyone. She was pretty frightened when Jo disappeared. We all were.'

Was Sam missing something here? Everything about this story sounded wrong to him. 'But – Jo came back, you said. Didn't she tell you where she'd been and why?'

'No. It was clear she didn't want to talk about it.'

'But if your mother subsequently changed her mind and altered her will to leave her house only to you, why wouldn't she have told Jo? Jo would have been pleased, presumably, to have got what she wanted.'

'I don't know that Mum ever did change her mind,' said Ritchie. 'I was just speculating.'

'If she did, though. Hypothetically.' It was the lack of communication, and Ritchie's presentation of it as normal, that interested Sam most. 'Why do you think she wouldn't tell Jo straight out?'

Ritchie considered the question. 'Hard to put into words,' he said eventually. 'I guess . . . if Mum thought the row about the will had upset Jo enough to make her do that, she'd have been afraid to raise the subject again, no matter what she had to say about it. When Jo decides a subject's closed, it's closed. If she doesn't want to talk about something . . .' He left the sentence hanging in the air.

'And you haven't asked your mum about the will since, when Jo's not been around?'

'No. It's not my place, is it?'

'You and Jo haven't discussed it between yourselves?'

'No way. She disappeared for the whole of Christmas Day,' Ritchie emphasised, as if Sam might have missed the point the first time. In his mind there was a causal link, clearly. Sam had yet to be convinced that it wasn't a coincidence. Often, when one thing followed another, people assumed a cause and effect relationship between the two that didn't exist.

'No way I'm bringing that subject up again.' Ritchie looked upset suddenly. 'The whole family was together, Jo had hired this mansion place in Surrey . . . we were supposed to be having a nice time.'

'Instead, you spent the day worrying,' said Sam.

'Yeah, and trying to persuade the police to give a toss. Not you. Surrey police. Whatever dealings I've ever had with local police, they've been great.'

Sam nodded, appreciating the concern for his finer feelings, wondering why he didn't disapprove of Ritchie as much as he imagined most people would, as much as he felt he ought to. He made a note to remind himself to check if Ritchie's details were on any of the police databases.

'I love Jo to bits and I see her all the time, like I said, but I learned my lesson after Surrey, however many years ago it was. Five or six, maybe? No, Barney was a baby, so more like seven years.'

Timekeeping for people without diaries, Sam thought. It sounded like the title of a novel his wife Kate might read for her book group. 'Learned your lesson how?' he asked.

'They still all get together every year, but I don't. I make an excuse, usually a pretty lame one. I don't think anyone ever believes me.'

'Excuse for what?' Sam asked.

'I've spent Christmas Day on my own, every year since then,' Ritchie said proudly.

~

Simon pushed Charlie out of his way when she tried to kiss him. 'This stops right here and now,' he said.

Don't follow him. Charlie stayed where she was, in the hall. She heard his coat hit the floor, the fridge door open and slam shut. 'Is that shorthand for "I want a divorce"?'

'It will be, if you can't get your jealousy under control.'

'Jealousy?' What was he talking about?

'Three text messages asking who Johannah Utting is, when you know I'm working and can't text you back and I haven't got time for that shit anyway. I'm sick of it. Every woman's name I mention . . .'

'You think I'm jealous of Johannah Utting,' Charlie deduced aloud.

'If I'd told you who she was, your next question would have been is she attractive.'

'No, it wouldn't.'

'You're not pathetic, so don't act it,' Simon raged on, impervious. 'There's no need to be jealous of every woman I meet. You're the one I'm with. I'm married to you. I don't give a shit about anyone else, and you know it, or you ought to know it. My whole life is you. You and work, but you mainly. Is that the sort of thing you want me to say? If I say it more often, will you stop interrogating me every time I mention a woman's name?'

Charlie took a deep breath. He scared her when he was this angry, but what scared her even more was knowing she could still provoke him. She lacked the soothing instinct that most women seemed to have. 'To answer your questions in order: yes, that's exactly the sort of thing I want you to say, though you might want to work on your delivery. But that's a minor quibble. Will I stop interrogating you when you drop strange women's names into the conversation? All right, yes. Unless there are extenuating circumstances.'

'What the fuck does that mean?'

'It means I still want to know who Johannah Utting is.'

'She's attractive. Very. Prettier than you, but so what? I don't love her and I never will. I love you!'

Charlie flinched. 'Going back to what I said earlier, about your delivery . . . Yelling it at me from the kitchen . . .'

'You're lucky I'm not yelling "Get the fuck away from me," because that's how I feel at the moment!'

'Now, you see, that detracts a bit from the otherwise romantic message you're hoping to put across.' So did the two-litre carton of semi-skimmed milk in his hand that he was about to take a swig from. Charlie decided not to mention it.

'Just because I don't . . . Ah, fuck it. Forget it.' He turned away. *In a different room, facing in the opposite direction.* He was the perfect poster boy for breakdowns of communication everywhere.

'Just because you don't what?' said Charlie. 'Don't have sex with me any more, if you can help it? Don't allow me to explain why I might have asked a question, but assume the worst and attack me instead? I don't give a toss what Jo Utting looks like! I'm not jealous of her and never have been. Did I mention that I have no idea who she is? Who is she? There you go, I asked again. I'm not getting the hang of this surrendered wife thing, am I?' Was it worrying that Charlie was only now getting angry? Her first reaction had been to try to accommodate Simon's unprovoked attack as if it were a high-maintenance house guest he'd invited to stay.

'Do you want to know the real reason I'm paying through the nose to see a hypnotherapist?' she said.

'Proust reckons it's nothing to do with wanting to give up smoking.' Simon put the milk back in the fridge.

'I can't give up anything. I'll never be able to. Not you, not cigarettes, none of the things I love that are killing me. I haven't actually asked her yet, but I'm pretty sure that if and when I do, Ginny'll tell me there's no way she can brainwash me so that I stop loving you and fall for someone normal instead.'

'Anyone normal'd run a mile if they saw you coming,' said Simon. He seemed calmer. Because he was thinking about something, Charlie realised. Her? Did she dare to hope? Probably work, she decided.

'I'm going to save myself some money,' she said, making the decision as she heard herself say it. 'I won't see Ginny again.'

'Our sex life. That's the problem from your point of view, right?' Charlie froze. Had she misheard?

'Everything'd be fine between us, except we don't . . . do it often enough?' Simon stood in the doorway, his body nearly filling the gap between the kitchen and the hall.

'I'm a little bit scared,' Charlie admitted. 'Are we really going to have this conversation?'

'I like sex as much as the next person.'

'That's not true, and if you don't want there to *be* a next person, you're better off admitting it,' she told him. Had she just threatened to have sex with someone else? She hadn't meant to. There had been nights when she'd thought about it, thought about leaving him asleep in bed and driving to the sort of place where she could easily pick someone up, someone she didn't know, would never see again and could screw for the sake of it, because it was what both she and Simon deserved.

She knew she'd never do it; the sexual practice involved in her revenge fantasy had a name, a sufficiently disgusting one to put her off making it a reality.

'It's not that I don't want to do it, and it's not that I want to do it with someone else,' Simon said. 'I swear to you. All right?'

'Er . . . not really. What are you talking about?'

'I should have tried to explain before.'

'Try now. Trust me, if you think your work is done on the explanation front, you couldn't be more wrong.'

'I'm actually attracted to you. Physically.'

Charlie laughed. He made it sound like a recent discovery, one that amazed him.

'I'd want nothing more than to go to bed with you if I didn't know it was what you wanted too.' He swore under his breath. 'I don't mean . . .'

'You don't mean you want to rape me,' Charlie clarified.

'No.'

'It's okay, Simon. I know you don't mean that.' She kept her tone steady. If anything happened to panic him now, they might lose this thread forever.

'I mean that your wanting it to happen means it can, and . . . I suppose I'd rather it couldn't because . . . it doesn't feel right. It's never felt right. Not because of you. None of this is anything to do with you. It's me, something fucked up in me.'

'Go on,' Charlie said.

'It doesn't make sense.' The line she'd heard so often, delivered with the same frustration. Except this time he wasn't talking about some bizarre murder scenario. 'There couldn't be anything more private, but it's not allowed to be, is it?' he said, angry again. Because it was easier than being embarrassed or ashamed? 'You have to do it in front of other people. Or, if you do it on your own, you're a pervert. There's—'

'Hang on. In front of other people?'

'I'm not talking about in public, in front of an audience,' Simon muttered, staring at the floor. Both his fists were clenched. 'Just . . . whoever you're with.'

Charlie got it. He'd meant her. She was 'other people'.

'You're saying it's private, so you're uncomfortable doing it in my presence?' *Don't sound as if you can barely believe it*. 'Even though I'm the person you're doing it with?'

'Which makes me a freak,' Simon said impatiently. 'Everyone does everything in front of the whole world these days. No one cares, no one thinks it's strange. If I need a piss while I'm at work, I'm expected to do it in front of anyone else who happens to be hanging around the gents' khazi. That's always been true, but now . . . Nothing's private any more. People are giving birth on telly, getting the results of paternity tests and lie-detector tests, accusing each other of all kinds of shit that they shouldn't be talking about in public. People are dying on-screen, celebrities having their deaths filmed, euthanasia advocates documenting their own send-offs. You can watch Saddam Hussein getting executed on YouTube, for fuck's sake! And, no, before you ask, I'm not comparing sex with you to a dictator getting what's coming to him. All right?'

Charlie saw the mistake she'd made: she'd assumed it was about her, that Simon didn't fancy her enough, or couldn't shake off the memory of how promiscuous she'd been when he'd first met her. When she thought only about him and took herself out of the equation, what he was saying made sense. No, she corrected herself, it didn't make sense and never would, not to her, but it was consistent with some of Simon's other hang-ups. Until a couple of years ago, he had been unwilling to eat in front of her; he still hated the idea of being seen eating by other people. If Charlie ever suggested they go to a restaurant, he would pretend he was too tired and suggest ordering a takeaway instead.

He locked the door when he used the bathroom, every time. Charlie didn't. Sometimes she didn't even close it. Simon had never walked in, not once.

His parents were people who trembled with fear when the

doorbell rang. Charlie had seen it happen, more than once. 'Who's that?' they said, or even sometimes, 'What's that?', as if they no longer recognised the sound of someone from the outside world wanting to interact with them.

Yes, it made perfect sense insofar as anything about Simon made sense. Charlie told herself to be happy that at last she knew, at last she understood what the problem was. Solving it could come later. There had to be a way.

'I know what you're thinking,' said Simon. 'I don't do that either.'

'Do what?'

'I don't mean private like that – with a porn film, or a wank mag.'

'I didn't think you did.'

'I'm not some kind of . . . deviant.'

'I know that, Simon. I understand, but . . .' God, this was hard. Being able to laugh would have helped. Or cry, or scream. 'You're kind of trapped then, aren't you? Your inhibitions apply equally to having sex with me – in front of me, as you see it – and to what you'd call being a pervert. Which a lot of people wouldn't think was perverted or wrong at all, by the way. Contrary to what your mother might have told you, it isn't a sin. Everyone does it. Not necessarily using pornography, but—'

'I don't.'

'Everyone else does. Ask around. And it's not an either-or, on your own or with someone. You can do both. Both come highly recommended,' she couldn't resist adding. The basics of sex explained, in nutshell-compliant format.

Simon pushed past her to get to the stairs. *Conversation over.* Charlie wanted to ask what the plan was. They'd discussed the problem openly; that had to be a good thing. Did it mean Simon would be more self-conscious and awkward in future, or less so?

She followed him up the stairs, then nearly fell down them when he swung round to face her. 'Jo,' he said.

'Sorry?'

'Jo Utting.'

'Even Jo Utting,' said Charlie. 'I'm sure she wanks up a storm.'

'*What?* That's disgusting. I wasn't, or I never will be again, talking about that. You called her Jo, not Johannah.'

'It's what she calls herself,' Charlie countered.

'You asked me who she is,' Simon snapped. 'If you don't know who she is, how do you know what she calls herself?'

'You'd have the answer to that question by now if you hadn't assumed—'

'Tell me what's going on!' Simon roared in her face. 'This is important.'

Unlike what we were talking about before?

'No,' Charlie said. 'Not until you apologise.'

'I'm sorry. All right?'

'Not all right. Too quick and therefore not at all satisfying. What are you apologising for?'

'I don't know.' He looked around, as if he was hoping to see the right answer somewhere near the stairs or on the landing. 'Anything, everything. Tell me. Please.'

'I need a drink first, and to sit down.' She wanted to add that she'd had a shock. It was true.

Simon sighed heavily, ran his hand over his face, and Charlie had a sense of a pulling apart, though they hadn't been touching. Some binding force had been broken, and it was a relief; she had regained the ability to move and think freely, independently of his movements and thoughts. He had liberated her. Temporarily. He would always be able to stop her in her tracks at will, twist her perceptions, warp her sense of herself. Crazy to imagine that the likes of Ginny Saxon would ever be able to change that.

They didn't speak as they poured drinks and went to sit in the lounge. Pretending to be civilised, normal people, Charlie thought, grabbing a beer and settling in for a nice relaxing evening. She knew she would have Simon's full attention as soon as she started to tell the story. That was the difference between them, one of many. Even as she told him about Amber Hewerdine and Little Orchard, part of her mind would be on what she'd discovered about him, what he'd confessed to. Was that how he saw it also, as a confession?

Would he think about it again later, or pretend to himself that the conversation had never taken place?

Charlie felt the need to match his confession with one of her own; if she could have added his shame to hers and felt all of it, for both of them, she gladly would have. She hoped he'd be able to forgive her what she now knew about him and not resent her understanding as another invasion of his privacy.

She told him about having posted copies of some of the Katharine Allen notes through Amber Hewerdine's letterbox the previous night. She started to apologise, but Simon stopped her, told her he didn't care, that he'd been thinking about doing it himself. 'What else?' he asked.

Charlie described her meeting with Amber at the internet café, the favour she'd refused to do for her, the email she'd sent to Little Orchard's owner.

'Why did you bother?' Simon interrupted her. 'So what if some French woman who once rented a house to Amber Hewerdine doesn't want to do it again?'

'That's what I thought with most of my brain,' said Charlie. 'But there was a tiny part of me that wondered if this Little Orchard place had something to do with Kat Allen, or the fire at Amber's house last night, or . . . I don't know. I just couldn't see why she'd ask me to do it, me of all people, unless it was because she knew I was married to you. I had a feeling she thought Veronique Coudert and her house were connected somehow – but she wasn't sure enough to talk to you about it, in case she was wrong, so she came to me with it instead. Almost hoping I'd tell you, or look into it, or . . .' Charlie shrugged. 'I couldn't see any other reason why she'd ask a police officer she hardly knows to do that.'

'Okay, so you sent an email to Veronique Coudert,' said Simon. 'And?'

'I sent an email to Little Orchard's owner,' Charlie corrected him. 'As an innocent holiday home seeker, I don't know his or her name.'

'And?'

'Stop saying "And". Shut up and I'll tell you the and. I got an email back saying yes, fine, when did I want to book for?'

'So Amber's hunch was right,' Simon said thoughtfully. 'She's the one who isn't welcome there, her specifically. And she had no idea why that might be?'

'No, but that's not the most interesting part. The email from the owner, an email that made unambiguous reference to her *being* the owner, wasn't signed Veronique Coudert. It was signed Jo Utting.'

'What?'

'Now, I'm guessing Jo Utting and Johannah Utting are the same person,' said Charlie. 'So I ask you again, with not a jealous bone in my sex-starved body: who is Johannah Utting?'

'Amber Hewerdine's sister-in-law and closest friend,' Simon murmured. 'Except Amber doesn't like her much.'

'If they're so close, how come Amber doesn't know that Jo owns Little Orchard? And who's Veronique Coudert? Simon?' She'd lost him to his own thoughts. 'Simon!'

'She was willing to let you book, you say?'

Charlie gritted her teeth. 'Forget it, Simon. I'm not—'

'Book it,' he said, standing up. 'Soon as you can. Is it empty at the moment?'

Should she pretend she hadn't noticed that no one was due to stay at Little Orchard this weekend? Too late; he could see the truth in her face.

'You could set off tomorrow,' he said.

'Me? Why me? No! No, I couldn't set off tomorrow. I have a job, and a—'

'Phone in sick. You've done it before.'

Nothing's been decided or arranged. Nothing can be, unless you agree to it. Don't agree. Don't. 'Why don't *you* go?'

'Jo Utting knows my name and my face,' Simon said. 'I'll meet you there, but she can't know it's anything to do with me. Whatever she's hiding . . .'

'This is crazy, Simon. There's no need to go tearing off to some random house in Surrey. You don't even know why Amber's so desperate to go back there. Why don't you talk to her, or Jo Utting, or both of them?'

'I'm going to. That's exactly what I'm going to do. And you're going to book Little Orchard for this weekend, so that I've got instant access, soon as I've spoken to Amber and know why I need it.'

Charlie closed her eyes. My entire life could legitimately phone in sick, she thought.

'What are you waiting for?' The sound of his voice chipped away at her attempt to form a judgement of her own. 'Open your eyes.'

Nowhere to hide. So much for privacy. And autonomy.

'Book Little Orchard,' he said on his way out of the room. A few seconds later, Charlie heard the front door slam shut.

Let's have a few minutes of silence, breathing slowly and deeply, calmly and quietly, letting go of all stress and tension. You too, Simon. I'm concerned that the jagged rhythm of your breathing's going to affect Amber. Breathe deeply into your chest, right down into your diaphragm. Better. Much better.

All right, good. Now let me explain why it's vital that we stay calm. A memory's surfaced and there's every reason to think it's an important one, but that doesn't mean it's the only one that's likely to come up. Often when you unlock one repressed memory, others spill out with it. So instead of getting excited about what Amber's remembered, let's put it to one side, take it for granted, start to talk about it as if it's part of what we've always known. Though of course it isn't, and that's what's so fascinating about repressed memories when they surface. One never doubts them. Amber, you say you're certain. This latest detail is an integral part of the scene as you remember it. Hard as I might try, I wouldn't be able to persuade you that you imagined it. And yet, five minutes ago, it was missing from your mental picture. Now that it's slotted into place, you perceive it as having always been there, but at the same time you know it wasn't. So if you didn't know it before, if it was totally absent, and now you know it as surely as you know your name is Amber, where did that knowledge come from?

That's how it feels when a repression breaks the surface: one minute it's not there at all, next minute it's always been there in its entirety. It's very different from the sense that something's hovering around the outer reaches of your memory, the 'Ooh, it's on the tip of my tongue' feeling. Those tip-of-the-mind memories are ones we've left lying around and forgotten about because they don't matter to us. When we realise we need them and look for them, they usually present themselves without too much trouble – first as a tickle in the brain, then a partial answer, then a whole one. Like a baby being born – first the head, then the shoulders . . . you get the idea.

Repression's different. We repress things for a good reason: to protect ourselves. Amber, you expressed disappointment because, although you've solved a mystery – yes, you have, whether you realise it or not – it isn't the mystery you were hoping to solve. You still don't know where you saw those words written on that lined sheet of paper. Relax. That might be the next memory that presents itself, now that we've oiled your unconscious mind's lock mechanism. And so what if it doesn't? Sometimes the right answer doesn't take the form you expect it to take. Going out on a limb, I'd say your disappointment is denial in disguise. It's a safety net. You're still trying to pull the wool over your own eyes because you're scared of knowing the truth. If you're disappointed, that must mean we haven't got anywhere today, our session has been a waste of time. But it hasn't. We have got somewhere. You've taken us somewhere, with the missing detail that you remembered, and it's somewhere that's frightened you so much, you're trying to put your awareness into reverse.

No, don't . . . sorry, Simon, you'll get your chance to speak to Amber afterwards, but . . . it's important that I continue to lead this session.

Amber, much as I understand the temptation, you mustn't give in to it. If you force yourself to deny what you know, you'll make yourself ill – physically, psychologically, or both.

So, what do you know? Let me throw professional behaviour out of the window again, because if I wait for you to put your new knowledge into words, I suspect we'll be sitting here for another year.

I'm going to tell you exactly what you've just told me. Listen, and see if you can hear how obvious the truth is.

When you, Jo and the rest of your party left Little Orchard in 2003 – sorry, on New Year's Day 2004 – the key to the locked study wasn't hanging from the nail behind the kitchen dresser.

Everyone was outside, getting into cars, saying goodbye, talking about what a lovely time they'd had, nobody mentioning the disappearance and reappearance of Jo, Neil and their sons. You and Jo were the last two people to leave the house. 'Can you get out?' Jo said to you, abruptly, as if you'd done something wrong. 'I need to set the alarm. You're standing in front of the sensor.' You were next to the door. Before you stepped outside, you glanced into the gap between the dresser and the wall, and you saw that the key wasn't there on its string, where you found it when you and William were looking for it on Boxing Day.

Jo keyed the code into the alarm, joined you outside, closed and locked the kitchen door. She then went to replace the house keys in their hiding place in the garage, and after telling us that she did that, Amber, your exact words were, 'I didn't see her do it, but I assumed she did.'

What do you assume now? Did or didn't Jo return the keys to their hiding place in the garage, to be collected later by the owner, or the cleaner? Or do you think she put them in her handbag and took them home?

You've already told us that the cleaner, when you went to Little Orchard yesterday, didn't recognise the name Veronique Coudert, said she wasn't the house's owner. I'd like to pick up something else you said before, too. Dinah and Nonie wanted to have a go on the trampoline in Little Orchard's garden yesterday, and you told them they couldn't. If they waited till the weekend, they could have a go on William and Barney's trampoline, which is exactly the same kind, and which I assume was chosen and bought by Jo, since she makes all the decisions in that house? And if Jo knows which she thinks is the best kind of trampoline . . .

Amber?

All right, since you won't say it, I will: I think Jo is the owner of Little Orchard. Jo and Neil. They didn't rent it for the whole family to stay in over Christmas in 2003 – they invited everyone to stay in their second home. Replacing the key on the back of the dresser didn't matter. Guests have to leave things as they found them, but if a house is yours, you can move whatever you like.

Simon, you're nodding. You knew? No, sorry, don't answer me. This can't become a three-way conversation.

Amber, keep your eyes closed, keep breathing slowly and deeply. Think about that locked room, Little Orchard's study. Think about what might be in it: everything in the house that proves it belongs to Jo and Neil. That's why Jo was so frightened when you wanted to go in there.

Think about what else you know. It's odd that Jo and Neil chose to keep their ownership of Little Orchard secret. Think about whether you know the reason for their secrecy. You know more than you think you know. Is anyone else in the family well-off enough to afford a large, luxurious second home? From what you've said, I doubt it. Jo and Neil might be embarrassed to be seen to be as wealthy as they are. They give money to Jo's brother Ritchie, you said before. Neil, who earns all the money, doesn't mind Jo supporting her work-averse brother. That would make more sense if they have plenty to spare. If they don't want people to envy their wealth, perhaps that also explains why they live in a house that you've said several times is too small for them.

Sorry, Simon, I know you're desperate to speak, but please just bear with me. There's more coming, and we need to get to it. It's starting to be a real problem, Amber, that you're intent on withholding so much. I wouldn't normally break confidentiality like this, but then I wouldn't normally have a detective in the room during a patient's hypnotherapy session, so what the hell. Before you arrived, Simon, Amber was telling me how much better she was sleeping at Hilary's house, Jo's mother's house, than she does at home. I suggested a reason for this and she got angry, told me I had no idea what the reason was, that *she* knew exactly what it was. When I asked her to set me straight, she clammed up.

Tell us now, Amber. Why are you sleeping so well at Hilary's, if not for the reason I suggested?

And for the hundredth time: what's the secret you told Jo? What does she know about you that you're so ashamed of?

11

Friday 3 December 2010

I am awake, and not in the usual way. Newly awake, without the scratchy sandpaper lining inside my eyelids that I've grown so used to. I feel substantial and defined – as if I've come back from some-where far away – a place you only know you've been to once you've got back safely. Luke sits on the edge of the bed, staring at me as if an authority figure has ordered him to guard me, watch my every movement. 'You've been asleep,' he says. 'All night.'

'Is that an accusation?' I miss the heaviness of sleep already – a blanket that has been pulled away.

'You got into bed, closed your eyes and slept. What's going on? How come you can sleep here and not at home?'

'I'll take that as a "yes". I was joking, but . . .' I'm stalling, and it's not fair. 'Forget my insomnia. Where are the girls?'

Luke gives me an odd look. 'At school. I put them on the bus ages ago. It's ten to nine.'

I nearly laugh. He sounds like a concerned doctor talking to an amnesia patient. I find it hard to believe that Dinah and Nonie got up and dressed and had their breakfast without waking me.

I crawled into bed at eleven o'clock last night. I've slept for nearly ten hours. Incredible.

'Did either of the girls . . . say anything this morning?' I ask Luke. I have to be at Ginny's by ten and I need a shower before I go anywhere, but this conversation can't wait.

'No, but it was pretty obvious there was something they weren't saying. Why did you take them to Little Orchard last night? What happened there? What's going on, Amber?'

I don't want to do this, but I have to. Even knowing it's going to

283

sound like a threat. 'I need an undertaking from you that you won't tell the police. No matter what.'

'The *police*?'

The panic in his voice irritates me. It shouldn't come as a shock to him when the word crops up in conversation. Someone tried to burn down our house; I was questioned in connection with a murder on Tuesday. Luke knows that our life at the moment involves regular contact with detectives.

'I don't want to hear that you've asked Dinah and Nonie to keep a secret from the police,' he says.

'Other way round,' I tell him. He looks as worried as I want him to look. He needs to know this is serious. 'I'm not saying any more until I have your unconditional promise: you don't say anything to anyone. It's not for my sake I'm asking you to keep quiet.' Dinah's harmed no one. If Simon Waterhouse finds out that his mystery words originated with her, he'll want to interview her. The idea makes me feel sick. It would make Dinah and Nonie feel even worse, which is why it can't be allowed to happen, not under any circumstances.

I must be a bad person, as both Jo and I have always suspected: I would let Katharine Allen's murderer go unblamed and unpunished to protect my girls from pain. Except that it's not as simple as that, not if whoever killed Katharine Allen also killed Sharon, and set fire to my house knowing that Dinah and Nonie were inside, asleep. What pain am I prepared to suffer – what pain will I inflict – for the sake of punishing that person?

This is such a strange feeling: I have a new, fast mind that can think quickly and strategically without hurting.

'Tell me,' says Luke. 'If it's in the girls' best interests for me to keep it to myself, I will. I don't care about anything else.'

'Kind, Cruel, Kind of Cruel,' I say. A refrain line I've been reciting for days, the chorus of my frightening, disrupted life. Will its echo in my mind ever stop, I wonder, and those words become ordinary words again? 'I know what it is and what it means. Dinah told me.'

'*Dinah* told you? But . . .'

'She invented it.'

Luke opens his mouth. No sound comes out.

'It doesn't mean she knows anything about Katharine Allen's death. She knows as little as I do.'

Not quite true. If you know who killed Kat Allen, then Dinah knows less than you do. My throat closes. I don't know anything. I can't know something that can't be true. It's impossible.

'I still have no idea where I saw the words written on lined A4 paper,' I tell Luke, hoping he can't hear the tremor in my voice. 'Dinah swears she and Nonie have never written them down, and I believe her. It was top secret, so they didn't risk committing anything to paper. They kept the lists in their heads.'

'Lists?'

'I was right, they were three headings. Kind . . .'

'Amber, slow down. I'm not following.'

'Dinah invented a caste system,' I tell him. 'Don't look at me like that. Do you want to know or not?' I shouldn't take it out on Luke; it's not his fault. 'Last year at school they had a special assembly about all the different religions. They learned about the Hindu caste system: the important people on the top rung of the ladder – Brahmins, is it? – and the Untouchables at the bottom, no mixing allowed. Do you remember Dinah coming home all steamed up about how wrong it was?'

Luke nods. 'Even more so than Nonie.'

'Dinah doesn't mind injustice as long as she's on the privileged end of it,' I say. 'Turns out what she thought was so unfair wasn't the idea of a caste system that values some people more highly than others, but its randomness: you're born high or low, and there's nothing you can do to change your ranking. She decided a caste system would be an excellent idea if it was based on how good people were, how kind. Or how cruel. So . . . she decided to invent one.' I sigh. In other circumstances, I might find it funny. 'A useful way of categorising her classmates.'

'I don't believe this,' Luke mutters.

'And the teachers. No one at school is exempt. Even the dinner ladies and the guy who drives the school bus. Even the head. Caste trumps position-in-school-hierarchy. Since Dinah and Nonie are both Kinds and Mrs Truscott's only a Kind of Cruel, they're superior to her. Kind of Cruel's the most interesting caste. It's a bit more complicated than Kind and Cruel, which are self-explanatory. It covers many diverse . . . personality types. Kirsty, for example. Thinking about Kirsty made Dinah realise she was going to need an in-between caste.'

'Kirsty? Jo's sister Kirsty? But she's—' Luke breaks off. Looks guilty.

'Too disabled to be kind or cruel or anywhere in the middle? Dinah and Nonie disagree. I've tried and failed to explain it to them. I think they've sort of . . . mythologised her. They think that because she's brain damaged, no one can tell if she's a good person or not, that her inability to speak allows her to hide her personality in a way that most of us can't.'

'For fuck's sake,' Luke says, staring at his hands.

'Mrs Truscott's in the Kind of Cruel bracket for a different reason. To quote Dinah, "She tries to be so nicey-nice to everyone, but she's not really being nice because then she'll say the complete opposite to the next person she wants to be nice to." Truscott can't be a Cruel, though, Dinah says. Only overtly horrible people are Cruels.'

'Don't talk about it as if it makes sense, Amber. It's sick.'

'Is it? I'm not so sure.' I'm only sure that I would want to defend Dinah and Nonie whatever they had done. 'If it was nothing to do with an unsolved brutal murder, I'd probably think it was a great idea. I'd want to put all our family members, friends and acquaintances in one of the three categories. I'd hound you until you joined in.'

'Stop,' Luke says.

I never stop when I ought to. He should know that by now. 'I've played worse games, especially at Christmas,' I say. 'It'd be more fun than one of your pedants' paradise general knowledge quizzes. How many pairs of socks did Clement Attlee have in his sock drawer in his house in . . . blah blah blah.'

'Nonie knew about this caste system too?' Luke asks, ignoring my meanness.

'Course she did. She's a big fan. Because it's fair: good people at the top, bad people at the bottom. Dinah made it their joint project from the start, knowing it would appeal to Nonie's sense of justice. I'm sure it's given them hours of pleasure, discussing particular teachers and children, debating which caste they ought to be assigned to. Oh, this'll make you laugh – Nonie insisted on one change to Dinah's system as originally conceived: people had to be able to move up or down a caste if their behaviour improved or took a dive.'

Luke isn't laughing. Neither am I.

'Dinah wasn't convinced at first. She preferred the idea of people being awarded safe-seat pedestals, or, at the other end of the spectrum, being condemned forever for something they did wrong years ago. But Nonie insisted. Quoting again, "Any good person can become bad suddenly, and any bad person can turn good if they try." '

'Did they . . .' Luke clears his throat. 'When they were telling you about it, did either of them mention Sharon's . . . you know, or Marianne, in the context of this caste thing?'

Sharon's killer, I want to say. Not Sharon's 'you know'. We need to start calling things what they are.

You first, then. Hypocrite.

I nod. 'Both. And the person who set fire to our house, assuming that's somebody different.' Which is the opposite of what I'm assuming, so why say it? 'The two fire-starters are both Cruels.' *Except that there aren't two of them. There's only one.*

I try to silence the voice in my head, tell myself I won't know anything for sure unless and until I can work out where I saw that sheet of lined A4 paper.

'Marianne *was* a Kind of Cruel,' I tell Luke. 'For pretending to care about Dinah and Nonie when it's obvious she doesn't give a toss. Hypocrisy and a lack of integrity are recurring themes for Kind of Cruels – Kirsty excepted, obviously. Two-faced people, anyone who lies to themselves about their own goodness.'

Jo. Jo is a Kind of Cruel.

'Marianne's a Cruel now, you'll be glad to hear. The girls downgraded her last time they spoke to her on the phone and she said something mean. They wouldn't tell me what it was, so I assume it was about me, or us.' I tried to convince them that they didn't have to protect me from anything. I think Dinah could have been persuaded, but Nonie wouldn't budge. 'I can't tell you a horrid thing someone else said without saying it myself, and I don't want to,' she said.

Sensing that Luke is waiting for something, I look at him – something I've avoided so far. Eye contact makes it harder. 'I think the school angle's an excuse. The caste system wasn't invented for school.' I can't help smiling. 'Though it comes in handy there. Dinah sacked some people from her Hector play yesterday, giving them no reason why. She could hardly tell them they'd been recategorised as Cruels, no longer worthy of the spotlight, however good their acting skills. Cruels are the lowest of the low. You don't play with them, help them with their homework, cast them in your dramatic productions. Kind of Cruels can associate with Cruels – and Kinds, obviously – but Kinds can't have anything to do with Cruels, in case it contaminates their kindness.'

'How many people know about this?' Luke asks. 'I've always dreaded parents' evening, but this is . . .'

'Oh, no one at school knows. It's embargoed information. Only Dinah and Nonie know about it. Which means they can't put most of their rules into practice, or they only can when they can disguise what they're doing as something else – bit of a drawback, but Dinah's not willing to risk anyone finding out and criticising her invention. She's smart enough to understand that once any system becomes common knowledge, it attracts opposition. That can't be allowed, not for something that's so precious to her. And equally precious to Nonie.'

I blink away tears. 'When they told me about it, they were so terrified I'd be angry – ask them to give it up, or try to tell them why it was wrong. They could have kept quiet, but . . . they knew it was important to me to understand what those words meant. I'd written them down on a newspaper. Dinah saw them, asked me about it. I tried to avoid answering, made a mess of it. She's clever. She knew I'd found out somehow and that something about those words was bothering me. She and Nonie couldn't understand it: if I knew about their apartheid system, why wasn't I bollocking them for it? Why hadn't I brought it up? They discussed it and decided to be brave and ask me, confess all, even if that meant me having a go at them. Which I didn't,' I add defiantly. 'And I'm not going to. I'd prefer it if you didn't either. Later, when things have calmed down, maybe I'll talk to them.' Or maybe not. Will fighting for the rights of Cruels ever make it to the top of my to-do list?

Luke hauls himself up off the bed and walks over to the window. 'You're right,' he says. 'It's nothing to do with school. It's about reordering the world, after Sharon's death. The girls need to know they can put evil in its place. Amber, it's heartbreaking. They need to talk to someone. A professional.'

'You say it as if we've never thought of it before.' Dinah has promised that if we make her talk to someone she doesn't know, she'll pretend her mouth's zipped shut and say nothing. Nonie bursts into tears and starts shaking at the mention of any kind of therapy or counselling, however Luke and I phrase it. 'At the moment, I'm less interested in who they might talk to in the future and more in who they've *been* talking to.'

'What do you mean?' asks Luke.

He's too focused on the girls; he isn't thinking about the police, about Kat Allen's murder. 'If Dinah invented Kind, Cruel, Kind of Cruel, and if she and Nonie – and now us – are the only people who know about it, and they've never written it down on paper . . .'

'They must have done,' Luke says.

'Except they didn't. They swore to me, and I believe them. They've never written down those words, as headings or any other way. Luke, they were at school on the day Katharine Allen was murdered. It was half term. They went to the Holiday Fun Club, the Holiday Your-Parents-Still-Don't-Want-to-Spend-Any-Time-With-You-Assuming-They-Haven't-Been-Murdered Club. You were at work, I was at Terry Bond's restaurant launch party in Truro . . . Dinah and Nonie were at school between eight thirty and four thirty. They weren't in the centre of Spilling, writing, "Kind, Cruel, Kind of Cruel" on a sheet of lined A4, while someone beat Katharine Allen to death in the next room!'

'Then . . . if they didn't write it . . .'

'They also swore, at first, that they hadn't told anyone their secret, but with slightly less conviction. It wasn't long before Nonie was asking for a guarantee that whoever else knew, whoever might have committed the words to paper, hadn't done anything wrong by writing them down and wouldn't get into any trouble.' I smile sadly. 'I think the trouble she had in mind was a strongly worded ticking off for joining in a game that involves defining people as morally untouchable rather than giving them the benefit of the doubt.'

'Who did they tell, for fuck's sake?' I can hear from Luke's voice that he's crying. 'Who do they know who'd kill someone? No one! This makes no sense, it's . . . fucked up.'

'The person they told didn't kill Katharine Allen,' I say. 'People, rather. Two of them, also children. They're as innocent as Dinah and Nonie.'

'Which children? Friends at school?'

'No.' I'm hating this. Hearing the answer is going to be even harder for Luke than it was for me. Nonie's right: you can't tell someone something that's going to upset them without being the person doing the harm. 'Closer to home,' I say. 'William and Barney.'

~

The first thing I do when Ginny opens the door is hand her a cheque for two hundred and eighty pounds: her compensation for having to encounter me again, after I was so unpleasant the first time. 'I don't mind if you want to pin it up on the wall so that you can see it while we're talking,' I say.

She looks puzzled, but reluctantly so – as if, in an ideal world, she would like to understand what I mean.

'The cheque,' I explain. 'In case you need a visual reminder of your incentive for putting up with me for three hours.' If she doesn't let me in soon, I might snatch it back. It's snowing out here. Warmth spills out of Ginny's little wooden room into the cold grey air. I want to be inside.

She smiles. 'If I wasn't putting up with you, I'd be putting up with someone else. Or do you think you're the angriest person ever to cross my threshold?'

Let me cross it first. Then ask me.

'I promise you, you're not. And if I was scared of anger, I'd be in the wrong job.' Finally, she stands to one side, makes an inward-sweeping gesture with her arm. She's wearing black leggings and a pale pink jumper, and smells of something I can't identify at first. Then I realise it's nutmeg. If I met an accountant or a lawyer who smelled of a cake ingredient, I'd assume they'd been baking. Ginny is a hypnotherapist, so obviously she's chosen nutmeg oil in preference to perfume.

Prejudices are comforting: everyone should make sure to cultivate at least three.

I walk in, stamp my feet on the mat beside the door. Snow slides off my shoes, turns from white to transparent as it liquefies. I take off my coat, hat, scarf and gloves, and try not to resent the hours I've committed to spending here. It's hard. If I hadn't come on Tuesday, if I hadn't listened to all the people who extolled the effectiveness of last-resort hypnotherapy . . . If it's so brilliant, why is it nobody's first choice? Why hasn't word-of-mouth pushed it up the league table?

'This is a first for me,' Ginny says. 'No one's ever booked in for a whole morning before.'

I adjust the reclining chair so that it's as upright as it can be, feeling more comfortable in this position, more equal. What is it about hypnotherapy that makes it work better horizontally than vertically?

Stop. Give it a chance.

'I'm sorry I accused you of lying,' I say to Ginny. 'I had no right to yell at you and storm out without paying. You were right, I was wrong. I just . . . I was confused. I thought you'd said something and asked me to repeat it and—' I break off, wondering how much she already knows. 'Did Charlie Zailer tell you about the case her husband's working on? Katharine Allen's murder?'

'She didn't, no, but I've since been interviewed by the police.'

'About me?' Why else would they talk to Ginny other than to ask about my state of mind, how I'd come to say the magic words, whether I'd looked and sounded like a murderer when I'd said them? 'What did you tell them?'

I don't like her smile. It's a pity smile, not the kind that anyone with any self-respect would want to be on the receiving end of. 'Amber, I'm really sorry, but I'm not comfortable with you asking me about my interactions with the police. Why don't we talk about what you'd like to do here today?' From her tone, it sounds as if she's about to offer me a choice of face-painting, skipping, or playing in the sandpit.

Stop. Seriously. How would you like to have to deal with you? Give the woman a break, for fuck's sake.

'Kind, Cruel, Kind of Cruel,' I say.

Ginny nods, as if it makes sense all by itself.

'I saw it written down on a piece of paper – three headings, with spaces in between. Lined paper: blue lines going across, one pink vertical line on the left, for the margin.'

'Why are you telling me what the paper looked like?' Ginny asks.

'I have a strong visual memory of it, but nothing else, no context. I need to know where I saw it. Hypnotherapy's good for making memories resurface, supposedly. I mean, that's what it's for, right? So . . . here I am.'

That sheet of paper is the piece of the puzzle that's missing. Dinah and Nonie didn't kill anybody; neither did William or Barney. Which means one of them must have shared the secret with someone else, someone who wrote those words on a notepad in Kat Allen's flat before or after they brought a metal pole down on her head. If I can remember where I saw that torn-off page, I will know who in my life is a murderer. *I'll know for sure.*

'Hypnotherapy's great for retrieving repressed memories,' Ginny says, 'but I have to be honest with you, Amber, because it won't help either of us if I'm not: I'm sensing a potential problem, and it's a serious one.'

I don't want to hear about what might go wrong. This has to work. 'I'm willing to do whatever it takes to find out what I need to know,' I say. 'I'll come as many times as I have to, and pay as much as—'

'Amber, Amber – stop.' Ginny holds up both hands, as if miming a window. 'It's not a question of insufficient time. It's more complicated than that. Our unconscious minds are their own bosses. Really, they are. Yes, repressed memories come up under hypnosis, but randomly. Though, actually, there's often a reason.' She sighs. 'I'm not doing a very good job of explaining this, am I? Look, to put it simply, using your case as an example: you want to know where you saw a piece of paper. Your conscious mind thinks that's what you need to know. It thinks it's *all* you need to know. Problem is, there's a strong chance your unconscious mind disagrees. It'll release other memories – not what you're looking for, things that strike you as entirely irrelevant . . . except they won't be irrelevant.'

I hate that knowing look in her eyes. This is my nightmare, not hers – my life in chaos, my girls in danger – and she thinks she knows more about it than I do.

'They'll prove they're not irrelevant by presenting themselves to your conscious mind over and over again, and you'll think, "Why does this stupid incident keep coming back when it's so insignificant?" Hopefully, that's when you'll realise it isn't insignificant at all. Whatever it is, chances are it'll be more important than where you saw your piece of paper.'

No, it won't. She knows nothing.

'What you need to know and what you want to know are two different things,' she goes on, enjoying the sound of her own wisdom. 'I think you'd benefit enormously from hypnotherapy. I'm certain I can help you, and that you'll solve several mysteries you don't know exist. Not murders – mysteries inside you, in your character, in your day-to-day life. What I can't do is guarantee that you'll remember this one particular detail, and . . . I have to say, the more you set it up as the big crucial thing, the less likely you are to remember it.'

'Fine,' I say, though it isn't. It's as far from fine as Mozart's *Requiem* is from a disappointing Eurovision Song Contest entry, but if I want to get anywhere, I have to try to cooperate. 'Fine. Look,

I told you, I'll do whatever it takes. If you think it'll help if I stop wanting to know what I want to know, I'll try to stop.'

Ginny presses the palms of her hands together. 'Why don't you lie back, relax, and stop worrying about results and outcomes?' she says. 'We've got three hours, so let's do some hypnotherapy, some free association, and see where it takes us. Okay?'

'You've got no personal experience of murder, have you?'

'No. Does that bother you?'

'What about your patients? I'm sure you've got abuse victims coming out of your ears, but have you got anyone else like me, where murder's the issue?'

'No, and—'

'Have you ever?'

'Amber, murder isn't the issue for you. You only think it is.'

'Funny how everything I think turns out to be wrong, isn't it?' I snap. 'Tell you what: why don't I go and get my legs waxed, and you can sort out all my problems on your own, since you seem to know more about me than I do.'

Ginny smiles as if she appreciates the joke. 'You think you want to know who killed Katharine Allen, but you don't wonder why it matters so much to you. You didn't know her, did you? It's the police's job to find her killer, not yours.'

I laugh. 'Are you serious? No, I didn't know her, but I know I've seen a piece of paper that was torn from a notepad in her flat. That means there's a chance I know her murderer, in case you're too dim to work it out.'

'Exactly,' says Ginny.

What kind of person says, 'Exactly' when you've just proved they're a fool?

'You came to me on Tuesday hoping I could cure your insomnia.'

I haven't got the patience for this. I know what I did on Tuesday; I don't need a recap. *Previously on* The Smug Hypnotherapist . . .

'You told me you knew why you couldn't sleep – stress – but made it clear that you were unwilling to discuss what was causing the stress. Now, thanks to a combination of circumstances that no one could have predicted, you've brushed up against a murder investigation and, again, you come to me with a specific, narrowly focused request: you don't want to get sidetracked, you just want to find out this one thing and then you'll be fine. Just as, on Tuesday, you believed that if I could cast a spell on you to make you sleep, everything else would be fine.'

She's unbelievable. And I'm a saint for not walking over and smacking her in the face. I imagine myself doing it, then saying, 'Sorry, but we don't all work in the caring professions.'

'You might not have been lying on Tuesday, but you are now,' I tell her. 'At no point did I say or think that if I slept, everything would be *fine*. What I thought, and sorry if I didn't make it clear, was that if I slept, I might not die in the next fortnight. See the difference?'

'Amber, I don't want to argue with you. We should stop this and get on with the hypnotherapy. The more I say, the more there is for you to twist.'

'And vice versa.'

'Your issue isn't insomnia and it isn't an unsolved murder. You're here now and you were here on Tuesday because there's something terribly wrong in your life and you don't know what it is. That scares you. That's the mystery I hope to be able to help you solve, if you'll let me. Why don't you lie back? Adjust the chair to make it go flat, close your eyes, and—'

'Wait,' I say. 'Before we start, there are things I need to tell you.'

'No, there aren't. You only think there are.'

Unbelievable. 'I feel like that tree,' I say, mainly because I know it will confuse her.

'Tree?' She looks at the botanical prints on her wall. None are of trees. *Guess again.*

'The one that falls in an empty forest. No one hears it fall. Can it be said to have made a sound if there was no one there to hear it?'

Ginny frowns. 'And . . . you feel like that tree?'

'Was there any point in my brain popping round this morning, if you're going to dismiss every thought it produces?'

'Your brain's a bully,' says Ginny. 'It needs to back off.'

'It feels the same way about yours,' I tell her.

'That's already an improvement.' She smiles. 'A feeling is always an improvement on a thought, in therapeutic terms. Look, I'll do you a deal: you tell me whatever you want, and then, from then on, I'm the boss. You switch off your brain and take orders from me? Agreed?'

'All right.' *Kind of.*

Now that she's given me permission, I don't know where to start. And then I do: with the mystery words. I tell her that when I blurted them out to her on Tuesday without being aware of what I was saying, my mind was on Jo's Christmas vanishing act seven years ago; I was trying to decide whether it was too showy, too good a story – did it count as a newly surfacing memory, given that it was so often in my mind?

I describe what happened at Little Orchard in detail. It's more of a relief than I imagined it would be. It doesn't help me to understand any of it any better, but it feels good all the same to arrange the facts and present them to someone who isn't a member of the family. When I've finished, the gaps in my knowledge seem more clearly defined.

I tell Ginny about Sharon's death, Dinah and Nonie, Marianne, the adoption that might or might not happen. There's no need, but I find myself wanting to say more, so I explain about Terry Bond and the residents' association, about my DriveTech course and the scam Jo and I pulled. I allow myself to rant about the hypocrisy of Jo's disapproval that extended only to me and not to herself, her claim that I'd betrayed Sharon by going to the launch of Terry's restaurant. By now it seems necessary to put Jo in context, so I tell Ginny everything I think she needs to know: Neil, Quentin, William and Barney, Sabina, Ritchie, Kirsty, Hilary, the too-small house stuffed full of people.

Over and over, I hear myself say her name: Jo, Jo, Jo.

I must change the subject. I go back to Tuesday, explain to Ginny how I ended up in Charlie Zailer's car; the notebook, DC Gibbs turning up at my house a short while later, being taken to the police station and questioned. My attempts to convey the awfulness of DI Proust make her laugh. Her expression turns serious again when I move on to the case notes Charlie Zailer posted through my letter-box, but she doesn't interrupt. She's a good listener. Her still attentiveness does more than anything she's said so far to convince me that I'm not wasting my time. Nobody in my real life would listen to me for this long, without trying to intervene.

Is that a good enough reason for me to start talking about Jo again, listing things she's done and said over the years, tiny inconsequential things? Why can't I stop?

I force myself to talk about other people: Simon Waterhouse, the shaving-rash bobby that he referred to as a 'police presence'. I tell Ginny about the favour I asked Charlie to do for me, her refusal, my embarrassment. How could I have thought, even in my wildest dreams, that she'd agree? I wouldn't have made that mistake if I'd had a good night's sleep, but that was before we moved into Hilary's house. It was after a night of no sleep at all, the night of the fire, the night I emailed Little Orchard's owner, having got it into my head that I had to go back, that I must have seen that lined sheet of A4 there, even though I knew I hadn't, which makes no sense to me – as little sense as Neil being woken in the early hours of Christmas morning and ordered to pack up the boys and go into hiding against his will, hiding from the people he and Jo had invited to spend Christmas with them.

Eventually, I run out of steam and fall silent. The information I'm holding back rings in my mind, so loud that I imagine Ginny must be able to hear it. I haven't said anything about Dinah's confession, about my knowing what Kind, Cruel, Kind of Cruel means. I try to convince myself this won't matter. Ginny can't imagine I've told her my full and complete life story, missing nothing out. There are other things I haven't mentioned, plenty of things, all unimportant.

'You were right,' she says. 'You needed to get all of that off your chest. I shouldn't have tried to stop you. I just want to pick up on something you mentioned in passing, before we start. You implied that, since moving into Jo's mother's house, you've slept better?'

This isn't 'before we start', I want to say. *We started as soon as I arrived.*

'Yes. It's only been one night, but . . . I slept really well.'

Ginny nods. 'Because of the police presence outside the house.' She smiles. 'You're off duty. Someone else is making sure Dinah and Nonie are safe, so you can sleep.'

No. I nearly don't bother to say anything. Then I decide it's important. I can't let her tell me things about myself that aren't true. 'I don't think it's that,' I say. 'In fact, I know it isn't.'

Ginny's shaking her head. 'You told me you, Luke, Dinah and Nonie climbed out of the window onto a flat roof.'

'So?'

'You might not realise it, but that's why you chose that house and not a different house. You saw that window and that roof and thought "fire escape".'

'True, but that's not what you said before. I'm not sleeping well at Hilary's because of any police presence.'

'For eighteen months, you and you alone have been responsible for making sure that what happened to Sharon can't happen again. That's how you've felt, anyway. That's why you've had to spend all those nights patrolling the house.'

I stare out of the window at the falling snow. It's starting to settle, thickening. 'What do you want, a gold star?' I say.

'Luke wouldn't understand. You haven't talked to him about it because there's no point. He'd only say it's crazy to think that whoever killed Sharon would want to harm Dinah and Nonie. If they had, they'd have left them inside the house with their mother before setting fire to it.'

'Can you please not—'

'What can you say to that? Nothing. He's right, but it makes no difference. Nothing he could have said would have persuaded you that the same wouldn't happen again: a fire, started deliberately.

Next time the girls might not be so lucky, so how can you sleep and take the risk? How can you ever sleep again?'

I clear my throat. I feel as if I've been run over by a truck. No one can see the bruises and breakages; only I can feel them. 'Thanks for clarifying that for me,' I say. 'I thought I needed therapy for insomnia. Turns out all I needed was a trustworthy babysitter, all night every night.'

'Which, at Hilary's, you have,' says Ginny. 'Which is why you slept last night.'

'No, it isn't.'

'Amber . . .'

'Fuck you and your patronising . . .' I'm on my feet. It's a good job I didn't get as far as reclining my chair. Hard to storm out in disgust from a lying-down position. *Can you lift me up so that I can leave, please?* 'Sorry, but you don't get to be right about everything. Do you really think I'd trust some teenage copper I know nothing about to make sure Dinah and Nonie are safe? That I'd trust *anyone* apart from myself to be a match for the kind of evil . . . Look, forget it. There's no point.' I stagger, reach for the door handle. Ginny is saying something about evil, but I don't hear it. All I hear is a clear insistent voice in my mind that seems to belong to nobody, that thinks it can explain the change in my sleeping habits, if only I would listen.

Shut up. Shut up. You're nobody's voice, you're not mine, you know nothing.

The police presence. That's what made the difference. Ginny's right. She must be.

Then why are you so angry with her? Why are you leaving?

It fills the room: the full weight of what I know for sure and can no longer deny. It fills my nose and mouth, until I feel as if I'm suffocating. I have to get out.

I pull open the door and run out into the snow, and into the arms of Simon Waterhouse.

Since you don't want to be patronised, I'm going to be absolutely frank with you: I find your request outrageous. Being treated as an equal is one thing; demanding that I tell you what shameful guilty secrets I was forced to confront as part of my own therapy is not acceptable. And I'm not going to do it. If that's your idea of a fair deal, you must have a bloody screw loose!

Listen to me: the therapist who verbally abuses her patients. What's the problem, Amber? I'm treating you as an equal: you have a go at me, I have a go at you. Perfect equality.

I'm not asking for your secrets because I want to get some dirt on you that I can use against you later. I'm asking you to face and state the truth for your own good. That's my recommendation as a therapist, but, frankly, I don't care whether you do it or not. If you want to be screwed up forever, stay in denial. Be my guest.

The reason I can't tell you my guilty secrets in exchange for yours is that we're not two people chatting here. I'm a therapist, and I take pride in my work. I've invested some time and considerable effort in trying to help you, and I'm damned if I'm going to wreck it by confiding in you as if we're best friends. If I start telling you about my life, my personal history, my mistakes, I become Ginny-the-woman, and believe you me, she's not going to be nearly as helpful to you as Ginny-the-therapist. I told you before: I'm a means to an end here, nothing more. My personality and experiences have got nothing to do with anything.

I'm sorry, Simon. You must be hoping I'll invent some lie to keep her happy, to get it out of her, whatever it is, but I'm not going to do that. Or maybe you're hoping I'll tell the truth? Share my intimate secrets with the two of you, all in the good cause of helping to catch a murderer? Well, sorry, but it's not going to happen. I've made quite a few exceptions today to my general rules, but this is a boundary too far.

Let's be very clear about this, Amber. If we make no further progress today, my unwillingness to share guilty secrets with you in exchange for yours is not responsible. You can blame your own unhelpful attitude. I was willing to set aside my whole morning for you. I even cancelled two appointments, and you swear at me and walk out, exactly like you did on Tuesday. Then Simon persuades me to give up my afternoon as well, and he persuades you to . . . I don't know what he got you to agree to, to be honest. Certainly not to cooperate. You strut back in here with a list of ridiculous over-the-top rules: I'm not allowed to ask any direct questions, I mustn't expect any answers, you'll talk when you feel like talking and apart from that you'll just lie there and let me do all the work, making it clear you think I'm a complete waste of space. And what do I do? I agree. I agree to your ridiculous counterproductive rules, I cancel yet more appointments, because I, too, want to help Simon. I have to go through my hypnosis script three times before I'm sure it's worked, because you're intent on interrupting me to argue about how many steps there ought to be in an imaginary staircase! You're positively garrulous when you see an opportunity to bait me, and silently, sneerily detached the rest of the time. Still, I give you the benefit of the doubt: I talk myself hoarse. I rack my brains for helpful things I can say, I describe the difference between memories and stories, I talk you through every detail of your life and your preoccupations, like some bloody *This is Your Life* host, in the hope of drawing you into a dialogue, but it doesn't work. You're determined to say only the bare minimum.

Yes, I want to help Simon, but I'm not sure I want to help you any more, if I'm honest. I'm not sure you deserve it. There, is that equal enough for you? Are you feeling sufficiently unpatronised?

Yes, I've got secrets. Haven't we all? Yes, there are things I feel guilty about and ashamed of, but I can promise you one thing: speaking my mind now will never be one of them. Now get out of my clinic, both of you.

12

3/12/2010

'Don't blame yourself,' said Simon. He and Amber were sitting in his car across the road from Ginny Saxon's house, with the heater on full blast, not going anywhere. Simon wasn't ready to move. Ginny might have kicked him out of her clinic, but he was entitled to keep his car parked outside it on a public road for as long as he wanted. 'She overreacted. You asked her to do something she didn't want to do. She could have said no without throwing a tantrum.'

'It won't work.' Amber leaned her head against the window.

'What won't?'

'Flattery. Massaging my ego. I had no right to ask.'

'You wanted to start a fight,' said Simon. 'Get us kicked out.'

'Think that if you want to.'

'It's not true?'

She shook her head. 'Ginny said she was willing to be unprofessional to impress me. I wanted to see if she meant it. I didn't do it to wind her up, or make her feel uncomfortable. I don't even want to know her secrets. She's nothing to do with me. I'd rather not know them.'

'Then why ask for them?' Simon felt uncomfortable. He'd spent too long listening to Ginny, had temporarily lost his ability to differentiate between interview questions and therapy questions. Did he ask that last one because it would help solve a crime or crimes, or because he was interested in the workings of Amber's mind? Too easy to tell himself they amounted to the same thing.

'I just . . . wanted her to understand what she was asking me to do,' Amber said. 'It's a bit too easy to tell someone they need to cut their heart open in public and let all the crap spill out in front of strangers. I wanted her to feel the . . . horror's too strong a word. I'll be moderate for a change and call it extreme reluctance.' She shifted in the passenger seat so that she was facing Simon. 'So extreme you feel it physically, not just as an idea, not a purely intellectual preference for secrecy over sharing. I may have cocked up our working relationship . . .' – she mimed inverted commas – '. . . but at least now Ginny knows how I felt every time she ordered me to reveal all for the good of my psyche.'

Simon nodded. How many therapy patients swallowed the for-your-own-good line? Nobody who genuinely valued their privacy, surely. He didn't want to risk alienating Amber – she seemed to be in favour of him where she was against everybody else, for some reason he couldn't fathom – but privately he decided her conditional stance was dubious. Either she could bear to talk about whatever the hell it was or she couldn't. If she could, if telling didn't feel absolutely impossible, why the hell wasn't she giving him the information he needed?

'I could have done with the moral support, to be honest,' she went on. 'Why should I be the only one parading my guilt? If a therapist can share his or her own personal story and make a client feel they're both in it together, equally frail and fucked-up, why is that such a bad idea?'

'Even if it is,' said Simon, thinking. 'Don't tell me training for psychotherapists doesn't include ground rules about how to deal with patients who cross the line and get too personal.'

'Like me, you mean?'

'There'll be a script. Ginny must know it by heart, like she knows the rest of her lines: "breathing slowly and deeply, calmly and quietly", all that shit. She should have been able to handle you without losing it.'

'You say that, but hardly anyone can.' Amber smiled. 'Only you.'

'Don't be daft,' Simon batted away the compliment, if that was what it was. It felt more like an encroachment. Which gave him an idea. 'What about me?' The words slipped out before he'd had a chance to think. Now it was too late. Was he about to make her a genuine offer, or would he cheat if it came down to it, make something up? 'Would it work if I did it instead?'

'Did what?'

Simon gestured towards the wooden clinic building in Ginny's garden. 'She's nothing to do with any of this. Someone kills Kat Allen, someone kills your friend Sharon, your house gets torched – it's nothing to her, is it? We're the ones this matters to, you and me. Forget Ginny. If I tell you something about me that I haven't ever told anyone else, will you tell me what you wouldn't tell her?' It wasn't strictly true that he'd told nobody, though the version he'd given Charlie had been minimal and stilted. Simon had sensed that there was a lot more he could have said if he'd wanted to, without allowing himself to wonder what that more might be.

No, he wasn't going to tell Amber. He'd sooner cut his tongue out.

'I was wondering if and when that might occur to you,' she said.

'You sound as if you're sorry it did.'

'I hate to sound noble, especially since I'm the opposite, but I can't let you do it. Wouldn't be fair. You don't want to tell me anything, and why should you? Ginny's a therapist. She dishes it out, she ought to be able to take it. You're . . . well, you're just an innocent bystander. She's the one who chose a career that gives her a free pass to crack open people's heads and poke around in all the icky stuff.'

'My job's not so different,' Simon told her.

She smiled at him. 'Shut up and thank me for digging you out of a hole. You'd only have had to dream up a convincing lie, and you'd have felt like shit if your scam had worked. I'll settle for being told how long you've known about Jo and Neil owning Little Orchard.'

'Since yesterday.'

'Charlie told you about our conversation in the café?'

Simon nodded.

'Why would Jo lie?' Amber muttered. 'Why not tell us they've got a second home? No one would have been jealous.'

'Did you know about Neil Utting's business? Hola Ventana?'

Amber nodded. 'Named by Jo. They make window films. *Rear Window* by Alfred Hitchcock.'

'Sorry?' Simon was confused.

'Doesn't matter. It's a stupid name for a company. It means "Hello, window" in Spanish. It's supposed to have an accent on the "a" of "Hola", but Jo thought that looked too foreign.'

'You didn't wonder where all the profit from the firm was going?' Simon asked. 'Why the owner of a business as successful as Neil Utting's would be living in a house that's too small for his family on a treeless street in the dodgy bit of Rawndesley?'

The surprise on Amber's face said it all. 'I had no idea there was any success or profit involved. To be honest, I could never work out how they afforded a full-time nanny. Neil doesn't talk about work, and Jo's always made it sound as if Hola Ventana was barely keeping its head above water financially.'

'Far from it,' said Simon, who'd been briefed by the Inland Revenue earlier about Neil Utting's recession-defying business.

'Did she think we'd ask for hand-outs? No.' Amber shook her head, arguing with herself. 'Whatever else you might want to say about her, Jo's not tight with money. The opposite. She's always treating people. She subsidises her brother Ritchie, says he's the baby of the family and she enjoys spoiling him.'

'You don't know the half of it.' Simon told her the story he'd heard last night from Sam, about Hilary's will and Jo's efforts to ensure that her mother's house was left exclusively to Ritchie. 'I've been trying to work out what it means,' he said. 'All the evidence says Jo's generous, but she doesn't want anyone to know she's got more than enough herself. So maybe she gets a kick out of being seen to make sacrifices. Or maybe she's worried you'd all be after her for more than she's willing to give if you knew how much she had. Whereas if you think she's skint, you'll be grateful for whatever she offers.'

Amber was shaking her head. 'No. I don't buy it. If you're that paranoid about your family finding out how rich you are, you're also the sort of person who imagines you can't spare a penny of your huge fortune. You give away nothing, don't even treat a friend to a pizza on her birthday.'

She might have been the voice of Simon's brain; that was exactly the thought process he'd followed, down to the last detail. He felt the need to create some distance between Amber and himself. Turning on the windscreen wipers might help; he would feel less claustrophobic if he had a view of something other than snow.

Amber nudged him with her elbow. 'Look,' she said. The blades had flicked away the whiteness to reveal Ginny standing at the wooden clinic's curtainless window, staring at them. 'What's she doing?'

'Wondering why we're still here. Wishing we'd leave.'

'I'm with her on both.' Amber sighed. 'But we're not leaving, are we? There's a reason we're sitting here instead of going somewhere else to talk, a reason you're not telling me.'

Simon said nothing.

'Jo sent Neil to bed alone so that she could talk to Ritchie and Hilary about Hilary's will,' said Amber slowly. 'If we put together everything we know, from all the different sources, that's our conclusion, right?'

'Probably.'

'So the argument about the will was the catalyst for Jo and Neil's vanishing act. It had to be. Ginny would say it was, for sure. Simon, if I—' She broke off.

'What?' He couldn't understand why he was being so patient. Normally by now he'd be doing everything he could to extract whatever knowledge she was withholding. What was it about Amber Hewerdine that kept him more focused on her needs than his own? He had to get himself together, remember what he was here for. 'If you're in two minds about telling me something, please could you do everything in your power to get into the one that's saying "Tell him, for fuck's sake"?'

Amber closed her eyes. Simon could hear her breathing: short, loud bursts. 'I think Jo set fire to my house,' she said. 'I think she killed Sharon. She couldn't have killed Kat Allen because she was on a DriveTech course pretending to be me, but she arranged for Kat to be killed. I don't know who she got to do it. Neil or Ritchie, I'm guessing. Probably Neil. Ritchie would have messed it up.'

'Why, why and why?' Simon asked.

'I can only answer one of those,' said Amber. 'This week's fire was a warning. She knew I'd be awake. I'm awake most of every night, or I was. It was a risk, but she'd have been fairly sure she wouldn't kill anyone. She doesn't want to hurt Dinah and Nonie. Though if she could be certain she'd end up with them under her roof, she might try to get me and Luke out of the way. If we adopt them, I wouldn't put it past Jo to suggest we make a will saying that if anything were to happen to us, we'd want the girls to go to her.' Amber laughed, covered her face with her hands. 'What am I saying?' she mumbled through her fingers. 'Tell me I'm talking shit. Please.'

'Slow down,' said Simon. 'Go back to the warning. Warn you off doing what?'

'Helping the police. Talking to you. Didn't really work, did it?'

'So . . . Jo killed Sharon and had Kat Allen killed, but you don't know why? No idea at all?'

'None. None for Kat Allen and only stupid ones for Sharon.'

'Such as?'

'Jo knew how close I was to Sharon. Jealousy. She wanted me to have no one but her.'

'Which suggests you're the prize she's after,' Simon pointed out the discrepancy. 'Yet you said she'd kill you to get the girls.'

'Why aren't you telling me I'm crazy?' Amber snapped. 'I must be wrong. I must be.'

'You weren't wrong about Jo owning Little Orchard. Ginny might have been the one who said the words, but you'd realised it long before she said anything. I could see from your face that you knew.'

She looked as if she wanted to deny it. 'I should have known at the time, in 2003. It was obvious to anyone with a brain. There were so many things: the way Jo went ballistic when I suggested opening the locked door, way out of proportion to the situation.

I should have known then that she wouldn't have gone so mad unless the private things in that room were *hers* – the cat well and truly out of the bag if anyone went in and started nosing around. Same bloody trampoline in the garden, the exact same model. Other things, too: an electric blanket on Jo and Neil's bed at Little Orchard, but none on any of the other beds. Jo's got an electric blanket on her bed in Rawndesley too. And . . . there was a manual for guests, explaining how to use everything. Jo didn't look at it. She *bragged* about not looking at it! "Those things are pointless," she said. "Any fool can work out how to live in a house for a few days."'

Amber looked as angry as she sounded. 'She talked about the locked study. How did she know the locked room was a study if she hadn't read . . . if she hadn't *written* the manual? How stupid am I, that I'm only thinking of this now?'

'You can't blame yourself for not realising,' said Simon. 'You'd been told it was a rented holiday house. It wouldn't have occurred to you to doubt it.'

'I saw that Jo hadn't put the key to the study back where I'd found it, hanging from the dresser.' Amber shook her head angrily, unwilling to let herself off the hook. 'I should have known then. I would have, except . . . I didn't want to. Denial – different from repression, remember? If I'd allowed myself to know the truth about Little Orchard, how would I have fended off all the other truths I'd been avoiding?'

Simon waited. Ginny was no longer at the window. He wondered if she'd be gratified to know that Amber was quoting her.

'I never really believed someone from the residents' association had murdered Sharon. Why did I try to persuade the police that was what happened? Not to save Terry Bond.'

'To protect Jo.'

'Even though I hate her. If she died, I'd be relieved. If I could prove she'd killed Sharon, I'd kill her with my bare hands.' Simon could hear that she was crying. He wouldn't look at her again until she'd stopped. Charlie hated what she called his 'crying policy', but nothing she said would ever persuade him it wasn't the right thing to do. Who wanted to be watched when they were in a state?

'I said nothing and did nothing for so long,' Amber whispered.

'We don't go round accusing people of murder if we can't prove it,' Simon told her. 'If it makes you feel better, I'm in the same boat, and I've had experience of murder investigations. Never like this, though. This is a new one for me.' He heard a sniff, hoped it signified the tears drying up, Amber pulling herself together.

'What do you mean?' she asked.

'When I interviewed Jo yesterday, I knew. Like you're saying you know, without understanding how or being able to rationalise it. No evidence, but that didn't bother me. We'll find it. Lack of evidence won't be a problem. But no idea about motive, no theories . . .' Would it be safe to look at her now? Simon decided to risk it. 'Like you, I know it's Jo I'm after, but I've no idea why. There has to be a motive. No one commits three serious crimes, two of them murders, without a motive.' He swore under his breath, then regretted it. He wanted Amber to believe he was more in control of this mess than he felt.

The next words he heard didn't register at first, so unexpected were they. 'I know what Kind, Cruel, Kind of Cruel means.'

Simon listened, stunned, as she started to explain. He'd have been angry if Amber had been someone else, someone who hadn't insisted on special treatment from the start and duped him into believing this meant she deserved it. Where was her apology for not telling him sooner, as soon as she found out? She was making up for it now, recounting the story in minute detail: Dinah and Nonie's school, their politically correct headmistress and her world religions assembly, the Hindu caste system that had inspired Dinah to invent one of her own. Amber kept interrupting her narrative to remind Simon that none of what she was telling him would help him, that she still couldn't remember where she'd seen the piece of paper that might have come from the notepad in Kat Allen's flat.

Interesting that she felt the need to tell him this so many times. He'd heard her admit to Ginny, however reluctantly, that she was sure she'd seen the lined A4 page at Little Orchard. He'd heard her confess to the irrational conviction that if she could only get into the locked study, she'd find it there. Didn't she remember any of that? Ginny had made a point of reassuring her, at the beginning of the session, that hypnosis doesn't affect memory or control: you know what you're doing and saying, and you remember it afterwards.

Simon was picturing Dinah and Nonie Lendrim inside Kat Allen's flat on the day of her murder, writing 'Kind, Cruel, Kind of Cruel' on the notepad, when Amber said, 'The girls swore to me they hadn't written anything down. Anywhere, ever. Dinah might lie to avoid trouble, but Nonie wouldn't.'

If she'd claimed both girls were incapable of lying, Simon would have discounted her opinion. As it was, he believed her. But if not them . . .

'They told two people, and swore them to secrecy.'

'William and Barney Utting,' Simon said. Wanting to prove he'd worked it out before she told him; stupid. He thought about William's explanation of transitive and intransitive relationships. *Dinah tells Nonie a secret, Nonie tells William a secret, William tells Barney a secret* . . . Did that mean Dinah tells Barney a secret or not? Indirectly, yes; directly, no. Did that make 'tells a secret to' transitive or intransitive? *Depends if it's the same secret.* 'Jo's sons,' he said. 'It all comes back to Jo.'

'It was half term when Kat Allen was murdered,' Amber said. 'The day of the DriveTech course. Jo was busy being me. Sabina would have been looking after the boys. But . . . could a woman have done it?'

'What, killed Kat Allen? You're thinking Sabina, at Jo's request?'

'No, I . . .' Amber looked and sounded flustered. 'Nobody would take two children with them to commit a murder. Especially not Sabina. I know it sounds mad, she's a nanny, but Sabina doesn't cope with kids very well on her own. She gets stressed and hassled. No one notices, because Jo's almost always there taking the pressure off, freeing Sabina to nanny the grown-ups in general and Jo most of all.'

'So . . .'

'If Sabina had sole charge of the boys for a day, she'd find it hard to unbearable, and take the easiest option: plonking them in front of the telly, probably, and disappearing off to another room to go on Facebook. She wouldn't attempt a trip to the shops, let alone a murder. And . . . she's a lovely person.' Amber said it as if she was describing an exotic and unfamiliar species. 'It's crazy that we're discussing it. Sabina couldn't kill anyone. It's just that I told you Neil or Ritchie must have done it, and then I remembered Sabina and felt guilty on their behalf, because I'd left her out. It didn't occur to me that a woman—' She broke off. 'Neil's not a killer either. Nor is Ritchie. Useless, yes, but not a murderer.'

Simon thought about Hilary, Jo's mother. Parents, in his experience, were the ones who committed heinous crimes to help their children.

Why? The question gnawed at his brain. Why was Sharon dead? Why Kat Allen? 'I need you to do something for me,' he told Amber. 'Leave your car here and come with me to Little Orchard. Charlie'll be there by now.'

'Charlie? What . . .'

'Ring Luke, tell him to collect Dinah and Nonie from school and take them somewhere where Jo won't know where they are. Away from Hilary's.'

'No.' Amber frowned. 'Not "no" to coming with you to Little Orchard, but "no" to the rest. Why can't I follow you in my car?'

'I want your car left here, where Ginny can see it. And I want your family safely out of Jo's reach. Surveillance or no surveillance, she knows where you are.'

Amber waved his words away. 'Relax,' she said. 'The police presence outside Hilary's house is irrelevant, nothing to do with why the girls are safe there. And nothing to do with why I've started sleeping better, whatever Ginny would have us believe. What is it with you and Ginny?' she asked Simon. 'Why does she need to see my empty car parked outside her house?'

'Why are you sleeping well at Hilary's?' Simon asked. It was happening after all, though no formal agreement had been made: trading information, trading secrets.

'Hilary's Jo's mum,' said Amber. 'She's sacred. Jo wouldn't set fire to her mother's home under any circumstances, not even if all her enemies were staying there.'

All her enemies. Simon wondered how many there were. Jo Utting struck him as a woman who might have plenty of groundless grudges. His biggest fear was that her motives for murder might be so irrational that he would never work them out, however long he puzzled over it. He could end up with all the evidence he needed to convict her, and her still refusing to say why; at that point, keeping her reasons to herself would be her only way of exercising power.

'If Jo wants to attack my family again, she'll wait till we're back at home.' Amber's voice broke into his thoughts. 'That's when she'll feel the need to, if she does – when we've escaped her grasp. For as long as we're at Hilary's, she's in control, or thinks she is. I know it makes no sense to you, but . . . Please.' She clutched at Simon's jacket sleeve. 'Let Luke and the girls stay at Hilary's. They're safer there than anywhere else.'

~

It couldn't be Simon at the door, thought Charlie. He'd texted half an hour ago to say that he and Amber were only just setting off from Great Holling. Who, then? Was Charlie about to meet the more-attractive-than-her Jo Utting, owner of the enormous house Charlie had been rattling around in for the last four hours, for no reason that anybody had bothered to explain to her? If this was Jo at the door, the first three questions Charlie would be asking her were: why was the study locked, where was the key and why advertise in the manual for guests that there was a locked room they wouldn't be able to get into? It was couched in more welcoming terms – 'Do feel free to use the whole house and all of the grounds, apart from the one locked room, our private study' – that put Charlie right off this woman she'd never met. The word 'study' on its own, fine; 'private study' sounded superior and excluding. Charlie had looked everywhere she could think of and found several keys, but none that worked.

The bell rang again. 'Coming!' she yelled, though she was still too far away for whoever it was to hear her. 'Give me a chance.' As she ran from the conservatory in the direction of the back door, she wondered about Little Orchard's give-up-and-go-home rate. It wasn't a problem for her in her small terraced house in Spilling, but here there was little chance of making it to the door before the person who'd rung the bell grew old and died. Tonight, the cause of death was likely to be hypothermia. Charlie's drive to Surrey had been dicey; Simon's was likely to be even worse. She'd texted him, pointlessly, to say he shouldn't risk it, that the official advice from the radio was don't drive anywhere. Simon had texted back four words: 'They didn't mean me.'

Fair point, Charlie had been forced to admit: no one who didn't know Simon personally meant him when they talked about people in general, since he was about as far from a typical human being as it was possible to be.

It was good that he was coming, even with Amber, though Charlie would have given anything to have him turn up alone, and didn't understand why Amber needed to come too. She was praying the snow would die off. All she needed was a text from Simon saying he was stuck in a blizzard on the M25 and likely to be there for the next eleven hours. Stuck in a cold car with only Amber Hewerdine for company.

Amber wasn't attractive, particularly, but she had something – a strange appeal, even for Charlie.

The bell rang a third time, longer and more insistently, as Charlie raced through the kitchen. She groaned when she opened the door and saw Olivia. 'What the fuck are you doing here?'

'What an amazing house!' Liv stared up above both their heads at the lit-up windows. The first thing Charlie had done when she'd arrived was switch on all the lights. 'No back door should have a doorbell, though,' Liv went on. 'Doorbells are for front doors. If you're going to have a permanent back door policy, it has to be knocking only, otherwise it defeats the object. Can I come in, ideally now? It's snowing out here.'

'I'd noticed.' Charlie stood aside, allowing the invasion. She was annoyed to find herself, after the initial shock, glad of her sister's company. 'How did you get here? You shouldn't have driven.'

'How else was I going to get here? Middle of bloody nowhere. You drove here. Your car's outside.' Charlie knew the tone well from her childhood: *you* did it first. 'I hope there are lots of beds made up, because I'm buggered if I'm driving back to London tonight,' said Liv.

'Lots? Won't one be enough for you?' Charlie asked. 'Or are you planning to move between rooms during the night, as you would if they contained men?'

Liv's the slag these days, she thought. Not me. I'm the faithful wife.

'Of course not. I just meant . . . I know Simon's coming. For all I know, other people are too.'

'Liv, this isn't a house party.' What was it, though? Charlie had no idea. She hoped to sustain her pretence that she knew what was going on until it became the reality.

'How many bedrooms are there?' Liv craned her neck to see beyond the kitchen into the hall. 'Can I have the tour?'

'No,' Charlie snapped. 'You can tell me how you knew where to find me, and why you wanted to.'

'Aren't you going to offer me a drink?'

Charlie had changed her mind about wanting her sister here. 'I'm not the hostess, Liv. My relationship to this house is no different from yours. I got here before you, that's all. The cleaner who gave me the keys said there was milk in the fridge, and there's coffee, tea, sugar and a kettle on the side there. Get yourself a drink if you want. You can do it at the same time as answering the question I've now asked you twice.'

Liv made no move towards the kettle. 'I rang Simon,' she said.

Charlie swore loudly.

'It's not his fault. I forced him to tell me where you were. I think his mind was elsewhere.'

'I bet it was,' Charlie muttered.

'I don't want to fight with you, Char.'

'Then what do you want?'

'I've found something out. I can't tell Chris. He mustn't find out it came from me, which means Simon mustn't either.' Liv straightened up, as if steeling herself for confrontation. 'It shouldn't be a problem. I'll tell you, and you can pretend it was you that had the idea—'

'Is this to do with Katharine Allen's death?' Charlie broke in.

Liv nodded. 'It won't occur to Simon that it's come from me. We can tell him the reason I came was to . . . sort things out between us.'

Charlie didn't get it. 'Everything you know about Katharine Allen came from Gibbs,' she said. 'I've told you nothing.'

'I never said you had.' Liv frowned.

'Then if you've found something out, why can't Gibbs know?'

Liv chewed the inside of her lip, stared down at the floor. 'It's too important,' she said.

Charlie laughed. 'You're worried his male pride'll never recover if he finds out his shag-on-the-side's a better detective than he is?' She walked over to the kettle and lifted it. It felt full. Not knowing how old the water inside was, she knew she ought to pour it out and refill it, but she couldn't be bothered. 'Go on, then, let's hear the brainwave,' she said. 'Look in that guest manual on the table, will you? See if it says where the mugs are.'

'I don't need a manual to find mugs in a kitchen,' Liv snapped. 'Open the cupboard nearest to the kettle.'

Charlie followed her instructions. 'More brilliant detective work,' she said, when she found herself staring at more mugs than she'd drunk from in her life, probably, if she were to add them all together.

She picked two at random and put teabags in them. She wasn't listening properly as Liv started talking. When she heard the words 'costume supplier', something twisted in her stomach as she realised she'd been wrong to treat this as a joke. Much as she would have loved to believe her sister had nothing significant to tell her, her discomfort was shouting loudly that it wasn't the case. She asked Liv to stop, start again at the beginning.

'For Christ's sake, Char! Did you hear any of it? You heard the bit about me ringing the school?'

'School?'

'Where Kat Allen worked.'

Charlie swallowed a heavy sigh. This was going to be bad. And something she should have thought of herself. 'No. I didn't. Why did you ring her school?'

'Because Kat was an actress when she was young. She was in films. I wondered whether she might have still been interested in drama as an adult, whether maybe she'd done it with her pupils at school.'

'So what if she did?' Charlie asked.

'Whoever set fire to Sharon Lendrim's house wore a fireman's uniform. A costume, maybe, from a costume shop. I thought . . .' Liv looked embarrassed. 'It was a long shot that I never dreamed would come to anything, but I thought that, if by some chance Kat had still been involved in any kind of acting-related activity, she might have access to costumes.'

Charlie could laugh at this at least. This couldn't be Liv's big revelation. It was preposterous. 'You decided that because she was a child actress, Kat Allen must have killed Sharon? Why would she? Is there even any connection between the two of them?'

'Yes. There is.' The look of mortification on Liv's face had given way to something else, something deeper. Guilt, Charlie realised, as a mixture of anger and envy surged through her. Liv knew she had no right to be the person who worked anything out first; she must have known how Charlie would feel. Yet what choice did she have? She couldn't keep quiet about it.

'There's a connection between Kat Allen and Sharon Lendrim?'

'Yes,' Liv said solemnly. 'The connection's somebody called Johannah Utting.'

Charlie gestured around the room. 'Owner of our mansion for the weekend.'

'Johannah Utting owns this house?'

Didn't know that, did you? Charlie felt childishly satisfied.

Liv pushed her out of the way and set about making them cups of tea, a task Charlie had realised was too boring some time ago. 'I rang Kat Allen's school,' she said matter-of-factly, as if she was reciting a series of mundane instructions. 'I was right: Kat was still a drama enthusiast. More than that: she was the teacher with overall responsibility for drama at Meadowcroft.'

Charlie stopped herself from asking just in time. Meadowcroft was the school's name.

'I asked if she ever hired costumes for school productions, or—'

'Wait a second,' Charlie interrupted. 'Why would the school talk to a random arts journalist about a member of staff who's . . .' She stopped, shook her head as fury sealed her mouth shut.

'Obviously, I couldn't say who I was. Look, I'm not proud of it, Char, but I had to think of something and I was so livid about the way he'd spoken to me . . .'

'He?'

'Sam. That's who I said I was: DS Sam Kombothekra, Culver Valley Police. Sam's a unisex name: Samuel, Samantha.'

'You didn't pretend to be me, then,' said Charlie. 'I suppose that's something.'

'I thought about it, but . . .'

'You decided it'd be an identity theft too far. Agreed. Go on.'

'No, it wasn't that. I . . . I wanted to make it as true as possible. You're not a detective any more, you're a suicide person.'

'And I owe it all to you,' Charlie murmured under her breath. 'What did fake DS Sam find out? I can't believe you got away with it. How many times must Sam have been to that school since Kat died?'

'He hasn't,' said Liv. She handed Charlie a cup of tea. It was too weak and too milky. 'Sellers did all the school interviews. Chris told me.'

'How would *Chris* feel if he knew you were telling me all this instead of him?'

Liv sighed. 'Kat Allen's best friend from Pulham Market, the village where she grew up, runs a costume business,' she said. 'Kat was in the habit of visiting her folks every couple of weeks for the weekend. All the costumes for Meadowcroft's nativities, plays – everything came from her friend.'

'Where does Jo Utting come into it?' Charlie asked expressionlessly. She wanted to get it over with, since there was no avoiding it.

Liv hid behind her mug as she answered. 'I asked the school if they knew this friend's name. They didn't, but they knew the name of her business: The Soft Prop Shop.'

'That's a shite name,' Charlie observed.

'Yes, let's talk about the name of the costume shop.' Liv shook her head. 'It's clearly the most important detail.'

'You rang up? DS Sam Kombothekra again?'

'I spoke to Kat's friend. Like the woman I rang at the school, she just accepted I was who I said I was. Wouldn't happen in London. Anyone'd demand some kind of proof of ID; a toddler would ask. People are more trusting in the middle of nowhere, I suppose.'

'Not for long, if pathological liars like you keep popping in.' *And not me. And don't call everywhere that isn't London 'the middle of nowhere'.*

'You wouldn't think it, would you?' Liv said. 'I'd be *more* suspicious if I lived in some rural hamlet, greenery all around me. I'd worry about truckers strangling prostitutes and leaving their bodies in woods near my house.'

Charlie could guess the rest of the story. 'You asked Kat Allen's friend if she had any fireman costumes.'

'As I was saying it, I was thinking, "You're mad, Zailer, get a grip." But I was right.'

There it was, the painful line Charlie had steeled herself to hear: her sister was right.

'She had two fireman's uniforms. I asked her if anyone hired either of them in November 2008, told her the date of the fire at Sharon Len—'

'Jo Utting,' Charlie said quickly. She wanted to be right too. More right, ideally. If there was such a thing.

Liv nodded. 'Johannah Utting booked one. She went to collect it four days before the fire that killed Sharon Lendrim. I was about to say thank you, get off the phone before something went wrong, but then she said, "How weird." I asked her what she meant and she said, "I remember her. Corkscrew curly blonde hair, pretty. Did she kill Kat?" Then she started crying. It was awful. I didn't know what to do.'

'Why *don't* literary journalists get any training on how to deal with loved ones' grief in the wake of a brutal murder?' Charlie wondered aloud. 'Someone's not thought this through.'

'Oh, shut up, Char. Do you want to know or not?'

What I want is for you not to know. Anything. Apart from your place.

Liv took her silence as a 'yes'. 'It was awkward for a few minutes. I was trying to cheer her up – well, not cheer her up, you know what I mean – and work out what was going on at the same time. First thought to cross my mind was how the hell does she remember a woman who hired a fireman outfit two years ago? Assuming she has a regular supply of customers.'

'How?'

'Kat Allen was there too. In the costume shop at the same time as Johannah Utting, four days before Sharon Lendrim died. They knew each other. They spoke. Kat's friend heard their whole conversation. She clearly remembers Kat being pleased to see Jo, and the pleasure being all one way.'

It was too much. Too much information to take in at once; too much good luck to fall into Liv's undeserving lap. No wonder she didn't want Gibbs to find out. He might as well give up the day job and take up carpentry or stone-wall building; that's how Charlie would feel in his position. 'Jo wasn't pleased to see Kat?' she said.

'Not at all. Apparently she was shocked, and not in a good way.

She said, "What are you doing here?", as if Kat was trespassing. She recovered quickly and turned on the charm, but neither Kat nor her friend could understand why she'd react like that. Jo knew Kat's parents lived in Pulham Market, the costume business belonged to a close friend of Kat's – why shouldn't she be there? Jo was the one who didn't live anywhere near and hadn't been before. Kat was a regular customer.'

'Stop, wait.' Charlie started to feel panicky as unasked, unanswered questions started to jostle for position in her mind. 'How do you know Jo knew that Kat's parents lived in Pulham Market?'

Liv thought about it. 'Kat's friend said. When she was quoting Kat. She told me what Kat had said to her at the time, after Johannah Utting had left the shop.'

'Which was?'

' "Silly woman, she looked like she'd seen a ghost. God knows why, she knows my folks only live round the corner." That's not word for word, but . . .'

'Did fake DS Sam ring Kat Allen's parents?' Charlie demanded. 'Ask how their daughter knew Jo Utting?'

'No.' Liv looked stricken, as if she'd been found guilty of gross negligence. 'I thought I'd done enough. Should I have . . .'

'They knew each other,' Charlie muttered, pacing up and down the kitchen. 'Which is also how *Kat* knew Jo lived nowhere near Pulham Market.'

'I guess so,' Liv agreed.

'What else did they say to each other?'

'Hardly anything, according to the friend. Johannah said, "What are you doing here?", Kat said, "I'm hiring costumes for my school play. I'm a primary school teacher now." '

'You sure about that? "I'm a primary school teacher *now*"?'

'Of course I'm not sure.' Liv's voice shook. 'I mean, I don't know if Kat's friend was sure. All I know is what she said.'

'Jo knew Kat a long time ago,' Charlie deduced aloud. 'They hadn't seen each other for years.' She turned on her sister. 'What else was said?'

'Kat told Johannah – Jo – that she'd got a job in her part of the world, in a school in Spilling. Jo didn't seem happy to hear the news. Kat and her friend had a good laugh about it when Jo had gone, how freaky it was. Why would a woman Kat hardly knows mind Kat being in the costume shop and mind her teaching at a school in Spilling? Apparently she really did seem to mind, both. It made no sense, Kat said. I asked her friend if she said anything more about who Jo was. I thought she might have said, "She's always been a loony, ever since . . ." and then mention something from their shared past.'

'They didn't have a shared past,' said Charlie. 'You just quoted Kat Allen as saying they hardly knew each other. Hardly knowing is still knowing, though.'

'Kat's friend *did* ask, but Kat just rolled her eyes and laughed to indicate that it was too boring,' said Liv. 'Before Jo Utting walked in, she and Kat had been discussing something more interesting to both of them, and they got back to gossiping as soon as they could.'

'So Kat wasn't worried by having seen Jo,' said Charlie. This was a good kitchen for thinking. It was long enough that you could walk laps, keep your brain on the go by keeping your body moving. 'No, she wouldn't have been. She didn't know she had any reason to fear Jo. She didn't know Jo had hired a costume from a shop hours from home because she planned to wear that costume to commit murder.'

Liv nodded. 'I was wrong. Kat Allen didn't kill Sharon Lendrim. Did Jo Utting kill them both, then? That's how it's looking, isn't it?'

'If Kat hadn't gone to her friend's costume shop that day, if she'd gone the day before or the day after, she'd still be alive,' said Charlie.

'Don't say that. It's too horrible.'

'It's true. The meeting at the costume place might not have swung it on its own, but when Kat said she was working in Spilling . . .'

'Jo Utting knew it was more likely she'd hear about Sharon's death, a local murder,' Liv completed the thought. 'Started by someone dressed in a fireman's uniform who turned out not to be a fireman. But why not kill Kat Allen sooner, then? Two years later? What sense does that make? You'd do it straight away or not at all.'

Charlie was shaking her head. 'Jo Utting's alibied for the day Kat died, Simon said. She was on a driver awareness course in place of Amber Hewerdine.'

'Char, you can't tell Simon any of this came from me. If Chris found out . . .'

'He'll have to learn to live with it,' said Charlie.

'Please. I'm begging you. I'll do—'

'Anything? End it with Gibbs?'

'Not that.'

Charlie sighed, pressed her eyes shut. 'Fine. In that case, how about throwing a rock through the window of a locked room instead?'

Re: Next week's appointment

From "Charlie Zailer" <charliezailer@gmail.com>
To ginny@greathollinghypnotherapy.co.uk
Fri, 3 December 2010 5.35 PM

Hi Ginny

Thanks for being so understanding about the short-notice cancellation. And, work permitting, I will do my best to make another appointment in the not too distant future, though based on past experience of never-ending workload, we might have to make that some time next century!

While I'm on the subject of work, I was wondering if I could pick your brains in relation to a man whose case I'm reviewing as part of my work as second in command to the Strategic Lead for Suicide for Culver Valley Police. This is unofficial and off the record, so if that's a problem feel free to tell me to bog off (many people do, all the time), but I'm not going to miss a chance to ask an expert: can you give me any kind of psychological profile on someone who is embarrassed/shy about the prospect of having sex even with someone he loves, because he perceives it as having sex in public – i.e. even a loved and participating partner becomes 'public' or 'audience'? But he wouldn't do anything sexual on his own either, because that would be dirty/ wrong? What sort of background/history/psychological problem might lead to feeling that sex is too private a thing to be done 'in front of' even a partner? I'm fairly certain no childhood physical or sexual abuse was involved, and also certain that it's not an issue of not enjoying sex physically. More a case of things working fine on the desire/physical front, but some kind of strong psychological aversion to having sexual desire/behaviour witnessed. Have you ever heard of this kind of thing before?

Thanks in advance, and don't worry, I won't quote you on anything.

Charlie

13

Friday 3 December 2010

For the third time in my life, I have arrived at Little Orchard. The snow is still falling, but it didn't stop us from getting here. I asked Simon on the way if he was worried about it and he told me he wasn't. 'Snow's never been a problem for me,' he said. 'I drive as if it's not there, and I'm fine.'

I know he's hoping the third-time-lucky rule will work tonight: I'll walk into Little Orchard's kitchen and it will come to me – I'll know where I saw 'Kind, Cruel, Kind of Cruel' written down, and Simon will have the link he's desperate to find between Jo and Kat Allen's murder.

As we trudge in silence through snow to the back door, I say a silent prayer: *Please let this not be all down to me. Please let Simon not be relying solely on my unstable memory.* Even if I do remember, what will it achieve? If I can't produce the sheet of paper, which was probably tossed in a recycling bin weeks ago, how can he prove that Kat Allen's killer tore it off the notepad in her flat? Even Simon Waterhouse is not a good enough detective to run DNA tests on a mental image.

Little Orchard's back door opens as we approach. In the doorway, backlit by the glow from the kitchen, stands a woman I've never seen before. The collar and cuffs of her coat look oddly inflated and puffed up, as if someone's injected them with the clothes equivalent of Botox.

'Liv,' says Simon. 'You made it, then.'

'Have you brought anything?' the woman snaps at him, as if he's done something wrong.

'Anything such as . . . ?'

'Food, wine, loo paper, soap? There are eight loos in this house and only two nearly finished rolls of loo paper. There's nothing to eat. Nothing!' She glances at me, decides I'm not important, and turns her attention back to Simon. 'Sorry to lower the tone. I know your mind's on higher things, but I seem to be the only person who's worked out that we're about an hour away from being totally snowed in here, so . . .' She marches out into the night, tries to push past him.

'Where are you going?' He blocks her path. 'You can't drive in this weather.'

'Says the man who's just stepped out of his car, and doesn't mind if we all starve.'

I hope he lets her go. I've heard enough of her voice already.

'Where's Charlie?' Simon asks her.

'In the locked study, which we've renamed the unlocked study. You can nose around in there all you like.'

My heart beats double time. I think about running into the house and up the stairs, picture myself doing it. I stay where I am.

'Charlie found the key?' Simon asks.

'There's a desk in there. Key was in the top drawer.' Liv smiles at me suddenly, as if she's decided it's okay for me to be included in this part of the conversation. 'I smashed the window earlier.'

'You did *what*?'

'I used a stone from the garden. Three, actually. It took three attempts, but I did it eventually. Char and I carried a ladder from the garage and Char climbed in through the smashed window. It was my idea,' Liv raises her voice as Simon marches into the house. I run after him. 'Charlie knew nothing about it until I'd done it!'

Through the kitchen, into the hall, up the stairs. *Don't think, don't think*. I can do this if I tell myself that all I'm doing is following Simon Waterhouse.

A minute or two later I am standing on the half-landing outside the study, looking in. I don't know what I was expecting. I see nothing that shocks me. The study contains two wing-back armchairs, a desk, a computer, a rug, a whole wall of bookshelves, but only the top two shelves have books on them. The rest are covered with family photographs: Jo, Neil, the boys with their grandparents.

There's a photo of me, Luke, Dinah and Nonie in our new house, just after we'd moved in.

I try to imagine how terrified Jo must have been in 2003, when I stood with the key in my hand, threatening to unlock the door to this room, joking about what fun it would be. What would have happened if I'd insisted? Overpowered Jo, gone in against her wishes? What would we all have said and done once the locked study of Little Orchard had been found to contain row upon row of photographs of us, Jo's family?

And Neil's. Neil isn't a killer, but he knew about this. No wonder he looked scared on Wednesday, when I asked about Little Orchard and said Luke and I were thinking of going again.

'Anything?' Simon asks Charlie, who is sitting at the computer as if it's her own.

'Just a bit,' she says. She hands him a blue envelope file. 'From a desk drawer.' The file has black handwriting on it, but I can't see what it says, not before Simon opens the flap and folds it back.

'Coming here turned out to be a good idea after all,' Charlie tells me.

I can't answer her. My sister-in-law, my husband's brother's wife, the woman who gives Dinah and Nonie their tea every Wednesday after school and usually once at the weekend too, is probably a murderer. And here I am in a country house in Surrey with two police officers, about to be snowed in. Who will tell Luke? Someone needs to tell him, everything.

'I should phone home,' I say. Simon doesn't look up from the papers he's studying. Telling myself that I don't need his permission to ring my husband, I make my way to the bedroom that was Luke's and mine seven years ago, when we stayed here. Only the bedding has changed: from white with a blue border to plain white.

'It's me,' I say when Luke picks up. 'Is everything okay? Are the girls okay?'

'Everything's fine,' he says. 'Are you going to tell me what's going on?'

'Yes, but . . . not now. I have to go. Can I talk to Dinah and Nonie, quickly?'

'No, you can talk to me.' I've made him angry.

'Don't let them out of your sight, okay? Until I get home.'

'That's it, end of conversation?'

'I have to go.'

'So why bother ringing at all?' he asks. 'You can't just say "not now" and—'

'Don't let them out of your sight,' I repeat, cutting him off, as anxious to get back to the study as I was to leave it a few minutes ago. I shouldn't have phoned Luke; all it did was make me aware of the distance between us.

Simon hasn't moved; he is still flicking through papers. 'Veronique Coudert was the previous owner of Little Orchard,' he tells me. 'She sold it to Jo and Neil.'

That's right, I think, as if his words have jogged my memory. *Of what?* Then I realise: whether he knows it or not, he is reminding me that I mustn't fall apart. There are things I need to find out. Things *we* need to find out.

'Looks like they had a previous second home before they bought this one,' Simon says. 'Little Manor Farm, in Pulham Market.'

'Where Kat Allen came from,' I say.

'They sold it in 2002, traded up,' says Charlie.

I force myself to listen as she tells Simon about a meeting in a costume shop: Jo meeting Kat Allen and not being pleased to see her. I don't want to listen. I want to know what all of this means, but without having to pay attention. Normally I'm good at paying attention, but tonight it's frightening, too hard. My mind is in pieces, held together only by taut threads stretched nearly to breaking point. For a long time, as Charlie talks, I feel unreal, too aware of myself, as if I'm a ghost no one else can see, but even that feeling isn't strong enough to prevent me from knowing what Charlie's story means, even though the precise details slide past me before I have the chance to grasp and grip onto them. It means that Jo is a killer. She hired a fireman's uniform from a costume shop in Pulham Market. She wore it to kill Sharon.

Jo killed Sharon. The idea rolls around in my head, echoing in black space.

Think about Dinah and Nonie. Think how much they need you not to do anything stupid.

Jo killed Sharon. Luke will have to find out. I can't let him hear it from anyone but me.

Kat Allen was murdered because Jo wanted peace of mind, Charlie is telling Simon. Jo knew Kat worked in Spilling, too close for safety. Kat's friend who owns the costume business said to Jo, 'Oh, you've come for your fireman costume, haven't you?' in front of Kat, who heard every word and was killed because of it.

'Amber? Amber!' Simon is shaking me. I think about the Tree Shaker, Ginny's hypnotherapy exercise. *If a tree falls in a forest and nobody hears . . .* 'Why would Jo kill Sharon? What did she gain from Sharon's death?'

'Nothing. I already told you the only thing I can think of. She wants Dinah and Nonie.'

'Would you and Luke ever make a will saying you wanted the girls to go to Jo and Neil?'

'Never. Even before. Never.'

Simon nods. 'And Jo knows that. Ginny said narcissists are shrewd when it comes to knowing who's for them and who's against. Getting her hands on Dinah and Nonie can't be the motive. There has to be something else.'

'There's nothing else,' I say tearfully, trying to pull away from him.

'I want to know whatever you're still not telling me. Now!' he yells in my face.

'I never wrote down her address,' Charlie says. I hear a new note in her voice: surprise, moving towards disbelief. As if she's in the process of working something out. She stands up. 'Simon, wait.'

'Whose address?' he asks, impatient. I'm no longer the focus of his attention. The relief is overwhelming.

'Ginny's. 77 Great Holling Road, Great Holling. I didn't write it down. I didn't need to. 77's an easy number to remember.'

'So you didn't write down Ginny's address. So what?'

'Did you, Amber?' Charlie asks me. 'Did you write it down and take it with you, the first time you went to see her?'

Why is she asking me this? What does it have to do with anything?

'Not only the address but the phone number too, in case you got lost on the way?'

'How do you know that?'

'Wait here,' she says, and disappears from the room. I fight the urge to run after her. Anything is better than being left alone with Simon.

You're going to have to tell him. He won't let you not tell him. You won't let yourself, knowing how important it is to him to know.

Why have I made this one man, this virtual stranger, my yardstick for measuring how I ought to behave? It's crazy.

'I'm waiting,' he says. 'I'll be waiting until you tell me.'

'It has nothing to do with any murders,' I say. 'I told Jo a secret. Something I did, a lie I told. I couldn't talk to Luke about it, or Sharon. They were the ones I was lying to. I had to tell someone, it was driving me crazy. I told Jo.'

'Whatever you told her, that's the reason she killed Sharon,' says Simon.

'No! No, it's not. It can't be. Look, just . . . take my word for it. I could tell you the whole truth, everything, and you'd have no new information.'

'How can that be true? If you tell me something I don't already know . . .'

'Because it's about Dinah and Nonie! Jo knew Sharon had made a will saying she wanted me to have Dinah and Nonie if she died. You've just said yourself, she wouldn't kill Sharon in the hope of getting her hands on the girls because she'd have no reason to think that would happen. There's no motive!'

'Jo *knew* . . .' Simon stops, hearing Charlie's footsteps stomping up the stairs. She reappears, out of breath, holding up a piece of paper with Ginny's address written on it. And her phone number. 'Is this your handwriting?' she asks me.

I nod. 'Where did you get it?'

'It was in my car, on the floor.'

Sitting in the driver's seat, looking at her notebook . . .

'It was in my jacket pocket,' I say. 'It must have fallen out when

I was . . .' I am trying to tell Simon and Charlie what they worked out long before I did. Speaking has become difficult. I stare at the piece of paper with Ginny's address on it and start to shake. *Pink line for the margin, blue horizontal lines.*

Charlie turns it round so that Simon and I can see the other side: the three headings written in handwriting that isn't mine, black ink instead of the blue I used for Ginny's address: 'Kind, Cruel, Kind of Cruel'.

Now I remember.

~

'When?' Simon asks me.

This is the same chair I was sitting in on Boxing Day 2003, when Jo said that there was nothing she wasn't telling us, nothing at all. The woman called Liv hands me a drink I don't remember asking for. I take a sip. Brandy. 'Last Wednesday,' I say. A week and two days ago. Simon can work out the date.

'Talk me through it,' he says.

'I was at Jo's. We go every Wednesday, me and the girls.' I may have said this already, or I might only have thought about saying it. 'I'd decided that morning that I had to do something about my not sleeping. Enough people had recommended hypnosis, I thought I'd give it a go. Jo agreed it was a good idea. I used her laptop to do a search.'

'A search for . . . ?' Simon's pen hovers over his open notebook.

'Hypnotherapists in the Culver Valley. Ginny was the only one with a Great Holling address. The others were all in worse places. I thought I'd give myself the incentive of going somewhere nice.'

'Did you mention this aspect of your thinking to Jo?' asks Simon.

'She asked me how I could choose when I knew nothing about any of them, and I said, "The one with the best address is bound to be the best." I didn't really think that . . .'

'Then why say it?'

Answering isn't a problem. Or it shouldn't be. I know the answer. The problem is that I know it too well; it's so woven into my consciousness that I've never needed to put it into words. I am playing a strange parlour game in this room where everyone congregated seven years ago for Luke's Christmas quiz. Everyone but me and William, who were looking for the key to the study.

Do William and Barney know their parents own this house? Have Jo and Neil trained their sons to lie, or are William and Barney lied to like the rest of us? Is the study kept locked against them too? Have they seen the family photographs on the bookshelves?

'Amber,' Simon says. 'Why lie to Jo about your reason for choosing Ginny?'

'I suppose I was nervous. About the prospect of going to any kind of therapist for the first time, being hypnotised. I hoped I could make it a slightly more pleasant experience by making sure I went to a nice place. It was probably silly of me to think I could make any kind of treat out of it . . .'

'The sort of hope Jo would trample all over,' Simon guesses correctly.

I nod. 'I still got the ticking-off: ridiculous, irresponsible basis for choosing a therapist, all that.'

'But you were protected. She was attacking a false opinion you'd offered up as a shield.'

Liv opens her mouth to say something; Charlie, sitting beside her on the sofa, taps her with the back of her hand. I recognise this way of telling someone you take entirely for granted to shut up, even though I don't have a sister.

What is Charlie's sister doing here? What are any of us doing here?

'I pretended to let Jo persuade me,' I tell Simon. 'I showed her the list of hypnotherapists, asked her which I should choose. She picked one in Rawndesley, near her. She lost interest as soon as she thought she'd got her way, went back to cooking. There was . . .' My throat closes on my words. I try again. 'There was a piece of paper next to me, next to the computer. A blank sheet of lined paper, or so I thought. It was creased, it just looked like scrap. It didn't occur to me that there might be something written on the other side. I wrote Ginny's details on it, put it in my handbag. Next day

I rang Ginny from work, made an appointment. I don't remember noticing the words written on the back, but I suppose I must have.'

'We don't register what we see if we don't think it's important,' says Charlie. 'Ginny's address has been lying in my car's footwell since Tuesday evening. It kept catching my eye without catching my attention. It didn't occur to me until just now that I never actually wrote it down. Or that it was written on blue-lined paper.'

'You were right,' Simon tells me. 'There was a link between Little Orchard and that piece of paper. Jo was the link. The page came from Jo's house. This place *is* Jo's house, her other house. If Ginny's right, if you knew on some subliminal level . . .'

'Kirsty.' As I hear myself say it, I know on every level that what I'm about to say is true.

'What about her?' Simon asks.

'She isn't in any of the photographs. In the study. Everybody else is in more than one. Even me.'

'Are you sure?'

I'm already ahead of him, too far ahead to answer. Jo wouldn't exclude her sister from the display by accident. She'll have chosen those pictures carefully.

'I was going to ask about Kirsty,' Charlie says. 'The mother, Jo's and Kirsty's mother, what's her name?'

'Hilary,' Simon tells her.

'You mentioned Jo and Ritchie when you were talking about Hilary's will, but not Kirsty. Doesn't she get left anything?'

'I don't know,' Simon says impatiently. He pulls his phone out of his pocket, but does nothing with it. 'She's as helpless as a baby. She doesn't care about money, doesn't even know what it is.'

Charlie laughed. 'Simon, she might not be hankering after a Ferrari, but she's going to need a lot spending on her care, isn't she? Full-time carers, residential homes – I don't know exactly what, but I'm pretty sure that the more disabled you are, the more expensive it gets. Hilary must have thought of that and made some provision for Kirsty in her will.'

I didn't think of it.

Simon stares at her. Keeps on staring, as if he's in a trance.

Charlie tries again. 'Wasn't Kirsty mentioned *at all* in the discussion about Hilary's will?'

'Breast cancer,' Simon says quietly.

'That can't be the answer to my question. Have another go.'

Liv and I might as well not be here. The two of them have sealed themselves into their own private universe.

'Amber was right, what she said to Ginny.'

Don't talk about me as if I'm not here.

'Kirsty can't speak, can't think properly. People treat her like she doesn't exist. They forget about her. Me included. I've been thinking only about Jo and Ritchie: are they going to sell Hilary's house and split the proceeds? Is Jo going to donate her half to Ritchie once Hilary's gone? Will she try again to persuade Hilary to leave it all to Ritchie, and why would she *want* to? No one's that generous. Kirsty didn't even cross my mind.' Simon shakes his head, angry at his own stupidity. 'But she was there too, on Christmas Eve.'

'Christmas Eve?' Liv asks.

'Kirsty is Hilary's child too,' Simon continues. I can hear meaning in his voice that isn't coming through to the rest of us. There's a transmission failure, one he seems unaware of. Even Charlie looks confused. We watch him in silence, the three of us, none of us daring to speak. He reminds me of a computer trying to process too much data, one that might crash if we add another command to the queue.

When he next speaks, it's to me. 'What about what Ginny said? About you thinking Kirsty might know something. She can't know anything. What, you think she's faking her brain damage?'

'No.'

'What, then?'

'I just . . .' Is there any thought or feeling that I'm allowed to keep to myself?

'I don't care if you've thought things about a disabled woman that you're not supposed to think. Why did you think Kirsty might know something?'

If I tell him everything, he can act as my brain and I can switch off. That would be a relief. I could sleep. The snow could pile up outside, over the roof of the house, and I could sleep on and on, for days. 'That Christmas, when Jo, Neil and the boys went missing . . . Kirsty went missing too.'

'What?'

'Only for a few minutes, but at first it looked as if there were five people missing, not four, until Luke found Kirsty.'

'Go on,' says Simon.

'She was lying in Jo and Neil's bed. She hadn't been there when I first looked, for Jo and Neil. She must have wandered in there while we were all searching the house and the grounds. Hilary was relieved. At least one of her children had turned up.' I shrug. 'That's it, really. Not much of a story, and no reason for me to think anything, but . . . it had never happened before, far as I knew. I don't think it's happened since. I see Kirsty a lot. It's not something she does, climb into other people's beds and just lie there. And then later that day, twice, she kind of broke free of Hilary and went into the kitchen and stood next to the cooker, exactly where Jo would have been standing if she'd been making Christmas dinner. The noises she made when Hilary tried to move her . . .'

'You thought she might have been trying to tell you something?' Simon asks.

I think she believed Jo was never coming back. I think it was her way of saying she missed her sister.

'Not really, no,' I say. 'I have a Sod's Law mindset, maybe that's what it was: you assume the one person who's physically incapable of telling you what they know is the only person who knows anything.'

Simon puts down his notebook and pen and walks over to the window. He opens it; snow blows in.

'What are you doing?' Charlie yells at him. 'Close it!'

'I can't think without fresh air. If you don't like it, go somewhere else.'

Less than a minute later, he and I are alone in the room. It's cold, but I don't mind. It helps me to think too, jolts me out of numbness. Is this what he wanted, the two of us alone?

'So Jo knew Dinah and Nonie were coming to you and Luke if Sharon died,' he says. 'That was your big secret?'

'Luke was the one who didn't know,' I say. 'And Sharon didn't know I hadn't told him. I lied to both of them. That was what Jo knew. That was what I was terrified she'd decide to tell Luke one day – if I said the wrong thing, if she thought I'd let her down or disobeyed her.' This feels like a dummy run. It will be harder to tell Luke. 'I knew how Sharon felt about her mum. She hated her, always said she was dangerous, and she was right. I've seen enough of Marianne first-hand to know Sharon was right about her. You probably don't know anyone like that, a parent who thrives on crushing the spirit of their own child and calls it love.'

'I probably do,' Simon says.

'Most people don't think about wills when they're young, but Sharon did, before she was even pregnant. She always planned everything way in advance. She wanted a baby, but she wasn't prepared to have one knowing that if something happened to her, the child would end up with Marianne. So she asked me if I'd agree to be guardian. And . . . I had to say yes. She had no one else to ask. I was her best friend.'

'She put pressure on you?'

'The opposite,' I say. 'She told me I should only agree if I felt totally okay about it. She knew how much she was asking. If I'd said no, she wouldn't have had a baby. Ever. She didn't say that, but we both knew it. How could she think it was fair to ask me? She should have known I wouldn't be able to say no!' I stare at Simon, astonished. Where did that surge of rage come from? 'I was single at the time. It was before I met Luke. Sharon told me to think carefully about what I was taking on. She was so . . . heavy about it. I tried to make light of it and tell her that she wasn't going to have a child and then die and leave it motherless, but she wouldn't let me say that. She said I had no idea what might happen, all kinds of unexpected bad things happen. If I agreed to what she was asking, she said, I'd have to tell any man I was ever serious about. I'd have to tell him about the promise I'd made to her.'

I see Dinah and Nonie's beautiful faces in my mind. 'The girls weren't even born,' I say, knowing logically that I didn't let them down but feeling as if I did. 'For them, I'd have been willing to tell any man to get lost if he didn't want them, but . . .'

'I understand,' says Simon. 'And then you met Luke.'

I nod. 'Sharon was pregnant with Dinah by then. Luke and I – it all happened so fast. I kept expecting Sharon to ask me if I'd talked to him about our . . . arrangement, but she didn't, not at first. Probably didn't think she needed to. We'd discussed it enough before she made the will and she always got upset, thinking about having children and dying before they grew up. By the time she got round to asking me, Luke and I were engaged. We'd set a date for the wedding.'

'And you hadn't told him about Sharon's will?'

'I couldn't make myself do it. I was afraid he'd . . .' I stop, try to remember exactly what I was scared of. 'I don't know why I dreaded it so much. I never allowed myself to think about it. Sharon was young, she was healthy. I told myself there was no point worrying about something that wasn't going to happen. But I did worry, I couldn't help it. And because I didn't want to feel guilty, I blamed Sharon. Why was she stupid enough to *trust* me?' I start to cry. 'I didn't *want* her baby. I wanted me and Luke to have our own children and *only* our children.' Strange: I can still tap into that feeling, even though it doesn't belong to me any more.

'When Dinah was born, she was so lovely. I loved her instantly, and I panicked. I knew I had to tell Luke now that there was a real baby, but . . . our wedding was coming up. I just couldn't do it. What if he says no? I kept thinking. Why would he be willing to take on my best friend's baby? What if this leads to me losing him, or losing Sharon?'

'So you took a chance,' says Simon thoughtfully. I'm grateful to him for not sounding as if he's judging me and deciding I must be the worst person in the world. Maybe he's good at hiding it. 'Understandably, you assumed Sharon would live and you'd get away with it.'

'Tempting fate. As it turned out.'

'You can't think like that.'

'When Nonie was born, my lie doubled in size: two children Luke knew nothing about his wife having agreed to provide a home for, two children Sharon adored and was prepared to entrust to me in the event of her death, and I was playing roulette with their future. What if she died and Luke point-blank refused to have them in his house? What would I do then?'

'You went to Jo for advice,' says Simon.

I laugh through my tears. 'The worst mistake of my life. She's used it against me ever since. She can't bring herself to admit that it *hasn't* caused a problem between Luke and me. He was brilliant when Sharon died. He loved the girls as much as I did by that point. He was happy to take them on, we both were. We agreed that we wouldn't have kids of our own; Dinah and Nonie became our children. But Jo couldn't let it lie. She'd go weeks without mentioning it, then, out of the blue, she'd say, "You know, one day Luke's going to find out that you knew about Sharon's will several years before he did. How's he going to feel about you deliberately keeping it from him?" She still mentions it sometimes. Often. Luke's no fool, she says: he's clever enough to work out that he'd have loved his own children as much as if not more than he loves Dinah and Nonie, if I hadn't deviously deprived him of the opportunity to choose to have them; I'm the fool if I imagine he won't see that as the ultimate betrayal.'

'Sounds like she managed to convince you,' says Simon.

I nod. 'When I say Luke won't find out unless she tells him, she says she won't, but I must. And that "these things have a way of coming out", one of her favourite lines for trying to scare me. All I've ever wanted her to say is, "Don't worry, everything'll be fine." Even if it won't be. Like now. Say it anyway.'

'Now?' Simon looks over his shoulder as if he's expecting to find Jo here in the room with us. I'm not talking about her any more.

'Say that Sharon didn't die because I told Jo about her will. Tell me that's not why she was murdered.'

Simon closes the window. I wipe my eyes. I understand without his having to tell me that, on this occasion, I can't have what I want.

'You should tell Luke,' he says. 'He won't be angry. He'll understand.'

'You've never met him.'

'I don't need to. I know the truth. That's enough.'

'Meaning?'

'You handled it badly, but it's worked out okay. You, Luke and the girls are a happy family.' Simon shrugs. 'Some truths are nowhere near as bad as you think they are.'

This makes me feel better for a few seconds. Until he says, 'Others are worse.'

I hear a muffled ringing. Simon pulls his phone out of his pocket. 'Sam,' he says. He listens for a long time, glancing at me at first, then making a point of avoiding my eye. His posture is rigid. He's worried. 'What's being done about finding them?' he asks.

Them. It might not mean anything.

'Get everyone on it – nothing else matters.'

I'm on my feet. 'Are Dinah and Nonie all right?' Luke wouldn't let me talk to them when I rang. Why wouldn't he? However angry he was, he would let me speak to the girls.

'Your husband's been in touch with my sergeant,' says Simon, putting his phone back in his pocket.

No. Please, God, no.

'When you rang him before and told him not to let Dinah and Nonie out of his sight, it was too late. Jo had already met them off the school bus and taken them out shopping and for dinner, to help him out. Luke was scared to tell you because you sounded worried enough already, and he was pretty sure whatever you were afraid of wouldn't include a shopping trip with Aunt Jo, but he also couldn't understand why she'd be so keen to take the girls shopping in the snow, and why William and Barney weren't going too.'

I feel myself falling. Simon catches me, holds me up. 'Don't assume the worst,' he says. 'The girls are going to be okay. My skipper Sam's the best there is. He'll find them.'

From: ginny@greathollinghypnotherapy.co.uk
To: Charlie Zailer
Sent: Friday, December 3, 2010 9.51 PM
Subject: Re: Next week's appointment

Dear Charlie,

Will tackle your question v. briefly, as don't believe I can really help much at a distance – you always need to meet a person and hear what they have to say. But . . . if his childhood contained no physical or sexual abuse, the first thing that springs to mind is what we therapists call 'emotional incest' or 'covert incest'. It's a controversial idea that we're careful not to bandy about. Many people object to the use of the word 'incest' when no physical act has taken place, and some deny existence of emotional incest altogether, but personally I believe it's a justifiable term to use. Emotional incest can be as psychologically damaging as overt incest, and certainly the symptoms for adult survivors are similar. From what you say about this man's sexual attitudes and behaviour, it sounds as if he could well be an emotional incest survivor. You should encourage him to seek therapeutic help, but only if you're prepared to be met with furious denial.

It's often single parents who commit emotional incest against their children, though not always. Frequently the abusing parent is addicted to alcohol or drugs – though, again, not always. An emotionally incestuous parent can be married (often the marriage is one in which feelings are not openly expressed and nobody's needs are met) or single, a substance-addict or not, but the important thing to remember is that parents who commit covert incest are emotional children. Their own needs weren't met in childhood and they've never properly faced this fact or dealt with the damage. They are needy, frightened, codependent. These parents do not know how to ensure that their needs are met in appropriate ways by appropriate people, i.e. other adults, so those needs spill out all over their children in a variety of ways: excessive worry and control, enforced lack of privacy ('No closed doors in this house', etc), inappropriate confidences – telling children things they're too young to hear, confiding about feelings to a child in the way that you might to a partner (therapists call this emotionally 'dumping' on a child). Sometimes there's an almost romantic adoration that puts the child on a pedestal, sometimes there's offensive nudity, i.e. opposite sex parent parades round house naked in front of child, who feels uncomfortable but cannot say so because has been told there's nothing shameful about nakedness. In fact, for a parent to inflict his or her nudity on a child older than three or four is severely inappropriate and can be very damaging. Equally (sorry if this sounds confusing), making a child feel guilty about his or her nudity or sexual feelings, or reacting with anger or shock if the child happens to walk in and see parent naked, is a violation of the child from the opposite direction. What the two have in common is that, in both cases, the parent's need, be that to 'flash' at his/her child or to believe that child would never feel something as dirty and shameful as sexual arousal, is the only one taken into account, and the child is forced to adapt, crippling his or her budding sense of self in the process.

Going back to your man, I'd guess it was his mother who did the damage, though in some cases it can be the same-sex parent. Did his mother impose on him the burden of meeting her emotional needs? To the outside world – and to the confused child, who feels deeply uncomfortable and 'invaded' without understanding why – the emotionally incestuous mother is easily mistaken for a good mother: attentive and devoted, loving, would do anything for child, spends a lot of time with child (often needs child to fill huge hole in her inadequate life). Smothering with love is one way to describe it – inappropriate love, because it's all in the service of meeting the parent's emotional needs and not the child's. These are the girls who are 'Daddy's little princess', the boys who hear, constantly, 'What would Mummy do without her special boy?'. These are the parents who kiss, cuddle and insist on sitting next to their children on the sofa because they, the parents, want that physical closeness, not because they sense the child wants or needs it. They are the parents who want their children at home all the time because, 'There are dangerous strangers out there'. If challenged (I'll show you my collection of battle scars some time!), these parents vehemently insist there's nothing wrong with hugging and kissing their children as much as they want to, or fearing for their safety – it's their way of showing their kids how much they love them. For 'love', read 'need'. Emotionally, the parent is overly involved with the child, overly invested in him, insufficiently respectful of his autonomy and independence, and unconsciously trying to create a neediness in the child equal to the parent's own, to guarantee that she will always be needed. The child knows he's the answer to her prayers, the cure for her loneliness, her protector, her confidante. It's far too great a responsibility, and to fulfil this obligation he never asked for, the child must deny his own needs entirely. It's incredibly damaging. This syndrome is so normal in our society that we assume these kinds of close relationships are healthy, but they're deeply dysfunctional. The best person I've read on this is Marion Woodman, who calls it 'psychic incest'. She describes it as 'unboundaried bonding', where parents use their children as a mirror to support their needs instead of what parents should do, which is reflect children's own selves back to them, as a way of supporting their development towards independence.

Healthy love from a parent to a child is love that meets the child's needs and always respects the child's boundaries. Meanwhile, the parent has his or her emotional needs met by spouse, friends, other sources, and demonstrates that she has her own healthy boundaries in place. Emotionally incestuous parents have damaged or, in severe cases, nonexistent boundaries, and are dishonest with themselves. They say, 'My child is the most important thing in the world to me,' and then instill in that child the belief that he must feel, think or behave in certain ways in order not to devastate his adoring parent. The child has to shut down parts of his true self in order to keep the parent happy. He experiences a loss of identity, and veers between feeling infallible and feeling worthless. And he has enormous problems with intimacy and sustaining a fulfilling relationship. He might put up huge walls, fearing being engulfed by his partner's emotional needs as he once was by his abusive parent's. Survivors of emotional incest often feel more comfortable being sexual with those they don't care about, or even those they actively dislike. Being sexual with someone they love feels wrong and taboo to them.

The adult child's feelings towards the parent who 'covertly incested' him (as we say, though we probably shouldn't) are normally a mixture of helpless rage and extreme guilt. Often, the adult children of emotionally incestuous parents are genuinely at a loss to understand why they so loathe, detest and fear the parent who gave up everything for them and claims to love them so much.

Hope this helps!

V best, and sorry that my 'briefly' wasn't so brief after all, but it's brief compared to the reams I might have written. Plenty more on internet if you're interested!

Ginny

14

9/12/2010

'The only thing I'm uncertain about is how you got hold of a key to Sharon Lendrim's house,' Simon told Jo Utting, who appeared to be present in the interview room in body only. Her eyes stared blankly ahead, empty. Occasionally the lids flickered.

'You're not going to get an answer from her,' said her solicitor, a young black woman who for the past half hour had been hectoring Simon in a tone that came across as more personal than professional; the two of them might have been exhausted parents, and Jo Utting their uncooperative toddler. 'She won't say a word to me and I'm on her side.' The underlined lack of enthusiasm gave the lie to her words. 'You've got your evidence and her confession from yesterday. Since when she's taken a vow of silence.'

'Amber didn't like the idea of you and Sharon meeting,' Simon continued as if he and Jo were alone in the room. 'She did everything she could to make sure it didn't happen. She was afraid you'd tell Sharon that Luke knew nothing about inheriting Dinah and Nonie, in the event of her death. She needn't have worried.'

He enjoyed interviews like this, the sort Sam Kombothekra hated: you direct all your questions and statements to a suspect who's pretending you don't exist, while blanking out the comments of the irate brief whose existence you're intent on ignoring. Enough obstacles inherent in the situation to keep you sharp, and no danger of anyone meeting the eyes of the person looking at them.

'There's no way you'd have told Sharon that Amber had let her down. What if Sharon had been angry enough to change her will? You needed those girls to be going to Amber if Sharon died. Without that, your whole plan fell apart.'

Was that a flicker of expression in Jo's eyes? How impatient was she to find out if Simon knew her secret? When he'd arrested her, she'd made it clear that his knowing she had murdered two people and attempted to murder four more was neither here nor there. In Jo Utting's mind, that wasn't 'it'; the crimes she had committed, everything that could be proved against her – that was the part she was willing, in an emergency, to concede. She had to be desperate, beneath that immobile exterior, to know if the truth she was determined to conceal, even on her way to multiple life sentences, was under threat of exposure. Simon decided to stall, make her suffer.

'Let's go back to how you got a key to Sharon's house,' he said. 'Amber says you used to try to persuade her to bring Sharon round for lunch, dinner. You couldn't stand the thought of Amber having a best friend you hadn't met. Unaware of anyone's needs and feelings but your own, you wouldn't have understood Amber's wish to keep you and Sharon apart. *You* knew there was no danger you'd tell Sharon that Amber had let her down by failing to talk to Luke about guardianship of Dinah and Nonie. It didn't occur to you that Amber might worry about that. *You* knew it wasn't going to happen.'

'What's this achieving, DC Waterhouse?' Jo's solicitor asked. Simon ignored her. He'd been told her name and chosen to forget it.

'I think you went round to Sharon's one day when you knew her girls wouldn't be there. You knew Amber had them for the day, was that it? You introduced yourself to Sharon as someone else – was it Veronique Coudert? Or did you only think of using her name when you got Amber's email about booking Little Orchard? Either way, you used a false name. You couldn't risk Sharon knowing your real name. You knew if your plan worked, the police'd want to talk to anyone she'd had contact with. You'd decided how you'd do it: like a coward, without direct physical contact and in disguise. Using a false name, you got yourself invited into Sharon's house on a pretext. Something to do with the residents' association, I'm guessing, and the ongoing saga of Terry Bond's pub. Maybe you said you were a new neighbour, you'd just moved in down the road and

344

wanted to know what was going on. Or did you say you were from the council? Environmental health?'

A heavy sigh from the solicitor. 'I hope you're not taking my client's silence as tacit agreement,' she said. 'Silence is silence. It means nothing, and gets us nowhere.'

'You weren't worried. You knew Sharon wouldn't recognise you, since she'd never clapped eyes on you. You weren't at Amber and Luke's wedding and neither was she. They got married abroad, thousands of miles from everyone they know, because of you, your attempts to make decisions about the wedding that weren't yours to make. And you didn't worry that Sharon might have seen a photograph of you at Amber's because there aren't any, are there? Just as there are no photos of Kirsty in your second home, Little Orchard. For the same reason.'

No response from Jo.

'You stole one of Sharon's spare keys. Amber says you'd have seen them if you went into the kitchen. DS Ursula Shearer who led the original investigation says so too. Mixed in with the fruit in the fruit bowl, weren't they? Six or seven loose keys, all exactly the same. Sharon had lots of spares. She tended to misplace them, leave them at work and in other people's houses, throw them out with the old papers. Did Amber tell you that about her best friend, not knowing how you'd use the information? She can't remember if she did or not. I think she did. Must have been easy for you to nick a key while Sharon was making you a cup of tea. You had your cosy chat with Sharon and then you left, with one of the many spare keys to her house and a feeling of infallibility. Don't tell me it didn't make you feel powerful, being with Amber's best friend without her permission, knowing you were going to kill her.'

'It's surely counterproductive to start sentences with "Don't tell me",' Jo's brief muttered.

'You waited. Whenever you saw Amber, you asked her about Sharon, the residents' association, the Four Fountains pub – just showing a friendly interest, or so Amber thought. She was upset, more reliant on you than usual. She and Sharon had fallen out. Over the pub, ostensibly, but Amber's guilt about lying to Sharon was the real cause, the guilt you stoked by telling her she'd betrayed her best friend. Amber couldn't handle it. She and Sharon went through a phase of not speaking, but Amber quickly realised that without Sharon in her life, she felt worse. They made up. You got to hear all the details, and still Amber said nothing about Sharon having had a visit from someone who lied about who she was, nothing about a key going missing. You'd got away with it. You were satisfied that no one but you knew you and Sharon had ever met. The next step was the fire. Where did you park? Not too near Sharon's. You wouldn't have risked your car being seen. And you'd have taken the fireman's uniform with you in a bag, changed into it only when you were inside Sharon's house.'

If a woman called Jo arrives at a house and a nameless fireman leaves, which of them is responsible for the crime committed in between? What was it Ginny Saxon had said: the house represents the self? Jo Utting owned two houses. Simon wondered how hard it was for her to locate and communicate with her true self after so many years of playing a part. He had the uncomfortable sensation that he was talking less to a person than to a survival instinct with a human face.

'What would you have done to Dinah and Nonie Lendrim on Friday 3 December, if you hadn't been interrupted?' he asked. Sometimes, if you changed the subject quickly, you could surprise an answer out of a supect. Not this time.

Back to Sharon Lendrim's murder. 'What you can't have known until you read about her death in the papers was that Sharon went out that night, until late – to the Four Fountains, of all places. If you'd arrived a bit earlier, you might have bumped into her, winding down after her night out or getting ready for bed. You were lucky. Less so when you tried the same again. We've got CCTV footage of your car on its way to Amber's house in the early hours of Thursday morning, on your way to start your second fire. Good footage, from several different cameras. You pulled over at least once, to reply to Amber's email about Little Orchard using your iPhone.'

'We've been over the evidence,' Jo's solicitor said in a bored voice.

'But not the motive,' said Simon. 'It's the motive – all the motives – that I'm most interested in. Amber thinks you torched her house as a warning,' he told Jo. 'She'd seen you on Wednesday 1 December, told you about being questioned in connection with Kat Allen's death. She'd asked your husband about Little Orchard, told him she and Luke wanted to book it again. How could your setting fire to her house several hours after those two conversations took place be anything other than a warning? That's the way Amber saw it, understandably. She was wrong, though. It wasn't a warning, it was revenge. Rage, jealousy, whatever you want to call it.'

Jo's eyelids fluttered closed.

'You had a bad shock that Wednesday. Amber told you something you didn't know, something you'd never have guessed. It made you hate her, made you think about her, Luke, Dinah and Nonie living happily ever after together: the perfect family, a family *you* created by murdering Sharon. Unnecessarily, as it turned out.'

'What do you mean, unnecessarily?' the solicitor asked.

Simon decided it was time to talk to the only person who was demonstrably listening. 'Amber thought Jo was jealous of her ending up with Sharon's girls, and she was right. Jo was the one who'd taken the risk and killed Sharon because she thought she had no choice, and Amber, who'd done nothing to deserve anything, was the one who'd ended up with Dinah and Nonie. Jo might not have wanted them herself – she had children of her own – but that didn't stop her resenting Amber for getting a perk she hadn't earned. Let me tell you something about the monster you're here to represent today: nothing makes her evil heart bubble over with envy like a perfect family.'

'Please.' The solicitor recoiled as if Simon had said something distasteful. 'There's no need for hyperbole.'

'I'll call her your client, then,' said Simon. 'The way she sees it, Amber's winning and she's losing. Not because Amber has anything she doesn't have. The opposite: Amber doesn't have, and will never have, what your client has and wishes she didn't.'

He could see the lawyer still didn't understand, and struggled to keep his impatience in check. It wasn't her fault. She hadn't met Jo Utting until yesterday, hadn't heard the whole story yet and couldn't be expected to fill in the blanks. 'Jo and Amber share a father-in-law,' he said. 'Quentin. Physically, there's nothing wrong with him; practically and psychologically, he's as dependent as a small child. He couldn't manage on his own after his wife Pam died. Jo and Neil took him in and have suffered ever since. I've met this man. Trust me, you wouldn't want him living with you.'

'I wouldn't want any man living with me,' said the solicitor, looking Simon up and down. He got the message: *especially not you.*

'On Wednesday 1 December, Amber told Jo she was a saint for putting up with Quentin,' he said. 'Jo said she'd had no choice but to welcome him into her home, that Amber would have done the same if she'd had to. Amber made it clear that wasn't true: under no circumstances would she have had Quentin under her roof, even if he couldn't cope on his own, even if she hadn't already had Dinah and Nonie to look after. She wouldn't be prepared to sacrifice her own quality of life in the name of family duty. That's what she told Jo, and she meant it. Jo could see she meant it. That's why she tried to burn Amber's house down, with Amber, Luke and the girls in it.'

'So?' the solicitor asked. Trying to sound bored, unwilling to admit she was curious. *She sounded like Charlie.*

'Jo and Amber had never discussed Amber's willingness to provide a home for Quentin before,' Simon said. 'There'd been no need. Amber and Luke were busy dealing with their new family arrangements and Dinah and Nonie's grief. It didn't occur to anybody that they might take Quentin on as well. Jo and Neil offered. Their family life was more stable, it was the obvious solution. Their house is small, but the boys were happy to share a room when Jo explained to them that sacrifices had to be made for Grandpa's sake. They could have sold their large second home in Surrey – Neil suggested it, he told me yesterday – but Jo didn't want a bigger house. It was important to her to be seen to have no space, and to be seen to be carrying the full burden of looking after Quentin.'

Simon turned to Jo, whose demeanour hadn't changed. Her eyes were still closed. 'Funny thing is, I don't know if I'd have worked it out without your son's help,' he said to her. 'William's been helpful in unexpected ways as well all the obvious ones. He remembers his last half term, going to the Corn Exchange building in Spilling, to the flat of a lady you needed to speak to. He remembers being parked in the lounge with Barney. You turned the telly on for them, closed the door so that the noise wouldn't disturb you and the lady while you were talking.'

Simon paused to compose himself. He wanted to yell at her, *What kind of mother takes her two kids with her to kill someone?* It would achieve nothing; Jo wouldn't react, and her solicitor would lose all respect for him. Simon knew the answer: the kind of killer who took her sons with her and put them in the room next door while she killed was the cleverest kind. Sabina was the only person who knew Jo wasn't on Amber's course the day Kat Allen was murdered; even Neil didn't know. He would have disapproved. If Jo wanted to break the law to help Amber, that was her look-out, but Neil would have thought it wrong of her to offer and then palm the risk off on Sabina. Jo knew Sabina was likely to hear that there had been a murder in Spilling that day. She knew Sabina wouldn't for a minute suspect her. Not only because the people we know personally and like and trust are never the bad guys, but because Jo had been with William and Barney – a bit of much-needed quality time away from a too-busy house, away from Quentin, alone with her children. Simon could almost hear Jo explaining it to Sabina: *You'll be so much better at pretending to be Amber than I would. You're braver than I am. I'd panic and give the game away.* The opposite of the truth.

'We showed William a photo of Kat Allen,' he told Jo. 'He identified her as the lady you went to see, said she was pleased and surprised when you turned up unannounced. He's also told us that you, he and Barney met Kat a month earlier – by chance, in town. What did Kat say to you? "We must stop meeting like this"? Did she mention that the last time the two of you had met, you'd been in Pulham Market hiring a fireman costume? William remembers her telling you that she'd applied for a new job – at Barney's school. That was the spur, wasn't it? That was the day you decided Kat had to be punished: for knowing too much, getting too close.'

Jo made a barely audible noise. She might have been clearing her throat. Or else Simon imagined it.

'Back to Kat's murder, your visit to her flat,' he said. 'William and Barney watched TV in the lounge until they got bored of whatever was on. That's when they noticed the notepad and pen on the table, and had the idea of playing a game Dinah and Nonie had told them about, one that involved dividing their classmates into three categories: Kind, Cruel and Kind of Cruel. Didn't get very far, did they? Suddenly, you were calling out to them that it was time to leave. William tore the sheet of paper off the notepad, folded it up and stuffed it in his pocket, to be continued at home later. Except he never got round to it. When you came into the room, you were shaking. You had blood and what your eldest son described as "stuff" on your clothes, and the game didn't seem important any more. The boys forgot all about it.'

Jo's wardrobes had been emptied, their contents taken away for analysis. With luck, some forensic material would have survived the washing machine, but it wouldn't matter if not. DNA found in Kat's flat after her murder matched the sample taken from Jo three days ago. That together with William's statement would be enough to send her to prison for a long time. Simon was unwilling to feel merciful towards her for a number of reasons; chief among these was his conviction that Kat Allen had suspected nothing. She'd said nothing to her boyfriend or any of her friends about a possible connection between a woman who used to have a second home near her parents' house and a murder in Rawndesley in 2008; as far as Simon could tell, Kat hadn't registered Sharon Lendrim's death.

'You told William and Barney that you and the lady had had a fight and she'd hit you – you'd had a nosebleed. You made them promise not to tell Neil or Sabina, who would only worry. The boys could see you were upset, and they were frightened. You reassured them that everything would be fine as long as the three of you forgot all about it as quickly as you could. Barney did. He's younger. He remembers some of it: the blood on your clothes, mainly. The invented nosebleed. William's older – he remembers a bit more. He asked you where the lady was when the three of you left. Why didn't she come to the door to say goodbye? Thanks to William, we also know that the reason he and Barney were with you that day was because Sabina had to go on a course. Doesn't take a genius to work out which course. Sabina denied impersonating Amber at first, then admitted it when it was pointed out to her how easy it would be to disprove her claim that she was at home on 2 November, having a day off while you took the boys out. Any number of DriveTech course participants might have identified her.'

Simon could have kicked himself for not working it out sooner. Sabina, who had adopted a Cockney accent when she'd met him and recited a typical 'suspect-to-detective' line, thinking it was hilarious; Sabina, who was at Jo's beck and call. Jo wouldn't have got a kick out of pretending to be Amber by playing the part of the course rebel and spouting outrageous opinions of the sort she believed Amber might hold. Sabina would. And did. Unable to reproduce Amber's Culver Valley lilt, she ditched her Italian accent in favour of an upper-class English one.

'I asked you why you didn't tell Amber about the speech you gave on the course, undermining the ethos of safe driving, do you remember? You had to think quickly. Why had Sabina missed out this detail, when she was supposed to have told you everything so that you could tell Amber what was meant to have happened to her that day? For what it's worth, the explanation you came up with was the right one: Sabina tried to get as much fun out of a mind-numbingly boring experience as she could, but it didn't occur to her that anything *she* might have said was important enough to relay to you. She told you what everyone else had said and done. Her mucking about and being provocative to entertain herself wasn't important enough to be worth mentioning. You must have been furious when you realised she'd failed to give you vital information and you'd nearly been caught out as a result. It's your God-given right to know everything, isn't it? Even when you reveal nothing.'

'You're the one intent on telling her everything,' the solicitor pointed out.

'She's hearing nothing she doesn't already know,' Simon said. 'Do you know how Sabina describes you?' he asked Jo. 'Her best friend. We've told her what you've done. She doesn't believe it. She trusts you, she says. You would never murder anyone. You didn't trust her, though, did you? She had no idea you owned a second home until we told her. Like Amber, she believed Little Orchard was a rental place you and Neil hired for Christmas 2003. Why wouldn't she?'

Simon was determined to keep asking, anything that came into his head. If he stopped, there would be nothing for Jo to answer if she changed her mind about talking. It was always easier to respond to a question than to volunteer information unprompted. He wanted her to tell him he was right. He didn't care when it happened as long as it happened.

'You don't even trust your own husband. You didn't tell him why he had to disappear in the middle of the night, why he had to pretend not to own first a house in Pulham Market and then a house in Surrey. You hardly ever go to Little Orchard, only when Sabina goes back to Italy. Even then, you need an excuse for the rest of the family, somewhere else you can pretend to be. Neil used to suggest selling. You'd never let that happen, but you couldn't tell him why, could you? Easier to attack him, burst into tears, leave the room. He doesn't bother any more. You know what he said to me? "I think it's important to Jo to know she's got a bolt-hole." That's not the word I'd use. Trouble is, there isn't a word for a house you think of as home but don't live in and hardly ever visit.'

Simon stood, walked round the table and Jo's chair, so that he was standing behind her. How would she feel if she could hear him but not see him? Would it change anything?

'I know what you did and I can prove it,' he said. 'I've got your DNA in Kat's flat, William's statement, a statement from the woman at the costume shop in Pulham Market, Sharon's house key in your jewellery box. How did you feel when Amber told you the police suspected Terry Bond? Did you get the key out and look at it, touch it? Wonder what was true and what wasn't? Hard to separate memory and stories, isn't it? Even harder when you've got three categories to contend with: memories, stories and lies. When you want to feel powerful, but not guilty. Hard. Think of the relief of telling the truth. Think about being able to live in the house that feels like home.'

Jo's head jerked back, then lolled forward.

'You think all I can prove are the facts, but you're wrong,' Simon went on, encouraged to get a reaction from her, even one he couldn't interpret. 'I can prove motive too. There's someone waiting outside ready to tell us all about why you did what you did. You don't think it's possible. You're so busy lying, you don't stop to wonder if you're being lied to. It doesn't occur to you that anyone might disagree with you when you're so right about everything, tell you what you want to hear just to get you off their back.'

'Can you please explain what you mean more clearly?' the solicitor said irritably.

'You chose a hypnotherapist for Amber. Or, rather, you thought you did. Amber seemed to think the one with the best address, in Great Holling, was probably the best. Instead of wondering if there was any rational basis for her assumption, you panicked. Amber always gets the best, doesn't she? Undeservingly. She's got Dinah and Nonie. You didn't want to her have the best hypnotherapist, so you chose one for her, the one whose address sounded least desirable. Amber pretended to agree, then went home and booked an appointment with Ginny Saxon, her original preference. You also booked to see Ginny. Having steered Amber in the opposite direction, you decided to claim her first choice for yourself. You'd never thought about hypnosis until Amber mentioned it, but if it could help with insomnia . . .'

Jo started to moan and slam her back against the back of the chair. Simon repositioned himself between her and the table so that he could see her face. The keening grew louder, its pitch changing as she let her mouth fall open. What was she doing with her eyes?

'What's she doing?' The solicitor sounded more disgusted than alarmed.

Simon raised his voice so that Jo would hear him over the noise she was making. 'Ginny's outside,' he said. 'If you talk to me, I won't need to bring her in.'

'What's wrong with her? Why can't she hold her head up?'

'She can. She's choosing not to.'

'Why the hell would she . . . ?'

'She's pretending to be her mentally handicapped sister,' said Simon.

~

'How well do you know him?' Ginny Saxon asked Charlie, eyeing the closed door of the interview room.

'Better than anyone else does,' said Charlie. 'Not as well as most wives know their husbands.'

'Simon Waterhouse is your husband?' Ginny's voice had changed; this was her wooden-hut-in-the-back-garden tone. Professional Ginny.

'If he wasn't, I wouldn't be your escort for the day. I'd be getting on with my own work.'

'You'd be trying to help that man, perhaps – the one you described in your email.'

Charlie could have done without the smug, knowing tone. She looked away. 'Him and others like him,' she said.

'Find the time, and make another appointment to see me,' said Ginny.

No. I'm fine. And you cost too much.

'I can help you. Both of you.'

'You could have helped Simon sooner by telling him the truth about Jo Utting.'

'He didn't ask me sooner. When he did, I told him what he wanted to know, after I'd talked it through with my supervisor.

Simon needs to learn to be more straightforward. He can't expect me to volunteer confidential information about a patient without knowing the full context. Why didn't he tell me Jo Utting was a suspect in a murder case?'

'Two murder cases,' Charlie corrected her.

'Instead, he has Amber Hewerdine leave her car outside my house, hoping I'll respond to his cryptic visual prompt by feeling guilty.'

'You already felt guilty.' Charlie hated it when she found herself quoting Simon. 'That's why you made sure to spell out your concerns about Jo's behaviour in great detail, why you lost your cool with Amber and kicked her out. Your overreaction made no sense unless you were hiding something.'

'Or unless I'm human,' Ginny said. 'Simon Waterhouse doesn't know everything. Though I've clearly entered a dimension in which everyone assumes he does.'

'You knew the information you were keeping to yourself mattered,' said Charlie. 'You can't have forgotten that Simon was investigating a murder. There he was, giving up hours of his time to listen to you and Amber dissect Jo's character in great detail. Don't pretend you didn't know she was a suspect.'

'I didn't *know* anything,' said Ginny. 'I wondered. If Simon was honest with himself, he'd admit that he also only wondered. Suspected. He can't have *known* Jo Utting was a client of mine.'

'He did. He's good at putting things together, things no one else would think to connect: you throwing a fit and kicking him and Amber out, your diagnosis of Jo's narcissistic personality disorder – made without having met her, allegedly.' Charlie's words sounded odd to her; she didn't think of herself as a boastful wife.

'What I told Simon was absolutely true,' said Ginny. 'It's possible to identify a narcissist simply by listening to his or her victims. I've done it many times.'

'Though, on this occasion, you'd met the narcissist herself,' Charlie reminded her.

'Yes, I had. My point is that Simon only *knew* that when he asked me and I told him two days ago. And if he thinks otherwise, he's misleading himself. Which I suppose he must have been doing all his life. Children of highly dysfunctional parents learn very early on to mislead themselves. Anything's better than facing the terrifying truth that you're not safe in your own home, with the two people who are supposed to love you most in the world.'

On balance, Charlie preferred being told to fuck off by teenage drug dealers, which was what normally happened in the corridors of the nick. Unsolicited psychoanalysis was rare. And unpleasant, she was discovering. Technically, she thought, you'd probably have to call it psychoanalysis-in-law, since Simon was the focus.

'The same children also learn to think and communicate cryptically,' Ginny went on. 'They become expert at reading signs, making sense of atmospheres. They pick up clues others would miss. They make great detectives, but they're badly affected by life's knock-backs because their sense of identity is so frail.' She smiled a brave-face sort of smile that made Charlie feel like the victim of a terrible misfortune. 'If Simon can't get Jo Utting to confirm the story he's telling himself about her – which, having met her, I don't think he will – I'd expect him to experience depressive symptoms and express them in a manner that's anything but straightforward.'

'Why don't you save your wisdom for your paying customers?' Charlie said impassively.

'All right. I'm sorry.' Ginny looked upset. 'If you don't want my help, I'm not going to force it on you.'

Charlie knew better than to come out with every disintegrating lunatic's favourite catchphrase: 'I don't need any help'. Instead, she said, 'If Simon says he knew, then he knew. What he couldn't work out was why someone with as many secrets as Jo would choose the same therapist as her sister-in-law. When we found out that Jo thought Amber had obediently gone elsewhere, it made more sense.'

The interview room door opened. Simon came out, shut it behind him. He didn't look happy.

'Change of plan?' Ginny asked.

'No. I need you to say what we agreed, even though—' He broke off. Looked at Charlie as if he hoped she might take over.

'Even though what?' she said.

'She's faking mental impairment – either mimicking Kirsty or pretending to be her. Why would she do that?' Simon demanded, eyeballing Ginny as if it was her fault. 'Where does it get her that "No comment" wouldn't?'

'Let's talk to her about it, shall we?' said Ginny.

Charlie hung back, hearing the animal-like noises that came from the interview room when Simon opened the door. He didn't close it once he and Ginny were inside; he expected Charlie to follow them. She thought about the piles of work waiting for her in her office, decided they would have to wait a bit longer. Simon needed her here whether she wanted to be here or not; things weren't going according to plan. Was that the answer to his question: *where does it get her that 'No comment' wouldn't?* Every detective was used to hearing 'No comment' and knew how to handle it. Was Jo Utting pretending to be her disabled sister to intimidate Simon, throw him off course?

Charlie didn't see Jo at first when she walked in. Simon and Ginny, in front of her, were blocking her view. When they moved, she saw a black woman in a trouser suit sitting next to a disabled white woman with shoulder-length curly blonde hair and a line of drool snaking from her open mouth down to her chin. Her eyes looked vacant; her body twisted in the chair. Even knowing it was an act, Charlie found herself doubting it.

Ginny sat down opposite Jo and leaned forward across the table as if she was keen to get close to her. 'Hello,' she said. 'You remember me, don't you? I'm Ginny Saxon. You came to my clinic.'

Jo moaned and flung out her right arm. Charlie stood beside Simon, in front of the door. She was aware of the tension in his body, perhaps more so than he was.

'I'm not here to help the police, even though I've had to tell them what we talked about,' Ginny said to Jo. 'I'm here to help you. I don't think this is a sensible idea, pretending to be something and someone you're not. I don't think it's good for you.'

'What about when she needs to use the bathroom?' the solicitor asked. 'What happens then?'

'I understand that you're tired of looking after people,' Ginny went on calmly. 'I understand that you want to be looked after, and you can be. I'll help you. So will other people. But not like this. If you keep up this pretence, it won't be you that's taken care of. It'll be the person you're pretending to be, who doesn't exist. What about the real Jo? Doesn't she deserve some care and attention, after all these years of caring for others? If you hide her, she can't get what she needs. Jo? I'm saying "her", but I'm talking about you. No one knows how it feels to be you, do they? Why don't you tell DC Waterhouse what you told me?'

'This isn't going to work,' Simon murmured. No one but Charlie heard him; the noise Jo was making shielded his words.

'When you came to see me, you were angry.' Ginny raised her voice. 'Where's that anger now? Don't put it into sounds, put it into words. Tell us about it.'

'Or go back to saying "No comment",' Jo's solicitor snapped at her. 'You're making a fool of yourself and wasting my time.' She looked over at Simon. 'You're all wasting my time.'

'How long do you think you can keep this up, Jo?' Ginny's firm unaggressive voice neutralised the lawyer's impatience. 'It's an impressive performance, but it's not sustainable. Nothing about the life you've been living was sustainable, and that's why you've ended up here, because you ran away from the truth instead of facing it. Jo? Why don't you tell DC Waterhouse what your mother said to you on your sixteenth birthday? Listen to me, Jo. I'm worried you'll make yourself ill if you . . .'

It was impossible for Ginny to compete with the noises Jo was making: pitiful moans punctuated by high-pitched yelping noises. No words, but a sense of words having been distorted and reassembled inside out. Charlie shivered. What made Ginny so sure Jo couldn't keep this up? How could she *not* maintain her act? It was unimaginable that she might at any moment wipe her mouth, straighten her contorted face and say, 'No comment'.

Ginny had abandoned her post and was heading for the door, gesturing to Simon that they needed to talk outside. Charlie was first out of the room, planning how to avoid going back in. Jo Utting's peculiar brand of insanity was the least attractive she'd encountered in her career so far.

'You've got a problem,' Ginny told Simon. 'A big one.'

'We've got three closed cases,' he countered. 'She's confessed.'

'And she'll spend the rest of her days in an institution. She won't hurt anyone else. That's what matters. But if you're hoping for a criminal trial . . .'

'Don't give me that unfit-to-stand-trial crap! You said it yourself: she can't keep this up.'

'I said that when I thought it was an act,' said Ginny. 'Or, rather, when I hoped that it might be.'

'What, you think it's for real?' Simon yelled at her. 'Bullshit! People don't just become mentally retarded when it suits them.'

'No, but they do have breakdowns. Post-breakdown, almost anything can happen. I'm not denying Jo's particular response is unusual . . .'

'No. I'm not listening to this shit. No!' Simon slammed his fist against the wall. 'You heard her brief! Even she's not falling for it.'

'Jo's spent her whole life seeing Kirsty everywhere, even when she's tried not to look,' Ginny said sadly. 'Hearing Kirsty even when she was determined not to listen. She's watched her mother devote her whole life to Kirsty and known that even the whole of Hilary's life wasn't going to be enough. Whose life was next in line to be sacrificed, once Hilary was gone? Do you know how that feels – somebody so dependent, who takes everything and gives nothing? It's like carrying that person inside you. Your constant awareness of them means you're never fully yourself. Imagine that scenario, then add the stress of facing a life sentence for murder, being separated from your children . . .'

'You feel sorry for her,' said Charlie. By which she meant that, listening to Ginny, anyone might feel sorry for Jo. And Charlie didn't want to.

'I feel sorry for everybody involved,' Ginny answered diplomatically. 'It's not an act, Simon. I'm sorry, but you need to go back in there and insist that that lawyer gets her client some proper psychiatric help.'

'Don't worry,' said Simon. He wasn't looking at Ginny. He wasn't looking at anyone. 'I'm going back in there. Alone.'

He disappeared into the interview room, slamming the door behind him.

Ginny turned on Charlie. 'He's going to terrorise her. I'm powerless here. You have to do something.'

'What did Hilary say to Jo on her sixteenth birthday?' Charlie asked. She'd thought Simon had told her everything, but apparently not. And Ginny didn't understand that she wasn't alone in being unable to stop Simon from doing what he was about to do; his special power was to render everyone around him powerless when it suited him.

'She made Jo promise to look after Kirsty, when she couldn't any more – something no parent should ask of a sixteen-year-old child. In a way, Hilary's responsible for all the murders and attempted murders that have taken place.'

Charlie wasn't having that. 'It might be different in your profession, but around these parts we have clear guidelines about responsibility for murder. The person who commits the murder is the one we blame.'

'Jo was a good girl. Of course she said yes. Hilary had instilled in her from an early age the value of family: more important than Jo herself, that's the message she got from her mother after Kirsty was born. As an individual, Jo didn't matter any more. Rationally, she knew she ought to matter – her life, the one she'd built for herself, the one she wasn't ever able to enjoy because of the duty hanging over her head. That's why she came to me. She wanted me to help her believe what she knew to be true. I think what she wanted was the courage to say, publicly, what Amber said to her without any guilt at all, though of course Amber hadn't yet said it at the point when Jo came to see me: no one has a duty to ruin their own life for the sake of someone else.' Ginny shrugged. 'Maybe I could have helped Jo to believe it, maybe not. We therapists call it dehypnosis. When a child's been brainwashed by a strong-minded parent to believe something that isn't true, you can't always undo the effects.'

'Does the same apply to police who've been brainwashed into thinking murderers should be punished?' Charlie asked.

'Jo told me she loved Kirsty. Nothing I said could persuade her to admit she hated her. Even to her husband, she couldn't admit that the prospect of becoming Kirsty's primary carer after Hilary died was unbearable. Yet she freely admitted she couldn't stand to touch Kirsty or be close to her. She couldn't be seen by Hilary to be singling Kirsty out for special avoidance, so she reinvented herself as a non-tactile person. Even her husband believed it. She broke her own rule only for her children, only when she thought no one was looking.'

'Strange kind of avoidance, having her mum and Kirsty round every day,' said Charlie. 'Inviting them to stay, cooking meals for them . . .'

'That was her cover,' Ginny said. 'Yes, Hilary and Kirsty were there all the time, lost in the crowd of ageing father-in-law, kids, brother, husband, sister and brother-in-law, nanny who's paid a fortune to do next to nothing. I think Sabina was Jo's last resort. If all her other plans failed, maybe Sabina could be persuaded to be Kirsty's main carer after Hilary died. Jo's certainly paid her enough over the years, for almost no work. That has to be why she's kept her on.' Ginny frowned. 'When I say "persuaded", I don't mean literally,' she qualified. 'As Amber so perceptively said, Sabina's job title might be nanny, but her role in that house has always been to attend to *Jo's* needs, having first deciphered them by osmosis, with nothing ever being stated explicitly. At the moment, with Hilary still alive, Jo's main need is for Sabina to keep Quentin entertained. Jo won't ever have asked Sabina to do this. She finds it impossible to articulate her own needs, that's her whole problem.'

'That and being a conscienceless murderer,' Charlie quipped irritably.

'Assuming Sabina had proved amenable – which we can't be

certain of, and personally I think it's unlikely she would have been for long – Jo would have taken full credit for looking after her beloved sister. Nobody would have felt able to point out that in fact Sabina was the one doing all the hard and intimate physical work, or that Jo was never seen to go near her sister.'

'How much of this did Jo tell you and how much are you making up?' Charlie asked. Simon had led her to believe that Jo's determination not to be saddled with responsibility for Kirsty was a known fact, but everything Ginny was saying sounded alarmingly speculative.

'She told me more than enough.'

'So having Kirsty in her house every day was good PR for Jo?'

Ginny nodded. 'Exactly. She could hide in the kitchen, defended by a mountain of cooking implements, knowing Hilary was there to provide the hands-on care Kirsty needed, and Hilary wouldn't suspect a thing. She *didn't* suspect a thing. No one did. Everyone thought Jo's house was full to bursting because there was nothing she wanted more than to look after everybody. Jo made sure to convince all those close to her of her devotion to Kirsty. If anyone failed to treat Kirsty as an equal, they got it in the neck from Jo, the loyal sister. Jo sacrificed her home and day-to-day life to her elaborate pretence. In her heart, the second homes she kept secret from her mother and was rarely able to visit – in Pulham Market, in Surrey – those were her real homes. She made an exception and invited everybody to Little Orchard once, for the sake of being seen to perform a grand gesture: hiring a mansion for the family to spend Christmas in. What better way to visit the home she loved but could hardly ever get to? What better way to cement her image as family goddess who loves everyone so much that she can't bear the idea of them not all being together for Christmas? Plus, she wanted Hilary to change her will in Ritchie's favour – pretending to have enough spare cash to hire an enormous mansion probably struck her as a convenient symbol of her and Neil's lack of need, in contrast to Ritchie's obvious neediness.'

'The symbolism didn't work on Hilary, evidently,' Charlie pointed out.

'No. Hilary said no, and Jo couldn't handle it. Still, she didn't consider being honest with her family about her wants and needs. Instead, she suffered a minor breakdown and decided to disappear with her husband and children. After a day and two nights on the run, she must have recovered sufficiently to realise it wasn't practical. She returned to her life, pretending nothing had happened.'

'Then what?' Charlie asked. 'Waited five years, then planned and committed a murder, then another one two years later?'

'Sounds extraordinary, doesn't it?' said Ginny. 'Unless you're Jo, and then it makes perfect sense. She didn't lay a finger on Kirsty. She knew how irredeemable that would make her in the eyes of her mother, and she had other options to explore first. Hilary's message throughout Jo's childhood was clear: taking care of Kirsty was all that mattered. Everything and everyone else was expendable. If Jo herself didn't matter, why should Sharon Lendrim and Katharine Allen's lives be worth anything? Why shouldn't Jo take the risk of committing two murders? She'd never heard her mother say that *she* mustn't end up in an institution: a prison, a psychiatric facility. Kirsty's the one who must always be kept at home, wrapped in the love of her family for as long as that family has breath in its body.'

Charlie stared at the closed door of the interview room. This part of the nick was new, well soundproofed. No way of knowing what was going on inside.

Ginny held out her hand. Charlie shook it. 'Thanks for your time,' she said. 'Simon ought to be the one saying it, but he never will.'

'Don't worry about me,' said Ginny. She gestured towards the door. 'Do what you can to help Jo. Whatever she's done. And don't deny your own needs. It's a fast-track route to tragedy.'

~

'Transitive and intransitive relationships,' Simon said as he paced the room. The solicitor had moved her chair into the corner, as far from the action as she could get. 'William explained it to me. Jo stands to gain from Sharon's death? No. *Amber* stands to gain from Sharon's death: she gains Dinah and Nonie. Jo stands to gain from *Pam*'s death, then? Still a no. Jo ends up with Quentin, but it's no gain. It's a burden, a nightmare.' He leaned over the table, stared into the vacant eyes of the drooling mess in front of him. 'Except that's your tactic, isn't it? If you're having a bad time, going through hell, then it can't be what you wanted – that's what we're all supposed to think, isn't it? You've compromised your principles to save Amber by attending a driver awareness course posing as her and you're terrified of being found out. You beg me not to tell anyone you did it, making sure it never crosses my mind that maybe you *didn't* do it. The perfect alibi: the extent to which you're visibly desperate to hide your guilty secret determines the extent to which I assume it must be the truth. Who bothers to hide a lie that never happened?

'If Amber and Luke have got their hands full with Sharon's girls when Pam dies, there'll be no question of them taking Quentin in as well. Their spare room's taken, it's Dinah and Nonie's bedroom. You, on the other hand, can put your boys in together and provide a bedroom for Quentin. Once you've got Quentin and a full house, how could anyone expect you to provide a home for Kirsty when Hilary carks it? Why shouldn't Ritchie do it? He's a man, true, and not an obviously capable carer, but it isn't as if he's got anything else to do, is it? You made sure of that: supporting him financially, telling him not to take any old job, to wait for something important to come along, something that'll give his life meaning. Something like looking after his handicapped sister. If you can persuade Hilary to write you out of her will and leave her house to Ritchie alone, all the better. The solution starts to look even more obvious: your unoccupied brother, with a big house all to himself, no children. Except it wouldn't have worked. You'd have seen that if you hadn't been desperate. Ritchie couldn't look after Kirsty. He can barely look after himself. You'd have had to think of something else, but what? Hiring a full-time professional wouldn't have been an option – you couldn't have done that without being *seen* to do it. Hilary would turn in her grave. Shall I tell you what would have happened, assuming you haven't already worked it out? A pillow over Kirsty's face, the only solution in the long run. Or an accident. As long as no one suspected you, the devoted sister, you could have made it work. Hilary-from-beyond-the-grave wouldn't have known any more than the world knew. No one has the power to get inside your mind and read your thoughts, not even a ghost. Especially not your mother's ghost. Alive, all Hilary's ever cared about is how you appear in the eyes of the world. That's how she sees you – she just looks at the surface, doesn't she? She doesn't want to delve any deeper. She doesn't care how you feel, doesn't even try to imagine. She *tells* you how you should feel. Isn't that right? Why should her spirit, after death, be any different?'

'Seems someone does have the power to get inside her mind,' Jo's solicitor muttered.

'You think about your dead mother a lot,' Simon said. 'Even though she's not dead yet. In 2003, she was diagnosed with breast cancer. They caught it early. You knew there was a good chance she'd be okay, but it focused your mind, forced you to confront a truth you hadn't faced before: maybe Hilary wasn't about to die imminently, but one day she would, and you'd be expected to make good your promise to her. To look after Kirsty, provide a home for her. You panicked – hence your apparently selfless suggestion that Hilary alter her will in Ritchie's favour. Her saying no must have been a shock. She told you and Ritchie it was out of the question, it was important to her to treat her children equally. But that wasn't the whole story, was it?'

Simon imagined himself grabbing Jo's hair, yanking her head back. He wanted to do it, but couldn't. 'I've spoken to Hilary,' he said. Jo's shoulders jerked. 'After Ritchie went to bed, Hilary told you the truth: she couldn't leave her house to Ritchie because you'd need the proceeds from selling your share of it to buy a bigger house for you and your family, one that could accommodate Kirsty. If Ritchie got the whole house, you wouldn't be able to afford to do that, or so Hilary believed. Kirsty would have to go and live with Ritchie, and Hilary didn't trust him to be able to look after her properly. She hadn't wanted to say so in front of him because it would have sounded like a vote of no confidence. But Ritchie knows Hilary doesn't think he's up to much. You're the dependable one, he's the disappointment. The failure.'

Jo had stopped moaning and fallen silent. She sat with her head tilted forward at an angle that looked painful, as if her neck was broken.

'Except that wasn't how it felt, was it?' Simon said. 'You felt like the failure. Your plan hadn't worked. Hilary wasn't changing her will. Kirsty was still coming to you. What did you do, when you saw that running away in the middle of the night wasn't going to work? Push it to the back of your mind? Tell yourself Hilary wasn't going anywhere for the time being, hope you'd think of something else in the meantime? And you did, didn't you? When Pam was diagnosed with liver cancer, you thought of plan B. Was Ritchie really so hopeless that he couldn't be trained to look after Kirsty? Surely Hilary would think about this, once she saw that you and Neil had had no choice but to take Quentin in. Surely she'd come to you then and tell you she'd decided your suggestion was a good one: Ritchie must have her house and responsibility for Kirsty's day-to-day care after her death, since you were already up to your limit. You needed your mother to transfer responsibility from you to Ritchie, officially. Ginny would say you couldn't allow yourself to have a need that Hilary hadn't allocated to you. No, what's the right psycho word?' Psychotherapeutic, he meant, not psychopathic. Assuming there was a difference. 'Validate, that's right. Hilary had to validate your need to say, "I've reached my limit" – your *right* to say it. She never did, though, did she? Why would she? She saw you cheerfully providing accommodation and food for the whole world and assumed you could cope with anything. Yesterday she told me she was never in any doubt about your wanting to look after Kirsty, you'd been that convincing: her saintly daughter who wanted her little brother to have a big house for purely altruistic reasons.'

Jo made a noise that subsided after a few seconds. Ginny had been wrong to say she wouldn't be able to maintain her act. The low energy version was easy. Anyone could do it.

'Transitive and intransitive relationships,' Simon said. 'I'd call this one transitive, though William might disagree. Amber stands to gain from Sharon's death: Dinah and Nonie. Her fully occupied spare room and emotional resources ensure that Jo gains from Pam's death – the dubious gain being Quentin, and no more room at the inn. With Hilary's blessing, Ritchie could then potentially have gained from Hilary's death: a big house, and full-time care of his sister. See how it's transitive? Follow the chain of causation back and we see that Ritchie gains from Sharon's death, and so does Jo, who gains from Ritchie's gain. Her gain is the loss of the burden of her sister. If Sharon hadn't died, Quentin might have gone to Amber and Luke, who would still have had a spare room in their house when Pam died.' Simon bent down, put his face as close to Jo's as he could stand to. 'A room Quentin would never have ended up in, as you found out on Wednesday 1 December. Unlike you, Amber wouldn't rather kill innocent people than say no to an unreasonable demand from an abusive mother.'

Jo's mouth tightened, then went slack again. Or was Simon seeing what he wanted to see?

'That's right: abusive,' he said. 'That's what Ginny reckons, and she's the expert. It's abusive to make one of your children feel that she has to look after another to earn your love and approval.'

'Hang on a minute.' Jo's solicitor hauled herself out of her chair, but stayed in the corner of the room. 'Is this a game you're playing that I'm not clever enough to understand, or are you seriously suggesting her motive for killing Sharon Lendrim was to fill the spare room of the only other person who might have offered a home to her father-in-law?'

'Never been more serious,' Simon told her. 'When Pam Utting's liver cancer was first diagnosed, Neil and his brother Luke, Amber's husband, had a conversation that Jo got to hear about and Amber didn't – because Luke was too scared of her reaction to tell her. Neil and Luke agreed that if Pam were to die, Luke would be the one to offer Quentin a home. Luke wasn't happy about it, but felt it was his duty. He had the room, Neil didn't. And Neil had two kids. Luke told Neil that Amber wouldn't be happy, but he thought he'd be able to talk her round. I don't know if he would have been able to or not. She says not. But Jo knew nothing about Amber's reluctance. All Neil told her was that she didn't need to worry, Luke had promised to take care of Quentin. Jo could relax, knowing her father-in-law would never be her responsibility.'

'So, according to your theory, she did the opposite of relax?' the solicitor asked.

'That being murder, yeah,' Simon said. 'Jo needed to be responsible for Quentin to be in with a chance of avoiding responsibility for Kirsty. When Sharon died and Amber decided she needed a bigger house for her, Luke and the girls, your client did everything she could to talk her out of it.'

The lawyer sighed and shook her head. 'Did she succeed?'

'No. It didn't matter, as it turned out.' He looked at Jo. 'You must have thought you'd got away with it. When Pam died, no one said anything about Amber and Luke having a house twice the size of yours. Luke's promise to look after his dad was never mentioned again – by you, Neil, Luke himself or anyone. Everyone knew how hard it was for Luke and Amber, adjusting to life with Dinah and Nonie. You made sure to draw the whole family's attention to how much they had on their plate. Poor, stressed Luke and Amber.'

'Why kill Sharon, though?' the solicitor asked. 'If you're right, wouldn't it have been simpler for her to kill Amber and Luke? They can't take Quentin in if they're dead.'

'If anything had happened to Amber and Luke, Jo would have automatically come under suspicion. If she kills Sharon – a stranger – who's going to suspect her? It looks to the world as if she gets nothing out of Sharon's death. And she's been indoctrinated by her mother so that she believes family's all that matters. To Jo, Sharon wasn't family; her life wasn't important.'

Jo's solicitor sighed. 'Look, there's no ambiguity about my client's actions, but everything you're saying that relates to motive is unprovable.'

'I've proved it,' Simon told her.

'You've *said* it. Saying's not the same as proving.'

'She's got photographs in her second home of every single member of her family apart from her sister. What does that tell you?'

'That Kirsty's not photogenic, and that you're clutching at straws.' Jo's lawyer took her by the arm. 'Interview terminated, an hour after it should have been. We're out of here.'

Jo stood.

'See that? She did what you told her.' Simon blocked their path to the door. To Jo, he said, 'You're going to be proved to be a liar and sent to prison.' He spat the words in her face. 'If you drop this act, you can talk to your children, explain to them why you did it. You can explain in court the pressure you were under. Ginny'll testify for you – mitigating circumstances.'

'What you mean is, if she drops her act, she'll be able to prove you right,' Jo's solicitor said. 'Clearly, that's not enough of an incentive for her.'

Jo yelped, moved her mouth as if she was struggling to make her lips meet.

'I can help you,' Simon shouted after her as her lawyer guided her out of the room, aware that he'd brought his stunted inner good cop into play far too late. 'I *want* to help you.'

'Help yourself,' the lawyer advised. 'Stop wasting your time.'

They were gone. He was alone in the room with the echo of a slammed door.

15

Friday 10 December 2010

'You're drinking wine,' Dinah tells me. She, Nonie, Luke and I are having dinner at Ferrazzano's in Silsford, our favourite Italian restaurant.

'I know I'm drinking wine.'

'If it's bad for Mrs Truscott to give parents glasses of wine at school shows, then it's bad for you to drink it.'

'No, it's fine for me to drink it,' I say. 'It's wrong for Mrs Truscott to *sell* wine at school shows and pretend to be giving it away. And actually . . .'

'Actually what?' Dinah asks.

'Nothing.' Luke and I exchange a look. We are both thinking that Mrs Truscott can do whatever she likes from now on, and we will continue to think she's a hero. Without the efforts of the headmistress I have endlessly derided, I don't believe Dinah and Nonie would be alive today. Jo wasn't the only one who had the idea of shopping in Rawndesley on the afternoon of Friday 3 December. Mrs Truscott spotted her with the girls in John Lewis and noticed that Nonie was crying, noticed that Jo seemed unresponsive to her distress. When Nonie spotted her headteacher, she ran over to her, ignoring Jo's loud orders to come back immediately, and said that she wanted to go home but Jo wouldn't let her. She was scared: Jo and Dinah were hatching a plan to go and play in the snow in Silsford Woods, and Nonie didn't want to.

Mrs Truscott went over to speak to Jo, who at first snapped at her to mind her own business, then changed her demeanour entirely and became almost sycophantically reassuring. Mrs Truscott told the police later that she'd found Jo's behaviour so alarming that she'd insisted on taking Dinah and Nonie away from her and driving them home to Luke.

Silsford Woods is about half a mile from Blantyre Gap. The council recently announced a plan to put a barrier there, to make it harder for people to drive their cars off the edge.

'Let's not argue about wine,' Luke says. 'Let's talk about the brilliant school show we've just seen, the brilliant play by brilliant new playwrights Dinah and Nonie Lendrim.' In the end, Nonie succeeded in intervening on behalf of Hector's ten sisters. Their final fate was less gruesome thanks to her: covered in mud rather than dead.

'So you liked it?' Dinah asks us for what must be the twentieth time. 'Really?'

'Really,' I tell her. 'We loved it. Everybody loved it – you heard the applause. You're both incredibly talented.'

'You would say that,' says Nonie. 'You're our parents.'

Luke squeezes my knee under the table.

'You *are* our parents,' Dinah insists.

'Tell them,' Nonie whispers to her across the table.

I force myself to swallow the food that's in my mouth. Last time Nonie ordered Dinah to tell me something, it was Kind, Cruel, Kind of Cruel. It wasn't something I wanted to hear. When she told me how scared she'd been when Jo had tried to force her to go to Silsford Woods in the snow, how she very nearly hadn't had the courage to approach Mrs Truscott in John Lewis, I didn't want to hear that either – it upset me too much. *Please let this be something good.*

'We've made a decision,' Dinah says, putting down her knife and fork. 'You don't need to adopt us. We're already a family, you're already our parents. We don't need a piece of paper to make it true.'

'You're right,' Luke says. 'And we'll be a family whether we adopt you officially or not.'

'But if you stop trying to, nothing bad can happen,' says Dinah. 'No one will say you're not allowed to.'

Nonie nods her agreement.

Luke looks at me, a question in his eyes. I transmit one back to him: is it up to me? I don't want it to be up to me. Or maybe I do, because there's no way I'm giving up, whatever Luke says. Whatever anyone says. 'If you knew for sure that we'd definitely be able to adopt you legally, would you want us to?' I ask the girls.

'But we don't know for sure,' says Nonie.

'She said "if". Don't you know what "if" means?' Dinah snaps.

'You would, wouldn't you?' says Luke. 'You're scared, like we are, that it's not going to go our way. That's why you want us to stop trying.'

Both girls nod.

'We can't do that,' I tell them. 'Luke and I are as frightened as you are, but if we all want it to happen then we have to try. And . . . it might be fine.'

'It probably will be,' says Luke.

'Amber?'

'What, Nones?'

'What will happen to Jo?'

'I don't know, love. No one knows at the moment. But . . . she won't hurt anyone else.'

'I feel sorry for William and Barney,' Nonie says.

'If things aren't fine, they'll still be fine,' says Dinah. 'We'll still be a family.'

We will be, from now on, a family whose members tell each other the truth without fear, knowing we will always be forgiven. When I said this to Luke last night, he laughed and said, 'That's a great policy for you and me, but the girls are going to be teenagers. Don't be too disappointed when you find lager cans and tattooed boyfriends hidden in the airing cupboard.'

'Yes,' he says now to Dinah. 'We'll still be a family.'

Thank you for coming to see me. It must have taken a lot of courage. I wasn't expecting you to agree, or even to respond to my letter, so that's great. It's great that you've got courage because you're going to need plenty of it to help the boys to survive . . . well, I don't want to say 'losing their mother', because that makes it sound as if Jo is dead. You know what I mean.

First of all, I want to tell you that in my one proper encounter with Jo – I tried to talk to her again at the police station, but she was unresponsive – when she came to see me here, voluntarily, we talked properly and it was clear to me that she adores you and the boys. She genuinely loves you, Neil. And William and Barney. I know she's . . . inaccessible at the moment – she's shut herself down in order to be able to survive the ordeal ahead – but I strongly believe she still loves you. You, William and Barney are the people in her life that she can love non-strategically, without calculation or complication. In a way that she *can't* love Hilary, Ritchie and Kirsty, because she sees them all as in some way responsible for her problems.

So, although I mainly asked you here to talk about the boys and how to make this easier for them, I also want to say something about Jo. Don't give up on her, Neil. She's done terrible things, I'm not denying that, but it doesn't make her a terrible person. Jo has never had the chance to get out from under her mother's brainwashing and become the person she once had the potential to be. With your help, and mine – or with the help of any good therapist – she still could. She has never been allowed to feel or express her own needs, which is why she did what she did. I know it must be hard for you to understand, but although Jo is, legally, a fully responsible adult, psychologically she's a frightened child fighting the annihilation of her frail identity.

We can talk more about this if you decide to come and see me again, but I'd like you to consider this: why fire? Why did Jo hire a fireman's uniform and kill Sharon Lendrim in that particular way? It can't have been the easiest option, surely. I know it's painful for you to think about it, but Jo made life difficult for herself by choosing to attack Sharon in the way she did. She first had to obtain a key to the house, then let herself in at night, when she hoped Sharon, Dinah and Nonie would all be sound asleep, but she couldn't guarantee it, could she? She had to change into her fireman clothes, get the girls out of the house . . . How did she know Sharon wouldn't wake up and catch her in the act? Why did she take that risk?

I think, and Simon Waterhouse agrees, that it was important for her to be able to focus on the 'rescuer' role and disguise she adopted. She was Dinah and Nonie's saviour that night, covered from head to toe in the protective clothing of the profession that does the *opposite* of the harm she intended to do. Symbolically, she protected herself from her crime – almost cancelling it out, in her mind. Do you see what I mean? She encased her whole body in this saviour costume, so that the real Jo was completely buried, and she rescued two children. That's the part she'll have focused on, blanking her mind to the fact that she was the cause of the fire, and to her true aim. She wouldn't have allowed herself to think about that. I believe that it was only possible for her to commit murder for the first time in this very specific way: literally, encased in an identity that cancelled out her true identity, and neutralised her abhorrent behaviour. It will have been as abhorrent to her, on some level, as it is to you and me.

I believe, though I can't prove it, that if it had been possible, Jo would have used the same method with Kat Allen, but Kat lived in a flat, not a house. She didn't have her own front door, accessible from the street. I probably shouldn't tell you this, but I disagree with the police about why Jo took William and Barney with her to Kat's flat that day. I know this is one of the aspects of all this that upsets you the most, but if it's any comfort, I genuinely don't believe Jo simply used the boys. Yes, a mother in charge of her two young sons on a day a murder takes place is less likely to be suspected of having committed that murder, but I don't think that's why she did it. She didn't want to fool others, she wanted to fool herself. She wanted to believe that, though she had to do something unpleasant, she was mainly having a fun day out with William and Barney. That she killed Kat during a day that was otherwise spent in the company of her beloved children would have made it just about bearable for her. She needed the boys with her for moral support, if you like.

I'm not justifying anything she did, Neil. I'm trying to help you understand what might have been going on in her mind, that's all. Outward appearances are more real to Jo than her own internal reality, which has never been allowed to develop, never received any validation. Does that make sense? What I'm trying to say is that Jo could *still* develop in any number of ways. I'm not trying to make her your responsibility – believe me, I'm not. I just wanted to give you the chance to think about it in a different way, that's all.

With regard to the boys, the most important thing is to help them understand that nothing that's happened has been their fault. They are children, and are in no way responsible for the problems of adults. Please do everything you can to drum that into them, because they'll need it. They'll be thinking back over the past and wondering what they might have done differently to prevent their mother from becoming so unhappy. Your job – the most important one you'll ever do in your life – is to make sure they know there was nothing they could have done to change anything. You can't arrange for them to avoid suffering altogether, but you can ensure they don't take on guilt that isn't theirs, as so many children do.

Let me give you an example: when I was a child, on my first day at school, I was nervous and shy and didn't really want to be there, so I hid behind a doll's house and pretended I wasn't there. I knew I was doing something naughty, and eventually I got scared and came out. My teacher spanked me with a ruler in front of the whole class, which is something I still find difficult to talk about. It's the most humiliating thing that's ever happened to me. When my mother arrived to collect me that afternoon, my teacher told her what I'd done, and my mother didn't speak to me – at all – for nearly a week. It was absolutely clear to me that, by doing this one thing wrong, I had forfeited my right to be loved by her. And yet, for years, the dominant feeling I had when I recalled that incident was guilt. If only I hadn't hidden behind the doll's house . . . It was my fault, I was horrible and worthless. It took me nearly twenty years to realise that the guilty people in the story were my teacher and my mother. The adults. I was an ordinary child who did something naughty, as children do. When I realised that, I got angry. And decided to become a therapist, so that I could help people like me, like you, like Jo. Like William and Barney.

With the right help and guidance, they'll be okay, Neil. They have you. Love them, look after them, and they'll be fine.

Acknowledgements

I am deeply grateful, as always, to my agent Peter Straus of Rogers, Coleridge & White (or Straus MD of the Princeton-Plainsboro Literary Agency as I prefer to call him, on account of his genius-maverick qualities), to my brilliantly incisive and supportive editor Carolyn Mays, to Francesca Best, Karen Geary, Lucy Zilberkweit, Lucy Hale and everybody at my wonderful publishers Hodder & Stoughton. Thank you to my long-standing copy editor, Amber Burlinson, after whom I cheekily named the protagonist of this novel without asking permission. Thanks to Montserrat and Jeromin, owners of the real Little Orchard – again: cheeky name theft, no permission. Thank you to all my international publishers who work so hard to distribute my peculiar brand of twisted fictional psyche all over the world. Thanks to Mark Pannone as ever, and to the Cambridge Stonecraft gang: Simon, Jamie, Lee and Matt. Thank you to Dr Bryan Knight, whose amazing website first made me think, 'Hmm, hypnosis . . .', and to Dr Michael Heap whose expertise proved invaluable.

The original *Hector and His Ten Sisters* was a short story I wrote with my children, Phoebe and Guy. I am grateful to Phoebe, also, for supplying Dinah's quip about the hypothetical baby who would only grow up and work in an office. Thank you to Dan for too many things to list (and I won't bother to try, in case he hates lists of things he's done as much as he hates lists of things I'd like him to do).

Last but far from least: major thanks to Emily Winslow for brilliant editorial advice and suggestions.

The following books have proved fascinating as well as incredibly useful: *Toxic Parents: Overcoming Their Hurtful Legacy and Reclaiming Your Life* by Dr Susan Forward, *The Body Never Lies* by Dr Alice Miller, *The Emotional Incest Syndrome: What to Do When a Parent's Love Rules Your Life* by Dr Patricia Love, *The Narcissistic Family* by Stephanie Donaldson-Pressman and Robert M. Pressman, and *Facing Codependence* by Pia Mellody.